To She

by Roland Ladley

The eighth of the Sam Green novels

For all Sam Green fans – you are the best.

Let the end try the man.

Henry IV, Part II

Prologue

Great Bitter Lake, Suez Canal, Egypt

October 1968

It was hot. Too hot. The handrail on the metal hull of the SS Asian Glen, which was a mixture of paint and rust, was good to touch to steady yourself. But it wasn't somewhere you could plant your exposed forearms. Not for long. Not without a blister.

This fucking sun.

He hated it.

He hated the glare from the sandy-white hold covers and the main superstructure. He hated the windless days and intolerable heat of the night. He hated the salty air which matted his black hair to a paste. He hated the interminable boredom – the routine. And he hated the way many of the crews had grown accustomed to where they found themselves. Some relished the pattern. They had become inventive – amused by their disposition, and keen to encourage others to feel the same way.

Like the Bitter Lake Olympic Games, just a few months ago, coinciding with the Mexico City jamboree. He hated sport. He *fucking* hated it. It was no surprise, therefore, that he hated it even more stuck on a ship in the Suez Canal, moored with fourteen others, where a couple of ebullient crew had decided what they all needed was an eight-nation competition to mirror the Mexico games. It was pathetic. Fishing and swimming and sailing and acrobatics and football. Germans and Swedes and Brits and Czechs and Americans and the fucking Bulgarians. And medals! Badly bits of chiselled wood presented to the winners, while overhead Israel flew jets so close you could see the pilots' rank badges.

And in the distance, the low *thud* of bombs landing on both sides of the canal promised that nothing was changing soon.

He hated that.

He hated *all* of that,

And he hated his father. He *particularly* hated his father.

Alcander Konstantos.

Greek shipping tycoon.

Owner of seventy-four ships, the second largest fleet in the world. 60 million tonnes of freight shipped annually to any port in the world. Real estate worth over 80 million drachma. Three wives. Twelve children. And two Greek hounds, the best hunting dogs in the world.

Theodor hated his father. Especially now.

But, it was fair to say, it wasn't always like that.

Once they had tolerated each other.

Theodor was the second son, third child, of his father's first wife. He lived a life of luxury in Alimos, Athens' most expensive coastal suburb. He'd had a British education followed by a playboy existence whilst his father primed his eldest son to take over the family empire. And there was some of the playboy in him. Theodor owned a Maserati. He had a Gold American Express card. And he had a face which allowed him unfettered access to all of Athens' hotspots.

He had women. Whichever ones he wanted.

And he'd travelled. After three years drinking himself stupid at Imperial College in London, where his father's funding of a new science facility had ensured that Theodor had finished his education with a piece of paper, he'd travelled. First to San Francisco. Then Los Angeles. And then, bless it, Las Vegas.

It hadn't taken long for him to be called home, though. No, *ordered* was a better word.

In disgrace.

His credit had run dry. He'd smashed up one too many rooms. He'd thrown up in one too many lifts. And a few women had made complaints to the police. His sexual practices were not to the Americans' taste, it seemed.

Landing in Athens, travelling only second class, he'd not spoken to his father. Instead one of the flunkies had packed him off to SS Asian Glen, a 7,000 tonne freighter running a constant loop between Hong Kong and Rotterdam. He'd been given the title of 'third officer' – a nothing. It ranked alongside senior cook and an older able-bodied seaman.

A nobody.

And everyone loathed him.

They loathed him because he was his father's son. And whilst none of them, other than the master, knew his father to talk to, Theodor had quickly learnt of his reputation among the crew. His father was tough and uncompromising. He ran his ships like his business – *his* way: nothing stopped the freight from hitting the quay on time.

Nothing.

A couple of months ago, during an evening of heavy drinking, the bosun had recounted the story of how an apprentice engineer, an Italian, had got his arm caught in

3

one of the turbines. It had ripped off his hand and 'the blood had spurted from the soggy end of his arm 'like a fountain'. The bosun, a fat, cheery Spaniard, was wetting himself as he retold the story, his right hand in a fist like a stump, and his left making spraying gestures. 'We stopped the bleeding, but the man went downhill quickly.' The bosun had swigged some more beer at that point. 'I told the master we needed to berth somewhere quickly. Anywhere. Otherwise the gringo would die. But he was having none of it.' The bosun had leant up against Theodor, his eyes bloodshot and his breath a mixture of stale tobacco and alcohol. He had tapped his nose.

'We follow Konstantos rules.' He'd nodded slowly, looking like he might fall asleep on Theodor's shoulder.

'What do you mean?' Theodor had asked.

'The only thing which stops a Konstantos ship ... is a torpedo,' the man had mumbled.

'Did the engineer die?' Theodor didn't know whether he felt nauseated or excited.

The bosun had nodded again. Drunkenly.

Then he sat bolt upright as if the King of Greece had entered the ward room.

'But ...' he hiccupped, 'we met our quayside slot in Valletta.' He'd smiled then, nodding with a face full of pride.

So the crew not only loathed his father – they were petrified of him.

And so they loathed his son. His second son. Not his chosen one. A worthless playboy. A useless merchant sailor. An idler. No more important than the cook.

And, if you were crew on SS Asian Glen, his daddy's spy.

Theodor had been surprised when the bosun had offered to have a drink with him those months ago. Because

4

everyone else avoided him. Their attitude was one of caution ... mixed with disdain.

Hmm.

Theodor looked out across the bows of the three ships which had been roped together. In the distance all he could see was the flat, blue-grey of the water, and then a shimmering sandbank which signalled where the lake stopped and Egypt started.

Not everyone.

Not the pumpman. The lowest rank in the engineering crew.

He was a thug of a man. A fellow Greek from the Peloponnese, likely from a large fishing family where there were too many sons and not enough boats. He had hands the size of portholes, and arms like a lifeboat's davit. If you got within reaching distance, there was no escaping him. There was no preventing him from doing what he wanted. Having his way. Theodor was half his size. He might have speed and cunning on his side, but close to, he lacked the strength to resist.

After the first degrading and painful episode he'd kept away from the pumpman. He'd only taken to his bunk when his cabin mate, the second officer, was sleeping. And he tried not to go below deck – particularly to the engine room – unless he had a direct order from the master. And then he timed his visits to coincide with the ape's off-duty roster.

That hadn't stopped the man.

With the Yellow Fleet – the colloquial term for the ships at anchor waiting the interminable wait for the canal to reopen – going nowhere, they'd reduced the crews to a skeleton. That meant more jobs for fewer men. Which meant more opportunity of finding yourself alone with the ape of a pumpman.

He could have complained. He could have made a noise. The master would have listened. And who knows? Maybe he would have done something about it. Maybe, even, he'd have spoken to Theodor's father and the pumpman would have been kicked off the ship, making Theodor's life immeasurably better?

Maybe.

The merchant navy was a man's world. Men were men. These things happened. Engineers got their hands ripped off and died a painful death rather than prevent cargo from being landed on time.

And, if nothing else, Theodor *was* a man.

Just thinking of the humiliation made the bile rise into the back of his throat.

No.

He wasn't going to give his father the pleasure of knowing his son was weak. That he couldn't cope. That he couldn't look after himself. That he was being abused and there was nothing he could do about it.

Because he could.

I will.

He was hatching a plan.

In the same way the Israeli air force had caught the Egyptians with their planes on the ground guaranteeing the outcome of the Six Day War – but not Egypt's belligerent scuttling of ships to shut the canal – so he too would catch the thug unawares. He had speed and guile. The ape was slow to react and easily fooled.

And ... when the pumpman's lacerated corpse was at the bottom of the lake, Theodor would then turn his ambitions to his father's empire.

That would be the next conquest.

December 1999

Everything about Heather hurt. And she was cold. Bitterly cold. Her fingers were like ice; they throbbed. Her right hip and shoulder, which were resting on unforgiving tarmac, leached what little heat she had left into the ground, heat which made easy work through a flimsy blouse and inadequate jeans.

The cold was one thing. The pain, however, that was specific and utterly draining.

Her neck, where men's hands had relentlessly pushed her head against the floor.

Her wrists, where nylon rope had bound her hands tightly behind her back.

And between her thighs. Where ...

She couldn't finish that sentence.

And now the cold. Which, as well as making every part of her body ache, was emphasising what she had endured. Her neck and her wrists, and the soreness below. They were magnets for more suffering, and the cold was recklessly exploiting their vulnerability.

What should I do?

That wasn't the right question. The right question was, 'what am I capable of doing?'

It was dark, the only light coming from a distant streetlamp which marked the edge of what she assumed was a village – there were some houses beyond the light. She was lying on a slim piece of pavement which serviced a narrow road that ran toward the village. She'd been in the foetal position for maybe fifteen minutes, having been launched unceremoniously through the sliding door of a van after a long journey, most of which she had no recollection of. Throughout she'd kept her knees forced tightly together – and that was so now. Nothing was going to separate them. Nothing but her own will, which was currently lacking.

She should do something, though. But she wasn't ready yet.

Not yet.

The whole thing had been unspeakable. Her mind recalling some things and then instantly forgetting them. She had no idea what day it was. She had no idea where she was. And she had no idea where she'd been. It was a blur of unimaginable suffering. The opening scenes of a Sunday night TV crime series. The ones her dad liked. The ones her mum endured.

That brought tears to her eyes – the comforts and familiarity of home.

The wetness stung cold as it dribbled over the bridge of her nose and dripped onto the grey-black ground.

I can't stay here all night.

She couldn't. She was shivering now. The semi-warmth of the back of the van's floor had been robbed from her. And now the deep cold was penetrating everything.

She was a student. She knew that. And she was studying – what was it? Her mind was a fog of memories which were being abruptly interrupted by a recent history of shocking violence and enduring pain.

Bioveterinary science.

Yes, that was it.

She knew how bodies worked. She knew that if she didn't move soon and find shelter she might well succumb to hypothermia. And that would finish the job they had started last night.

Or was it the night before that?

Or had it been both nights?

She had no idea. It was all a smear.

Sure, she remembered popping an Ecstasy tablet at the club in Aberdeen. Maybe two? And by the time they'd wrestled her into the back of the van she had had far too much to drink. But ... not so much she didn't know she was being taken against her will. Not so much she couldn't scratch at the man and dig her fingernails into the top of one of his hands.

But enough to be caught unawares. For her reactions to be dulled and her legs and arms hapless in a brief struggle.

There had been a cloth with a strange smell, pressed against her face ... and then nothing.

She had no idea how long she had been out for. She had no idea where they had taken her, although she thought she remembered a slow rocking sensation, as if she had been on a boat?

And then ...

No, she couldn't make herself do it.

It was musty, with grey, heavy stone walls.

And candles. *Yes, candles.*

And the smell of burning wood. A big fire, maybe. In a large hearth?

Yes.

And ...

No. She didn't want to go there.

How long, though? Could she remember? It had been Friday night, that was for sure. What day was it now? Was it Saturday? No, that didn't make sense. The journey seemed as if it had been interminable. She had drifted in and out of consciousness. And when she had woken, had she shouted? Screamed, maybe? And had a man in the back of the van suffocated her again with the smelly cloth?

Chloroform?

Was that it?

A smell of ether?

Could she remember?

In the past, vets had used the drug as both an anaesthetic and an analgesic, particularly for horses. She knew that from her studies. But it was toxic to the kidneys and liver. Yes. And – *and why is this coming to me now?* – it was carcinogenic for dogs in particular. She'd learnt that. She remembered that.

And wasn't it also used to drug victims of kidnap?

Or was that only in black and white films?

She had been conscious through the ordeal in the musty place with the stone walls and the hearth. Her mind skipped that with an alacrity which surprised her. And then another long journey home? Another smelly cloth to her face. Another heavy-handed smothering by a man with large hands and ... *a tattoo*? On his forearm. Blues and reds etched into white skin, entangled with horrible ginger, wispy hair.

This time, when she'd woken on the journey, she hadn't screamed out. It had seemed pointless. This time the swaying was accompanied by a rotational heavy *thump* of water against metal. It was slow and gentle. Melodic almost. As though the vessel she was in was easily capable of withstanding whatever the sea was asking of it.

How long? She couldn't say. She was in no state to judge. She thought she had possibly slept on and off. So it could have been a couple of hours. Some on a boat? Some time driving? The ordeal was eventually broken by the metallic *grate* and then a *clump* as the side door of a van had been dragged open and smacked against its buffers.

The man with the tattoo and the ginger wisps had picked her up as though she were a doll. And dropped her on the pavement.

That was maybe half an hour ago.

That journey, then. She had done that twice? That made it easily longer than a single night? So it was Sunday, she was sure of it. Sunday night. Early Monday morning, perhaps?

She had to get up. Her cheekbone, the one resting on the tarmac, was numb with cold. Her teeth were chattering in overtime. And she couldn't feel her toes, and the ends of her fingers ached as her blood refused to meet its obligations at her extremities.

I have to get up.

She had to face the future.

That was the issue, though. Wasn't it?

It wasn't that the ordeal had happened. It wasn't that she had been kidnapped, drugged, taken miles away – almost certainly over water – repeatedly abused by more than one man in a room which looked like it was from a mediaeval film set, and then drugged again, thrown into the back of a van and eventually deposited on a pavement in who knew where.

That wasn't the issue.

That was all *her* secret.

My secret.

She could reimagine most of it. Or, more likely, she could forget it. She was already accustomed to ignoring the horrors of the assault.

The men with the masks.

No. The problem wasn't what she had been through. It wasn't the shame or the already burgeoning remorse. It wasn't the indignity. Or the residual, physical pain, which she knew would eventually slip away.

It was what came next.

What was she going to tell her friends? If her parents found out, what would she share with them? Could she really recount the story?

Really?

Wasn't that better left untouched? Hidden?

Wouldn't it be best if she pulled together something more believable? Something more imaginable?

I don't know, possibly ...

A fling. A one-night stand with an older man. It was fabulous, but rough sex. It was delightful, but painful.

It was transient.

That was easy. It could be a story lost to her in a mist of a weekend of Scotch whisky and Irn-Bru. Of cheesy chips and slutty passion.

That would explain everything.

It was her fault.

Her choice.

...

There was a light. No, two. *Headlights.* A car. Heading her way, toward the village. There was no way the driver could avoid seeing her.

She had to do something.

So she did.

She forced herself to sit up. It was a struggle, but she managed.

The car was on her now, on the other side of the road. It pulled up. The driver's window lowered. The lights from the car's interior lit up a face. It was a man. Initially

Heather flinched, her chin dropped and her shoulders hunched.

'Are you OK, lassie?' the driver called out kindly.

It was a gentle voice. And when she lifted her head, the voice was accompanied by a sincere face. An older man. It might have been that of her father.

She didn't answer to begin with. And then, with ice-cold tears forming again, she shook her head.

Leaving the engine running, the man opened the door of his car and got out. He walked to her and dropped to his haunches.

'Can I help you? Can I phone someone? Your parents maybe?' His accent was soft.

She nodded meekly, hoping that would answer both questions. And then she asked him. She had to know.

'Where am I?'

His neck stiffened and his face became etched with confusion.

'Kingseat.'

'Is that ... near ... Aberdeen?' she asked, her chattering teeth breaking the question into pieces.

'Yes, wee one. A few miles north.'

She should have known of the place. But Aberdeen had a draw for the students. It had everything they needed within walking distance. Its environs were for the locals.

She was just about to ask a second question, but she stopped herself.

...

I have to know.

'What day is it?'

The man was still on his haunches. The car's engine was purring away nicely and Heather felt the draw of the warmth of its interior, like a sailor to a siren.

13

'Monday,' the man replied. 'No. Tuesday morning.'

Kindred

Chapter 1

Present day

Jane glanced at her watch. It was 11.17 am. She was running late. The Chief had asked to meet her away from Babylon. He had phoned her mobile, not her work extension. It was all highly unusual.

There was a pair of benches right on the Thames near the Buxton memorial. She knew of them. They were to meet there at 11.15. She could see them now, 30 metres in front of her. They were empty. Both of them.

Damn.

Where was the boss? Why this cloak-and-dagger stuff?

She was by the benches now. She glanced out at the Thames. It was high tide and the river was brown, wide and sluggish, a slight wind developing a swell which was struggling to be bothered.

Jane looked around. The park was hardly busy. Business people were using the path to cut through from Millbank to Westminster. A couple of Pacific Rim tourists were taking a selfie by the memorial. A jogger, heading south, lolloped past her, hardly out of breath.

But no Chief.

No Sir Clive Morton, Chief of Secret Intelligence Service, who had called for a clandestine meeting with Jane Baker, once a high flyer in SIS and now, even after the success of Sarajevo, responsible for 'Special Projects'. Whatever that meant.

Her phone rang. It was in her coat pocket. She retrieved it.

It was the Chief.

She connected.

'Yes, sir?'

'Bin to the right of the benches. Yesterday's *Mail*.'

The phone went dead. Jane stared at it, her mouth forming an oval as if she was about to say something.

Something like, 'What the hell?'

She put her phone away, took a long look around the park, and then moved to the bin.

There it was. A copy of the *Daily Mail*. She reached for it, folded it and stuck it under her arm, like a busy commuter about to rush for a train.

I need to find a more discreet place.

She knew London well and she knew this part of the city like the words of every 90s pop song she had ever memorised ... and never forgotten.

Tate Britain.

The gallery had a coffee shop. She'd used it before for client meetings. It was a pretty perfect spot. She was visiting. And she needed a coffee. That's all.

It took her three minutes to walk to the Tate, looking behind every so often to check that she wasn't being followed. It took her a further ten minutes to look as though she was coming to the gallery for a good reason. She busied herself, popped to the loo, and then grabbed an espresso and parked herself in the far corner of the vaulted Djanogly café. Its coffee was, apparently, made from beans that were roasted in a World War II Nissen hut in the gallery's grounds.

17

Jane took a sip from the tiny white cup.

It was good.

She looked around. Slowly.

Nothing.

She opened the tabloid and then carefully, a page at a time, glanced through its contents.

There.

The crossword was partially done. The Sudoku was complete.

The inky words scribbled on the crossword gave nothing away. Not yet. Not now.

However.

Some of the numbers of the Sudoku were … wrong. She was doing her best mental agility thing, looking for the patterns, checking for duplicate numbers in a line which would immediately identify a mistake.

There was one obvious one. Third row down. There were two fours and two threes, where there should be just one of each. The line was, like all Sudoku, nine numbers long. This one started with a seven followed by eight other numbers, including two fours and two threes.

The puzzle had been completed with confidence.

But this one line was wrong.

A mobile number?

Jane was in her element. This is what she did for a living … or used to.

A burner phone. Use once and throw away.

All UK cell numbers start with '07'. And then nine digits follow. That's where the pattern stopped. From there, there was no wisdom in the numbering. UK network providers bought random blocks of thousands of numbers, which they then assigned to customers. But anyone can change providers and take their number with them. So you couldn't get much from a number, other than from which operator it had been originally assigned.

Jane reckoned the Chief had led her to a burner.

She checked the crossword now.

No. Nothing there.

Yet.

She got out her phone, added '07' to the front of the nine-digit number which wasn't a correct entry into yesterday's Sudoku in the *Mail*, and sent a text. It read: *How can I help?*

She drank a touch more of her coffee. The liquid was intense and bitter. And it was getting cold.

Her phone vibrated. There was a response.

We need to meet. 1D and 3A. Come as soon as you can. Watch your back.

Jane had placed her phone on top of the paper, her head now resting in both hands. She glanced at the crossword.

One down: Saint. Three across: Giles. The clues and the scribbled answers didn't match. She'd missed that.

St Giles. Just under a mile away. Due north. She had a mental map in her head and she was really pleased with the way the synapses were twitching. Just months ago she'd have struggled to make her way into the office. Her life had been in tatters. Emotionally she was a wreck. Last year's events in Southeast Asia, which had culminated in the villa in Lao Chai where she had tried to take her own life, had taken a hatchet to what anyone might consider to be 'normality'. Her rescue from the villa at the hands of Sam Green had complicated matters further. Whilst it had saved her life, it had heightened her anxiety and further undermined her own value of worth.

Post Hanoi it had taken her eight months to find the strength to come back to work. To a job which was nothing more than a fill-in, when previously she had been destined for much greater things.

She had been at the bottom in Asia. There was no further down she could go.

And so she had surprised herself by wanting to get involved with an emerging threat. She had surprised herself further by disobeying the Chief's clear instructions that she wasn't well enough, or indeed competent enough, to be operational.

Yet … three months ago she had met The Box man just up from where she was now. She had been standing next to him when he had been pushed onto the rails.

And she had said and done nothing … other than use the intelligence he had shared with her. She knew that being at the scene of the murder of an MI5 officer would complicate any investigation, so she ignored it. Instead she had travelled to Paris to meet Louis Belmonte. And then on to the Balkans to meet up with …

… there she was.

Sam Green. Waiting for her outside the embassy in Sarajevo. The same Sam Green she had rescued from a burning hostel in Kenema a lifetime ago. The Sam Green who months earlier had dragged her out of the villa in Lao Chai.

Mayhem had followed in Bosnia. And death. By the end of which, bizarrely, she was beginning to feel better. Not fixed. No, fixed would be an overstatement. But better. More in control. More steady.

Jane had stayed in Sarajevo at the end. Because they needed her. They needed all of them. But Sam hadn't. She had immediately moved on to Africa. In the Balkans they had blown apart one despicable criminal activity. But Sam was already onto the next. Jane had implored her to stay. She wanted her by her side. Sarajevo needed her energy and efficacy.

That conversation had been short and one-sided and Sam had flown to Nigeria. Another massive operation, this time effected by the Israelis with Sam in cahoots.

It was a success – from what the UK government could fathom. Neither the Israelis nor Sam had shared any details, so they couldn't be absolutely sure. But Mossad don't mess about. And the Nigerians weren't offering a view. It was all too messy. Too close to home for them.

Jane got Sam's drive. What they were all involved with – the Balkans and Nigeria – was only picking at a scab of a wound which was too deep to heal. They, that is Sam and her and Frank and, well, everyone who was on their side, were trying to bring down an organisation which had roots everywhere. Which knew everything. Which was more powerful than governments. Which spanned continents and infiltrated the intelligence and police services across the world.

And now they, Sam and Frank and Jane – they were targets. They had kicked what they thought was a mule, but the mule had turned out to be a dragon.

Jane had warned Sam. Post Nigeria, her friend had been in Greece, camping. Jane had called her. Told her that they were all in danger. Told her that the SIS needed Sam back in the fold. They could use her expertise and hoped they could exploit her recent connections with Mossad. Jane was in the middle of the call when Sam had become distant. The phone had gone quiet. Then she could hear the rasp of Sam's breath and the thump of feet on sand.

She was running.

And then nothing. The phone had gone dead.

That had been three weeks ago. Jane had tried to call Sam again, but the number was no longer recognised. Sam was either off-grid, or something more unthinkable.

Three weeks ago.

That was a very long time in her business.

Jane and Frank had continued to work together on the aftermath of Sarajevo. They had tried to piece together what had gone on in Nigeria. The Israelis were permanently schtum and none of SIS's allies had much more than they had. Sam knew everything. Clearly. But they didn't know where Sam was. If, indeed, she were alive.

It was all very unsatisfactory, and with ranks closing and her circle of 'people she could trust' losing its shape and reducing to no more than a handful, Jane gets a call from the Chief for a clandestine meeting. Which leads to a burner phone, an out-of-date copy of the *Daily Mail*, a badly completed Sudoku puzzle, and a crossword which was going to send her on another journey.

She assumed it was St Giles in the Field. A little bit on from Covent Garden. She'd be there in half an hour, maybe less. That was as good as 'as soon as possible'.

Jane picked up her phone and thought of replying to the SMS but didn't. Standard procedure would be for the Chief to remove the SIM, break it, and then drop it down the drain. He'd wipe the phone with a cloth and shove it in a bin. Even if someone discovered it they wouldn't be able to make a connection to the messages which had been passed. And starting the process with a fresh dead drop which connected to a single-use mobile number, the whole meet was as secure as you could make it.

The Chief was clearly worried about something.

Frank was ... what was it? *Anxious*. That was it. Anxiety was part of his life. It was central to who he was. It had been like it since school. He was a nervous child. He was a sensitive teenager. And he was an anxious adult. That hadn't prevented him from doing well at his studies, getting a decent degree and finding a really good job as an analyst in SIS. In some ways it helped. He struggled with failure. He hated being told off. He disliked company, but was always keen to share his success with others. He had an eye for detail. And plenty of logic up top. And now, with twelve years' experience, he was very good at what he did.

So anxiety was an ever present colleague.

But the anxiousness he felt now was different.

This wasn't about whether Marcus, his boss, would be happy with the German report he was working on. Or how Frank felt about the pile of unfinished work on his desk.

This was much more fundamental.

This was about trust.

It had all started a year ago. Post Korea. There was an emerging ideological struggle in the UK. There was division. Politics was loud and angry. And it had percolated down through communities and families. People were wearing their support openly. You were either one side, or the other. And the press and social media had amplified and encouraged the division.

At first the intelligence services assumed it was just the way it was. People's previous disregard for politics had been pricked by populism. Leaders across the world had tapped into a hitherto uncharted vein of support by heightening individuals' fears, and telling them that they were the people to fix it. Social media – and some mainline news stations and papers, particularly in the US and UK – had amplified the struggle. Facts had become anti-facts. Truth was what someone said, not necessarily what could be verified.

Conspiracy was rife.

Facebook was the go-to place to feed the theories. But there were many more devious – and dangerous – corners of the internet.

QAnon had emerged as the internet frontrunner for peddling subterfuge. It was a cauldron of fake news and deception. Its theories became flesh by way of a disorganised and unled army of all manner of people who wanted to believe something, even if that something was plainly nonsense. The 'anons', as they were known, formed their own subgroups on Facebook and other social media platforms, and from there they organised campaigns against seemingly sensible and honest activities. And those groups disintegrated as quickly as they had formed when their energies were lost to another cause.

It had been impossible to predict where the next QAnon theory might lead. And which group of people might decide it was a banner under which they would march. The madness was that anons were not just unhinged loners, living out their lives in the depths of the Appalachians, building nuclear bunkers and stocking shelves whilst waiting for the apocalypse. They were 'hockey moms' and, over here and across most of the West, they were often professional people – working mothers, grandads and university students. The last intelligence from MI5 was that there were 213,000 dedicated anons (that is, subscribing to a QAnon social media page or site) in the UK. And they were busy.

The latest conspiracy was that the UK's nuclear deterrent had been compromised. HMS Vengeance, one of the four Trident-carrying Vanguard-class submarines had, apparently, gone missing. There were multiple photographs of sea-wreckage and Geiger counters measuring seawater radiation levels well above normal. A leading marine biologist (who had been recently sacked from his job at Plymouth University for embezzling funds) had put his name to photographs of dead seabirds off the coast of the Hebrides. They had, apparently, succumbed to radiation poisoning.

There had been protests outside Faslane, the home of the UK's nuclear deterrent. There had even been a question raised by a Labour MP in the Scottish parliament.

But it was nonsense.

Frank knew where Vengeance was. And it wasn't at the bottom of the ocean.

Vengeance was the first of the four missile submarines to begin the Trident renewal programme. That work was being undertaken by BAe Systems at Barrow-in-Furness. The boat was safely in dry dock getting an upgrade, before the subsequent launch of the brand new Dreadnaught replacement class in 2030.

The UK took the intelligence surrounding its nuclear missile submarine programme very seriously. And there was no way this latest conspiracy was going to be quashed by a tour of the facilities. That wasn't going to happen.

In any case it wouldn't last. Next week there'd be a new conspiracy. And the week after, another.

In some ways the haphazard nature of the QAnon phenomenon was no more than an irritation: a distraction from the day-to-day business of keeping the nation and its interests safe, both here and abroad.

But it *wasn't* haphazard.

Not anymore.

And that was the unnerving thing about it.

The Belmonte Paradox was still a thing. The YCA – the Young Crofters' Association, that was still a thing. SIS and the Bosnian police might have dismantled its organ harvesting and transplant set-up a month ago. And Sam, whatever it was that Sam did with the Israelis in Nigeria, would have hurt them further. But the YCA – the group of international billionaires currently fashioning governments for their own ends – was still doing what it did. Frank was convinced of it.

It was clear to him that with Michael Connock, the Australian media mogul, in the YCA's ranks, and with the widest influence which only billions of dollars could buy, QAnon was no longer a spontaneous and unaffiliated social media construct. It was no longer a banner under which any old influencer had the opportunity to manipulate others with unsubstantiated stories and fringe views.

Not now.

Now there was a clear linkage between the endless Q-drops and the YCA. QAnon, which pushed back against organisations, which prided itself on undermining the rich and powerful, had now unwittingly crossed over to the dark side. It was now a vehicle for a small, elite group of the rich and powerful. The soccer moms, who last year marched against the Federal poisoning of their children because the US government was putting too much fluoride in their domestic water supply, were being set up and manipulated by the very people they were purportedly fighting against.

Frank was sure of it.

But that wasn't why he was feeling anxious.

He was anxious because it was now also clear that the division in society – right versus left, Christian versus Muslim, Brexit versus pro-Europe – was no longer just an issue of ideological belief which, if you weren't that bothered or easily influenced, you could ignore. You could distance yourself from the rhetoric by keeping off social media and ignoring anything other than the centrist agenda. You could ignore sensitive subjects when you were in the pub with your mates, or around your in-laws for Sunday lunch.

That was workable.

But when it reached into the very organisations you worked for, the organisations set up to protect you and the country you loved, then it became much more difficult to ignore.

Frank's remit was UK nationals involved with right-wing terrorist organisations abroad; particularly, but not exclusively, in Europe. His work had exposed him to Louis Belmonte, the French DGSI officer, who had originally uncovered the YCA. That had led to Jane's meeting with the man in Paris, and subsequently the dismantling of the YCA's organ harvesting and transplant set-up.

The intelligence which had come back from Sarajevo had been cluttered and huge, and he'd immediately started to dissect, label and compartmentalise it. It was a month's work. But it was going to be an important, potentially key, month's work.

That was until Marcus had pulled him into his office two weeks ago.

'You're off the Belmonte investigation. *Comprendez*?' his boss had said.

Frank was too shocked to say anything immediately.

'Pass everything you have to Bradley. Today. Got it?' Marcus was sitting behind his desk, his chin resting on clasped hands.

Frank couldn't stand the man. He'd loved working for Jane, every day had been a pleasure. Once she'd left to tour Southeast Asia, Marcus Trafford had been posted in. He was an old-school case officer who had spent most of his time working at Langley. He was obtuse and lazy. Among others, that was two very good reasons not to like him.

'But, but … I've been working with Jane,' he spluttered. 'And Bradley's a baby!'

'Jane's off the case too. And Bradley will work straight to me.' Marcus had sat back in his chair, but his hands were still clasped.

'Any problems with that, Frank?' It wasn't a question. Not one that he expected an answer to. It was a statement of intent. Frank was to pass everything to Bradley. End of.

'And I want the Stuttgart report on my desk pronto. Savvy?'

Frank hated him even more when he used words like 'pronto', 'savvy' and '*comprendez*'. He felt like he was in an episode of *Only Fools and Horses*.

He waited for a second, chewing on his lip.

'Yes,' he'd said sheepishly.

'Good. Report. Sharpish, yeah?' Marcus had tapped at his desk.

Frank nodded as he turned. He'd walked quickly back to his desk, his shoulders more hunched than normal, overwhelmed by a feeling that his brief had been taken from him because he was one of the good guys.

It had taken him the rest of the day to produce a pack for the cadet, Bradley … and into the evening to complete the German report Marcus wanted. He'd bought fish and chips on the way home, and had supped at an alcohol-free Bud whilst he waited for the bath to fill.

That was two weeks ago. Two weeks for his anxiety to spike.

Since then he hadn't stopped working on the Belmonte investigation. He had just worked smarter, and stayed at his desk for longer. Not that Marcus noticed. He was always in late and left early.

But the episode had deeply unsettled him. One of the early takes from the Sarajevo operation was that the YCA had reached into many nations' security infrastructure. The only way they could pull off what they did was if they were able to influence national police forces and prise information from their intelligence services. Louis Belmonte was convinced of that. So was Jane.

But not SIS?

Not here? Surely?

The demographic mix was too diverse. They recruited pan-belief, pan-religion, pan-sexuality, pan-everything – specifically to recruit the best people, whilst noting that this grouping would never unionise around a particular cause. There were too many oddballs. Too many loners.

He was wrong, though, wasn't he?

Marcus was proof of that.

Wasn't he?

Or was this Frank's very own conspiracy? That SIS was riddled with YCA acolytes? That some staff had Q-badges sewn into the inside breasts of the jackets? And that Her Majesty's Secret Intelligence Service was no longer independent?

It could no longer be trusted.

That's why he was anxious.

So much so he had started to think about finding another job.

But first he had work to do.

His phone buzzed.

Frank picked it up.

It was Jane. He pressed the green phone icon.

'Hi, Jane. Everything OK?'

'Are you on your own?'

That's odd.

Frank looked around unnecessarily.

'Yeah.'

'Get out of there, now. Bring a secure laptop and any personal effects you can get away with. Make sure you have the latest on Belmonte on your hard drive, and delete it from everywhere else. And be discreet.' Jane's voice was uncompromising.

Frank looked around again. His eyes rested on the left-hand of his three screens. On it was a list. It read:

YCA

- *Duke of Nairnshire, Edward Grinstead; UK; landowner and founder; net worth – £43bn*
- *Elias Bosshart; CH; bank, art and watches; net worth – £45bn*
- *Jimmy Johnson Jr; US; oil, minerals and metal; net worth – £81bn*
- *Edouard Freemantle; SA; unknown; net worth – c£50bn*
- *Marc Belmonte; FR; wine; net worth – £32bn*

30

- *Sheik Rashid bin Nahzan; UAE; oil; net worth – £94bn*
- *Theodor Konstantos; shipping; GR; net worth – £21bn*
- *Michael Connock; AU; international media; net worth – £76bn*

'What's this about, Jane?' he asked whilst saving the document to his laptop's hard drive and deleting it from the secure cloud.

'Meet me at your favourite restaurant. I'll be there at 6.30 tonight. Come straight there. Do not go home. And follow usual procedures.'

'But ...?' Frank was shaking his head, whilst gathering his things together. There were three people in his life whom he trusted completely. Jane was one of them. The Chief was the other. Sam Green was the third.

'Just do it, Frank. And ...' it was Jane's turn to sound unsure, 'be careful, Frank.'

Then the phone went dead.

Chequers (Prime Minister's Official Country Residence), Missenden Road, Aylesbury Buckinghamshire, UK

Dominic Bianci was finding his way. On one hand he couldn't be more excited. On the other he was six days into a job which frightened the hell out of him. Chequers was it. As a newly appointed valet and someone desperately keen to make their way in the 'personal attendance' business (his ambition was to become a butler in a large country house, or on a whole-floor apartment in Belgravia), he could have pinched himself when the pale cream envelope dropped onto the mat of his mum's house. His name, and the address, was beautifully etched on the front in some senior gothic font. On the back was the Lion and Unicorn armorial, under which was the number '10' and the two words 'Downing Street'.

He'd stared at it, not wanting to know what was inside, whilst desperately keen to discover his fate.

'Is that it?' his mother had whispered over his shoulder.

He could only nod in reply.

Any other potential employer would have phoned, or dashed off an email. But not the office of the United Kingdom's prime minister. No. Only a formal response would do.

'I'll make some tea,' his mum had said. 'Bring it into the kitchen.' She had already turned and was scuttling away down the narrow hall.

Ten minutes later, halfway down a cup of Earl Grey (of course) – no milk – his fate was known. He was to become the second valet to Prime Minister Geoffrey Fordingly, based at Chequers, the prime ministerial retreat. Prime Minister Fordingly, a Conservative, was eighteen months into a fixed five-year term – although fixed, as Dominic was quickly learning, was a moveable feast. Should two-thirds of MPs vote in favour of an early election, or the government lose the confidence of the House, then a general election could be called at any time. These details were important. Especially to a newly appointed valet. A new prime minister, say, a woman, might want a female valet at Chequers. Or, like Gordon Brown, who only used Chequers for major visits, the staff might be slashed in an instant.

And 'second', in terms of the hierarchy of valets, was because the premier valet was based in Downing Street, a job Dominic already aspired to.

Chequers was absolutely stunning. According to James, the current and long-serving butler, the house was set in 1,000 acres of prime Buckinghamshire countryside. The 16th-century, red-brick manor house had become the country residence of British prime ministers in 1921 when the estate was gifted by the then owner, Sir Arthur Lee, for exactly this purpose. .

With an index finger touching his nose, James had then told Dominic that, 'Chequers is why you want the job.' He'd paused then, and looked wistfully at a silver centrepiece. He'd added, 'Dennis Thatcher told me that.'

Dennis Thatcher!

Dominic *was* impressed.

It had taken him five days to get his bearings and start to recognise who was who among the house staff, the gardeners and the security personnel. He was a quick learner and he already knew the details of the prime minister's wardrobe, and that of his fourth wife, Maisie (née Knowles), a young blonde lady who had already delivered one child and was due a second anytime soon. Dominic had rehearsed the prime minister's toiletries, his towelling and his favourite snacks and drinks. They had two resident chefs – a number which, James had said, rose to six or eight for major functions – who could provide most meals to order, and *any* meal given two days' notice. But the valet's, sorry *second* valet's, job was to fill the gaps: a can of full fat Pepsi; a Warner's London Dry Gin (at £150 a bottle – Dominic had googled it) with Fever-Tree tonic, and a slice of lime, not lemon; a cut glass tumbler, half full of Shetland Reel whisky, all the way from islands, with two blocks of ice; and an espresso made with Whittard Jamaican Blue coffee served with two Oreos. These were just a few of Prime Minister Fordingly's favourites. He had many more, and Dominic was onto them.

There was still much to learn. But there was also so much to be distracted by. What particularly caught his attention were the photographs. They, like the prime ministerial tenure of the house, traced back a century. There were hundreds – too many to pick a favourite. If pressed he particularly liked the one of Margaret Thatcher and George HW Bush. Sure, the more, heavier, historical collectives – including Dwight Eisenhower with Harold Macmillan, among scores of others – were impressive. But, notwithstanding the current occupant, Prime Minister Thatcher was his favourite. He had so far counted fourteen photos where she was either the subject of an image, or was with a group of dignitaries. Only Winston Churchill had more. That was some accolade.

So, he might find himself distracted.

But not today.

Today was a special day.

The prime minister, his wife and their first child (his sixth, Dominic noted) were due at Chequers for the weekend. Apparently the family came as often as they could which, unfortunately, wasn't that often.

'Pressures of state,' James had said. 'They like to consider the place as their holiday home. So when they come we try to make it as relaxing as possible. Other prime ministers, like Gordon Brown, only ever came here with VIP guests. He wasn't comfortable using it.'

'Do you know why? It's such a fabulous place,' Dominic had asked. He wasn't sure if it were yet his place to press for answers from a man with a wealth of experience.

'Gordon Brown was my first. And I never really had the chance to get close to the man, so I can't say why for sure.' They were in the dining room laying the table for supper. For a casual weekend where staffing was at a minimum, all hands were on deck. James was polishing a red wine glass. He raised it to the window so he could check for smudges.

'I suppose it might have been his socialist principles. Possibly uncomfortable with being waited on. I understand his wife, Sarah Jane, was more at ease ... but I get it. I think.' James placed the glass on the table, forward right of the placemat. He then nudged it into its rightful space.

Dominic wasn't sure. The office of the prime minister was the most eminent position in the United Kingdom. And if this house, and its staff, came with that role then the top person deserved the accolade. He was certainly going to try his best to make the family's stay as comfortable and relaxing as possible.

And now was that time. It was 8.23 pm. He and James were standing, three steps up, in the mellowly-lit, square-pillared entrance of the house. The procedure was for them to step off onto the gravel once the second car, an armoured Jaguar XJ Sentinel, pulled up in front of the alcove. James would take the nearside door, Dominic would walk quickly around the back of the Jag to the offside. They would open the doors and stand back for the occupants. The prime minister always sat nearside, rear. His CP (*close protection* – Dominic was getting into the vernacular) always travelled in the passenger seat in front of the main target, so they could jump out 'into the line of fire', or drop the window to provide immediate armed support.

Tonight should be no different.

Three sets of headlights. Three cars in the motorcade. Again, normal routine, as described by James. The lead was a security vehicle, an unmarked police Range Rover. Next was the Jag, known as the executive car. And then the tail security vehicle, another Range Rover. James had also told him there were two regular patrol cars clearing the route five minutes ahead of the motorcade, but they didn't pull into Chequers. Apparently three weeks ago RASP (*Royal and Specialist Protection* – another learnt acronym) had tested a low-light drone to follow the convoy. It had hit a mobile phone pylon and burst into flames before they'd got out of Westminster. So that had gone back to the drawing board.

The lead Range Rover pulled past them, and the Jag stopped right in front of the entrance, its wheels skidding slightly on the gravel.

James moved first, catching Dominic off guard; it took him half a second to get back on task. He took off quickly, around the back of the huge car, and was by the offside rear door a couple of seconds later. By the time he pulled the thick, heavy door of the Jag open and caught a flash of a silky smooth calf extending from under the hem of a blood red dress, the prime minister was out of the car, his hand on James's shoulder.

'Good to see you, James. I hope Margaret is well?' The prime minister's voice was deep, but smooth. It rang with confidence, but was also laced with compassion.

'Very well, sir. Thank you. I hope you all had a good journey?' James responded.

There was a beat ... it happened so quickly.

The prime minister's young, vibrant and pregnant wife was out of the car, her back to Dominic as she worked on something still inside the vehicle. Dominic was poised ...

'You must be Dominic?' The prime minister hadn't replied to James's question. Instead he had turned and, across the roof of the car, addressed Dominic, the Jag's quiet engine hardly registering from a bonnet which seemed miles away.

Dominic was caught. He was half bent forward and was about to ask the prime minister's wife if she needed a hand.

Should he help the lady, or respond to the question? With his mind already spinning with the excitement of such an important role, he was in a quandary.

He lifted his head and found Prime Minister Fordingly looking directly at him, as though he was the only person who mattered in the world.

'Yes, sir. Thank you, sir.' The 'thank you' was a stupid thing to add. The prime minister ignored it and moved on.

'Good to meet you, Dominic.' The prime minister stuck up a thumb. 'We look forward to getting to know you. Now, can you give Maisie a hand with the baby?'

The prime minister has recognised me.

That's all Dominic could think of. He was starstruck. His heart was filling with more blood than it had ever before. Still caught in a half-bent stature, he nodded and said, 'Sure ... sir,' another poor response. He must do better.

And then the great man turned away, at the same time as the red dress, with its big tummy and a baby so soft and warm and cuddly it might have been a Disney cartoon, was facing him.

Maisie Fordingly looked flushed. But she managed a smile and held the child in front of her in both hands.

Does she ...?

She did. Maisie Fordingly was clearly expecting Dominic to take the young girl into his arms.

Which he did, with as much care as if he were handling an unexploded bomb.

He was going to really, really like this job.

Chapter 2

Sam was resting her arms on the white block wall which overlooked the Danube. Behind her was the city's castle, an ugly, square, white building, four storeys high with a thin red-tiled roof and four slim square towers – one at each corner. Even though it was 9th century, it looked brand new and boxy, as if last week a local primary school had run a competition to design a castle and this was the outcome. But in front of it the views over the wide river were spectacular. Forward left was a slender modern bridge at the end of which was the officially named 'UFO Lookout Tower'. The slim tower was part of the suspension mechanism for the bridge, on top of which some comedian of an architect had placed a frisbee-shaped restaurant. It looked as though a drunken alien had popped down to Earth and hadn't bothered too much with parking and, as a result, had skewered their craft on an inconvenient pole.

She loved it.

Bratislava didn't take itself too seriously. The main shopping street was decorated with bronze statues of life-sized men and women in poses which were in sympathy with where they found themselves. Sam particularly liked the 'man at work' one – a metal guy emerging from a manhole, his hard-hatted head resting on his arms as he took a break before he pulled his torso from the underground doom.

And it was late in the year, so the place had that pre-Christmas feeling. It was cold and crisp. The trees had lost their leaves, so you could see more. People were wrapped up well and the shops were awash with sparkly lights and winter ornaments. As she stared across the Danube to a flat, pale green and grey landscape beyond the city limits, for a nostalgic moment Sam was in a ski resort. She had her boots on and a set of skis and poles resting on her shoulder. She had just finished a hard day on the piste. Under her helmet her hair was damp with sweat, but brittle where it was exposed to the freezing air. She had stopped outside a bar and ...

She shook her head and mumbled something incoherent which probably included an expletive. It was pointless. She couldn't begin to imagine any future which included the freedom to ski without fear that someone would be following her, intent on doing her harm.

There'd be a man on the ski lift with her. Or the chair behind. Or they'd be someone in a dark corner of a bar.

She had been chased on the slopes once before, in Alpbach, Austria. A man, a faster skier than her, had caught her on the Red 8 and knocked her off her skis. There was a gun. And a fight. She had escaped that time.

That time.

This time, though, the odds were different. Then it was one man and his thug.

Now she was being chased down by possibly ... probably, the largest and most capable criminal syndicate in the world. A group of businessmen with more money than the combined worth of a G7 country. They had spectacular resources. They had agents embedded in every major intelligence community. They had bought influence in police forces.

And they chose governments.

What chance did she have?

They had found her in Greece, on the campsite in the Peloponnese. And she was sure they had clocked her as she crossed the border into Albania. The border guard, who was handling her Israeli passport, had spent far too long conferring between his old, boxy cathode-ray-tube computer screen and her document. His hand had wavered over a dirty telephone handset, before eventually he had scribbled down a note on a spare piece of A4 and thrust the passport back at her. Nervous, Sam had not got back on the overnight coach to Tirana which had been waiting outside. Instead she had walked across the road to a taxi rank and offered an elderly man $50 to drive her to the capital.

She had stayed in Tirana for a week, in a rundown hostel on the outskirts of the run down city. She had used that time to breathe. To regain her humour and get fitted out for what looked likely to be a long haul of cat and mouse. She had left the Peloponnese with nothing other than the essentials she always carried in her daysack and waist-belt. On foot. With black smoke rising from the campsite in the middle distance, and the man on the beach looking her way with a pair of binos, she was convinced her campervan had been torched – and that the man had spotted her. She was sure of it. So, with a stomach wound which had been expertly sewn by an Israeli doctor two weeks previously but was still woefully short of time to heal, she had run as fast as she could into the local forest. And then, never completely happy that she had lost the man, or men, she had spent thirty-six hours tracking the road until she had reached a town.

By which time she had felt wretched. She was tired, hungry, her stomach was sore and she needed a shower.

And the town was too close to where she had been spotted. It was too exposed. She needed to get further away. Much further away.

Patras, Greece's third largest city with its bridge from the Peloponnese to the mainland, was ideal. There she could get lost in a crowd, regroup and form a plan. But Patras was 150 kilometres away and she wasn't yet ready to chance public transport.

It was an instantaneous decision borne from necessity. She didn't like it, but there was no other choice.

She'd stolen a car. It was an old Mark 1 Fiat Panda. It was blue. Well, rust and blue-ish. It was beyond midnight when she had made her way from the shrubby bushes at the edge of town into a small urbanisation. And she hadn't had to try many cars before she found one which was open, with its keys under the visor. This was Greece, not Grantham.

Before she left for Patras she'd had to fill up with fuel and get some cash, which had meant using a card. That would have tied her to a place and a time, information any decent intelligence service would have within an hour. For her, though, it was about priorities. And, in any case, they knew she was in this part of Greece. They just didn't know where she was going next.

She had abandoned the car on Patras's seafront by a bus station, and bought a ticket to Igoumenitsa, on the Albanian border. It had been a fitful, six-hour coach trip. Followed by another to Tirana – until a dozy border guard had spooked her. She had then taken a taxi the remainder of the way.

During all that time she hadn't slept in a bed, or used a shower. She'd eaten sparingly and drunk from streams, which would highly likely come back to haunt her. Thankfully, though, her week in Tirana had bought her some space, refilled her stomach with much needed food, and allowed her to shower.

Once she'd begun to feel semi-human, she'd crossed into Serbia, and then on to Hungary. Whilst she carried with her her four Russian and Latvian aliases (as well as her British passport), she continued to use the Israeli cover which Mossad had set up for her after the Abuja operation. Micah, the field agent with whom she had worked, had assured her that the blue and gold embossed passport was supported by a credible history. He'd given her two pages of notes which detailed the background of a Neta Peretz, a thirty-two-year-old unmarried history graduate from Jerusalem. She had read it once and then set fire to it. So far her disguise was holding water. Her only footprint was her bank cards, which she had used sparingly.

But probably not sparingly enough.

With a simple set of keystrokes Cynthia, SIS's mainframe, would be able to track and compare bankcard locations against cross-border travel. It would sort through tens of thousands of border checks against ATM and other transactions, matching passports and ID cards, to credit and debit card usage. There would be, maybe, 15,000 names that matched her itinerary in the same timeframe. That was nothing for a decent analyst. Add in gender, age and half-decent facial recognition, and the list would be down to no more than 100.

If it were Sam, she would then check among the 100 for Brits, Russians ... and Israelis. The first two because of her history. The third because of her recent Israeli linkage, one the YCA must have made after the Abuja operation. There was, after all, the unmistakable Israeli Air Force's insignia of a blue Star of David set in a white circle on the side of the Hercules transport plane which had rescued them all from the Grandom Tech compound.

That would cut the list down to, say, five.

That was an easy number. For any idiot. Provided they were doing their job properly.

She had to assume, therefore, that her passport had been compromised.

Thankfully she was now in the European Union, where you could move across borders transparently. Provided she stayed in the Schengen zone she might go unnoticed. Other than her two VISA cards, which limited her to a cash withdrawal of 300 euros – and leaving aside CCTV, because no organisation could search every CCTV camera in central Europe – she was close to invisible.

Other than my bank cards.

Sam had to use her card again soon. The previous time had been in Serbia. That 300 euros had lasted ten days. It had found her a coach journey, lodging, food, some winter clothes and a couple of burner phones, neither of which she had used.

She was now down to her last forty euros. That was enough for one more night. And then she'd need to use an ATM – and find some other city to get lost in.

Sam turned to face the castle, its shockingly white façade made brighter by the brief appearance of the low winter sun.

What to do?

She could, if she wanted, live like this indefinitely.

If she wanted.

But it was rubbish. It wasn't living.

It was running.

What other choices do I have?

Jane had phoned her at the beginning of this saga. On the sun-kissed beach, just down from the campsite. When she had been walking to the local taverna for some food.

Jane had warned her. Told her that they were all in danger – that Sam was in danger. That SIS wanted her back in the fold. Back at Vauxhall. Jane had been close to pleading.

It was an option.

But it wasn't an attractive option.

There was another. And it wasn't without risk, both physical and emotional.

But it might be the best of some alternative, crappy options.

Nando's, Streatham, London, UK

Frank was looking dazed. And jittery, if that combination was possible. Jane couldn't blame him. In less than twenty minutes she had taken his world and turned it upside down until everything had fallen out of its pockets. In quiet tones, because even Nando's' walls have ears, she had recounted her earlier conversation with the Chief, and then what had happened on the steps of St Giles in the Field directly after their meeting.

'If you're struggling to believe me, open the BBC news app, Frank,' she'd said a few minutes ago.

Frank had a fork in one hand and an earlobe in his other. His mouth was ajar. Thankfully there was no half-eaten burger in it.

'I don't have the BBC App. I have the *Guardian*.' His voice was emotionless. His pale face in need of some Vitamin D.

'Open it.' Jane was eating chicken in something. She hadn't paid any attention to the menu. Food was important, but not as important as getting Frank on side and then coming up with a plan. Which, in the forty minutes that had spanned the Chief's arrest and her meeting Frank, had failed to materialise in her head.

Frank had put his fork down and was dabbing and swiping.

There was a pause.

'What the hell?' It was a quiet 'what the hell', almost under his breath. 'You're right. He's been arrested?'

It was all part of an incredible story which made every sense, but then no sense at all. Her meeting with the Chief had been short. He'd looked under pressure. He lacked his usual calmness. His brief had been sharp but, ever the professional, not rushed.

'The YCA are pulling the strings of this, and other, governments,' the Chief had said. They had been sitting together on the 'friends and family of the bride' side of the church. 'They are slowly but competently removing references to the YCA, the Belmonte Paradox and the Sarajevo and Abuja operation. It's thorough. And it's everywhere.'

'What do you mean, everywhere?' Jane had asked.

The Chief was staring ahead, an eye catching the light from a distant candle.

'Tom Ridden is on their payroll,' the Chief said flatly. He'd glanced at her at that point.

Tom was the Chief's de facto deputy, although his actual title was Senior Operations Coordinator. Jane knew him well. She'd have bet everything in her bank account that the man was straight.

'No. That can't be so. He's ...'

The Chief had raised a hand.

'I don't have much time, Jane. Just trust me.' His face reinforced the line. 'The YCA files make many sensitive claims, such as the group's influence in choosing this country's prime minister. Add in the work poor old Louis Belmonte did ...'

'What do you mean, "poor old"?' SIS staff were trained to be specific. 'Has something happened?' Jane recognised her voice was too much of a shriek. She made a note to go back to whispering.

The Chief hadn't reply. His face continued to tell the story.

'No!' She spat it out, and then checked herself. 'I had dinner with him. His brother is a YCA member. They wouldn't ...?'

'He was found this morning, head down in the Seine. It was made to look like suicide. And the *gendarmerie* will quickly come to that conclusion. That's the YCA's way.'

Jane brought her hands together as if she was about to pray.

'My God.' This time it was quieter than a whisper. 'If Belmonte ... then,' she had struggled forming words, 'why not me?'

The Chief put a hand on her forearm.

'Get everything you can from the file. Get Frank. And find Sam, if they haven't got her already. I can't help you with who's on the payroll, and who isn't. Because I really do not know who else in this country to trust. But find somewhere safe. And then start afresh ...'

'How?' She was exasperated. And scared. 'How do we do that without recourse to the resources in Vauxhall? And why can't you come with us?' It was all a whirl of conspiracy, and, she found a more apposite word, fear.

'I am no use to you. Not where I'm going.' There was finality to what he said.

'What do you ...?'

The Chief had stood, not letting her finish her sentence. He placed a hand on her shoulder. She looked up at him, her eyes damp with forming tears.

'Get Frank. And Sam. Other than Marcus and a new lad, both of whom I am confident are on the payroll, there is no one else with access to the YCA file. It's always been on close hold. Find somewhere safe. Regroup. And then decide what you are going to do next. And if the answer to that question is a Costa Rican beach, then I won't judge you.'

She had tears now. Full blown, rolling down your cheek tears.

She had been making progress. She was getting close to believing she was becoming a normal, fully functioning human being. Sarajevo had done that for her. Given her focus and a renewed zest for life. Now there was every danger that that progress was about to be shattered. The Chief's revelations over the YCA's control, whilst hardly a massive surprise, were still monumental. But the fact it seemed he was about to leave them was too much. Sure, eighteen months ago it seemed possible she might eventually take his successor's place on the throne. But a lot had happened in eighteen months. And she wasn't in any way ready to step up and take that level of responsibility, especially if that role were divorced from Vauxhall.

A beach in Costa Rica?

She was a family woman. She had a mother and a brother, who had a wife and a daughter. She liked going down the pub. She set up her Christmas tree in a certain way with decorations she had collected over the years. She had an old red sit-up-and-beg bicycle on which she used to potter down to her local coffee shop on the rare days she wasn't overwhelmed with work.

She had a mortgage. And gym membership.

Was the Chief really suggesting that she was to give all of that up because a French DGSI officer had met a watery death?

Jane looked at him, his hand still on her shoulder.

'And if I don't?' It was no more than a bleat. She knew what the answer was.

'Think of Louis Belmonte, the man who started all of this. Think of his fate.' The Chief took his hand from Jane's shoulder and turned, reaching into his jacket pocket to pull out his phone. He dialled a number.

'Tom. It's me.'

Jane couldn't hear the reply.

'I'm out front of St Giles. The police can pick me up there.'

He had moved out from the pews and was in the aisle. He looked back at her.

'There have been some very unsavoury revelations made about me. I will struggle to refute them. The police are coming to pick me up now.'

He didn't wait for a response. Instead, he dashed off a sign of the cross in the direction of the altar and then walked to the back of the church.

Jane had sat still and watched him go. A minute later one of the west doors opened and the Chief slipped

49

through the gap. As he did she heard the distant sirens of approaching police cars.

And still the tears came.

...

Frank was staring at his phone. Jane could read his lips.

'SIS's Chief arrested on paedophilia charges.'

He looked across at her. He was about to say something when she passed her phone to him. It was the third article on *Le Monde*'s news app. This time she didn't need to read Frank's lips. The only words which mattered were 'Louis Belmonte' and '*mort*.'

Frank stared at the phone and then looked up at her. Without taking his eyes off her, he handed the phone back.

Neither of them said anything for a few seconds. Both of their plates remained half eaten. Frank then looked back down at his own phone. And then back up at Jane.

'What do we do now?' he asked.

She knew the question was coming. Frank was a doer, for sure, but he wasn't a strategist or a leader. He was an outstanding analyst, but he wasn't trained for field work. Both times he'd left the office he'd been in support of Sam Green.

Who might be dead.

Frank and me.

Against the world.

It was a movie title.

They didn't stand a chance.

The Costa Rican beach was looking more and more attractive as the day wore on. As she stared at her friend it was becoming more attractive still.

'That's a very good question, Frank.'

Dominic was taking a breather. He was in the corridor between the kitchen and the main hall. And he was on his own. The prime minister had fallen James out. 'Dom's fine on his own. We won't bite him!' The smile had followed, and James, who had a wife waiting for him, had headed off home.

The Fordinglys were together in the 'snug', a room whose size belied its title. It was three times as big as his mum's living room. But in some ways, snug was an apt description. There was a huge wrap-round sofa, easily big enough for a family of four and associated pets, a flat-screen TV the size of a small cinema, and a thick pile carpet which you could lose your feet in. There were other bits of furniture and a Bang & Olufsen hi-fi which likely cost the same as a small car – and the lighting was calming and relaxed. It was the ideal place for a busy family to unwind.

In the case of the prime minister, it was a family of three and a half – the baby was asleep in her mother's arms, resting on what would soon be either her brother or sister. The scene, which Dominic had experienced half an hour ago as he'd delivered a tray of 'lesbian tea' – he'd laughed at what the prime minister had called a herbal infusion – was idyllic. Just the three of them, some bedtime drinks and a late-night chat show.

The scene was pretty perfect.

In fact, the whole thing was.

The first family (he knew that was an Americanism, but it just made sense), the house, the exquisite food, the

51

expensive drinks ... and his role in it. *So far, so good*, he thought. Earlier on he had helped the prime minister unpack a small overnight case, reminded him of where his 'Chequers clothes' were, and asked if he needed anything, to which the response was, 'a strong Scotch please, Dominic. Or should I call you Dom?'

'Your choice, prime minister.' He'd paused. And then, 'Only my mum calls me Dom. But I'd be delighted if you're comfortable with the same.'

'Dom it is then.' The prime minister had stuck up both thumbs, a popular trait of his, along with his disarmingly wide smile.

Dominic had nodded, smiled sheepishly in return, and then beat a retreat to the small bar to prepare the top man his Shetland Reel ... with two blocks of ice.

Half an hour later James and he had served supper in the small dining room. It was Beef Wellington, new potatoes and various delicious *al dente* vegetables. He knew it was fabulous because the chef had made a spare which James and he had shared – this was, apparently, how things worked. And James had let him serve the wine and accompanying water. Dominic had previously worked in a pub, and then moved on to an upmarket wine bar in Clapham where he had discovered he had a nose for wine and skill as a cocktail maker. It helped that he was good-looking. At six-two, slim, but with an olive complexion passed down from his father's Italian-Lazio lineage, he had no problem charming anyone – male or female. His Italian surname, Bianci, disguised the fact that he was born and bred in southeast London. At school, an average state affair with its own share of problem families, he had stuck with an accent which matched his postcode; it was safer that way. But his local area's lack of finesse grated for as long as he could remember. His grandfather had been a tailor of some repute – everyone knew the Italians made the classiest suits. But the Mediterranean country's inability to run itself effectively forced his would-be father to look for a job somewhere with a functioning government.

And the UK was it.

The rest was history although – and he didn't share this with anyone – his father was a good-looking rogue who couldn't keep it in his trousers. His mum, an English nurse, had left him not long after Dominic was born. She brought him up on her own and had never remarried. He saw his father now and then, but hadn't made a connection. There was only so much love you could muster for a drunken philander.

Dominic had managed to pass a handful of GCSEs and then went to the local college to study hotel management. He worked hard, got his national diploma but, in the end, jobs were scarce. Hence the pub and then the wine bar.

His break came when he had been serving a couple of yuppies one Friday evening. They'd had one too many, but weren't being offensive. Dominic had laid on all of his charm with the hope of a decent tip ... and, in many ways, he got that and more.

The affair with Richard, an early-thirties merchant banker, was beautiful. There was no other way to describe it. He was intelligent, great company and generous. But Dominic wasn't stupid. He knew that he gave Richard a lot of what he wanted, but not *all* that he wanted. Likewise, Dominic loved the man. But he had his own ambitions. And being a wealthy banker's love interest was an opportunistic interlude, but it wasn't fulfilling. It was no surprise then that after two years they found themselves naturally drifting apart.

Just before the inevitable break-up Richard had returned to his expensive apartment (never *their* – but then again, he had never allowed Richard to call him 'Dom') one evening with a suggestion.

'A pal of mine's parents have a small estate in Gloucestershire. They're looking for a manservant – full time.' He'd paused at that point. Dominic thought Richard was waiting to see if he screwed up his face. He hadn't. 'The thing is, and we both know this, "us" is going to end soon ...' he paused again, waiting again for comment, '... and you'd be *so* good supporting a family. You have such a wonderful way with people, and you have fabulous taste. It's a decent job, as I understand it, with good money. And a stepping stone to better things. Which is what you want, isn't it.' Richard had paused again, treading carefully. 'I always thought you'd be better managing a family rather than running a hotel. It's always been personal for you.'

Richard had stopped talking.

Dominic's brain whirred ... and then he smiled and put out his hand.

'Where do I apply?'

The sex that followed had been deep and loving. In retrospect, it had been the night of his life.

Until tonight.

The summons' bell rang. It was in the kitchen, but the high-pitched ring easily reached the hall.

Dominic straightened his black bow tie and checked his white shirt was correctly tucked into his immaculately creased black trousers. Below them was an expensive pair of black brogues, his mother's present to him for getting the job.

He turned away from the kitchen and set off towards the snug ...

... where he met the prime minister in the hall.

'Ah. Good. Dom.' The top man had a hand up, as if he was waving for a bus.

'Yes, sir?' Dominic took three strides and came to attention a few feet from the prime minister. He put his head on one side and smiled.

'Ah. Yes. Good. Well.'

One of the most endearing traits of Prime Minister Fordingly was his ability to hide his sharp intellect within a clown-like persona. His hair was never quite tidy and his shirt was often untucked. To Dominic that was an attraction. The top man didn't look like most politicians. He enjoyed a beer ... well, certainly when the cameras were rolling. And a laugh and a joke. He joined in with people. Made them feel at ease. And he wasn't afraid to make a fool of himself. There was no starch on him. And he could speak to anyone. Anyone.

Except ... he was struggling to communicate now.

Dominic knew the prime minister hadn't had too much to drink. He'd drunk a whisky and possibly half a bottle of 2008 Chateau Ramafort.

Unless he had a stash hidden in the snug.

No. This was how he was.

'Look, fella.' The prime minister had put his arm around his shoulder. It wasn't a threatening gesture and Dominic felt completely at ease.

'You have a car? Yes?' There was that disarming smile which prevented Dominic from even beginning to understand where this was going.

'Yes, sir. I do,' he replied.

'Here?'

He did. There was enough staff accommodation for ten. Dominic didn't have a dedicated room, but there was a spreadsheet on which he could secure a bed. He had booked a small suite until Monday morning. His car, a 2015 Audi A2, was parked in the staff car park.

'Yes, sir.' Dominic had begun to identify some possibilities. Maybe the prime minister wanted something that either wasn't in the pantry, or the wine cellar? A trip to Waitrose in Aylesbury might be necessary? Dominic hadn't touched any alcohol, so that would not be a problem.

'Good. Excellent. Look, this may seem to be a bit of an odd request ...' The prime minister paused. He was staring at Dominic directly. His manner was affable. But his eyes were sharp. There was an edge to them. Dominic kept his gaze, hoping that he wasn't being too familiar.

'... good. Good lad.' The prime minister moved his head close to Dominic's; he still had his arm around him and their faces were now inches apart. 'I need you to drive me somewhere. Not far ...' he added quickly.

Dominic imperceptibly pulled his head back. His face must have shown some surprise.

'It's all perfectly normal.' The prime minister's sentence was rushed and he dropped his arm from Dominic's shoulders and put out two flat hands. 'I do this every so often. My valet drives. It's a bit below the radar, but needs must. National security and all that. Got it?' The prime minister had bent forward so he was looking straight back at Dominic.

Who smiled, the smile of a man who was caught between doing two things, one of which was standard fare, the other carrying risk but offering enormous reward.

And then ...

'I'll go and get my car, sir?' There was only ever going to be one response.

'No. No.' There were the flat hands again. 'Let me get my coat. And then I'll follow you out the back.' The prime minister now had a single index finger raised which he quickly accompanied with another mischievous smile.

Dominic didn't know what to do. Or what to say. So he stood stock still and then forced a smile.

'Mum's the word, hey?' the prime minister said, his still straight finger now touching his nose.

Chapter 3

They weren't getting very far. They were sitting diagonally opposite each other on their respective single beds, their knees no more than a foot apart. The smell of peroxide was still lingering, even though both windows were open to their maximum, which wasn't wide enough to make a difference. Frank was on his laptop, typing something. Jane was looking dead ahead at the slim gap in the curtains. They were on the third of five floors of an unremarkable Travelodge which had set them back over £100. They had booked in as a couple, Mr and Mrs Brown, and paid with cash – as they had for the Burger King they'd just finished out the front of St Pancras. Having only picked at their Nando's earlier, Jane was insistent that they eat something before they got their heads down. It was among many straightforward rules which had been reinforced time and again on her case officer training at Fort Monckton. Eat when you can.

Another was, check your escape routes. Sure, it was 'Janet and John do spying', but having the training ingrained into your day-to-day life ensured you didn't forget the essentials when the chips were down.

Like now.

And Jane had checked their escape routes.

The Travelodge had a lift, a set of stairs and two fire escapes. She'd asked for a first-floor room so, if necessary, they could use the window if the standard routes were blocked. Unfortunately the floor was fully booked. Fire escapes it was then. Both were alarmed and both gave a different aspect from which to make a run. She'd done her best to look at that too.

Cash was also key. They had £568.30 between them; Jane had made them count it once they were into the room. They could both draw more cash tomorrow and that would bring the total to over a thousand pounds. Enough to leave the country, but probably not enough to secure a future in Central America.

And they had toiletries and some spare clothes. Frank had insisted he go home and collect a few things which 'are important to me.' Jane had ummed and ahhed, but there was no stopping him – she was not his keeper.

He had needed an hour.

Whilst Frank was doing that, Jane had popped into the local Tesco superstore and bought a second set of clothes, some underwear and the makings of a first aid kit. She'd then bought two pay-as-you-go SIMs (they'd both disconnected their old phones in Nando's). Next, to give some CCTV protection, she'd dashed into a late night tat shop and bought two un-matching baseball caps ... and some hair dye. For all of her transactions Jane had used her card because she needed to keep as much cash as possible. Doubtless the purchases would have thrown up a flag somewhere but, in a city as big as London, provided they kept moving they'd be safe enough.

She'd met up with Frank outside St Pauls; he was carrying a medium-sized brown-leather satchel. They'd taken the N17 bus to King's Cross, and eaten a late night burger. They then booked into their hotel and, once Jane had checked routes out, they helped dye each other's hair. Now, close to one in the morning, exhausted and with no plan to speak of – they had both independently decided that whilst tomorrow's itinerary was the elephant in the room, it could just bloody well stay there – she was close to falling asleep.

'I'm going to get my head down, Frank. Are you OK?'

Frank stopped what he was doing and looked up. In the low wattage lighting from the bedside lamps his face looked even more drawn than earlier.

'I'm not sure I can do this, Jane.' His mouth was tight, his narrow lips lost against the flatness of his face.

She knew. And she couldn't blame him.

Jane didn't think she could do it either. Wouldn't it be better to go into work and face whatever music was playing? Surely they couldn't pin some ghastly event on the pair of them? OK, it might mean that dear Louis Belmonte had died for nothing. But ...

A blue flash from between the curtains caught her eye. Then another.

Jane ignored Frank, stood and quickly walked over to the window. She gently pulled back one of the drapes ...

... and then dropped it as though it was too hot to touch.

This can't be happening?

They had been *so* careful. The last time she had used her card was a couple of hours ago, over a mile away.

She chewed on a knuckle.

They had both used their Oyster cards for the bus, hadn't they? Tap on the yellow card reader ... and tap off.

Really?

Come on.

The Met were the only organisation that regularly checked the use of travel cards to determine criminal movement. It was beneath The Box.

And here they were. Outside their hotel.

'Pack your things, Frank. We've been compromised.' It was a bark. There were two police cars out front of the hotel. And she was sure she spotted a black van across the road.

Frank turned to her, but didn't move.

'What?' There was no energy in his reply.

'Pack ... your ... things. Now!' She pointed at the window. 'The Met are outside.'

Jane didn't wait for a response. She was quickly pulling her own stuff together.

Frank, however, was still stationary, his fingers hovering above the keyboard.

Jane stopped what she was doing, exasperated.

'You have two choices, Frank. Be arrested or, worse still, end up in the Thames. *Or* come with me. If it's the latter then move now. I can't wait for you.'

Jane gave him a second, and then, still exasperated, got back to the business of shoving her stuff into the small rucksack she used for work.

He still didn't move.

She sighed inwardly, but still kept packing. Next she was in the bathroom. Her toothbrush was all she was short of.

'I'm coming.' It was a frenzied call from Frank. Jane was out of the bathroom just as he closed his laptop and reached for his satchel. She slipped past him to the window.

The police from the first vehicle had left their car. They were probably inside the building. The second still had its lights on. *A chase car.* And the van's back door was open and ...

Oh my God.

It was an SCO19 firearms team. The guy holding open the van's rear door had a weapon slung, barrel down, but his laser designator was on. A bright red spot dabbled around the tarmac as the man swung his shoulders.

And Frank wasn't moving quick enough.

'Come on, Frank!' She squeezed past him again to the bedroom's main door. She pulled it toward her and peered out.

The corridor was partially lit. Forward right was the lift. Next to it was the stairwell. Beyond that, at the end of the corridor, was the backlit green and white sign of a fire escape.

Option 1.

The closest.

Option 2 was in the other direction. It meant a longer run, down the corridor, right at the end, and then down another long corridor to the second fire escape.

She'd made up her mind.

She turned … and there was Frank. He was the same height as Jane, but just now he seemed a lot shorter.

She looked back to the corridor.

Left.

'With me. Pull the door behind you.'

And then she was off – at a sprint. She reached the corner in a couple of seconds, looked back and saw Frank a few paces behind, his satchel swinging like a kid being chased across the playground by the school bully.

Jane turned the corner. Ahead of them was a 20-metre dash and then the fire escape. The only issue was whether or not SCO19 were covering the exits.

Maybe.

She was running, her heart beating faster than it had for months.

62

There.

The bar-push door.

Jane looked over her shoulder. Frank was with her.

She paused. Frozen for a reason she couldn't comprehend. Was she frightened of what was on the other side? She was running from the British police. How crazy was that? If she went through the door she would be a fugitive. If ...

Too long.

Frank elbowed her out of the way and slammed his hip against the bar. The door burst open and a rush of cold air swooped into the building. In one movement Frank grabbed her by the elbow and they simultaneously took a step onto the caged metal stairs.

The cold air hit her.

She had crossed the Rubicon. There was no going back.

She glanced around.

Nothing. Maybe ...

Too long again.

'Come on, Jane!' Frank pushed at her back and she almost toppled down the first set of stairs.

Come on, Jane! she screamed to herself.

And then they were off; both of them had momentum. Down one set of stairs. Then another. Then another.

One more.

Jane had planned an escape. Of sorts. It was SOP. It's what spies did.

Make it to King's Cross underground.

As well as overland trains, King's Cross serviced six metro lines. As an escapee that was a choice of twelve different underground directions. Provided they had some distance between them and their pursuers, if the chasers saw them enter the station the odds were still in their favour. She had planned it that way.

It was 600 metres as the crow flew.

She had a more circuitous route of sorts in her head. *Of sorts.*

'Which way?' Frank whispered. He had both hands on his satchel.

'We're going to King's Cross underground. Make it up from there. Follow me!'

Jane turned to her right. As she remembered it, Verman Rise led to Penny Circus. And then north onto Great Percy Street. It was the wrong direction for the station to begin with, but it led them away from the front of the hotel and all the noise.

She ran, keeping close to the buildings where there was some shadow. But they couldn't stay on this side. Not with her plan.

Cross the road, now.

It was a dangerous manoeuvre. A dash across the road would expose them ... for a few seconds.

She glanced back. Frank was right behind her, still clutching at his satchel.

She looked beyond him, over a row of parked cars.

It all looked clear.

'Run!' she growled.

One second, two seconds, three seconds ...

They were across the road, moving toward the circular park that was Penny Circus.

Left. Then left at the first junction.

Frank was with her. Right on her shoulder. Neither of them were athletes, but anyone chasing them would be wearing a stab vest – at least. And other heavy police paraphernalia. They had an advantage.

Left now. Great Percy Street. She was breathing hard. She glanced over her shoulder again. Frank was a few paces back, but still with her.

How far?

Maybe 250 metres. *Then left at the end?* That would lead to the A501. Left there and then half a mile to the station.

Shit, blue lights!

Turning into the road ahead of them.

They were running along one of those streets where the houses had cellars, or cellar flats. A sharp, black metal railing was between them and a drop of a couple of metres into a well of darkness.

They had seconds.

Avoiding a tree she skidded to a halt, her black flatties a decent match for an uneven pavement. She took a breath, her brain trying so hard to work through the machinations of the choices she faced.

'Get over, Frank!'

But he was ahead of her. In fact he already had his torso over the railings and was twisting his legs over the top. Then, hanging on to a spike with one hand, he held out his spare.

'Come on, Jane.' Frank's face was etched with determination.

She could have cried.

Jane grabbed two of the spikes and with no sense or fear as to whether she might puncture some key part of her anatomy, she pulled herself up and, for a second hanging in no man's land, she felt Frank's hand on the neck of her jacket. And then she was over. They both were.

And down.

Into the darkness.

Safe?

The blue rotating lights of the police car moved slowly, flashing left to right, high above them. Their journey seemed to take an age. At one point Jane thought the car had stopped opposite them to check something out, the strobe of blue catching the black, leafless branches of a tree which the pair of them had avoided a few seconds earlier.

And then it was gone.

Jane breathed out and closed her eyes, the beat of the blood pounding through her veins a frantic reminder that they had just used one of their nine lives.

'What do we do now?' Frank's words were raspy, forced out between multiple breaths.

'Wait ... for ... a minute.' Jane had her eyes closed. She kept them that way.

They needed a plan. It seemed possible that the Met had the local area swamped; and so far the pair of them had been lucky.

Possibly.

Two squad cars and a van full of SCO19? It was a decent crew, but not big enough. She and Frank were already a couple of hundred metres from the hotel and every minute they moved further from the centre point, the search area would become more and more unworkable. It was an R-squared rule. She remembered it from A-level maths. Every unit of travel from a point, squared the area it subtended. Or something like that.

They were making a bigger circle. That's all that mattered.

She and Frank had changed their clothes, their hair was a different colour and they had baseball caps. Provided they didn't use their cards, at dawn they would be lost in a growing crowd of commuters.

But the Met had found them once at the Travelodge.

How was that possible?

Jane didn't get it. When Frank had been doing his thing, she had contacted her mother via SMS using her old phone: *Can't make it this w/e. Work calls. Sorry. J xx.* She'd then turned her phone off and she'd not opened the new ones. And they were at least half a mile away from King's Cross when they had last dabbed their Oyster cards. In Central London that was a population in the tens of thousands.

She had no idea.

...

'Oi! What the fuck are you doing?'

There was a man in a dressing gown outside of his front door looking down into the well. He was late middle-aged, paunchy, but clearly happy to take on two trespassers.

'I'm calling the police.' He fished a mobile from his dressing gown pocket.

'Sir!' Jane was on her feet. She stepped over Frank toward the man. 'I'm with the security services. Here's my card.' She had walked a few paces to a small set of concrete steps which led up to the bridge between the man's front door and the pavement.

'What?' The man was confused.

'Here.' She thrust her card high and forward. 'Can you let us out, please? It's a long story involving high-level national security. We took refuge here ...' She was struggling with an alibi, but at least the man had dropped his phone from his ear and was squinting at Jane's SIS ID card.

Jane slowly took the steps which led from well. The only thing that now separated her and the man was a gate and a padlock.

'Oh. Wow. That's ... well, something. I'll get the key.'

Jane looked over her shoulder. Frank was directly behind her, his satchel to his chest.

The man was back a second later.

'Here. I'll let you out.' He was fumbling with the padlock. It took him a few seconds and then it was open. He pulled the gate ajar.

'Thank you, sir. It's been a bit of a ...'

'Who's that, George?' The voice was a woman's. It echoed from the hall behind the front door of the house. The door opened fully. Jane looked in. The woman, who looked older than the man, was also wearing a dressing gown, her hair in curlers. It was something from a 70s sitcom.

She stopped short of the door ... and stared.

There was a moment.

'Come in, George.' Her tone had lost its inquisition. 'Leave these good people alone. Let them go.' Any hint of her initial confidence had gone. It was now all timidity.

'What?' the man barked over his shoulder.

'Come in, George. We want nothing to do with these people.' And then she lifted her chin to indicate that she was no longer talking to George, but to Jane.

'Please leave us. Please,' she added.

Was she pleading?

And then a penny seemed to drop with George. He stood up straight and pulled his shoulders back as though he was creating a shield for the woman behind him. He stepped backward. One step. Two steps. And then he was in the house, and the door shut quickly.

Frank was about to say something, but Jane put out a hand to stop him.

She listened.

It was faint. But she heard it.

'Those are the two criminals we saw on TV this evening. They're armed and dangerous.'

Jane looked at Frank, his face screwed up in a grimace.

'We need to go, Frank.'

Lay-by, A413 south of Aylesbury, UK

Dominic drifted in and out of sleep. It was intermittently cold in the Audi, depending on whether or not he had the engine running. He had just over half a tank of fuel, easily enough for a couple of hundred miles, but he didn't know what was going to be asked of him next.

Or when.

They had left Chequers two hours ago. The prime minister sat in the front. He was wearing the jeans and polo short he had changed into earlier, and had thrown on a Barbour jacket. He had taken a narrow-brimmed fishing hat from his pocket and pulled it down over his forehead. It was hardly a bombproof disguise, although Dominic assumed it was a half-hearted attempt at that.

In any case the gate guard, who stayed in the hut, lifted the barrier without a second glance. James had told Dominic that the whole place had discreet cameras with vehicle recognition software and the guard only ever took a cursory look at occupants of the car. It was possible that the top man had left the grounds without being seen. Or maybe the guard was in on it?

For the short journey the prime minister had kept his eye on his phone, issuing simple instructions for Dominic to follow. Twenty minutes later – it might have been twenty-five – he was told to pull into a layby and, 'turn off the engine, Dom.' Dominic had done as he was asked. He kept his hands on the steering wheel and his eyes to his front. But he could see the prime minister from the corner of his eye.

The top man's phone had *pinged*. He'd glanced at it and then grimaced.

'I'm getting out. There's a car coming to pick me up. Now ...' he had leaned towards Dominic and put his hand on his shoulder, 'there's nothing to worry about, and nothing untoward going on. This is all common practice. I'm in no danger. You have to trust me.'

There was that smile again, under the brim of his green floppy hat.

The prime minister then opened his door. He got out and stuck his head back in.

'I might be gone for a couple of hours. You stay here and keep warm, Dom. Hey?' He stuck up a thumb.

'Sure, sir.' He was about to add something but the prime minister stopped him.

'Mum's the word.' He tapped his nose again. 'Not anyone. Not even James. You got it?'

Dominic nodded, unsure as to exactly what was going on, or what he felt about it.

The passenger door closed and the prime minister moved round to the back of the car.

Nothing happened for a few minutes. Dominic kept an eye on the rear-view mirror. The boss looked disconsolate and fidgety. The man kept looking at his phone, and then back down the road. A couple of cars and a juggernaut belted past the layby. On all occasions the prime minister looked away.

And then a set of headlights, from behind. It was a slower vehicle. The lights pulled in and the main beam flashed. The prime minister moved to the rear passenger side of the vehicle – it looked like a big car – and got in.

The car pulled away. Dominic recognised the marque straight away. It was a big Bentley, which immediately made him feel better. A series of random answers to the obvious question had buzzed at him in the last half an hour. The most unsettling was that the prime minister was meeting another woman – or, indeed, man. Dominic had no barriers in that regard. The top man was already on his fourth wife. He obviously enjoyed the institution, but maybe only up to a point. A mistress? It was the simplest answer. But, that would have upset Dominic. To him there was something a little seedy about important men playing away from home – maybe using their power to gain favour. And he didn't want to feel that way about his new boss.

In his mind a big Bentley was unlikely the car of a prostitute, or a wife of a good friend. It was more likely a business meeting which couldn't be held within the confines of an official residence. Dominic could cope with that. Politics was a messy business. Secret alliances for the good of the country. Spies and agents. Big business. It all made sense. And a long wheelbase Bentley could only be afforded by a rich organisation – one wanting to impress the British prime minister.

Yes, that was it.

The next two hours were lost in cat naps, chills and then a little too much warmth from the Audi's excellent heater. At one point he had to get out of the car and pee in the bushes. When he got back in he checked his tie was straight in the mirror and ran his fingers through the top of his black, spiky hair. He was still looking good.

He glanced at the Audi's LED screen. It was 2.15 am. Then back to the rear-view mirror.

A pair of headlights slowed as they approached the layby. They looked similar to the original set.

Dominic immediately started the car.

The lights pulled in. There was no attempt to turn them off.

A long pause followed – possibly four, maybe five minutes.

And then the rear passenger door opened and the frame of the prime minister got out of the car. He ducked back down into the body of the vehicle. And then out again. He closed the door, standing on the verge at the edge of the layby. His shoulders were hunched.

The vehicle took off. And, yes, it was the same Bentley. This time he caught the rear of it in the Audi's headlights.

Dominic inadvertently made out the registration. He wasn't looking to. It just happened that way. It was a private plate: two letters and three numbers. He immediately tried to associate the initials with someone famous, but got nowhere quickly.

The prime minister was back beside his car. He pulled the door open and jumped in.

Dominic looked at him.

It was difficult to tell in the light from just the dashboard, but …

… the man who had got into the car wasn't the same ebullient one who he had served a whisky to before supper.

What was it?

Tiredness? Stress?

Both?

Neither of them said anything for about a minute, the setting on the Audi's heating control delivering a perfect 22 degrees.

'Let's go home, Dom, hey?' There was no immediacy to the prime minister's tone. It had a resigned ring to it, as if he'd just lost a lot of money at cards and was working out how he was going to tell his wife when he got home.

Maybe that was it? It was as good an answer as any.

There was no smile. No thumbs up. Just a man staring at the halogen-lit blackness ahead of them, a couple of moths already dancing with the headlights.

Dominic pulled the car onto the main road. There was a roundabout half a mile ahead. He would turn around there.

As they picked up speed the prime minister put his fishing hat back on. And then he reached for his phone, dabbed at it, stared at it, and then put it away. He sighed through his nose, gently shaking his head.

Dominic felt anger then. Not at the man who had taken him into the night. Not at the same man who held the highest rank in the land – who had already shown him such kindness.

No.

He was angry with whoever was in the Bentley with the fancy number plate. At whoever had set the conditions to change the demeanour of one whom he thought of as one of Britain's greatest leaders.

He was furious with them. He *hated* them.

Whoever they were.

It was, surprisingly, as Sam remembered it.

When was it?

Four and a half years ago.

She had been running away from the thug on the skis. It had started in Alpbach, Austria. She'd scarpered down the valley to Innsbruck – or close enough – and then a direct train journey to Munich.

She had found refuge then.

She hoped to find refuge now, something she knew she had no right to.

In the post-dawn light she could report that the house was still the largest on Flemingstraße. It was still white-rendered, the bottom floor with tall symmetrical windows, and an entrance defined by a large, raised porch, its triangular balustrade supported by four Roman columns. And between the ornate gate and the house was the same large garden, with its Narnia-style street lamps and under-control rhododendrons.

It was as if the devastating fire hadn't happened.

Sam's memory was first-class. She never missed a thing. And, at untold cost to her mental health, she never forgot anything. If she'd been asked by an artist to describe the house, this is exactly what the finished sketch would have looked like – before the fire. She hadn't been inside when it had been engulfed in flames. Frank had. And the way he described it afterward was something close to Armageddon. It had been razed.

And now ... it had been 'raised'.

Maybe the German planners were particular with rebuilds?

Maybe.

What was different was the intercom. Last time it was voice only. A button and a speaker. This time there was a camera.

No, two cameras.

One above the bell button. And there was a low-light – possibly thermal – pod, set high on a dark green stalk a metre or so back. It was well hidden. But not that well.

She looked around some more.

She spotted another camera. And a fourth.

She wasn't surprised. If money were no object, and she was convinced it wasn't, she'd have built a three-metre wall topped with anti-intruder spikes, dug a deep ditch, fashioned some tank traps and bought some crocodiles.

Nobody would have blamed her.

She was about to press the call button when, above the low-level background noise of the gently rubbing branches in the slight wind, she heard a metallic *whirr*.

Sam looked to the low-light pod. The lens was focusing.

She smiled at it, a gentle, almost apologetic smile. And she raised a single hand in submission.

I'm sorry I haven't been in touch.

I'm sorry about Ingeborg.

I'm sorry about everything.

The lens shimmied … and there was a soft *clunk* and the ornate gate glided to her left into a recess which was neatly hidden among rhodies.

She waited, unsure now.

She looked back up at the camera. It refocused on her, as if it were a cyclopic animal, working out whether she were a friend … or dinner.

Oh well.

It took her a minute to cover the 25 metres of curved gravel drive to the entrance porch. There she took the four steps two at a time, and was about to come to a halt and wait for further instructions, when the left of the two front doors opened mechanically away from her.

She stepped in.

Inside was a facsimile of her previous visit. Even the grand family portraits were the same. The old pine double staircase, which rose in front of her … that was the same. It was remarkable.

As she took in her environment the heavy door closed behind her.

Clunk.

Then there was nothing.

Just a clinical calmness – an enveloping quiet.

She glanced over at a highly polished side table. In any other house such a table would be used to discard car keys and wallets. Here, as before, was a Royal Copenhagen lamp with a hexagonal cloth lampshade. Next to that was an old, probably ancient, Chinese blue and white porcelain vase.

Everywhere she turned was class.

And everywhere she looked was immaculate.

Germans were known for their fastidiousness, but this felt creepily off the scale. It was like a shrine to a previous life. A life with a mother. And a gorgeous girlfriend.

Am I going to regret this?

A noise. A door opening, from a corridor off to her right. And then a light rumble, as though a child pushing along a plastic tractor.

She saw it then.

It was a droid. White and grey. Four wheels, a cylindrical body and a head like an upturned pudding bowl, in the centre of which was an LED screen. It was something straight from a Japanese tech company.

It rolled up to Sam, the pine floor no obstacle for its grey, rubber-coated wheels. It stopped short of her and then – and she almost laughed out loud – the LED screen blinked and a pair of electronic eyes appeared.

'*Guten Tag, Fräulein Green.*' The male voice was straight from a satnav.

The screen blinked again.

She snorted.

'Good afternoon.' She paused, taking in the robot. 'What do I call you?'

'My name is Lukas. Would you like to follow me?'

Before Sam could answer, Lukas had spun around so quickly he must have got dizzy. And then he headed off at a bit of a lick back the way he had come. Sam had to half-jog to keep up.

She had stayed at the house previously and, being curious as to how the other half lived, she had nosed around. Currently they were heading for the kitchen, although there was a door to a cellar on her left up ahead (she'd not ventured there). She and Lukas ignored the cellar door and, as they turned left to walk the short corridor to the kitchen, the droid stopped on the spot, as only rubber-soled robots could. Sam managed not to trip over him.

What now?

And then it became clear.

Lukas had halted short of a set of large floor tiles which looked discoloured enough to have been laid when the house had been built. They were off white and grouted in grey. But the grouting cleverly disguised a break because, as woman and droid waited, the tiles fell away as if joined to the remaining unmoving floor by a piano hinge. What once was floor was now a hole big enough to swallow a small car.

This isn't happening?

The blackness of the cavity was soon filled with a square, horizontal metal plate. An aluminium cage was lifting up through the void, raising with such precision and grace she could hardly hear the mechanism.

Clunk.

The cage stopped. In front of them was an opening – human-sized. Lukas whirred in. He spun again. And blinked.

Whatever.

Sam followed.

The next three or four minutes was something out of a Bond movie. At first she thought they were using a new entrance to the cellar. Maybe the stairs in the original were too severe for Wolfgang? But, no. The cage dropped to a concrete-encased corridor which headed away from the main building, not back on itself into the cellar. And Lukas immediately rolled away.

Her army training made her count the steps whilst she followed the robot down the long, dimly but adequately lit corridor, hoping to make some sense of where they were going.

After forty steps she knew they had travelled 28 metres. It was a military skill. There was no gradient, and they were heading east, parallel to the road. They were easily into next door's garden.

Lukas stopped at a door which was blocking further travel. It was heavy. Metal. No handle. And no controls.

It didn't matter. It opened towards them, its thickness similar to a bank vault.

After another short corridor they left behind the present and time-warped to the future. It was Father Christmas does high-end electronics. The room was the size of a low-ceilinged squash court, with open entrances to three side-rooms. Sam spotted a set of tall computer towers through one of the openings, the machines' multi-coloured lights flashing with an intensity which she assumed meant that a lot of computering was going on.

A bitcoin factory?

That's what it looked like.

The main room seemed to reaffirm that. The walls were covered with screens, desks, more towers and, on the furthest wall from her, a bank of air-conditioning units, and a wide ceiling duct, which accepted more wires than seemed really necessary. The power being consumed by the electronics in these rooms was enough to light up Bavaria.

'Have you seen the news?'

The accent was clipped. The 'th' more like a 'z'.

She turned.

And there he was.

'Hello, Wolfgang.' She smiled and then let out a gentle snort.

He was exactly as she expected. Still rakishly attractive. Still impeccably, if somewhat country-gentlemanly dressed: mustard cords, a collared, red and white striped cotton shirt – open at the neck – and a deep-green, woollen waistcoat with leather buttons.

But not *exactly*.

His leg had been badly smashed up in Munich, so much so that even after the best surgery affordable, he had needed a stick. That had been six years ago when, among other horrors, his mother had been shot dead in front of him … and her. And who knew how deep the mental scar was after his futile attempt to rescue Ingeborg from the intense heat of the house fire?

But the physical result was clear.

He was sitting in a high-end wheelchair. Even through his expensive cords, one leg looked painfully slim. The other failed to deliver a foot from the bottom of his trousers.

What other damage were his clothes hiding?

'Have you seen the news? You must see the news. Now.'

The wheelchair coasted past her.

'Follow me!' He hadn't looked back.

It took Sam a second to finish taking in the room. Most impressive, and in the centre, was a four-metre long, two-metre high, semi-opaque screen – all glass. It was inset with electronic images, maps, words and notes. A scribble board for the 21st century.

'Come on, Sam.' Wolfgang had driven his chair to the far corner of the room. In front of him, hanging from the wall, were three large wrap-around screens, below which was a desk with an inbuilt keyboard, a mouse wheel and two tablets. Wolfgang was manipulating one of those. As he did the main middle screen, which must have been a 54-incher, was coming alive with information.

She moved cautiously towards him.

The screen filled. And then froze.

She was behind him now.

She immediately recognised the faces in the two news stories. A second later she had read the headlines.

She felt her knees lose a little of their stiffness and she involuntarily placed a hand on Wolfgang's shoulder.

'We need to help them, no?' Wolfgang asked. He had turned his head and was looking up at her. It was then, in the reflected light from his massive screen, that she saw that much of his face must have been reconstructed after the burns. The surgeon's work was excellent, but there was no way they could completely hide what Wolfgang had been through.

Sam closed her eyes, her hand still on Wolfgang's shoulder.

So much was going on.

They had so much catching up to do.

And yet, the screen presented something infinitely more pressing.

He was right.

These people were her friends. And whilst much of her wanted to hunker down somewhere safe – here maybe? – until this had all passed, that was no longer possible.

Was it?

She opened her eyes and looked down at him. He was here for her again. There was no explanation required. Twice he had been to hell for her. And it seemed possible that, because of who she was and whom she knew, he was about to embark on another journey the outcome of which might be just as, or even more, horrendous.

Sam was still looking directly into his intense eyes.

Count Wolfgang Neuenburg II.

A superb violinist. A world-class hacker. A member of German royalty.

Almost a lover.

Her friend.

She blinked.

'Let's get on with it then.'

Chapter 4

Chequers, Missenden Road, Aylesbury Buckinghamshire, UK

It was as if nothing had happened. Dominic had managed to get a couple of hours' sleep and was up to make sure early morning tea was delivered to the main suite. He then helped the chef sort out breakfast and served and cleared the table afterward. The workload was all prearranged. James had made it clear what his responsibilities were and so far, other than an illicit night-time drive, it was as he expected.

The prime minister's principal private secretary, an intense, middle-aged woman, arrived towards the end of breakfast with a red box. In it was a wealth of papers and letters, some multiple tagged. The boss seemed to make light work of the whole lot, skimming through pages and pages before signing something, or making a comment to which the woman scribbled a note on an iPad. His demeanour was light and jovial. There was none of the resignation Dominic felt he'd brought with him into his car last night.

Whilst the prime minister attended to matters of state at one end of the table, Maisie fed herself and the baby. The young thing was eating pureed apple, which the chef had knocked up in a mixer. She seemed to love that, as she did a mashed up Weetabix with soya. When he wasn't serving, Dominic stood in the doorway, keeping an eye. One part of him wanted Maisie to ask him to take over. He would have really enjoyed that.

Maybe in time.

Once the red box had been dealt with, the prime minister and the woman disappeared into the study, and Maisie and the baby popped along to the snug. The tiny girl, wearing just a pink and red hooped t-shirt and a nappy, was strapped into a baby walker and placed in front of CBeebies whilst the prime minister's wife flicked through a magazine. With her husband catching up on work, it could have been any middle-class family's Saturday morning routine.

James appeared mid-morning which gave Dominic a couple of hours' break and, whilst he could have gone back to his room, he decided to use the small staffroom which was off the kitchen. He chose the latter because, while he was happy to take the rest, he also wanted to be in earshot should he be needed. And to be honest, he wanted to stay close to the action. After all, he still had a huge amount to learn.

The staffroom was big enough for a small sofa, a central table and three chairs. There was a well-stocked fridge (no alcohol), tea- and coffee-making facilities, and a microwave. Next to the fridge was a full-height larder which held enough food to make a snack, not that any of them were ever hungry enough to need extra rations – the chefs made sure of that. And there was an additional worktop which acted as a desk. On it was a laptop, for which James had furnished Dominic with a password. Next to that was a printer.

He plumped himself down on the sofa, and closed his eyes. He rehearsed how breakfast had gone – in a self-critical way. Had he served correctly? Was his manner right? Had he got the correct balance between, as James had coined, 'deference versus duty'?

'They don't always know what they want – or they don't always know which is the right thing to do,' James had told him on day one. 'Sometimes you have to make that decision for them. There's a balance. "Deference versus duty", is a key phrase. On occasions it's much bigger than selecting the man's socks for him. But often it's just that, plain or patterned, if you get what I mean.'

Dominic thought he had.

This morning he had made some decisions for the boss, like refilling his coffee cup when he was in the thick of reading through his briefing notes. Ordinarily that might have warranted a question beforehand.

Nah.

He thought he had got that just about right.

Still with his eyes closed, but with his ears aware of the chef attacking some vegetable with a sharp knife, his mind returned to last night.

It was what it was. The prime minister had asked him to do something which wasn't strictly in his job description. And he had made it clear that he wasn't to tell anyone.

But how could the man know to trust him? How could he know that someone he'd just met – just employed – would hold close a secret which seemed to Dominic to be pretty senior? And surely Dominic wasn't the only one in the gen? Surely his wife knew? She must have done? She hadn't retired by the time he and the prime minister had left the building. And the pair of them shared a bed, so she would have noticed. Wouldn't she?

Why trust his newly appointed valet?

Why not James?

Unless the secret wasn't really a secret of note; that it was nothing that would shame the prime minister, or his office. But ... was popping out in the middle of the night without CP something which could be played fast and loose with?

Dominic didn't know.

He didn't.

But he knew something.

He knew the number plate of the Bentley.

He opened his eyes and looked across at the door into the kitchen. The chef was still murdering something, loudly.

Dominic took out his phone. It was connected to the Chequers' Wi-Fi. He was about to thumb and finger a search in Google, but he stopped himself.

Instead he went into settings and turned off the Wi-Fi. It took a second for the phone to recognise there was no mobile signal in this part of the building.

Blast.

A little frustrated, he leant back in the seat and put the phone on his lap.

No.

He wasn't prepared to leave it be. And he had nothing else better to do.

He turned on Wi-Fi and typed in the Bentley's registration – two letters and three numbers.

Nothing, other than links to companies selling similar plates.

So he searched for famous people with the initials from the plate: DG.

The first site offered 2,412 names. Each one was ascribed a nationality. He glanced through the Brits to see if he recognised anyone. Would one of the names have a good enough reason to hold a clandestine meeting with the UK's prime minister – in the middle of the night?

No. Not as far as he could tell.

He only recognised one name: David Gilmour, the vocalist and guitarist in Pink Floyd. The forty-three others were unknown to him. He made some notes on a scrap bit of paper.

Footballers won out. There were eighteen of those. There were eleven other musicians, five actors, two authors/poets, three rugby players, one botanist, one architect, and one snooker player. And a Davey Grant, a handsomely rugged MMA Fighter. Dominic had Googled him separately ... just because.

Could the prime minister have met with any of them?

If so, which one?

'Could you give me a hand with something from the freezer?'

It was the chef. And of course Dominic could. He'd have another think about the list later.

He sprang to his feet, putting his phone in his pocket ... leaving the scrappy list on the arm of the sofa.

'On my way!' Dominic chirped.

But he stopped, placing a hand on the door frame of the staffroom.

He'd forgotten the paper with the list of names on it.

He turned around sharply, spotting where he'd left it. He shook his head, jogged over and picked it up.

Therfield, Hertfordshire, UK

It was a quintessentially English village, but not quite something from the set of *Midsomer Murders*. That is, it wasn't achingly beautiful. But it was green and pleasant and close enough to London to be commutable.

86

There was a large triangular village green with its resident pub. And a small shop, a red telephone box-cum-community library and, down a narrow cul-de-sac banked by expensive houses, there was a church: St Mary's. They were just short of it now.

Jane stopped beside a freshly painted, wooden gate which blocked a wobbly paved path to a red door, with its brass door knocker. Either side of the gate was a shoulder-high yew hedge over which Jane could pick out a typical retiree's English front garden: a tidy lawn, a couple of rose bushes and a flowerbed, empty of summer life whilst maintaining some colour with sprays of clematis and honeysuckle (in her early days her dad had done a good job at plant recognition in their own garden).

The house was as she remembered it. She'd been once before. It was a work barbeque, one beautiful summer's evening. The senior crew had all been there – a professional and happy team. The juxtaposition between what she remembered as 'then' and where they found themselves now jarred so hard it brought a lump to her throat. It had taken less than a decade to turn everything on its head. Sure, she could only blame herself for what had gone on in Southeast Asia. But the recent transformation of SIS from an inclusive, diverse and incredibly professional organisation, to one infiltrated with people intent on doing the country harm, had been as swift as it had unlikely. It now reflected the society it served – ideologically divided, with the loudest voice rising above the rest.

What have we become?

She didn't know.

Jane opened the gate, checked behind that Frank and his satchel were still with her, and walked the short path to the door.

87

There was no bell. Just the knocker.

Her hand hovered above it and then dropped to her side. Did she really want to do this?

As had been the case since she and Frank had met up last night, it was he who snatched the lead. He reached around her and slapped the heavy brass handle against its setting. Three times.

They waited.

There was shuffling.

And then the door opened wide.

Nobody said anything for a second. It might have been longer. The pair of them, in their dishevelled clothes, sporting badly-dyed blond hair and unflattering baseball caps looked as if they'd just got off the plane from Bali at the end of a later-age gap year.

Then ...

'Hello, David,' Frank said from behind her.

David Jennings' face, which at first told a story of mild disbelief, broke into a smile. But it didn't last. He looked beyond them, then tilted forward, glancing up and down the small lane.

'Come in, both of you.' David made sharp encouraging movements with the hand which wasn't holding the door.

Jane and Frank shuffled in. She knew where the sitting room was. She headed for it.

The door closed behind her.

'Who is it, dear?' Jane recognised the voice. Sally Jennings. David's ex-barrister wife. She'd met Sally on a number of occasions at various work dos in London, as well as the barbeque. Jane remembered her as the consummate late-middle-aged woman. Kind, sincere – and as incisive as a scalpel.

The three of them were in the sitting room. David was pointing to various soft chairs.

'Jane and Frank, darling.' David raised his voice enough to be heard. He paused as the guests found a seat. 'I think we're going to need some tea ... and supper,' David added.

Jane sat down at one end of a three-seater, cream and paisley sofa. Frank was on a wooden chair which supported a muddy red cushion with tassels, his satchel still acting as stomach armour.

David nodded to himself as though he was content with the outcome of his direction. He then sat in the larger of two soft chairs, his elbows resting on the arms. Before anyone had a chance to say anything, Sally had come in. She was wearing an apron and what looked like gardening gloves.

She smiled, nodded at Jane and Frank, and then put her hand on David's shoulder.

'Remember, dear. We have guests coming next week.' She paused, forcing a further smile. 'And we have children and grandchildren, whom we love. And they love and need us. I know you understand.' Her tone wasn't patronising. It was just a statement of the obvious ... and it was meant for all of them.

Jane completely understood where she was coming from.

Two rogue SIS agents who were accused of selling state secrets to China were on the run. And, however unlikely it seemed to anyone in the know, they were armed and dangerous. Nobody in their right minds wanted these two fugitives on their doorstep, let alone in their sitting room.

Nobody.

Except ... David Jennings was the only option Jane could come up with. He had been her boss for seven years – up until his retirement. He left after being poisoned during the height of the Church of the White Cross operation, struck in the leg by a dart from an umbrella. He had nearly died. He'd made it through one major crisis where he had been personally targeted. It wasn't in any way fair that as a man who had given almost everything to his country, he might put his life on the line again. Not now.

Not when he should be enjoying his grandchildren.

But what other choices did she have?

Sally looked at both of them. Her smile had gone. She nodded curtly.

'I'll make sure there are some beds made up for tonight. Just tonight,' she added. And then she was gone.

It seemed natural to wait for Sally to leave the room before anyone said anything.

David broke the impasse.

'How did you get here?'

It was the most important question. David was an unlikely search option for the authorities, certainly to begin with, unless someone threw huge resources at the problem. Jane assumed the media assault on their reputations was deemed more than enough to force Frank and her to lie low, as well as ensuring that the Met, and whoever else was with them, had the broadest possible eyes and ears. Especially as, having checked social media on one of the two burner phones, there was a £10,000 reward leading to an arrest.

Each.

Jane took off her cap.

'We had an SCO19 encounter last night at a King's Cross Travelodge. We then walked, in a roundabout way to

Victoria, where we caught the earliest coach to Cambridge, via Royston. We paid cash …'

Frank interrupted.

'It was due to get in at ten-ish this morning, but the A10 was blocked by environmental protesters. That added an hour to the journey.'

Jane nodded.

'And then you walked?' It sounded a little bit like a plea from David. His village was 5 miles from Royston. There was an irregular bus service. And, of course, taxis. But both of those choices would have exposed them further.

Jane nodded.

'I had to ask directions, just the once. I came for the barbeque, if you remember, but couldn't recall the detail. And I didn't want to overuse a phone. We walked across the golf course and through the trees. We saw one couple out walking their dogs. And passed five cars. I think we're pretty clean.' She looked across to Frank. She squeezed out a nod.

David leant forward just as a tray full of tea arrived. It was china mugs and an earthenware teapot; Jane reckoned it wasn't the best set. David pulled out an occasional table from a stack of three. Sally rested the tray down gently.

'It's builders'. If you'd like anything else?' She paused, looking at her now not so welcome guests. Both Jane and Frank shook their heads.

'That's fine, thank you,' Jane and Frank replied in unison.

'Good. I'll prepare some supper. Any allergies?'

Jane knew Frank was a vegetarian, but he didn't say anything. *Bless him*. They both shook their heads again.

And then Sally was gone.

David set about pouring tea at the same time as he asked, 'So, tell me what this is about, noting that I am no longer classified for secret or top secret material.'

Jane looked to Frank, who raised his shoulders ... and she started.

It took Jane half an hour and a second cup of tea to complete the briefing. Frank thought she'd found exactly the right line between what David needed to know, and what she could actually tell him. Certainly she committed a few indiscretions, like the disclosure of the organisation's name: the Young Crofters' Association ...

'Young Crofters' Association? They're taking the mickey!' David had been sipping at his tea. He had almost spat some out.

She'd gone on to mention the likely CEO of the YCA, by title – the Duke of Nairnshire – but not by name. That brought no reaction from David, who at that point looked as if he was stewing on all of the intelligence, just like the remaining tea in the pot.

By the end David had as much as he needed to know ... and a little more. Jane had sat back in her chair and Frank had, eventually, taken off his baseball cap and put his satchel on the floor, resting against a leg, catching the satchel's strap around his foot, *just in case*.

'No sign of Sam Green?' David asked.

Jane had mentioned Sam's central role in the 'Balkans operation' and her subsequent move to Nigeria, where there was clear evidence she had become involved with a 'Mediterranean nation's security organisation'. No telling tales there, although it only led to one grouping: Mossad. She'd told David of the last time she'd spoken to

Sam, which was almost four weeks ago. Since then the trail had gone cold.

'If they can murder a French agent, frame the Chief as a paedophile, and then trump up charges against us,' she had used a finger to point at her and then Frank, 'I'd say the likelihood is that she's down.'

Frank felt his stomach tighten. He closed his eyes, opening them a couple of seconds later to find David Jennings staring at him. There was softness in the man's face. Compassion, for sure. It had ever been thus. Frank had not been invited to the Jennings' summer barbeque because he was just an analyst. As was Sam. But that didn't mean that David Jennings didn't know all his staff by name; he would often pop along to their desks for a chat.

David sat back in his chair. Jane had her hands in the prayer position, her fingers marginally separated widening the fan. Frank remained tense. He'd purposely chosen a wooden, dining room-type chair, because he hadn't thought it was his place to opt for a more comfortable one. After an hour and a half, he was beginning to regret it.

'So.' David looked sincere. 'I think Sally's made it clear that this can only be a short visit ... let's make the very best of the time we have. What do you want from me?' There was a beat and then he looked at Frank. 'Frank ... you've said very little. You first. What about your mum? Sorry, I'm assuming she's still with us?'

It was something that a man four ranks senior to him remembered that his mum had been alive when they had last worked together. And, by asking just about his mum, had also remembered that his dad has passed away some years previously. That was leadership.

'Mum's in a home, David. She's got great care. I see her once every month and we talk regularly via WhatsApp. In her current state, if she's seen the TV I'm not sure she'll recognise me.' He paused and looked to Jane. He then sighed a deep sigh as though he were about to give up his deepest held secret.

'Last night I was very willing to give myself up. It all seemed so futile. So hopeless.' He paused. Then, looking down at the floor, he said, 'You know I'm not a field agent, but …' He looked up again, his jaw setting to the way he felt: determined. 'I'm going to find Sam. Or …' He coughed to hide how he felt. 'I'm going to find her body, if that's all that's left. Once that's done I'll reconsider my position. But nothing's going to stop me from making that happen. Nothing.'

He was close to tears. So he blinked. And sniffed.

David spotted his discomfort and quickly added, 'That's clear, Frank. Thanks. Eh, Jane?'

She seemed less emotional.

'The Chief passed the responsibility to me. For me to do whatever I felt sensible. If that meant escaping to a beach somewhere, he said he wouldn't judge.' She paused. 'My mother will know that I'm innocent, as will my brother and his family. Goodness, they've been through enough. I do worry that they, the YCA's acolytes, will use them as levers to call Frank and me in. But I cannot believe, I *really* cannot believe, they will harm them. Marcus Trafford is an unpleasant man, and I can absolutely see why they want us out of the way. But hurt my family? I can't see it myself.'

David didn't say anything.

And Frank was staring at his feet, thinking of ways he might track down Sam.

Jane continued.

'I'm with Frank. We've made some progress since the Balkans operation, and Frank assures me he has everything on a hard drive. Sam has a whole new chapter – and contacts in the Middle East we do not have. She has got to be our first priority. Maybe, and I know you want us out of here tomorrow, we give ourselves a week to work on that – quietly – and then regroup?'

Frank knew that Jane's last line was a question.

David Jennings was the obvious port in a storm. Mostly because Jane trusted David with their lives. And Frank trusted Jane. But David was also a full-term SIS operative with the widest possible experience. As such, Jane's question was the one they both wanted to ask: *what would you do, David*?

There was a call from further within the house. Supper was on the table. Frank hoped there wasn't too much meat on offer.

David put up a hand.

'Let's eat. We all need food. After supper we'll explore ways of how we track down Green – doubtless Frank already has some ideas. And I have some contacts.' He paused. 'I think the first thing you both need to realise is that nowhere in this country is safe. Not even here, not with the exposure you've had. Other than, no operational pun intended, a remote croft in the Hebrides, there is nowhere to hide. I have a pal who runs Tilbury port. He owes me a favour, so I am confident we can get you abroad. The options may be limited, but you will be better out of this country for now.' David stood and stretched his back. Age was clearly catching up with him. 'And I have trustworthy pals at Langley, and with the French DGSI and the German BND. I will make some enquiries. Tonight. And we should plan on getting you out of here no later than this time tomorrow. I can make that happen.'

David had his arm out, directing them through a pair of glass doors which he'd opened. The gap led to a beautifully set dining table. Frank couldn't stop himself from scanning the fare for unmentionables.

Sally was pulling out chairs.

'I took the liberty of assuming that one of you might be vegetarian, so it's a beef chilli without the beef. I hope that's OK?'

Frank didn't know what to say.

People like David and Sally added much needed positive context to his current state of mind – that his country, one he dearly loved, had gone to the dogs.

Maybe there was hope?

Flemingstraße, Munich, Germany

Sam was studying the glass briefing wall whilst Wolfgang tapped away at his computer in the corner. She was good at a number of things. But hacking wasn't one of them. Wolfgang, on the other hand, was known to be one of the best and acknowledged as such by governments, including her own. Since she'd last seen him – and with him squatting in a basement for a couple of years under someone else's house – she could only think he would have got better still. She hoped so. He was currently working on two things: the paedophile charges against the Chief, and where Frank and Jane might be. He hadn't waited for any instructions and, whilst Sam had pressed him on his methods, he had turned to her and replied with a smile, '*dies und das*'.

This and that.

96

Looking at Wolfgang's summary board it was clear that the world's struggle with the YCA wasn't on his radar. There was no need why it should be. And so far there had been no time to mention it, although she would when the time was right.

However, what the board did show was two things, neither of which was a surprise.

Four-fifths of the opaque, orangey glass board, was electronically etched with the details of the – she hoped now defunct – Church of the White Cross. She recognised a couple of names and, by following beautifully constructed flow lines seemingly scraped into the glass by streaks of yellow light, she was able to make the connections to others. Among maybe sixty entries there were three FBI agents. Another was the CFO of an Italian defence company, which appeared to manufacture small arms ammunition, based in Trieste. A third was a lone German man with what looked like no ongoing connections.

Some of the information was vividly displayed. Images were full colour, and the text in black.

Other pieces were greyed out, as if in draft.

Or no longer operational?

And it was crammed with information. But like a beautifully written music score, it was all eminently readable.

Sam had reached the final fifth of the board. Beyond her was one of the three doorless openings that led off the main room into further space. Earlier she'd established that one of them opened into the server room. That was behind her. The one in the wall to her right was more interesting – a sort of padded room. She didn't want to be rude and poke her head in, so she leant forward.

She was pleased to see it wasn't set up as an infirmary for those with violent mental health issues, although that would be a good way to describe it. It was hexagonal, about the size of a family kitchen. On one wall was a music mixing bank and some speakers. Next to it, on another of the six walls, was something she recognised straight away. It was Wolfgang's Karl Höfner violin. It hung from the wall, a section of the padding cut away to allow the instrument to be displayed as if it were a piece of art in a gallery.

Bruch's Violin Concerto No 1.

That was Wolfgang's favourite.

There was a similar room to this in Schloss Neuenburg, Wolfgang's family's estate in the Bayerische Wald on the German/Czechia border. That one was much more grand, but just as round. On one of the few days Sam was there, Wolfgang had demonstrated its acoustics. The noise of his violin – the sound piercingly clear – had sent an arrow through her heart. It was all part of his attraction: good-looking, intelligent, musical, charming, a Saville Row-clothed count. That feeling hadn't lasted. Future destabilising events in the forests on the outskirts of Munich had dislodged the arrow, and any romantic notion sewn between them had become unstitched.

She didn't regret it.

Knowing Wolfgang's attention to detail she reckoned the acoustics in the padded room would be at least as good as those in the castle's *Runden Raum*. If they found time, she would ask him to play.

The third opening, to her left, looked as though it led to a bedsit. She could see the end of a sofa, there was a TV on the wall. And a kitchen.

As she dropped her shoulders to get a better look, Lukas zoomed out and skidded to a halt at her feet, his eyes blinking as his LED screen looked up at her.

'May I get you something?'

A less irritating voice?

'Eh ... no thanks.'

'Would you like a cup of tea?' Lukas added.

I wonder if you can do droid and chips?

Maybe with some mayo?

'No, thanks.' She grimaced at the machine. She was going to struggle to get used to this.

She turned her attention back to the last fifth of the wall.

There was a timeline, no title. A map: Europe top left, heading south to sub-Saharan Africa, and then east to Japan. A series of twenty-six black dots were joined together by those yellow, under-lit lines; she could count that quickly. Below that was a simple table: one column was dates, the second a location. There were twenty-six entries.

Sam touched on one of the dots on the map in Europe. A dialogue box appeared next to it. It gave dates, times, a flight number and other information. At the same time the table scrolled so that the date of the flight, and the corresponding information to its right, moved to the centre of the columns, its font colour changing from black to red. Map and table were linked.

She then touched a dot in Vietnam.

The same thing happened.

Now Africa.

The same.

She knelt down and scrolled the table contents up until the final entry was the latest date.

It was yesterday.

Location: Bratislava, which was now blinking at her on the map. In the left-hand column were details of the ATM she had used and the account number from which the 300 euros had been taken.

'Hence, I knew you were coming.' Wolfgang's wheelchair had glided to her.

'Like last time,' Sam replied without looking at him. Instead she had put her finger on Abuja, in the centre of Nigeria. The dialogue box next to it displayed her Russian pseudonym, flight number and other details. But there was a second box. It contained three Facebook screenshots of the Israeli Hercules as it disgorged the Shayetet 13 Special Forces that had come to rescue her, Micah and Hannah – and the unfortunate women. Sam knew the YCA had covered their tracks and electronically removed any hint of an attack on their facilities and the subsequent rescue by Israeli commandos. There was nothing on the web.

But Wolfgang had them.

In fact it looked highly likely that Wolfgang had the whole of Sam's life, since Venezuela, detailed on one-fifth of his briefing board ... and who knew what other information he had on her?

She didn't feel threatened.

He had done the same post the Munich warehouse incident seven years ago. His answer then was that he had been keeping an eye out for her.

Is it creepy?

She looked down at him. He returned her gaze.

There was no deep affection there. She didn't get the same resonance she'd got when she was with Frank. That, as he had said to her face, he loved her. This, here, with Wolfgang, was different.

Sure, they had been close. At one point she thought it might actually come to something. But the kidnap and murder of his mother, an action which had stemmed from Sam's role in SIS, had burnt any romantic bridges.

Sam was on the autistic scale – somewhere – and she was often emotionally discordant. She knew that. But she didn't miss everything. Looking at Wolfgang now, she knew the attachment between them was much more sibling-to-sibling than might be lover-to-lover.

And she was more than happy with that.

'I can see that,' she said with a small nod.

'You've been busy,' he added.

She glanced back at the map.

Too busy.

She nodded again and, for distraction purposes only, she tapped on one location after the other, checking on Wolfgang's accuracy.

'If you knew I were coming ...' she was looking at the Seoul entry. Extraordinarily there was a separate dialogue box containing a good deal of detail of the attack on the presidential train at Munmu Station, 'then, so do they. Don't you think?'

'Who are they, Sam?' It wasn't a trick question from Wolfgang. Sure, he had followed her around the world and sensibly associated local crises with where she had been. But there was nothing in any of the blurbs which mentioned the communist 'Gang of Four', for example. And, as far as she could tell, there was nothing here on the YCA. Why would there be? Wolfgang might be a world-class hacker, but there were some databases he could not reach.

She ignored the question. Instead she pointed at the four-fifths of the board which weren't a geographical shrine to Sam Green.

101

'You're still targeting the Church of the White Cross?' Sam waved a finger.

He nodded. 'It depends, of course, what you mean by targeting?' There was no emotion in his voice.

'Everyone on the board is a Church associate?' she asked.

'Absolutely. And there are more. But not many.' Wolfgang had moved his chair down the board about a metre. 'This guy here, for example. He's a Slovak builder. He runs a small firm in Detva. He is, or was, a Church member. Plus two of his friends.'

It had been Wolfgang's turn to point. His finger had stopped just short of a small dialogue box – one coloured the grey scale of orange, not as vibrant as some others.

'Was?' Sam asked.

'He's in prison now. Convicted of fraud, and some other more casual crimes. Down for five years, apparently.' Wolfgang was looking quietly pleased with himself.

'You did that?' It was the obvious question.

He turned to her, his face now set hard.

'I did. He was an active Church member. And now he isn't. There are, at the last count, 143 other people in his shoes. Some with important jobs, some less so.'

'You set them up? Cook the books?' Would she be bothered if Wolfgang had, or hadn't acted as God?

Possibly.

'Where it was necessary. I have to say that for most of them, my investigations quickly led to something illegal. Interestingly, I'd say one in three of the male members had been involved in sex-related crimes … which tells you all you need to know about the Church.'

His face had softened. It was almost sad.

She turned to him and there was a moment, as though the information on the briefing wall, Sam's place on it, and the disclosures over the Church of the White Cross, filtered between them as if they were joined together by a network cable.

'Why are we under someone else's house, Wolfgang?'

There was a pause. Wolfgang looked down at his hands as though he was uncomfortable with the question and was working out whether to reply.

'After the fire and my long spell in hospital, I was told that I have a compromised immune system and, among other things, would have to spend the rest of my life in a wheelchair. You won't know, but you have been expertly sanitised on the way down here. I can, at any time, access your vitals. If you had even the slightest of temperatures, or your breath showed signs of an infection, Lukas would have kept you in the main house. This place is, to all intents and purposes, hermetically sealed. Provided I stay down here,' he pointed to the floor, 'and provided I eat sensibly and follow a strict exercise regime,' he looked to his legs, 'I should live out a normal life – from the waist up. And I want to do that.'

Sam got it.

'You haven't answered my question,' she said.

'This isn't someone else's house. It's mine. I bought it within a year of the fire. It's currently rented out to a quiet professional family. They don't know that they have a bunker under their backyard. And there's no reason why they should ever know.' He smiled, a contented smile.

'By why not convert your cellar? And why rebuild the house exactly as it was before the fire?' Sam thought she knew the answer to the first question. She didn't know the answer to the second.

'Frank and I were in the cellar when we were bombed. You know that. It didn't keep us completely safe then. Hence this extension.' He waved a finger in a circle. 'I have, actually, rebuilt the original cellar as it was, with all the same technology, but the screens and databases are a diversion to what's happening in here. It's running via an algorithm. Should someone break into the house to find me, they would be welcomed by a semi-lived-in, old Munich dwelling, with a state-of-the-art cellar displaying nonsense. They would never be able to connect there,' he now pointed to the floor, 'to here.'

'And next door's decoration? The family portraits?' Sam pushed.

'Us Neuenburgs are a sentimental lot, Sam. You should know that.'

She did.

'Now,' Wolfgang continued, 'let me show you what I'm up to ...'

Other than persecuting members of the Church of the White Cross?

'... stay where you are.'

Wolfgang was back at his corner desk. As he prodded and swiped, the current briefing screen's maps, images and lists dissolved. In their place, covering only about a quarter of the screen, was new information.

Sam took a step to it. Wolfgang joined her.

'It's not much at the moment,' he started. 'Let's do the easy bit first.'

He had a laser pointer in his hand. A blue dot swung a circle around two boxes. One was a map of London and its environs. The second was a series of words and numbers. There was no title.

Sam had to lift her chin to read it.

'Drag it down,' Wolfgang said.

She did.

It took her no time to work out what the map and dialogue box showed.

How the hell?

'This is Jane's and Frank's recent ATM and Oyster card use.' She was staggered. 'How did you ...?'

'Unless you want an unnecessary and long answer, because most of the computer coding would be lost on you, don't ask. I've gathered the information. You, as I remember you describing, now deliver the intelligence.'

I will.

But in the meantime ...

'What's this, Wolfgang?' Sam had dragged a second series of boxes to eye level. There was coding, IRLs and what looked like profiles from a dating site. Except, it wasn't a dating site. It was ...

... she felt her stomach lurch.

'It's one of seven dark web paedophile sites. There is some discussion as to how many of these exist, certainly for European use. The current thinking, according to *Bundesnachrichtendienst*, the BND, is that this list of seven seems enough ...'

Sam had so many questions.

'How did you ... and have you ...?' She was pointing at the head-shot of a late middle-aged man, set in an innocent-looking dating profile under which was the line: *Preference – infant, female.* Her finger moved right to a piece of screen where a myriad of information had been greyed out.

Wolfgang nodded.

'Again, don't ask me how. But, as you have guessed, yes, I have used sites like this to help neutralise some members of the Church.'

Sam didn't know what to say, so she didn't say anything. Instead she looked at all of the information on the board and systematically started to internalise, reduce and re-form it into intelligence. This was something she was particularly good at.

It took a minute.

'Why this site?' She was pointing at the dark web, paedophile website.

'It's actually the most difficult to find, and it's close to impossible to hack – I haven't been able to, although I do have coding running with the aim of finding a trap door.'

'And you think this is the site that someone like, and I mean *like*, Sir Clive Morton might use?' Sam was convinced the Chief was no paedophile.

Wolfgang had a remote keyboard on his lap. He was typing into it.

'It's the one I would use if I wanted to create a fake profile with your ex-boss's name on it. For sure.' He was still typing.

'What are you doing now?' Sam's tone had a hint of accusation. She was a little frustrated that Wolfgang had set off on his own and, regardless of the early results he had delivered already, he was now off again without recourse to her views or ideas.

He stopped. And looked up at her.

There was another moment. And he smiled.

'I'm ordering supper. And wine – I have an app here. The menu's not vast, but it is incredibly good. Let me surprise you. Lukas and Matilda produce it to order.' His smile had morphed into gentle smugness.

'Who the … ' Sam checked herself. Then more softly, 'Who is Matilda?'

'You've not met her yet, have you? Let me introduce you …' And with that, Wolfgang's chair purred past her and headed for the bedsit.

Chapter 5

Dentles Drive, Bradley Stoke, Bristol, UK

Heather couldn't sleep. She rarely did. How long had it been like this? She did the maths, but she didn't need to. She knew how old Fi, her daughter, was.

Fiona Grace Hutton.

Born on 3rd September 2000 in the millennium year, but a Generation Z baby. Brought into the world during a recession. According to the experts her sort were meant to be pragmatic. Millennials, a little older, were optimistic … apparently. She, Heather, was Generation X. If they used her actual personality to define that group of people, they would be anxious and remorseful.

Remorse.

Such a powerful and adept word.

She always took an age to get to sleep, and then often only catnapped … ever since her lovely Fi had come into the world. Initially the pain she carried had just been with her. But within weeks she knew something wasn't right. At nine weeks and having missed twice, she had no option other than to buy a test. Two hours later – the worst two hours of her life, and that was saying something – and with more tears than any woman could bear, she knew what she already knew.

She was pregnant …

… with a child conceived from the most horrendous of assaults. She had no idea who the father might be. And it was impossible to say how many men she might have to choose from. Was it five? Or six? Or a couple, multiple times?

She didn't know. She couldn't know.

Nor could Fi. She must *never* find out. Ever.

Of course she looked for traits. Which sane mother wouldn't?

So far, thank God, Fi had grown up to become a kind and caring young woman. Sure, there were times during her early teens when Heather worried that the moods and sulkiness were the start of her daughter's transformation into something, someone, she might be unable to love, or certainly not like. But that had passed. And since sixth form she had been, pretty much, the model daughter of a fretful single mum. A mum who worried about everything and everyone.

Anxiety which had got worse.

It had been fine when Fi lived at home … hadn't it?

Maybe.

Possibly not. If she were honest, she found herself being too strict with her daughter on sleepovers and parties. She was a permanent, and willing, taxi, often arriving an hour before pick-up, like a suspicious lover checking on a partner who had gone for a night out with the girls.

She never left anything to chance. She was always alert.

Suspicious.

Heather had struggled, for sure.

But that was nothing in comparison to when Fi had chosen to go to Birmingham University.

'I'll move with you. I can get a job there. You can live with me. Wouldn't that be great?' The sentences had come out in a splurge.

Of course she couldn't follow her daughter to university. It was a ridiculous notion.

So Fi had left home, under one proviso: that she told her mum where she was going of an evening, and always gave a time when she would return to her halls. And then, when she got back to her room, she would text.

Was that too much to ask?

It was.

At first Fi had been compliant. It was all she knew. Why wouldn't she let her mum know where she was going, who she was with and when she was due back?

But it hadn't taken long.

By halfway through Fi's first year, they had fallen out. By the end of the year there was a danger the split might be irrecoverable.

'You're too controlling, Mum. I know you're worried, but … all my friends' mums are worried. You have to trust me. You have to let me go. It's not fair.'

That was all understandable. Heather deserved the tirade.

She got it.

But it didn't change how she felt.

How could it?

The summer break was even more difficult than term time. Fi was flitting about all over the country. She had only come home twice, for a couple of nights at a time. On the second visit Heather had suggested that they fit a 'Find My Family' app to her phone so that, if nothing else, Heather knew where Fi was without having to speak to her.

They'd rowed about that, with both of them in tears, followed by a hug and apologies that had lasted for half an hour.

'Trust me, Mum. Please.' The damp words had come when Fi's head had been resting on Heather's shoulder.

She had tried. God, how she had tried.

Everything had come to a head a couple of months ago. Fi had failed to hang up after an evening call and Heather had overheard a conversation between her precious daughter and a male voice. It was then she realised she was in danger of losing Fi once and for all.

'It's my mum,' Fi had said.

'Is she all right?' The male voice had sounded considerate.

'No. She needs to get a fucking life.'

Two months ago. The longest two months of Heather's life.

Since then she had tried *so* hard not to be controlling. She had vowed never to pick up the phone and dial Fi's number; that she would wait for her daughter to call.

She had tried. Because she had no choice. She either let Fi loose, or lose her altogether.

It was gut-wrenching.

And now, three months into Fi's second year, she had absolutely no idea where her daughter was. They hadn't spoken for over a week, although there had been two WhatsApp exchanges with plenty of smiley-face emojis.

But who knew where Fi was? Who knew what she was up to?

Get a fucking life.

Heather rolled over and stared into the semi-darkness of her bedroom.

A life.

That would be nice.

Heather had avoided relationships from the start. Her work – she was a legal secretary in the centre of Bristol – was interesting enough, and it kept her mind distracted during workdays. In the early days it had been easy. The evenings and weekends were all about Fi. There was no time for Heather's own ambitions. No time for hobbies.

No time for men.

Even now the thought made her skin crawl.

Her relationship with her parents had deteriorated quickly after they discovered she was pregnant, and that the baby had been conceived as a result of a one-night stand. Her dad was actually better about it than her mum. But, after she moved away from her family home in the north of England to Bristol – was it to be as far away from Aberdeen University as was geographically possible? – even that relationship had struggled. Her mother, who had always been a drinker, now started at lunchtime, and didn't stop. Her father, bless him, spent all of his time down the allotment. Heather knew that the pair of them only just survived each other.

She saw them once, or maybe twice a year. They never came to Bristol – Mum couldn't cope with the empty-of-wine shelves in Heather's larder.

And, whilst there had been plenty of relationship opportunities, she had not crossed that threshold.

Sex?

That was never on the cards.

If it came on TV she had to switch it off.

She was an avid reader. What else was there to do when you couldn't sleep? But the moment the author heading for an erotic scene the pages were skipped. Sometimes the book was banished to the charity shop.

As for anything long term – even something platonic, or gay? – well, who would want to share their lives with an anxiety-stricken single mum?

Who held a distasteful secret.

Get a fucking life.

The words bounced around her head every day.

Heather closed her eyes. Not to sleep. But to escape.

She had reluctantly gone to see a doctor about her anxiety and sleep pattern. The meeting had been cursory, and the outcome was some pills which had made her feel lethargic, but didn't help with sleep. So she dropped those.

She squeezed out a tear.

Could she live the rest of her life like this?

When would it end?

When Fi got married … to a man Heather approved of? But you couldn't trust any men, could you? He might, on the face of it, seem like a nice guy. But what was he doing when he was away from home?

She sniffed.

Will it ever end?

It was a curse.

…

If only she hadn't got drunk. If only she hadn't taken the drugs. If only she'd stayed with her pals, or …

It was no use.

This was the way it was going to be.

Wasn't it?

She wiped her eyes with a hand, sat up in bed and put the light on. She checked her phone. It was 01.12. She hadn't slept. And the way she felt, she knew she wouldn't. Tomorrow was another day. She'd try to find time for a walk, come back, pick at some food, watch some telly – during which, blessed relief, she might catch a nap for half an hour – put a chop under the grill, catch the news, and go to bed.

Get a fucking life.

Her finger hovered over the phone, its wallpaper a lovely shot of her and Fi a couple of years ago, big smiles for a selfie.

Get a fucking life.

Fi was right.

She was absolutely right.

Heather opened Google. Her finger now hovering above the horizontal white bar.

She typed in: assaults in Aberdeenshire.

There were 677,000 results.

The first read: *Police say serious sexual assault in Banchovy …*

She was about to open the tab to find out what the police said about the serious assault in Banchovy, but stopped herself. Instead she got out of bed, threw on a dressing gown and made her way to her small kitchen in her two-bed flat. She put the kettle on and, as it boiled, she found a notebook and a pen.

If she was going to do this, she was going to do it properly.

Flemingstraße, Munich, Germany

It was gone 2 am. Wolfgang was back in his corner. Everything he worked on was being shadow displayed onto the main board. He would throw something up and Sam would bark something across at him in return. If necessary they'd have a conversation, and then he'd crack on as she prodded and swiped, enlarged and reduced, as she thought helped. They'd been at it for a couple of hours.

Supper had been like eating at the International Space Station, but without the views. Sitting at a pristine white table which was easily big enough for the two of them, their crockery, glasses and a fabulous bottle of *Goldtröpfchen Piesporter* Riesling – which tasted like honey percolated through a glacier – she'd made the point.

'Don't you miss a view, Wolfgang? This, however lovely it is,' she'd used wide hands, unbothered that she was waving her cutlery about like a conductor, 'needs some context, don't you think?'

Wolfgang took a mouthful of schnitzel, made from veal which had clearly been fed for its short life on mother's milk and lush alpine grass, had chewed and then replied, 'You're right.' And then, out of nowhere, he tapped on a previous invisible pad on the table, looked up at her and forced a smile.

Wow.

Two things happened.

First, the whole wall to their left, one of the shorter pair, but still as big as anything you'd find in a conventional dining room, lit up with an image of a Caribbean beach. Apart from the clarity, what was clever was the perspective. The whole picture was as if they were looking out through bi-fold doors onto their own piece of paradise. Everything looked real – there was a 3D aspect which she couldn't get her head round. And it moved. There was a pelican. And, on the horizon, a yacht made its way gracefully from left to right, its spinnaker bursting with wind.

But that wasn't all.

Sam had felt it almost immediately. And then she'd smelt it. There was a warm, salty breeze. A *caw* from a distant bird. And the hypnotising sound of gentle waves caressing a white beach.

It was as real as if she were there.

She forked two identically sized chips and studied them. Beyond them and slightly out of focus, she noticed Wolfgang staring at her.

'What?' she said.

'This isn't going to end well, is it?' There was no regret in his voice. Just a touch of sadness.

Whilst 'Matilda', a couple of very neat holes in the wall and an eye-line, inbuilt tablet, delivered supper from who knew where – or how – Sam had given Wolfgang a detailed enough outline of her life since Minden. Her employment with what turned out to be a branch of Mossad. The princess and her failing liver, and her titled brother. Copenhagen, Sarajevo and then Abuja. The murder of the MI5 man. And, of course, the YCA. As Sam recited the eight names she knew of – Frank might have since uncovered more – Wolfgang had reached for his remote keyboard that was stored on the side of his wheelchair. He'd typed in their names asking her to spell Bosshart, the Swiss man, and the sheikh, Rashid bin Nahzan.

Eight names.

The YCA.

Wolfgang was right.

It wasn't going to end well, was it?

The Chief was in a cell somewhere. Like her, Jane and Frank were on the run.

If they poked deeper into the YCA's affairs, they would become the focus of a tirade of investigation which would inevitably lead to violence.

Against them.

She knew it didn't matter that they were hidden, deep underground in a nuclear-esque bunker. The YCA and their affiliates would find them.

Her and Wolfgang.

Eventually.

She put the chips in her mouth. They were too long to go in sideways, so Sam attacked them from enfilade. Small bites, like a hamster.

'You don't have to do this.' Sam's words came out between chomps.

He had a beautifully cut crystal wine glass in his hand.

He smiled.

'I wouldn't miss it for the world.'

He nonchalantly took a sip of his Riesling, as though signing up for a battle against adversaries whose arsenal was infinite, against an armoury equipped with three packets of sparklers, was hardly a commitment of note.

She finished chewing, took the napkin from her lap and, as he had taught her all those years ago, dabbed her mouth clean and placed it beside her half-eaten plate.

'Well. Thank you for all of this. And a special thanks to Matilda,' she nodded in the direction of the two holes, 'but I think it's time we got on. Don't you?'

Wolfgang had nodded, drained his wine and did the same with his napkin.

'After you, Sam Green.' He had held out a hand.

And that had been, how long was it? A couple of hours ago.

Now, still standing – sometimes, crouching – by the info wall, she was starting to flag. She had been in Bratislava just before lunch. A through-train had allowed her some time to rest, but she had always been on edge. Her stomach ached. That never went away. She needed sleep and, if that didn't happen soon, her brain, as it did, would shut down for her. She had looked around for a second bed, but couldn't find one. There was a huge double in Matilda's office, and she had no problem with that.

She might soon need to warn Wolfgang that she was running out of steam.

'Look at this!' The alarm in Wolfgang's voice caught her off guard. His wheelchair spun as a new image appeared from the left of her vision and slid across the wall. It slowed and then stopped pretty much at eye height in front of her.

She focused.

It was a middle page from *Le Figaro*, dated eleven days ago. It took Sam a second to find the relevant article. Using two hands, she enlarged it.

Un officier du renseignement français retrouvé mort.

Underneath, in the text, was the name *Louis Belmonte*.

'I'm guessing this is the same Louis Belmonte, brother of YCA member, Marc Belmonte, you mentioned before supper? As in, the Belmonte Paradox?' Wolfgang was at her side now, his voice at a gallop.

But she wasn't paying attention to him.

In fact, she hadn't been paying attention at all.

Since she'd arrived.

She had been overwhelmed by where she found herself. By the house. The electronics. The damn robots. The delightful *Goldtröpfchen Piesporter*. By Wolfgang's enthusiasm. His energy.

She grimaced.

A couple of hours ago she had been looking at the map of her wanderings on the board. Bratislava, her last

118

location, had been blinking. Wolfgang had said, 'Hence, I knew you were coming.'

Of course he did.

And now Louis Belmonte was dead.

And the Chief had been arrested and, if he survived a trial, would spend the rest of his life behind bars.

And the 'armed and dangerous' Frank and Jane were on the run.

They were all in danger.

They were all in danger – now.

'Mind out of the way.' Without any politeness, Sam ushered Wolfgang aside. She wanted to look at the south of England map which showed Jane and Frank's last movements.

It was too high for her so she dragged it down, other bits of information parted and reset themselves to allow for the map to move.

She studied it for a second. The purr of Wolfgang's chair announced its arrival by the side.

Sam chewed on a lip.

'If I give you a house address, can you find a UK landline?'

'Sure. Why?'

'I know where they are. And if I know, so does everyone else.'

Therfield, Hertfordshire, UK

The phone rang. David woke with a start and checked the time on his old analogue alarm clock: it was twenty past three. As he reached for the handset, he wiped his eyes and simultaneously tried to lift himself up. That was at least one action too many at this time of the morning. He was on the wrong side of seventy. What did he expect?

As his spare hand moved from his eyes to his temples, he rested his head against the knuckles of the fist which was holding the receiver.

'Jennings.' Sometimes he would say 'Jennings' residence'. Sometimes 'David Jennings'. But at 3 o'clock in the morning 'Jennings' was good enough for whoever on earth was phoning at this time. He hoped it wasn't one of their children in crisis.

It wasn't.

'Have you got company?' It was a female voice he didn't immediately recognise.

'Who ...'

No.

No need.

He now knew who it was.

His brain had settled on a name.

It was Sam Green.

'Well?'

It was *definitely* Sam Green. Even his children didn't talk to him in that tone. In fact, he couldn't recall ever being spoken to this way. Well, not for a while.

What did she want? Did she want to speak to Jane? Had she some revelation about this nonsense which would help? Did she want to meet up?

After supper he, Jane and Frank had only managed a couple of hours of work before it was clear they needed to sleep. They were both dead on their feet, which was no surprise considering the previous night. Jane and Frank had spent the time trying to work out where Sam might be. Without recourse to SIS resources that had been pretty futile. The last report they'd had – and Frank had been checking daily – was the use of an ATM card belonging to an Israeli national who, via the bank's CCTV, looked as if it might be Sam. The particular cash machine was in Belgrade. Jane and Frank had pored over a map of Eastern Europe, trying to establish a pattern. But they hadn't got very far.

Then they'd looked at what Frank had removed from Babylon on his hard drive. David had not wanted to be immersed in the detail, so all he got was that they had a good deal of information on the eight YCA members' corporate and personal bank accounts, plus some other info such as family details and personal and corporate properties. It was then Frank had fallen asleep with his head resting on his hands.

The pair of them had agreed to pick it up after breakfast.

As they cleared the dining room, Jane surprised him. She'd told Frank to shower, repack and sleep in his clothes. She made it clear that they'd already had one narrow escape so they needed to be prepared for another.

David had had the benefit of working with a full night's sleep and had continued after his visitors had hit the sack. He'd sent his DGSI pal, a retired deputy, a heads up. It was an innocuous email breaking the ice, so to speak. David was confident the chap would come back to him by the end of the weekend.

Next was the American. It was a Saturday afternoon in Langley and David had taken a chance and given his old CIA pal, the previous-but-one RoW (*Rest of the World*) chief, a call on his cell. His friend had connected and, as David had expected, it had been like old times.

But he'd kept it short.

'Hi, Chuck. It's David Jennings. It's been a long while?' He'd let the question hang.

'David!' The single word reply extended for almost a sentence. 'How's it going old man?' Chuck's accent was old school East Coast. He sounded relaxed and content.

'Are you watching a game?' David knew his pal was into baseball.

'No, sir. I'm driving to the mall with my granddaughter. I'm in spoiling mode.' David heard the granddaughter say something which included the word, 'grandpappy.'

'Anyways,' Chuck continued with a laugh, 'I'm guessing you want something?'

David hadn't spoken to Chuck for six years. Of course he wanted something.

'I need to pick your brains. Have you heard of an organisation called the Young Crofters' Association?' David asked, grimacing to himself as he did.

There was a pause … which was a worry.

'Is that a country and western group?' Chuck asked with another laugh. That sort of put David's mind at rest.

Sort of.

'Look, Chuck. I really don't want to mess up your shopping trip, but maybe on Monday you could talk to a live contact at Langley, and see if there's any gen which they might want to share with you? And maybe call me back?'

There was a further pause. His pal might have been negotiating a traffic light.

'Sure, David, of course. I don't have much sway anymore and my security clearance isn't what it was. But I'll ask anyway. Can I mention your name?' Chuck asked.

David looked at the Vienna-style wall clock which had once hung in pride of place in his office. The organisation had presented it to him on retirement.

'No, thanks. And ...' he paused, 'be sensible, Chuck. Pick those you ask carefully. Please.'

David heard Chuck breathing out heavily.

'OK, David. I get it. I'll be fine,' Chuck had replied.

They had finished off with more pleasantries, and then David had made his most important call, the one to the COO of Tilbury container port. There was a favour owed, and he intended to call it in.

And he didn't care what day or what time it was.

The conversation had been short. There was a German freighter leaving the port tomorrow – *no today* – at 1725. It was headed for Rotterdam and then on to Navi Mumbai, via Suez. His contact could get Jane and Frank onto the ship and could then disembark them on the other side of the wire at Rotterdam. But if they wanted to go all the way to Mumbai, they'd be on their own in India once they were quayside.

By the time David had secured the deal, his two visitors had been sound asleep. He would share their future itinerary with them in the morning.

Which had already arrived sooner than David had expected.

'Yes. I have visitors.' David didn't need to say anymore. There was always a possibility his landline was tapped.

'You must ask them to leave, now.'

What on earth?

David formed a few sentences in his mind but didn't utter them. Instead he said, 'I need more than that. I can't just throw my visitors out into the night.'

Sam's response was immediate.

'You have to.'

'Give me more.' He wasn't having any of it.

There was the shortest of pauses.

'I'm with my *noble* friend.' Sam's voice, which emphasised 'noble', was direct and laced with frustration. 'We have a map running. It's displaying nearly every UK mobile *ping*. There's a convoy of at least three cars. It's just turned off the ...' she paused as if looking at something, 'A505, heading south. They'll be with you ...'

David didn't hear the rest from Sam – he'd slammed down the phone. He also didn't hear his wife turning next to him, moaning something along the lines of, 'who's that, dear?'

Jane and Frank were in the twin room – minimal fingerprints to clean up once they had gone. David threw on the bedroom light, moved between the beds, and shook them violently. Jane woke immediately. It took him three attempts to raise Frank.

'What, what?' Jane spluttered.

'Sam called,' he was still shaking Frank, 'Come on, Frank, wake up.' The man stirred and coughed out some words. 'She's with Wolfgang. They know you're here. And so does everyone else. There's a convoy on its way. I reckon you have five minutes to get out of here.' David had grabbed Frank by the shoulder and pulled him up. Jane was already slipping on her shoes and reaching for her bag.

'Take my wife's Micra.' David was helping Frank disentangle himself from the bedclothes. 'The keys are on the hall table. It's on the drive. The gate will open automatically. Head out and turn right at the end of the road, not left. That's the direction they're coming from.'

Jane was out of the room. David was now helping Frank tie his shoelaces.

'Come on, Frank,' David hurried to himself.

Then Frank was up, satchel to his chest, moving quickly down the hall to the stairs. David chased after him. As they reached the end of the landing, David heard the front door open followed by the sound of feet on gravel. The pair of them followed on.

The lights of the Micra lit up as the car turned over. As Frank rushed around the bonnet to get to the passenger door, Jane's window dropped.

'Did you get us on a boat?' It was a plea.

David was beside her now, his hand resting on top of the car, his lungs working a little harder than he would have liked.

'Tilbury docks. 1725. It's a German freighter, the BBC Seville. The master's name is Klaus Bracht. He's expecting you both. First stop is Rotterdam. Then you're on your own. Now go!'

'Did you get all that, Frank?' Jane turned away from David to look at her passenger.

'Yup,' was the reply from inside the car.

She forced a smile at David, and then, with the gates taking slightly longer to open than David would have liked, the Micra disappeared around the yew hedge and into the darkness ...

... but his work wasn't done. Not yet. He waited for the gates to start to close and then he jogged back to the house. His wife was waiting in the hall, as fresh as if she'd had a shower and just finished her muesli.

'They're coming?' she asked matter-of-factly.

'Yes,' he replied, pulling the door to.

'I'll go and sort out their bed and wipe everything down. You turn off all the lights. We'll keep the bastards at bay.'

David looked at his wife, nodded his head and smiled.

How lucky am I?

Dentles Drive, Bradley Stoke, Bristol, UK

Heather was in the kitchen putting another pod in the Tassimo. She hadn't pulled the blinds when she had gone to bed, and the scene through the kitchen window was the black outline of the houses behind her garden, backlit by the yellowy-grey of Bristol's night-time sheen. She loved Bristol. And she liked living in Bradley Stoke. Her house was comfortable, her work was a twenty-minute bus ride away, and everything she needed was in walking distance. She was lucky. She knew that.

The coffee machine had stopped its heavy gurgling. She took hold of the mug's handle and stared at the bubbles as they swirled and popped, and popped and swirled some more. It was decaf this time in the vain hope that, once she'd finished what she was doing, sleep might come.

That was unlikely, though. Especially after what she had found.

She had carried out maybe fifty Google searches, and as a result had a notebook full of stuff which wasn't, in any way, heading for a conclusion. But it was pointing towards further research. The decision she had to make now was whether to push on or try to get some sleep and come back to it later?

She already knew the answer to that question.

What had surprised her was she hadn't thought about Fi at all. Not really. It had been just her, sitting at her small pine dining room table accompanied by a laptop and an accumulation of notes in a gradually filling reporter's pad. Fi hadn't bothered to text to let her mum know she was safe.

Heather had no idea where she was.

Ordinarily that was enough to send her mind into spasms. By now she would be pacing her bedroom, probably on her third or fourth coffee. Sweating, probably, that cold clammy sweat which made her nightdress hug her shoulders tightly.

But there was something about the cathartic nature of what she was doing – focusing on herself, her life, her angst – which was tugging at her arm, distracting her from her usual daughter-focused anxiety.

It was way too early to jump to any conclusions. But, as of now, she thought she just might be … *getting a fucking life*. Although, to be fair, if Fi knew what she was up to, Heather was unconvinced she would agree that was necessarily the case.

Heather sat down, took a sip of coffee and stared at her reflection in the patio doors. A 160 centimetre tall, slim built woman stared back at her. For someone in their mid-forties, she was still pretty, in an angular and no-make-up fashion. And her hair, probably her best feature, hung dark and sheeny, curving to her shoulders. She was proud of the way she looked. It was important to her. Not in a flirty way, although she reckoned when she dropped her hair across one side of her face and pursed her lips, that might be the case – that thought involuntarily made her shoulders shiver. But more like, 'I might be middle-aged, but I look after myself'. She wanted to do that. To be seen to be doing that … for Fi. She wanted her daughter to, well, like her. Much more important, she didn't want her daughter to think poorly of her.

That's why the dilemma, between giving Fi her freedom and keeping a close eye on her, was driving Heather slowly deranged. She knew the right thing to do. She just couldn't make it happen.

Until, maybe, now?

Maybe?

Maybe.

What did she have?

First, she had tried to catalogue assaults on women in Aberdeenshire between the pretty arbitrary dates of 1998 to 2004. She had seventy-four names. She'd interrogated those and had come up with three potential fits. After some further clicking it was clear that none of the three involved kidnapping. She made a note of them anyway.

She'd then widened the search. This time she extended it to all of the counties above the Caledonian Canal, and then cross-examined that search. She quickly found one name that might be a match. The girl was called Wendy McFort. The details appeared in the now discontinued *Sunday Highland*. The article, which included a photo of Wendy, described how she had claimed to have been kidnapped after a night out, driven somewhere in a car, raped, and abandoned. Her abduction had taken place from Arisaig, on the west coast, and she had been dropped on the A9, at Tacher. Heather had checked the map. That was 100 miles away. It hadn't been explicit in the article, and Heather had had to do some maths, but she eventually worked out that the date of the assault was 14/15th, and maybe the 16th of December in 2003. The report hadn't given all of the details.

Heather had been tapping her teeth with the end of her biro at that point.

Her own assault was in mid-December.

When, exactly?

Why didn't she remember this?

Because I don't want to?

Then she had it.

16th of December – that was it.

Four years later.

A coincidence, surely?

She didn't know.

Heather then broadened the search to include every year from 1995 – *how long could a man, or men, keep at this for?* – until 2020.

That was a whole new ball game.

It had taken her an hour to start to bring some order to the widened list of names. She had decided not to worry about the age of the victims. But, to begin with, she had skipped past anything which didn't include abduction. She had been scrolling down the list having jotted down fourteen new names ... and then had to stop.

It was a newspaper article on the assault on a woman in Wick in 2006. Heather had spent ten minutes on this one report.

The woman had been attacked by two men on a Friday night in April. She'd been thrown into the back of their car and taken to a remote beach where she had been repeatedly assaulted. It sounded horrific. She'd searched for more information and found a subsequent article on the trial. Both men had been found guilty and sentenced to long prison terms.

Their mugshots were in the paper.

'Could it be you who kidnapped me?' She had pointed the cap of her pen at both men in turn.

She blew out through her nose. There was nothing in the article which spoke of drugging, or backs of vans, or sea journeys.

So ... possibly not.

She carried on.

Heather's notebook was filling up, and her perseverance seemed to pay off when she had a third potential breakthrough.

It was from 2009. A young woman, Steph Landown, had gone missing from Thurso on a Friday night ... *in December*. After a boozy session in one of the town's pubs – karaoke and everything – Steph had not turned up for her shift in a high street café the following day. Her friends had immediately spoken to the police of their concern. Two days later the local force had deemed Steph a missing person. The police's interest had waned and, three weeks later, the case was closed as inconclusive. Sometimes people leave home and don't come back.

That was, until a month later when the body of a young woman had been found on Sanday, one of Orkney's northernmost isles, a good 25 miles from the mainland's coast. The woman's body had been attacked by fish, and whatever was left had all but decomposed. But the remnants of clothing and the dental records confirmed it was Steph. The local coroner couldn't rule out assault but, in the end, the death had been classified as 'misadventure'.

Two things had got to Heather. Leaving aside the sadness of the poor woman's death, the potential abduction had happened in December. Second, the body had, to all intents and purposes, been found at sea.

She wrote it all down, and carried on.

An hour later it was time for another cup of coffee – decaf. And now, as she stared at her reflection in the glass of the patio doors, she was ready to start again.

Heather put her coffee on a placemat and scrolled down, searching for the next possible article.

No.

No.

No.

Wait.

No.

No.

No.

Hang on.

She scrolled back.

To the right of the http web address, the blue Google headline read: *Journalist found dead*. It was a BBC Scotland link dated just over two years ago.

Why was that in the search?

She clicked on the link.

The journalist was a Peter Lynch. He was an independent reporter, but provided articles for a number of Scottish papers and journals. He was 'well liked, diligent, and in favour of Scottish Independence'. She didn't know why the latter was important. He had been knocked over by a car which hadn't stopped. He was declared dead at the scene.

There was a photo. It was the man's bust. He appeared to be a little older than her, he had a beard, glasses and a second chin – a sort of bespectacled and bearded Robbie Coltrane in his *Cracker* days.

Heather was about to close the tab and move on when, for a reason she didn't quite understand, she double-clicked on the image.

131

She stared at it.

Peter Lynch had a friendly face, which was humoured by slightly wonky teeth. And a greying beard.

She sighed.

And then stopped breathing.

The shot was a promotional one. Behind him, slightly out of focus, was a poster. On it was a photo of him holding a book, against a backdrop of distinctly Scottish scenery. There was some other blurb, but she couldn't pick out the details.

But she could read the title of the book.

The Unsolved Mystery of the North Coast's Abductions.

Heather closed her eyes. And then opened them again.

The image was still there.

She reduced the tab and opened a new Google search. She typed in 'The Unsolved Mystery of the North Coast's Abductions' and pressed return.

There was nothing relating to the book.

She typed in 'Peter Lynch'.

He wasn't the first on the list. Nor the second. In fact it wasn't until page 6 that she found any reference to him. It was the same link to the BBC Scotland article. She clicked on it. Unsurprisingly it was the same page.

She clicked back and scrolled further. There were a couple of other links to articles Peter had written, but none of them referred to any abductions.

She dithered.

And, for the sake of it, typed in 'North Coast abductions'.

There was plenty of stuff, most of Canada based, but none referring to the enigmatic Peter Lynch and his book.

Nothing.

What the hell?

Heather looked up at the patio doors just as her phone pinged. She glanced at the screen. It was a single line SMS from Fi: *I'm back safe xxx.*

She put the phone down and stared back at her laptop's screen.

She cleared the search.

What now?

Chapter 6

Wolfgang massaged both of his thighs, screwing up his face as he did. It had been a long day and, so far, a long night. He didn't mind the lack of sleep – he was used to it. It was the pain in his legs which got to him. His right was complete, but useless. Early on he and the physio had tried really hard to get him to use it effectively: one leg, two crutches. But there were more falls than was sustainable, one of which had broken his arm. In the end they'd agreed that a wheelchair was the way forward and that, maybe, sometime in the future, they'd have another go.

His left leg was a stump, although his phantom lower leg continuously reminded him that the bottom of his foot itched. He could probably have coped with that distraction, but the pain running down his sciatic nerve and disappearing into the oblivion which was below his knee, was difficult to ignore. So he had some pills. Which he was careful with.

His legs were playing up now, crying out for some relief. Tiredness always brought on the worst.

In terms of treatment, next up would be some form of spinal block. He was doing his best to ward off that opportunity for as long as possible. At the moment, at least, he could lift himself in and out of his chair using one leg as a pivot. When that was gone he might have to call in full-time help.

And that would expose his lair. And he couldn't have that ...

... because he was doing good work. Wolfgang was convinced he was the only intelligence operative in the universe still tracking and dismantling the Church of the White Cross.

He *was* an intelligence operative, wasn't he?

He nodded at that thought.

That had been a full time job, until he realised that Sam Green's recent route, north through Eastern Europe and then stationary for a few days in Bratislava, the gateway to the West, pointed to only one outcome. She was running away – as she often did – and she needed a safe haven.

He knew it wouldn't last. Just as he knew the moment she dropped down into the cellar his cart would not only be horseless, but it would be turned on its side. She would bring with her all manner of hurt and disquiet, which would grow ... and grow. So much so that his refuge, under a neighbour's house in Flemingstraße, would become a target for who knew what.

It was going to be the outcome. He knew it.

Sam Green.

She was sleeping now, on the bed in Matilda's room. Flat out, as if she hadn't a care in the world.

'I've got to get my head down. Wake me at four. I need to phone David back.'

Other than a forced smile, there had been no softness in her request. In fact it was an order. An order which Wolfgang had accepted with good grace. She was the boss. He was her adjutant. It might not have started out that way all those years ago, but it was now. Then they had been partners, dashing across Europe in an Audi Quattro, pursued by men with guns and evil intent. If Sam hadn't been there when they murdered his mother in that warehouse in the Munich suburbs, he would have died –

135

either from a combination of his wounds and the cold, or from a broken heart.

She had saved him, and from that point he had been in her service.

That's why he followed her.

He wasn't a stalker, not in the pervy sense of the word. He followed her so that, when it was necessary, he might intervene.

Surreptitiously where possible.

He had once ... recently. She had been in Albania. Wolfgang had hacked into Tirana's police database. He'd run a programme to search for any enquiries which were looking for the whereabouts of an Israeli woman, Neta Peretz, Sam's latest alias. A ping had come back within half an hour, from an HP desktop in the Albanian *Shqiponjat*, or 'Eagles' quick reaction unit within the *Policia e Shtetit*. He had overridden the information on the computer so that the CCTV which had spotted Sam was now 2 kilometres across from her hostel, rather than on the street corner by the refuge's front door. He'd had another long night, searching the police system for news of her arrest. In the end he only knew he'd been successful when he'd seen her card being used at an ATM the following day.

He kept an eye on her.

And helped when he could.

Now she was safe. With him. In his bed.

Sam Green.

His very own *Lorelei*.

With her, however, came a new challenge. An important challenge. One that threw shade over his petty and, at times, vindictive – he knew it – attack on the members of the Church of the White Cross.

Sam had given him eight names. Eight billionaires, from all over the world. His job was to find out everything about them. After she had spoken with David, and before she had collapsed into his bed, she had given him three priorities: locations; communications; and finances.

He was in his element. This is what he did. He had already used his well-worn coding to target the eight of them. It would take – *how long?* – forty-eight hours? There would need to be some tweaking, but he would sort it. Wolfgang reckoned by then he would have all primary and secondary properties, email addresses and phone numbers, recent movements (his coding looked back one month; he could go further), close family members, and the billionaires' recent accounts, both business and private.

It would be a mountain of information.

And that was where his expertise stopped. The information would be in many languages, most of which he didn't speak. And the sheer scale would overwhelm him. Wolfgang was a technician. He wasn't an analyst. Sure, give him a small business owner in Texas – one man, with links to the Church – and he could disassemble his background. The man's life would be 'virtually' in his hands and there'd a chink somewhere which he could exploit.

But eight international billionaires?

The CIA would have a floor of analysts on such a job.

It was too much for him. And, whilst Sam was a brilliant and indefatigable analyst, he knew it would be too much for the pair of them.

That hadn't stopped him pressing the return key. And it wouldn't prevent him from doing the best he could. Because that is what Sam wanted. And that was good enough for him.

What next?

His eyes darted from the green-on-black cursor which was blinking by the DOS prompt, to the time on the bottom of the screen.

It was 3.58 am.

I'd better wake her.

He twisted the joystick on his chair to turn it away from his screens.

And there she was. Standing behind him.

Ready for action.

She placed a hand on his shoulder and smiled.

'Thanks,' she said.

It was all he needed.

'No problem,' he replied. 'Can I get Lukas to make you some tea? Or do you want me to connect to David now?'

She smiled again.

'Get David, can you? I need to be clear that Jane and Frank made it away in time.'

Wolfgang spun his chair back round and dabbed away at the keyboard. It took a few seconds for the ring tone to echo from his desk speakers.

It rang four times before it was picked up.

'Jennings?' David didn't sound too happy.

'Did the guests leave?' Sam still had a hand on Wolfgang's shoulder. She was leaning slightly forward, looking at his black screen with the green cursor. To their right and left, his two other screens were alive with incoming information on the eight billionaires.

There was a sigh all the way from England.

'Yes, yes. They've left.'

'Good.' Sam turned to Wolfgang. She reached forward and pressed the microphone mute button. 'How secure is this?'

He shook his head.

'Can you make it more secure?'

'Sure,' Wolfgang replied. 'Get him on any Windows laptop in the house, preferably with an Ethernet cable, and I can remotely access his screen and, whilst it's not completely bombproof, the key-encryption I use is the best in the world.'

Their microphone might have been mute, but David's wasn't.

'Thank you for calling.' There was sarcasm in David's voice.

'Don't hang up.' Sam had unmuted the German end of the line. 'Get onto a Windows machine as soon as you can, one with an Ethernet cable ...' she glanced at Wolfgang, 'Does he need any special programme running?'

Wolfgang shook his head.

'We'll be in touch in a couple of minutes,' Sam said.

'But ...' David remonstrated.

'I need to speak about the visitors.' Sam hadn't let him finish his sentence.

There was a pause.

And then another sigh.

'OK.'

The phone went dead.

Therfield, Hertfordshire, UK

It took David five minutes to put his dressing gown on, make his way downstairs to his study and boot up his ageing laptop. It was a standard, non-work Dell. And it was connected to the wall of his house by a yellow cable. He

139

knew enough about stuff to know that's what you called an Ethernet cable.

It took a couple of minutes for the machine to grumble its way into being.

As the small men inside the machine switched on the lights, his wife arrived.

'Fancy a cuppa?' she asked.

He reached for her waist and pulled her close. He knew that what he was doing, however marginal in the fight against the YCA, was putting her life in danger. There was no escaping that fact.

He hugged her tighter still.

'Yes please,' he replied, a small lump growing in his throat.

The machine was almost ready. The last few icons were finding their place.

Then the screen went blank just as his wife gently prised herself away and disappeared to the kitchen.

'David?'

That was really off-putting.

'Yes?' he replied, without conviction.

'I need to know where Frank and Jane are heading. Can you tell me?' The response from Sam was as sharp as if she were in the same room.

'You understand I'm putting my family in danger. And that I gave that up for a game of soldiers a good while ago.' She needed to know.

There was a pause. But not a long one.

'Where are they, David? I, that is, we, need their help.' Sam wasn't taking no for an answer.

'How did you know the Met were coming?' David tried to take back control.

There was a mumble from the other end of the line.

'Wolfgang has a programme which can pick the pings from most mobiles, pretty much anywhere in the world. He can't yet ascribe numbers to them, but he gets a saturation picture. One of the three cars came directly to your house. The other two blocked the south and southeast route out of the village. There wasn't a ping from the north route towards Cambridge. So either the posse didn't have enough cars, or there was a block in place but we couldn't pick up the mobile.'

David had run the events in his head a couple of times. He was convinced Jane and Frank had managed to get out in time. The main squad car had arrived about three minutes after they had left. It had purposely taken him and his wife a further five minutes to make it downstairs. There was a tense 'what the hell are you doing here?' couple of minutes, and the inspector and the sergeant had not accepted an offer of a reconciliation mug of tea. But they had asked to look around.

They had left without comment half an hour later.

'Did either of the block cars move while the main car was with me?' David asked.

His wife had returned with a cuppa. She placed it next to him and then sat down on the only armchair in the study.

'No,' Sam replied.

'Well I reckon they got away then.' He felt good about that.

'Where did they go?' Sam pressed.

David looked across at his wife. She was stern-faced, holding her mug with both hands just short of her lips.

'They're catching a boat out of Tilbury tonight. It's a German freighter, the BBC Seville. It should dock early morning, tomorrow. Rotterdam. I'm assuming they'll get off at that point, rather than stay on the ship until Mumbai.' He couldn't be sure.

'Is there anything else the three of you discussed which might help us here?'

There wasn't. David had spent most of his time chasing his own contacts.

'No. I've been in touch with old pals of mine at Langley and with the DGSI,' he said. He could feel the penetrating stare of his wife burning through the back of his dressing down. 'If I get anything, I'll let you know.'

There was a further mumble from the other end. Then ...

'Wolfgang is putting together a message now. It will tell you how to contact him. If you leave your machine on, there will be a live, secure link, where we can get in touch. It is, according to Wolfgang, as safe as it comes.'

David didn't believe Wolfgang. But he'd started on this journey and there was no turning back.

As he replied, 'OK,' the dark grey screen came alive with a paragraph-sized set of lime-green words. He was receiving his instructions from his latest boss.

And he didn't know how he felt about that.

Dentles Drive, Bradley Stoke, Bristol, UK

Heather woke with a start. She lifted her head from her arm, yawning as she did.

What time is it?

The patio doors told the story. There was a low, deep blue, early morning light above the rooftops, the TV aerial on her neighbour's chimney reflecting an orange glare from the waking sun. She reckoned it was seven-ish.

142

Heather picked up her phone.

Two things.

First, it was 6.55 am.

Second, she'd had another SMS from Fi. It followed the one from late last night saying she was back, to which Heather had not responded. She had been too engrossed in a story which had stopped dead towards the end of Chapter 2 with just a semicolon.

The SMS was a single word: *Mum?*

Heather always responded. She always responded almost immediately, such was her state of mind. Last night she hadn't. And now it was Fi's turn to show some concern.

Heather speed-tapped in a reply: *Sorry. Got caught up in something. Glad you made it home. Love you so much. Mum xxxxx.*

She prodded at the 'Send' icon.

Was that enough?

Possibly. After all, she had other things on her mind.

She stood, stretched and took her half-empty mug to the kitchen. Coffee was needed.

As she found a suitable pod and washed out her mug, she thought through where she'd got to. It wasn't very far.

Peter Lynch might as well have never existed. She had Googled his name and his book's title a number of times. She had scrolled and scrolled. But there was nothing other than the three articles she'd found at the beginning. The first was the BBC Scotland link to his death, by hit and run – *with that photo*. The other two mentioned articles he'd written in the past. One was on the economic arguments for an independent Scotland. The other highlighted the killing of birds of prey on Scotland's grouse moors. She recognised that both were contentious subjects.

143

But that's what journalists did, didn't they? They reported on issues of contention. Otherwise nobody would read their stuff.

She'd tried Facebook next. No sign of him. Then Instagram. Nothing. She wasn't a Twitter user, but tried there anyway. Nope.

Peter Lynch, a reporter whom she knew had published on three things – Scottish independence, the grouse moors, and, critically, abductions 'on the north coast', wherever that was – might as well have not existed.

She had been stuck at that point, her fingers hovering over her keyboard.

But it had only been a brief interlude.

She'd reopened the photo of the man and his book.

And enlarged it.

She dragged the photo around looking for clues. Anything.

Nothing.

No ...

... hang on. There it was.

The publisher's moniker.

It was bottom left on the front cover, almost indistinguishable. Letters followed by a logo. She had squinted at it.

No.

She breathed out deeply.

It was definitely two words, the same length, maybe six letters each. And the logo was, what was it? A tree?

Her fingers were ahead of her thoughts. She had already typed 'publishers' logos' into Google and switched the search to 'images'. Life would have been so much simpler if it had been a puffin or a penguin.

Actually, maybe not?

Again, she was ahead of herself. Would one of the big houses engage with her about the work of a dead author?

Probably not.

She scrolled. Stopping, opening a link, closing it, and then scrolling some more.

She must have been at it for half an hour ...

... and then she found it.

Downy Birch.

The logo was a black circle with a yellow circumference. Inside, etched out of the black, was a yellow-leafed tree atop a white- and black-scarred trunk.

She typed in 'downy birch'.

The images changed. She now had pictures of rows upon rows of trees. It probably wouldn't help, but she clicked on an image which took her to a website: *Trees of Scotland*. There was a short blurb under three pictures. The downy birch was, among others, an indigenous tree of Scotland.

Of course it was.

Heather then reset her search and typed in, 'downy birch publishers'.

Their website link was number one on the list.

She clicked on it.

The website looked modern, complete, and up to date. She clicked on 'Contact Us'. There were all manner of ways to get in touch, including an email address, a telephone number and an actual address: a street in Inverness.

Relief washed over her. She had an opportunity – an opening.

The question was, how should she take this forward?

A few hours ago Heather hadn't wanted to answer that question. It was too much for her very tired brain. Instead, she had pushed her laptop to one side, laid her head on her arms and was asleep within minutes.

The Tassimo had stopped gurgling. She shook her head, trying to find some focus. That didn't work.

Coffee then.

She and her mug retired to the lounge and spread out on the sofa. Heather reached for the remote and put the telly on. It was early morning *Bargain Hunt*. She flicked through the channels. There was nothing.

And then she came to the news, which wasn't really her thing. But neither was *Aussie Gold Hunters*, nor *Hey Duggee*, two of the other choices. So she let the channel wash over her whilst she focused on the steam rising from her mug.

Beyond the smell of freshly brewed caffeine, it seemed that the world was still a mess. The talking head was interviewing some so-called expert about the dangers of remote assistants, such as *Google Home* and *Alexa*. The expert's view was the devices recorded and shared their information with some central computer. Apparently everything we said, even if we didn't think they were listening, was heard. An argument with a spouse here. A discussion over which vacuum cleaner to buy there. The talking head said that there was uncorroborated evidence from a couple in the US. The pair had been talking about which baby buggy to buy. Shortly after the husband had gone online to read an article from a work magazine ... and the first of the ever-changing adverts which interspersed his reading was from a certain brand of buggy.

He'd been working from home and had immediately asked his wife if she had searched on any of their devices for buggies. To which the answer had been 'no'. She'd then gone onto YouTube, and there it was. The first advert. Buy such and such a buggy.

Heather had got halfway down her coffee at that point.

This is madness.

But was it?

She knew that if she previously e-shopped for something, adverts for similar stuff would appear in various threads on her social media accounts. People sort of expected that nowadays, didn't they?

What were they: cookies?

But that was when you're actively online, wasn't it?

She refocused on the TV.

There was a different talking head now.

'... the issue is, Jeremy, if Google or Amazon are listening to your shopping ideas, are they paying attention to your political views? Or your sexual preferences?'

Heather had snorted some coffee through her nose. Her *Google Mini* would struggle if that's what it was hoping to establish.

'And do you think ...' it was a question from the presenter, Jeremy, 'the police or security agencies might be able to use this to find criminals? Maybe even before they commit crimes?'

Heather thought it was a good question.

'I think, and I know the US Senate is looking to pass a restrictive bill here, people are just as worried about rogue states or criminals having access to these devices. A good question is, for example, "Does our prime minister have Alexa?" We know he and members of his cabinet have been pretty liberal with their use of WhatsApp for conducting formal business. So who knows whether they're careful in the kitchen with our secrets? Do you see the problem?'

Heather saw the problem and thought it was all now getting a bit ridiculous. So she pressed the red button on the remote. In any case her brain was churning now and she had much more immediate and personal things to grapple with.

She reached for her phone and opened her emails.

She typed her boss's name in the 'To:' box and titled the email, *'Time Off'*.

Heather was due plenty of leave. Only last week her boss had pressed her to take a break; to book a last-minute holiday somewhere and catch some rays.

As she typed she was already thinking about her next search: this week's weather in Inverness.

McDonald's Drive Thru, Wembley, London, UK

Dominic presented his card to the cashier's machine. There was a low volume *beep* and the young girl at the window in the wall checked the machine for payment. She then passed the Big Mac meal to Dominic's now waiting hands. He carefully placed the paper bag on the passenger's seat and drove off. He couldn't have a large coke toppling over on his immaculately presented Audi.

There!

A free space in the main carpark.

He needed to stop ... soon. And he needed to eat. It had been a longish day, after an awfully long night. Fast food, a shower and then bed. That would be the tonic.

The afternoon had passed without incident. The prime minister, his wife and daughter had left Chequers after lunch.

'Thanks for everything,' the boss had said. There was a slight nod and a wink as he shook Dominic's hands just before he'd got into the armoured Jaguar. The prime minister held Dominic's hand longer than was really necessary. Which was nice. But it was a little disconcerting, wasn't it? After that he and James had cleared the lunch table and, whilst James had sorted out the downstairs, he'd tidied the prime minister's suite. That had taken him an hour – he had been careful, and particular. Because that was what he was like.

When the jobs were done, he and James had shared a quick cup of tea. James had complimented him on how he'd conducted himself over the weekend, and had then passed on a couple of pointers from a list in his notebook.

'Stand a little further away from family members. The rule of thumb is, unless you're directly serving, if their outstretched hand could meet yours, then you're too close.' James had ticked off point one from his pad.

There had been four others, none of which were significant issues, and all of which made sense. It was good to work for someone who gave constructive criticism.

'Anything for me?' James had asked as he folded his notebook away.

Well, last night ...

Dominic had taken a deep breath and blurted out, 'No, nothing. Thanks,' a little too quickly. James had frowned, but only for a second. He then smiled, stood and reached for his coat.

'Back at ten tomorrow, OK? We'll do the silver. And we can talk about how we can get you up to Downing Street for a couple of days so that you can get to know the big man a little better. You'd like that?' James rolled his shoulders so that his double-breasted British Warm woollen coat held closer to his frame.

'Perfect,' Dominic had replied with an honest smile. *Perfect.*

He'd left fifteen minutes after James and, now very tired – and hungry – he'd parked and was reaching across to retrieve his Big Mac, fries and coke. It wasn't going to touch the sides.

But he stopped mid-reach because his phone rang. It was on a cradle to the right of the steering wheel.

Unknown number.

He pressed the red cancel icon and reached again for his meal.

Peep, peep.

He stopped again, blowing out through his nose in mild exasperation.

What does a man have to do?

There was a message on his phone.

He opened it.

Hi Dominic. Please pick up the phone. Jack.

Who the hell was Jack?

Peep, peep.

A second message. This time it was an image. An ID card. He'd only glanced at it when his phone rang again. *Unknown number.* He looked across at the brown paper bag which was doing its best to keep his early supper warm. And then back at the phone.

The ID card had made the space between his shoulder blades turn to ice.

He pressed the green accept icon.

'Hello?' he asked.

'Hi, Dominic. This is Jack Downing. I'd like to meet with you if I could.'

The voice on the phone gave no explanation.

'Who are you? And why?' Dominic asked, unable to hide his frustration … and a touch of fear.

'I work for the British security services. The ID card makes that clear. I think it would be helpful to have a chat.' The voice was unthreatening; kind, almost. Dominic's mind was running down so many avenues whilst the smell of warm relish, soft meat and salted chips filled the Audi's interior.

'I don't … I don't understand?' It was all Dominic could think of.

'That's why we need to meet. We can do it wherever you feel comfortable. Let's say after work tomorrow?' Again, the tone was casual. As if Jack, whoever he was, was asking to meet Dominic to talk about life insurance.

'What if I don't?' A spark of anger set the question in motion.

'You will want to. I'm sure of it. And if we don't meet now, we will inevitably meet later. And, trust me, out of the two options you really want to meet now.' Again, the tone was unthreatening.

Dominic took his eyes off the phone and looked out at the darkening scene of northwest London. A splatter of rain had started to fall on the windscreen. It was going to be a very autumnal evening.

Like last night.

Mum's the word …

The words came back to him.

That's what this was about, wasn't it? An illicit drive in his A2, with Prime Minister Fordingly in the passenger seat.

And a blue Bentley, registration DG555.

The rain was falling harder. He'd need to turn on the windscreen wipers when he set off.

Did he have a choice?

Did he *really* have a choice?

He didn't.

'I'll text where and when we can meet. I need to think about it.' Dominic paused, waiting for a reply.

'Good. I look forward to it.'

And then the phone went dead.

What had he got himself involved with?

Dominic's appetite had deserted him.

Vandelingenplatz, Vlaardingen, Rotterdam Port, The Netherlands

Sam drummed her fingers on the steering wheel of the silver 2011 Mercedes CLK. She'd had a selection of cars to choose from. The garage, where Wolfgang kept some of his late father's collection, was set back in the grounds, remote from the house. It was large enough for five cars; not quite as big as the ten-car garage at the family castle on the Czechia border. There, all those years ago, Wolfgang had selected an Audi Quattro to effect their escape.

This time the list was shorter, but still pretty spectacular.

It hadn't taken her long, though.

She had ignored the burgundy 1922 Rolls Royce Silver Ghost, the yellow Ferrari California, the quirky NSU Ro80, and the Mk1 Golf GTi. Instead she had chosen the least ostentatious and most invisible of the five: a CLK 500. It lacked the bling of the top-of-the-range AMG version, but was quick enough to eat up the autobahn miles. And it would take three people, plus baggage … unlike the California. And, as with so many German cars, the boot was clean of nomenclature, other than the three-pointed star. Only a petrolhead could tell by the twin chrome exhausts and the width of the car's bottom sills that this was the 5-litre, V8. Well, a petrolhead and a woman who read and saw things she could never forget.

The drive had been pretty effortless. She and Wolfgang had checked the BBS Seville's itinerary using *vesselfinder.com*, and established the ship was due to berth in 2e Petroleumhaven, Rotterdam at about 1.20 am. With a flick of his wrist Wolfgang had dispatched GoogleMaps to the orange display board, where Sam had spent time manipulating the images, establishing best routes, and then using Google Street View to get a better idea of what she would be facing when she got there. It seemed that each section of the port was independent, with its own entrance/exit for vehicles … and, she guessed, foot passengers.

Sam had calculated times and distances and immediately appreciated that, with an eight-hour drive ahead of her, she needed to get a move on.

'The garage is set at the back of the grounds. Lukas will take you there. There's a hidden rear gate. Once the garage door is lifted, a subtle row of lights will direct you to the exit. The cars are all fuelled up, and each is fitted with a ham radio, which is in the glove box. Are you familiar with amateur radio?' Wolfgang had asked.

No.

Which was unusual.

'CB radio for wide-girthed men in big trucks who call themselves rubber duck? No, not really,' Sam had

153

replied. The confines of the cellar and the impending road trip was making Sam impatient.

'Really?' There was triumph in Wolfgang's voice.

Sam pricked his balloon.

'VHF/UHF. So I guess between 49 and 870 megahertz. Used by wide-girthed men in big trucks who call themselves rubber duck. That's what I have.' She smiled at him from halfway across the room.

Wolfgang had turned his chair away from his corner station.

'That's all correct. Importantly, though, it's the least intercepted of all voice comms. So it's ideal for keeping conversations like ours away from policemen with big ears.' Wolfgang was using his fingers to push his ears out wider.

Sam had ignored him. She was fishing out one of the mobiles she'd bought in Belgrade. It would be a last resort, but Wolfgang needed the number. Sam reached up for a spare bit of board and, using a special stylus, penned SAM, followed by a 14-digit number.

'You and I know, Wolfgang,' Sam had the stylus's lid between her lips, 'I'll be out of range by the time I get to Ulm. So here's my number.' She'd nodded at the screen. 'I'll put it on every hour for two minutes to send and receive texts, OK?'

Wolfgang was nodding.

'That's fine, Sam, but we shouldn't need that. Provided you have the engine running the radio will push out two kilowatts, that's three times the German allowable limit. And, if you make sure it's on SSB, single-sideband, we should be able to have a conversation. And if not, there's a message facility, via a PDA attachment. We should be OK.'

Sam was impressed. She knew about SSB from her military comms training. SSB used under half of the available bandwidth which helped it cut through background noise for things like Morse code. That was something else she'd taught herself and never used. She didn't mention it to Wolfgang.

'The frequency is set and the car's callsign is on the front of the radio. I'm delta-alpha-two-zulu-zulu-tango. Do you need to ...' Wolfgang stopped mid-sentence as Sam had dispatched a withering look.

No, I don't need to write it down.

'And take this,' Wolfgang said, offering an ID card from across the room.

'What's that?' Sam had taken the five steps to be at his side. She took the credit-card-sized slip of plastic.

'It's a German ID. It's a copy of my niece's. She looks like you.' He raised his shoulders as if expecting a volley from Sam. Nothing came immediately. 'It should be good enough, provided the authorities don't press too hard.'

Sam studied the card. It was similar to a British driving licence, but a lighter pink. The woman's face wasn't a perfect match, but it might do.

She looked at Wolfgang.

'You appreciate that my German isn't great. And aren't you worried about mixing ...' Sam looked back at the card, 'Fräulein Hoxter, up in some potential international conspiracy?'

Wolfgang had snorted.

'Hardly. She's a micro-biologist, working in Polynesia. She'll be safe enough.'

Sam waved the card in front of Wolfgang's face.

'Have you had this for a while ... for me?' she asked.

He nodded, a little sheepishly. 'You know what they say about preparation?'

Indeed.

155

Sam hadn't replied. Instead, she turned and made her way to her daysack which was lying against the far wall, next to Matilda's room.

'Keep in touch,' he added.

With her back to him she threw up a hand in recognition, picked up her daysack and called out for Lukas. As if anticipating her call, the robot skated across the polished concrete floor, stopped at her feet, and blinked.

She sighed.

'Take me to the garages.'

Lukas blinked again, spun around, and headed for the cage Sam had descended in just under a day ago. She was on the road fifteen minutes later in the wondrously comfortable Mercedes.

Making good time Sam had stopped at an *autobahn tankstelle* this side of the Dutch border, filled up with fuel, bought herself a coffee and, with the Styrofoam mug secure in a cup holder on her door, opened up the glove compartment.

I'd better have a go at this.

Radios weren't a problem. You can't go anywhere in the military without using one.

The one in the glove compartment was branded 'Whistler', a company she'd never heard of. Other than that it seemed straightforward enough. Sam turned over the Merc, and then played with some buttons on the radio's front panel. She then took hold of the handset and pressed the pressel.

'Hello, delta-alpha-two-zulu-zulu-tango this is delta-alpha-two-zulu-yankee, over.' The handset crackled with interference.

Nothing.

Then …

156

'Delta-alpha-two-zulu-zulu-tango, copy, over.' Wolfgang's voice was faint, but workable. It was, in its own way, remarkable. She nodded in congratulations to Wolfgang's preparedness.

Well done, Wolfgang.

She pressed the pressel again.

'Delta-alpha-two-zulu-zulu-yankee, I'm an hour short of the location. Out.'

That was enough for now. No electronic communication is secure. None of it. And at two kilowatts, everyone within 150 kilometres on the same frequency would have had their ears burnt.

She put the handset away, switched off the radio and started on the final leg to Rotterdam.

And now here she was ... short of a turning that led to a long, tarmacked road that only went to one place: *Kooye Tankstorage.* She had pulled the Merc off the road and parked it behind an advertising hoarding, mostly out of sight of the main drag. She'd got her binos out.

She knew the port of Rotterdam was enormous. And now she was experiencing it.

Covering 100 square kilometres, after Singapore and Shanghai it was the third largest port in the world. At its centre was a huge petrochemical set-up, but there was still plenty of room for container ships of all sizes. Having checked earlier, what fascinated Sam was its strategic position on the Rhine estuary. The port handled three times as many inland ships than it did seafaring ones. The river Rhine – and hundreds of canals – fed much of this part of Western Europe, and particularly Germany's industrial heartland, the Ruhr. As a result huge barges, built in the shape of massive skateboards, plied up and down the waterways delivering everything from coal to crisps. And as

157

Sam scanned the near horizon, she could see plenty of them now, chugging away to keep this part of the Continent functioning.

It was 00.45 am. The BBC Seville was due to dock in the next hour or so. If she had a smartphone she could have checked the website and confirmed the details, but that wasn't a luxury she had. Instead she would have to use the Mark 1 Eyeball. And some decent binoculars.

As of yet, no sign.

Sam used the binos to establish the entries and exits. From where she was the road ran straight for 300 metres. It led to a kiosk, which serviced a large set of gates. There was a turning circle in front of the gates and, off to one side, a dirt car park – Rotterdam might be a very modern port, but it was tatty around the edges. Beyond the gates an unbroken high fence headed endlessly left and right. The dock area was scattered with pipes, containers and Portacabins. But there were plenty of wide-open spaces of cracked concrete and large puddles. And a massive amount of light. Everything was lit. Which was good … and bad.

Small elements of the dock seemed busy, with the odd container lorry here and a yellow-vested worker there. Other parts appeared desolate.

Sam had to assume that Jane and Frank would walk through the gates in about an hour's time? What was their plan? David hadn't given any indication as to what the pair might do next. Was someone meeting them? Or had the whole thing been so quickly put together that they were to fend for themselves?

She didn't know.

And then none of that mattered.

A blue flashing light caught the low, dark cloud off to her right. It was heading her way.

The Merc was reasonably well hidden, but that didn't stop Sam from starting the car's engine, and then dropping down in her seat.

The police car came straight at her, reached the turning to *Kooye Tankstorage*, and headed down it.

Sam sat up, binos to her eyes.

The police car was an Opel Astra, almost certainly the 1.6 – she could easily outrun it in a drag race. Two occupants, one taller than the other. It reached the turning circle, pulled into the gravel car park, and turned off its lights. The driver got out – a man. He lit a cigarette and stared in the direction of the empty berth, the one Sam had assumed the BBC Seville would be docking at ...

... and there it is.

Wasn't it?

She had caught it in her peripheral vision.

A medium-sized freighter. Blue hull, cream gas domes and a spider-like array of pipes and tubes. It had just started turning into the fairly large dock, maybe 500 metres from the berth.

Sam flipped the binos back to the policeman. He had his head inside the car. He was having a conversation with his oppo, who then got out of the car.

A woman.

The bounty hunters had spotted their prey.

And, unless Sam intervened, it would all be over in under an hour.

Chapter 7

What a palaver. Frank was exhausted. The drop from the deck of the freighter to dockside was, he reckoned, about 20 metres – which didn't sound a lot. But it blooming well was when they had to scale down an almost vertical ladder, afforded only the slightest protection by a steel-mesh tube. The wind, which had made the crossing uncomfortable to say the least, whipped through the gaps in the ladder's cage. He was wearing jeans, a t-shirt, a charity shop jumper and an old khaki, fur-rimmed parka, which he knew had far too many badges. Unless Jane had decided to head south from here, he'd need to get himself some warmer clothes.

He jumped the final two steps onto the dock and was relieved to remove his bitterly cold hands from the icy-steel handrails.

It had been tepid in Hertfordshire; it was positively arctic in Holland.

How does that work?

Distance?

Really?

It was 120 kilometres as the crow flies.

Frank was also glad to reposition his satchel, which was dangling from around his neck. He shouldered it and pressed it against his chest. There was something immensely comforting knowing the things he valued most were that close to his heart. He gripped it tight with his left hand.

Jane was ahead of him. A couple of steps. She was following the route the master had outlined to them. The man had been pretty nonchalant about having two stowaways on board his boat. Frank guessed he didn't really understand the gravity of what he was being asked to do. If he had …

Anyhow, they were safe now. The white hatched path led down the dock between the boat and the large, pipe-laden, cylindrical containers, to an open area. From there it cut to a gatehouse where they'd be asked to show their passage documentation, which had been prepared by the master. They would get their passports stamped and then be on their way. It really was that simple, wasn't it?

He had to hand it to David. It's not what you knew.

Jane and Frank had discussed the 'what shall we do next?' question as they had eaten heartily from the wardroom's excellent kitchen. The stainless steel buffet had all manner of food and drink on hand. Jane had helped herself to steak and chips; Frank, a veggie lasagne. They'd shared a bottle of German red, another revelation. Frank thought the Germans only did white.

By the time they'd reached the route's midpoint – somewhere between Essex and the Continent – a combination of wine, the yawing of the boat and their failure to come to any conclusion, had begun to make him feel very uncomfortable.

'We should head for Central Europe, Sam's last locstat,' Frank had suggested. He'd not been affected by the cold continental blast at that point, so the likely temperature drop which would follow a move east hadn't registered. And Sam was his main effort. There would be no dislodging him.

'I reckon we hole up in Rotterdam. Buy a laptop, find some Wi-Fi with distance between our accommodation and the router, and do some more research. Maybe try and find Sam via her various aliases ... get onto the dark web?' Jane had suggested.

Frank wasn't convinced. But he knew he wasn't the lead here. Jane was much better at the bigger things. He would probably do as he was told.

'Or maybe head south. Somewhere warm,' Jane had added. 'At least that way we can enjoy any downtime. And Spain's extradition laws are among the tightest in Europe. It's an option.'

At which point Frank was no longer in a position to hold a conversation. A trip to the 'heads' was more pressing than a strategic discussion about how two British fugitives might remain undetected and un-extradited, whilst trying to bring down possibly the most comprehensive criminal network the world had ever seen.

That was then, mid-ocean.

He felt a little better now.

But a lot colder.

He needed some more clothes, no matter which direction they intended to travel.

Frank shuffled along a little quicker in order to catch up to Jane. She was striding purposefully, following the *alleen voetgangers* white hatching.

And then he heard it.

Shouting.

Female shouting. In a language which he recognised, but didn't understand.

They turned the corner at the end of the last gas – *or is it petrol?* – tank.

Frank saw the commotion first.

162

Beside the gatehouse.

A man and two women.

One of the women, the shorter of the two, was creating merry hell. There were arms and a poke to the chest, and shouting. Lots of shouting.

In Russian?

The man then pulled a gun ... a pistol!

The policeman *had pulled a gun*.

That was now clear.

Shit!

The world coalesced, like the twisting of an out-of-focus lens. Frank knew exactly what was happening.

He grabbed Jane, who had slowed and was mouthing 'is that Sam?' by the arm. He hoiked her backwards so they were out of line of sight of the gatehouse.

And the policeman with the gun.

And the policewoman.

And Sam Green ...

... who had, and this shouldn't have surprised him, found them, rather than the other way around.

Sam Green.

The woman he loved.

Shut up.

There wasn't time for that.

Jane had a flat palm out waving in the vague direction of the gatehouse.

'Was that Sam?' she whispered.

'Yes. I think so,' Frank replied unnecessarily quietly. The wind, which was snaking through the pipes and around the containers, easily drowned out any noise they might make.

Then in a protective way – which was very un-Frank – he put a hand on Jane's forearm to hold her back as he gently leant forward around the metalwork, so he could get another look at the fracas.

He pulled back sharply.

The policewoman had Sam in some form of arrest hold. The policeman was now looking back in their direction. He still had his gun out but, thankfully, it was no longer pointing at Sam's chest.

He was looking *for them.*

And Sam, bless her, was creating a diversion.

Frank turned, his hand still on Jane's arm.

'There's a male and a female police officer. One of them has a pistol. They've come for us.' He was looking directly at Jane. Her face was wide and disbelieving.

'How ...?'

'I don't know.' Frank tried to slow his voice. Calmness was required. 'But Sam knows we're here. She must have spoken with David. She's creating a diversion. We have to get out a different way.'

Jane was nodding. But Frank sensed she wasn't quite getting it.

Was he surprised?

Loa Chai, her rescue, the danger to her family, death in the tube, the Sarajevo operation, and now all of this. It was enough to unhinge the most stable of characters.

Jane would be fine, though. She always was.

She just needed some time.

So it was his turn now.

Jane was struggling to keep up. It wasn't that Frank was running quickly, it was that he was turning this way and that, through the pipes and containers and small buildings which ran alongside the ship.

He had her hand in his and every time he made a turn he yanked at her arm which pulled at her shoulder. *Ow!* ... then a few seconds of running ... *Oi!* She hoped it would stop soon.

Meanwhile her brain ran away with any number of things.

Sam is here!

Jane had seen her. She was alive.

They had turned again, Jane pivoting around Frank's wrist, then he slowed ...

... thank heavens for that ...

... then he stopped ...

... and Jane pulled up beside him, her flurry of disconnected thoughts hitting a wall.

Frank, whose shoulders were rising and falling with his staccato breaths, had his head around the corner of a wide cream pipe which appeared from the sky, twisted 90 degrees at the floor and ran back towards the ship. As Jane waited for Frank's next move she felt the patter of rain against her cheeks, the buffeting cold wind making easy work of cooling anything it touched.

Sam is here.

With two policemen. And a gate.

And a gun.

What would *she* do?

Find a secluded bit of fence and vault it? That's what Sam would do. Jane looked over Frank's shoulder. The fence in the middle distance didn't look too high. Maybe a couple of metres. It was doable.

Would we lose Sam, though?

Could they find a piece of fence which wasn't covered by CCTV? And, once over, they'd be on foot.

What happens on the other side of the fence?

And what about Sam? Would they leave her behind?

None of her thoughts would rest long enough to be interrogated.

What?

Frank was clicking his fingers in front of her face.

'Jane, Jane!'

She hadn't been listening.

She focused ... as best she could.

'This is what we're going to do.' Frank was all hands and determination. 'The male policeman is through the gate. He's heading down the walkway to the boat.' He was pointing over his right shoulder. 'In a few seconds he'll be between the boat and containers. He's the one with the gun.' Frank was nodding his head as he spoke. Jane's own head was beginning to nod in unison, her mouth slightly ajar. 'They may both have guns. Two guns.' His head shook now. 'Anyway, once he's out of sight we're going to head straight for the gate. Bypass him. OK?'

This doesn't make ...

Jane's brain wasn't examining the outcomes of Frank's plan anywhere near quick enough. Then it didn't matter.

'Let's go.'

He had her hand again.

They were running across cracked concrete slabs, decorated with large, dark, rainbow-filmed puddles. The gate was ten seconds away.

'Sam!' Frank cried out. Jane could see everything clearly now. The policewoman had Sam's arm locked behind her back, Sam's face pushed onto the roof of the police car. In front of that, on the road, was a silver car, possibly a Mercedes.

And there was a new man.

He had come out of the gate house. He was wearing blue official clothing. He looked stocky, and a little confused. She and Frank would be having a conversation with him any moment now. She had no idea how that would turn out ...

... but, all of a sudden, that didn't matter.

Sam's disposition had changed. Markedly.

She was no longer in an arm lock. And the policewoman was prone on the floor, an outstretched arm held taut by Sam, bent in a direction which looked as if it hurt, Sam's foot on her back.

Frank had slowed to a jog just as Sam bent down and retrieved something from the policewoman's belt.

A pistol.

One-all. A draw.

'*Beweg dich nicht,*' Sam shouted at the guard from the kiosk, the pistol aimed chest height across a distance of around 20 metres.

The man shimmied ...

... as Jane and Frank's jog became a walk.

Sam screamed, 'Don't move!' this time in English. And then their own procession slowed and stopped. They were now just a few metres from the guard who was tentatively raising his hands in submission.

The policewoman then moved – she might have been trying to get comfortable – but Sam pushed her arm northwards and she let out a yelp.

'Frank!' An order from Sam. 'Get in the gatehouse. Unlock the gate. Then take anything which looks like comms equipment and rip away the handsets.'

Frank was already moving, both hands now free of his satchel which hung around his neck like a St Bernard carrying a small barrel of cognac. Jane was really curious to know what was in there.

'Jane!' A shout from Sam.

What?

Jane wasn't sure what she was capable of.

'Find the guard's mobile. Approach him from behind, remember? And then tell him to get onto the floor. German should do.' Sam was thrusting the pistol at the guard, as if Jane needed directions.

Maybe she did?

A new sound. A *clunk* from the passenger gate. And then grunting and ripping from inside the gatehouse. Jane was mesmerised by the noises.

'Jane! Do it!' Sam's voice had immediacy and authority.

OK, OK!

Jane took a couple of tentative steps to the big man, got behind him and fished out a mobile which was in a chest pocket of his jacket.

'*Runter*!' Jane's order to the guard was a little louder than a whisper. The man ignored it. She closed her eyes, briefly. Anger welled up inside her. Tears and tiredness. The chilly wind. Her mum. The Chief. The red laser designator on the SO19 rifle she'd spotted at King's Cross. It was a blur of heightened frustration. She was grinding her teeth.

As Frank came back out of the gatehouse, a handset and curly wire in hand, something snapped inside Jane.

She kicked the back of the man's knees at the same time as she pushed hard against his shoulders. The kick was for all the angst, all of the toxic bitterness, which had built up inside her. The push a 'sod you, big man, with your smart uniform, the sweet smell of cologne, and your arrogance to disobey my order'.

The guard's body had no choice.

It was a near perfect arrest move from Jane, taught many years ago during her case officer training. Ordinarily she would have grabbed a hand as the man fell so that she, like Sam, could twist the wrist, pull the thumb towards the forearm and lock out the elbow. From there she could have broken the guard's arm in a second, or forced submission by pushing the thumb towards the man's wrist.

But Sam hadn't asked for that. So Jane had let the man fall to the ground.

It wasn't over, though.

The guard, originally prone, was now raising his chest from the floor.

Idiot.

A disdainful thought.

Jane knew where his kidneys were. She knew where to cause the most pain.

She kicked again – her teeth gritted – with her toe leading.

The man fell to the floor, groaning.

'Good work.' Frank was beside her. 'Come on, Jane.' He had her hand, leading her through the gate, letting it shut with a click behind them.

Jane glanced to her left. Sam was busy with the policewoman. She was handcuffing her to the fence. It seemed effortless. And thorough. She was now moving back to the police car ... diverting to one of the wheels.

'Get in the Merc. Turn it around.' Sam spat out more direction to no one in particular.

Then Jane heard something else.

'*Halte, halte!*' She looked for the voice, which was weakened by the gusting wind.

No!

The policeman had turned the corner by the containers and was running back towards them.

'*Ik zal schieten!*' The man was closer. The voice was louder.

And he was waving his gun.

The world spun. Things were moving much quicker than she could keep pace with. Sam had let the air out of a tyre and was now moving into the body of the police car. Jane didn't know what Sam was doing in there, but it seemed likely that more damage would be done.

And now the Mercedes was moving. Quickly. Frank was driving. It was spinning around, gravel thrown up by its wide tyres.

'Get in!' he shouted through a lowering driver's window.

Then ...

Crack!

Jane instinctively ducked.

Gunfire.

She had been in firefights before, most recently at the organ-harvesting plant in Bosnia. She knew what a bullet sounded like as it flew overhead. And now she found herself caught between following Frank's orders and watching the latest episode of 'Sam Green destroys a small corner of another continent'.

'Get in, Jane!' Frank bellowed again.

Three places to look. Sam, Frank and the policeman.

She chose option three. He had stopped running. He had the pistol at the end of an outstretched arm, his spare hand resting under a locked elbow. He was looking directly down the barrel towards …

… her.

The second *crack!* wasn't as loud as the first because Jane was toppling to the ground, pushed over by Sam who had thrown herself across the tarmac, wrapped an arm around Jane's waist and followed her trajectory to the floor.

That hurt, was all Jane could think of.

And then the silver car accelerated backwards and spun so that it was between the shooter and them. Sam already had the rear passenger door open. She grabbed Jane by the waist, and in a bundle of torsos, arms and legs they squeezed into the back of the Merc.

Crack! Followed by a *tinkle* of shredded glass.

And then the throaty roar of a big engine as the Mercedes spun and accelerated down the road away from the gatehouse.

Crack! Crack!

No additional noises.

Jane tried to lift her head from the back seat cushion, but Sam pushed against her move with a flat hand.

'Stay down!' she barked … then, 'Left at the end!'

More driving. A sharp turn. Acceleration. More orders from Sam. And then Sam clambered between the two front seats. It took a couple of seconds.

…

'Fucking hell, Frank!' Sam's voice was full of fear and angst. 'Pull over!'

'What's happening?' Jane asked, lifting her head. She was too out of it, too scared to want to know the answer.

The Mercedes slowed and drifted right. It bumped up a kerb and came to a halt.

Sam was out of the passenger door in an instant, round to Frank's side, the door springing open. All Jane could see was the back of Frank's head … and now Sam's face and hands, looking at him. Searching.

'Come on. Out. In the back.' Sam's voice was sharp. Frank's movements accompanied by a groan.

'Make a dressing, Jane. Now!' Sam ordered as she directed Frank rearwards.

That anger again. It came to her in a sharp wave. One minute Jane was inert. Next, she was all focused.

Move. As she pulled out a spare blouse from her rucksack, she made room on the backseat for an incoming Frank.

She saw it then.

Blood on his neck. Lots of it.

'It's a heavy graze, Frank. It's nicked a vein which is no longer returning blood from your head to your heart. You'll live.' Sam was squeezing Frank into the back. He looked tired and a little grey. 'But we need to dress it. Lots of pressure, Jane. But you're going to be fine.' Sam had tried to take the blouse from Jane, but she snatched her hand away.

Her and Sam's eyes met. It was a moment.

'Drive, Sam. Get us out of here. Make a plan. I can look after Frank,' Jane said with newfound conviction.

A little surprised, Sam nodded a few times.

Jane then ignored Sam, pulled Frank tight towards her so his head was in her lap, and began the business of stemming the flow of blood from Frank's neck.

Police Scotland, Tulliallan Castle, Kincardine-on-Forth, Scotland

Lieutenant Colonel Lewis Kennedy wasn't so sure about these 8.30 starts. On a good day it was an hour and ten minutes from Edinburgh to Kincardine. He was fine with early doors, even if 'early' currently meant leaving home and getting back in the dark. But the commuting was rubbish. All those years ago he'd joined the army because he wanted a life of adventure, not a nine-to-five. And it was an honest assessment to say that he had achieved that. He'd spent nearly all his time with soldiers. And quite a lot of that on postings and tours where he was either at the sharp end, or was exposing young men and women to the excitement of adventure training. Climbing a peak here, canoeing in difficult waters there.

He snorted gently.

Even he had to recognise that that was some time ago.

It was four years since he'd finished with the regulars. Now he was 'Full Time Reserve Service': FTRS.

Like a soldier.

But not quite.

As the JRLO (*Joint Regional Liaison Officer*) for Scotland, his role was based solely in the UK, and nearly exclusively in Scotland, his home country. He wore a uniform, but not always. And he kept his rank, which he tried very hard not to hide behind – although, at times, it was a useful badge.

The police understood him and what he could bring to the party. The ambulance and fire services, not so much. 5 and 6? The spies couldn't give much of a damn. But, and that's why he loved this particular job, if anyone – *anyone* – wanted aircrew, sailors or soldiers, and the equipment they brought with them, they had to come through him. And they had to have a bloody good reason.

At staff college – *when was it, 1995?* – they'd continuously played down the role the military could and should contribute to the day-to-day running of the country. Sure, the infantry were all over Northern Ireland at that point, but rarely, if ever, were there boots on the ground on the mainland. Nobody, particularly the government, wanted to see camouflage uniforms on the streets. When that happened, the political system had failed. The government had failed.

And, to be honest, his bit – the army – were a pretty blunt weapon. Soldiers carrying rifles on street corners? No thanks.

But that had changed. Slowly to begin with, like in 2001 when the forces organised and supported the operation to stop the spread of foot and mouth.

Then the series of fireman's strikes.

More recently: ambulance drivers, fuel tankers, support to the NHS in other ways, such as mobile testing, builders of car parks ... and, a very new but a growth industry, operational planning in support of all manner of government departments. Oh, and he'd forgotten the madness that was the Salisbury Novichok poisoning. That had created a bow-wave of work which had kept his southwest oppo busy.

Lewis was beginning to think that the forces were the fourth emergency service. Certainly the government had few qualms about directing MACA (*Military Aid to the Civil Authorities*) on a whim. They just signed the cheques.

We'll be delivering takeouts next.

Clearly, there were some specialised military support which you couldn't find anywhere else. UK Special

174

Forces, which included 22 SAS, the SBS and the SRR, delivered an effect that no other force in the UK could, maybe even the world. Special signals support, very clever surveillance aircraft, helicopters and drones, NBC specialists from Porton Down, bloody big submarines, and a pretty useful psyops group were also on tap.

But they had to ask nicely.

And Lewis thought that today might be one of those days.

The meeting, held in the Police Scotland's main secure briefing room, cast as wide a net as was possible. Led by a DCC (*Deputy Chief Constable*) at Gold Command level, the room was brimming. There were at least a score of boys in blue, a couple from the ambulance service and a senior-looking fireman – Lewis, who was sitting close to the back, couldn't pick out the rank. He recognised the reps from 5 and 6, a woman and a man. They were the most casually dressed, standing at the side of the conference room using the wall as a prop. And there were four other civilians who stood out from the crowd. Two had squeezed past Lewis earlier, carrying coffee. Their badges, which included their names, designated them as 'Secretary of State for Scotland' civil servants. Harmless.

The third was a bespectacled bloke from the COP26 team – the people actually running the climate change conference. He was their director of security and resilience. He mostly did as he was told.

The fourth was an outlier, in Lewis's mind. A woman from the Cabinet Office, all the way from London. She wore no badge. She didn't need to because after the first of these conferences all those months ago, when they'd gone round the room asking for introductions, she'd made it clear who she was, and her role. In short, she was the PM's man –

she'd actually said that – in the building. And since then, her job hadn't needed amplification. People just knew.

She was right at the front, sharpening her teeth with a file.

There was something different about today, though. Lewis could sense it. The same lead PowerPoint slide was being beamed to the screen: *COP26 – Security*. And the same lecterns were waiting for their presenters. But the mood was different. The convivial atmosphere, which, *bless them*, Police Scotland had tried very hard to engender, was missing.

There was a sternness. A seriousness about the way the police were holding themselves. There were whispers behind hands, and an exchange of last-minute briefs between junior officers and the big boys. Something was afoot.

He'd find out in a minute …

… he'd find out now.

The DCC had hopped up onto the small stage.

He tapped on the microphone. The noise was amplified by a competent audio-visual system.

The senior policeman leant forward.

'Can we make sure the doors are closed, please.' The DDC pointed to the back of the room.

There was a kerfuffle beside Lewis, followed by a thumbs up.

The DCC pressed a button on the dais. The slide changed.

And then things got interesting.

It took the policeman, with occasional exchanges across to the MI5 rep, half an hour to explain what had changed. JTAC, the London-based Joint Terrorist Analysis Centre, had issued an event-specific alert, raising the threat level from 'substantial' to 'severe'. There was clear intelligence that the event was now being targeted by a terrorist cell based in the UK, but likely with international support.

A 'severe' threat level was defined as 'an attack was highly likely'. There was only one further level, and that was 'critical', just before the shit hit the fan. The MI5 rep said that he expected that level to be reached mid-week.

Apparently the threat came from climate activists, but not your usual 'supergluing yourself to a 737's fuselage' type, or those blocking an A-road roundabout by lying on the zebra crossing. This was in an altogether different league.

The slides were nonspecific, but worrying.

And then the conclusion slide. The three bullets focused Lewis's attention:

- Attack window: D-1, D Day and D+1.
- Attack ambition: discrete targeting of world leader(s).
- Attack methodology: seaborne.

The DCC had little to amplify on the slide, neither had the 5 rep. But, it was clear that everyone was taking this *very* seriously.

'The US Secret Service were due to arrive on Wednesday. Usual score.' The DCC looked as though he needed some time off. But he stuck to his own brief. 'Now, it seems, they're coming mob-handed – this afternoon. I'll be asking a number of you to stay on call for a likely introductory meet with them at 1600.'

Lewis assumed that he would be included in the attendance.

177

The DCC moved along.

He threw up a supplementary slide entitled 'Additional Resources'. There was an ask for more policing support from south of the border. One of the blue jackets at the front had asked for more details on the size of the request. The DCC had given some large, almost certainly arbitrary, number.

And then it was his turn.

'Lewis?' The DCC pointed at him. Lewis raised a hand in response.

'We need, I don't know, a couple of troops of SBS. Maybe the odd frigate?' The DCC was fishing, no pun intended.

'How about an aircraft carrier?' asked the second policeman on the stage. There was humour in his voice, but he'd have been delighted if Lewis had replied, 'yes, of course, I'll talk to the admiral.'

Why do they always do this?

'What effect do you want, sir?' Lewis raised his voice above the crowd.

The police still struggled to get their heads around how the military did their business. Don't ask for troops, ask for an outcome. We'll then sort out the most efficient way of meeting your needs. And that may not include the SBS ... or an aircraft carrier.

'Good question, Lewis.' The DCC looked resigned. 'Let's have a chat straight after, shall we?'

That's more like it.

Universitätsklinik Mannheim, Theodor-Kutzer-Ufer 1-3, Mannheim, Germany

Sam restlessly checked her watch. It was 11.55 am, just twenty minutes later than when she had last looked. She stood, walked the few steps it took to reach the opposite wall of the grey and clinically clean corridor, turned and rested her back against it. Opposite her were three bright yellow polyprop chairs, joined at the hip, with two small speckled-grey tables attached at each end. The hospital was full of them.

Jane was asleep on one chair, her head flopped backwards against her own bit of wall, her mouth slightly ajar. Her backpack was resting on the floor, snuck between her calves, and the table to her left held a half-empty cup of cold vending machine coffee.

The corridor ran on forever in both directions, the grey walls broken every so often by a half-glazed door which opened onto a private room. Frank was just down from them. He'd been gurneyed out of theatre half an hour ago, drips 'n' all. Sam had caught a glance. There were lots of bandages but, thankfully, the surgeon had given a thumbs up.

Which was a relief because in the end it had been touch and go.

Within minutes of the shooting Jane had been pretty insistent that they drive to the nearest hospital.

'He's lost a lot of blood, Sam. I've stopped it as much as I can, but he's losing consciousness.' Jane's tone was sharp and efficient, which Sam hoped meant that the pair of them were in the same hemisphere. 'We should get him to a hospital straight away. If not he might go into shock and we could lose him.'

Sam, who was driving the Merc as furiously as she could without breaking too many speed limits, caught Jane's eye in the rear-view mirror.

179

And then she ignored her.

She'd had her own priorities.

First was to get the hell out of Holland. There might be no borders across much of Europe, and the one between the Netherlands and Germany didn't exist other than on dusty old maps, but there were very clear police jurisdictions.

Second was to steal some number plates, buy some tape and mask up the bullet hole in the rear window.

Third was to phone Wolfgang to see if he knew of any friendly doctors.

She'd managed all three – just. Although getting Frank to a hospital in Mannheim, 200 kilometres south of the border crossing, was accompanied by an ever rising note of panic in Jane's voice.

'How long, Sam? I can't feel a pulse. Hang on ...' Jane was struggling with Frank's limp arm in the back, '... no, I have it. It's very weak. How long?' Jane's voice was something close to controlled shrieking.

Still in the zone, though. Good.

'We're here.' Sam screeched the Merc into the hospital turning area which was clearly marked, *nur Krankenwagen.* She got out of the car in a dash, and scrambled into the back for a bloodied Frank who, as she turned, hung from Sam's arms like a pile of wet bed linen. She barked at Jane, 'Move the car, out of sight. In the centre of town. Then come and find me.'

She was running now. A couple of paramedics looked on wide-eyed.

As the huge double doors of the A&E department sprang open, Sam discovered that Wolfgang had been as good as his word. Which hadn't surprised her.

'Doctor Fischer will meet you at Mannheim's university hospital's A&E. He will look after Frank.' Sam had had one hand on her CB radio handset, the other on the Merc's steering wheel as she blared out their secrets across the airwaves. Needs absolutely must in some cases.

And Fischer was there. He had a name badge to prove it. He had quickly taken control.

That was, how many hours ago?

And here they were.

Frank was fixed, and probably very sore but with a helluva story to tell his grandchildren – should they ever materialise.

Jane was asleep …

… and Sam was frustrated, and dog tired.

She tapped her fingers against the wall, her closed lips contorting as she did. She looked up the corridor one way. And then down the other.

You had to hand it to the Germans, their hospitals were efficient and quiet.

She tapped some more.

What a mess.

Why hadn't she taken a shot at the policeman? He'd been 20 metres away. Sure, the Walther PP99 was an area weapon at that distance, but a double-tap would have found somewhere below the man's crotch, provided the mesh fence hadn't deflected the round.

He'd have lived. And he certainly would have cowered.

But he was just a man.

Doing what he was being paid to do.

He had no idea what influences had caused his boss to issue the instructions to arrest two British fugitives from a German freighter. He was just following orders, during a night shift, before he went home to his family. He didn't need a thigh full of 9 millimetre.

Even if he'd done exactly that to Frank.

Which frustrated her.

And she was frustrated with Jane.

Why had Jane dithered? If she had got in the car when Frank had called, he'd have had no need to put himself between her and the shooter. Sam stared across the corridor at her.

What shall we do with you?

Nothing, just yet.

Sam pushed herself away from the wall and walked down past Frank's door. She didn't look in.

A few metres further, set back in an alcove, was a nurse's station: a desk, a chair, some files, a computer, and a large, stern looking woman who was writing something in an official log.

'I'm using the phone.' Sam picked up the blue receiver from its cradle.

The woman stared at Sam, initially in shock. Then her expression changed. She was now chewing on a wasp.

'Munich. *Alles ist OK*,' Sam said, as she briefly held out a flat hand to deflect the nurse. She then typed in Wolfgang's voice-over-IP number, which pinged the signal via almost every continent.

He picked up straight away.

'How's the boy?' was his first question.

The nurse had stood now. She looked ready to say something, but Sam put her hand up again. She didn't have the energy for an argument in a language she wasn't fluent in.

'He's going to be OK. Your man Fischer was excellent. Thank you.'

'He's an old family friend. He'll keep your lad safe. What's your plan?' Wolfgang's voice was distorted by the contortions of the internet.

'Can you get Frank to your place? When he's fit? He'd be a good ally. And, according to Jane, he has lots of stuff on a laptop.' Sam had a thumb up now. The nurse, who had spat out the wasp, was shaking her head.

'And you and Jane?' asked Wolfgang. Sam thought she picked up concern in his voice, but it might have been something else.

'Which of the eight players have you got the most information on?' Sam answered his question with a question.

There was a beat. Sam assumed Wolfgang was checking something.

'The Greek, why?'

'Good. Because I'm going to track down one of these people and have a chat with them. I can't be doing with sitting around waiting for something to happen.' Sam now held up two fingers to the nurse. She'd be off the phone soon.

There was a longer pause.

'OK. I'll gather what I can here, and sort out Frank. He can help when he's ready. You're taking Jane with you?' Wolfgang asked.

It was Sam's turn to pause.

'Yup. I think so. Two heads and all that. I'll put my phone on as we discussed, but you need to think of a better way of keeping in touch. By the way …' She sighed. She was running out of batteries. And restless was an understatement. But she now had a plan – she wanted to get on with it. '… we've ditched the car. You need to ensure there are no traces that might come back to you.'

'Done that already. There's no link to me now. Instead it's owned by a man from Berlin.'

'A White Cross man?'

'Indeed.'

Did she just tut?

Sam was about to put the phone down, but held on to it for a second.

'Thanks,' she added.

'My pleasure. Keep safe.'

Even through the multitude of connections, Sam could feel the regret. Wolfgang wanted her in the cellar. Her, him ... Matilda and Lukas. A brother looking after his little sister.

She hung up the phone, turned her head to the still very earnest and still disbelieving nurse, and smiled.

'*Danke*,' Sam said, with a nod. She didn't wait for a reply.

Instead she jogged down to the yellow seats, again ignoring Frank's door. Jane was still flat out, a dribble of spittle drying at the corner of her mouth.

Sam stood to one side of her.

Jane Baker.

What is going on in your head?

Could she trust her to stay calm?

No, that's not the question.

If Sam left her, could she trust Jane not to be compromised?

Sam worked best alone. The last thing she needed was a passenger.

But ...

She breathed out heavily through her nose and then, after a long blink, grabbed hold of Jane's closest shoulder and nudged her.

'What? Eh! Who?' Jane's eyes were full of sleep. She shook her head and started to right herself. 'Oh. It's you.' It took a further second for Jane to find a smile. She then glanced in the direction of Frank's door. 'Is he OK?'

'He's fine, Jane.' Sam had taken her hand from her friend's shoulder. 'We have to go.' She tried to sound as sisterly as she could.

'What? And leave Frank?' Jane's reply wasn't accusatory, which was a relief. But it was filled with concern.

'Yes. He's in safe hands.' The last thing Sam wanted was a protracted discussion about this.

'Where are we going? Munich?' The 'Munich' was stifled by a yawn and a stretch.

Good. She's over leaving Frank behind.

'No.' Sam let Jane finish her stretch. 'We're off to see the Parthenon.'

Kinetic

Chapter 8

On a train between Edinburgh and Inverness, Scotland

Heather didn't know whether to soak in the views – a low, oblique sun was throwing elongated shadows across the most desolate of moorlands – or close her eyes and pray.

This was her first time back in Scotland since she'd graduated. How she had made it to the end of her degree without a full-on breakdown remained a mystery to her. A year and a half of purgatory. A desolate, barren time when friends became scarce and all she had to focus on was her work. And her next chance to get away from Aberdeen. Pencil crosses on her calendar which could never come round quick enough.

A wedge of cold formed between her shoulder blades at the thought.

But the views were magnificent. Scotland was a ruggedly beautiful country. That's one of the reasons she'd taken the offer from Aberdeen, rather than a placement down south in Plymouth, where the weather was warmer and the days longer.

It *was* beautiful. And it was still beautiful, the fawns, browns and greens of the mountainsides, forced apart at their feet by the deep blue of slithering and snaking lochs, and further scalpelled by bright, white waterfalls, overflowing with recently fallen rain.

Isn't it?

Or was there foreboding in this remote place?

Wasn't it a country of angry clans, marauding Vikings and hardened crofters? Weren't the men, men, and the sheep frightened? Wasn't this a place of beards and broad shoulders? Of hunting and killing? Weren't the women wee lassies – cooking, cleaning and, on Sundays, segregated to the upper floors of the kirks, leaving the men to their God whilst the womenfolk thanked the Lord for small mercies?

And wasn't it the land where men kidnapped vulnerable women, forced them into the back of a truck, sailed them somewhere indiscriminate and then gang-raped them in a musty cellar ... multiple times?

Could it be worse?

Was it a fair assumption that those particular men had been doing this for a generation? That there were untold and unsolved abductions in the north, most remote area of the kingdom? And that – and Heather struggled with this recurring thought – the one person who had started to uncover those crimes had been mysteriously killed in a hit and run, just as the true nature of those heinous events were about to be disclosed?

That was the only conclusion Heather could come to.

Peter Lynch. The dead journalist. Too close to a story.

It was a strong hunch. No more than that.

A hunch.

The sun had lost all of its intensity, and what power it had left had given way to a light rain which, according to the clouds, might become heavy in an instant. It would be dark in no time. And, as she leant her head against the window, the reverberations of the train played an atonal tune in her head which gave Heather no comfort at all.

Inverness was forty minutes away. Forty minutes out of a ten-hour journey which had started in Bristol, switched at Birmingham, again at Preston, and finally at Edinburgh. And it wasn't cheap. She could have taken a budget flight from Bristol to Inverness and it would have cost her a tenth of the price. And she'd have landed at Inverness Airport in daylight.

But, that would have meant flying over Edinburgh a few days before the start of a major climate conference. And, if nothing else, she was an environmentalist. Her daughter Fi was, Heather hoped, a few years from marriage, and slightly further away from having a child. Heather longed for a grandchild as much as she had ever wanted anything. But that would wait. It would have to wait because, in the meantime, somebody needed to get a grip of the planet … otherwise, what would be left for the generation but one?

Heather thought the current government seemed much more interested in personal gain than making the world a better place for all of their grandchildren. Staying in power was their unwritten manifesto. And that man Fordingly, who she didn't mind saying she couldn't stand, would do anything to keep his job. That made unpopular environmental decisions impossible unless a tsunami of evidence forced his hardened supporters to sit up like meerkats. Insofar as climate change was concerned that meant either their own back gardens were ablaze, or a tidal wave was heading down the Thames.

In Heather's anxious world, the current politics wasn't helping.

But …

… and it was a huge but.

189

She felt better, sitting on this train, heading north to her own Waterloo. She felt more in control. More than she ever had since that fateful weekend. She had purpose – a mission. When Fi had been growing up, there was always a reason to get up in the morning. She had a child to raise. Supper to cook. Clothes to wash. Since Fi had left home, work had filled the gap to an extent, but her anxiety had peaked.

Now, in a flash of internet research in the dead of the night, she had found a way ahead. It might be temporary, and it might come to nothing. But it had taken her mind off all the hurt, and banished her fretfulness to the back room. She had done something.

I am doing something.

She had booked an appointment with one of the literary agents from Downy Birch in Inverness. The meeting was at 9.15 tomorrow morning.

'I'd like to talk to you about Peter Lynch. Face to face, please,' she'd asked. Heather was already on the way to Inverness at that point. There was no getting off now.

A long silence followed.

'I'm afraid …' the agent, a woman, was struggling to find her words, 'We can't. No. It's not possible. Sorry.'

Heather's temper had flared.

'I'm one of Peter's unsolved north coast abductions.'

She let the comment hang.

There was more silence from Inverness.

'When can you get here?' The woman's voice had changed. Now it was quiet, furtive almost.

They'd agreed to meet tomorrow morning, but not on the premises. The woman had chosen a Costa Coffee in the town.

So Heather had a purpose. And that purpose enabled her to stare out into the gloom of the Scottish Highlands without flinching. Looking over a land of men.

A land of secrets.

A land of conspiracy.

A land of hurt.

Her phone buzzed. It broke through her gritty determination.

It was an SMS from Fi: *Hi Mum. Hope u r OK,* followed by a red heart emoji.

Heather swiped open her phone and typed: *Fine, love. You'll be pleased to know I'm getting a fucking life.*

She stared at the phone. She almost pressed send. Almost. Then she quickly deleted the 'getting a fucking life', and replaced it with: *taking a break. Off to Scotland to revisit old haunts. I love you so much. Give me a call when you can. Mum xxxx.*

She pressed send.

And then she put her phone down and stared back out of the window.

Men.

She hated some of them. Actually, at the moment, in this dank but beautiful country, she hated all of them.

Physical Energy Statue, Hyde Park, London

Dominic was sitting on a metal and wood bench. He had a takeaway coffee in one hand and a sandwich in the other. Across from him was a naked bronze man on a rearing horse, his hand shielding his eyes from the sun. He was definitely looking in Dominic's direction.

Dominic had chosen this place because Hyde Park was where his teenage self would come on the weekends when the weather was nice. The park had a specific grandeur; it was comfortable in its own nostalgia and reverence. The horses trotting along Rotten Row. The statues and follies. The rowers on the Serpentine. It was familiar. And it was resolutely middle-class, something in his teens he aspired to be.

And he had made it.

He dressed impeccably. Today he wore brown woollen trousers, a cream cotton shirt with a cut back collar, brown brogues, a red lambswool V-neck jumper, and an A&F trench coat in pale grey. This was, of course, after-work attire. His black and white garb was still at Chequers. He hadn't been there today. James had texted him last night to say that they were expecting him at No 10 at 11.00 am. He was due for a very quick and casual look over the prime minister's London workplace and then, as the main man was away for the day, a chance to familiarise himself with the flat above No 11 where the prime minister had decided to take up residence.

There was no staff accommodation in Downing Street; everyone went home after work. But the prime minister did expect his team to be on call throughout the day, including his primary valet. Dominic, therefore, needed to acquaint himself with the layout for when the man took leave. Today had provided that opportunity.

It had been a whirl. The primary valet, a chap named Geoffrey, was nowhere near as kind or accommodating as James. But, with lashings of deference, Dominic had made it work. By three in the afternoon things had run their natural course and it had been time to leave. Dominic, who had known he would be out of the building by

4 pm whatever the case, had SMSd the man with the ID Jack Downing, and agreed to meet him here … about now.

That arrangement had been made at lunchtime: 4.30 pm, just as it started to get dark.

Which it was.

He was due to meet the man with the ID card in the dark.

Was that an issue? There were plenty of ornate streetlights and, thankfully, no small number of people walking, running and cycling past the bench.

Should he be worried?

He didn't know.

It was all virgin territory.

And it was all highly unsatisfactory.

And … it was getting cold now.

He could leave, couldn't he? He should leave. He was under no obligation to meet the man.

But Dominic, if nothing else, was a man with integrity. He was honest and he would do as he was asked.

However.

Let's get on with this.

He took the final swig of his coffee, reached across to the bin by the bench, and stuffed his cardboard mug and sandwich tray through the slot …

… and took a metaphorical step back.

There was a man by the bin.

It was Jack Downing.

OK, it was dark and the light only threw relief on half of his face, but Dominic recognised him from his ID.

It was him.

He was dressed casually: jeans, sneakers and a branded hiking coat. And he was wearing a beanie, with a peak. The colours of his clothes were washed with darkness, so Dominic wouldn't have been able to give a decent police Photofit. But, he knew clothes. So he thought he had the measure of the man, who smiled and thrust out his hand.

'Jack,' he said with confidence. 'Jack Downing.'

Dominic didn't know whether to get to his feet, to remain seated, or dance a merry dance. He was at a loss. And was now more uncomfortable than he hoped he might be.

He stayed sitting, and replied, 'Hi. You already know who I am.'

'Indeed.' The man hadn't moved. 'Shall we walk? I think it would be good to walk.' He offered a hand by way of direction.

Dominic was still unsure. He stood hesitantly, brushed down the seat of his coat, and followed the man's offer to walk down the path towards the Royal Albert Hall, one of Dominic's most favourite of places.

For the first few paces the man with the ID card didn't say anything. He just walked slowly with Dominic at his side.

And then the ice was broken.

'We'd like you to work with us,' the man said.

That was it. He didn't add anything by way of explanation.

Dominic didn't reply. What could he say?

After a few more paces the man continued.

'I know this may seem highly unusual. A little frightening, perhaps. But we have a job to do and we think that people like you are willing to support us.' Jack Downing's accent was 'posh'. He came across as well-educated, even if his dress sense belied the notion.

Dominic decided not to respond. Not yet. So far there had been no mention of the Bentley and the DG number plate. Maybe that would come in time?

So they walked a further ten or fifteen paces in silence. A local running group came towards them in a splodge of cantering legs and pumping arms. They split either side of the two men, leaving behind the smell of hot bodies and spent breath.

'We will pay. We know your background and there is nothing there to coerce you with ...' the man let that hang, '... so we can come to some form of financial arrangement. We pay you. You help us keep the country safe. It's that simple.'

Jack Downing had ushered them off to the left down a lesser used track. The Albert Hall's glorious dome was no longer a feature at the end of a new tunnel of trees.

Dominic stopped, which caught the man off guard. It took Jack Downing a second to pivot and face him.

No hint of an illicit meeting with a dark blue Bentley.

Did they approach all senior politicians' personal staff? Or just this prime minister's?

It then occurred to Dominic that he was sort of enjoying this. Not much. And not in a 'centre of attention' way. Nor was he attracted by the money – he was doing OK financially, thank you very much.

But it was about the power.

Wasn't it?

He, Dominic Bianci, the son of an Italian immigrant from an estate in Sidcup, was being courted by two huge offices of state: the prime minister's and the security services. Both were admirable institutions. Both undertook roles of huge importance.

And Dominic was in the middle.

Or, did he need to choose sides? And if so, when did he need to make that decision?

It was the power, wasn't it? The influence.

It was in his hands.

'How can I help?' Dominic asked the man with the ID card.

Flemingstraße, Munich, Germany

Wolfgang was tired. The pain, which started at kidney level, worked its way down his leg and didn't stop. It niggled most of the time. But it was worse now. Worse than any tablets he could take.

That was because he was standing up, one flat hand on the briefing board, the other on the side of his wheelchair. It was the first time he'd stood for as long as he could remember.

Sam Green had done that. If you knew of her own background, of what she'd suffered – and he didn't know the half of it – that history, her history, inspired you to do better.

She had kept him alive once, for almost forty-eight hours, locked in a freezing shipping container on the outskirts of Munich. She had wrapped him up, checked on him, chatted to him. She had been suffering herself. But she looked after him anyway.

She was indefatigable. Unstoppable. Like a clockwork machine with a tightly but constantly wound spring.

She inspired you to do better.

Sam hadn't said anything. She hadn't needed to say ... 'I think you should get out of your chair more, you hopeless individual'. It was an unwritten script. It was in her expression; her mood. He knew she didn't pity him. But the point was, she didn't want Wolfgang to pity himself.

So, having transferred his latest data dump onto the info board, he was determined to spend at least an hour on his feet. To get the blood circulating. Work the muscles. He didn't have to walk anywhere. He just had to stand.

It can't be that difficult, can it?

Maybe.

He was thirty-five minutes in. Twenty-five to go.

He sighed, a deep sigh, his head drooping forward so it rested on the board.

He scrunched his eyes together, took a deep breath and righted himself.

What did he have?

He blinked.

Quite a lot, as it happened.

He had primary and secondary residences on all of the eight members of the YCA. One of the first things Sam had done was to scribble the list on the briefing board with a stylus. She had done it quickly and without reference to any notes. He was looking at that bulleted list now:

- *Duke of Nairnshire, Edward Grinstead; UK; landowner and founder; net worth – £43bn*
- *Michael Connock; AU; media baron – £76bn*
- *Elias Bosshart; CH; bank, art and watches – £45bn*

197

- *Jimmy Johnson Jr; US; oil, minerals and metal – £81bn*
- *Edouard Freemantle; SA; unknown – c£50bn*
- *Marc Belmonte; FR; wine – £32bn*
- *Sheik Rashid bin Nahzan; UAE; oil – £94bn*
- *Theodor Konstantos; shipping; GR – £21bn*
- *Chibuike Grandom; oil and minerals; NG – £34bn*

He had a pretty full list of companies, of which there were 143 associated with the nine men, 112 of which were registered in overseas tax havens, such as the Cayman Islands. His machines were currently pinging all 143 for back doors. He had nine sets of company accounts and countless *Financial Times, WSJ* and *Bloomberg*'s articles on the men's businesses.

He had sixty-one telephone numbers, four of them private.

And he had started the family trees, and was checking on the dependants of the nine.

There were also countless non-business newspaper articles which someone would need to trawl through. Probably not him.

Probably Frank.

According to Doctor Fischer, who had been as good as his word and treated Frank without documentation, Frank could be discharged tomorrow afternoon. All he would need then was rest and some antibiotics.

Rest.

They couldn't afford that. Frank needed to have his best analyst's head on as soon as he could put his boots on.

There was *so* much information, Wolfgang was swimming in it.

The question was, how did you get Frank to Munich without compromising the cellar? He had thought of sending him to the *Schloß,* and working with him remotely. Wolfgang paid for personal fibre which provided a direct and unbroken link between Munich and his family's forest estate. Wolfgang could mirror the work on the screen.

But that wasn't like having him in the same room.

Old pals and all that.

They'd been together in the cellar next door when an RPG had torn through the house. They'd been side by side when they'd crawled up the stairs and along the corridor, their mouths covered with damp cloths. And Frank had been at the front of the house when Wolfgang had emerged from the inferno, carrying Inge's limp and charred body.

Frank had taken her body in his arms.

Wolfgang had fallen to the floor.

The rest was still a blur.

Frank was his *Brüder*.

And Frank needed to be here.

Wolfgang had a plan. It involved friends of friends, and Tomas, the *Schloß*'s butler and life-long pal. It was the 'get Frank to the cellar' equivalent of routing information around the dark web. The more links the better.

He had passed the problem to Tomas. It would be fine.

That left Sam and Jane.

He'd told Sam to go for the Greek shipping magnate, because not only did Wolfgang have the most information on him, he knew where he was. He was at home. In Athens.

He knew that for two reasons.

First, the man was subject to a tax-evasion court case which was currently underway in the city. Second, Wolfgang had already hacked the video-alarm system on the man's Alimos home. It had been easy.

Had it been too easy?

Possibly.

Wolfgang would need to highlight that to Sam when they next spoke. In the meantime he had to assume it was a reflection of the Greek's relaxed approach to internet security. And with it, Wolfgang had a fireside view.

And it wasn't a pretty one.

Theodor Konstantos lived in a beautiful 12-million euro house, with its own coastline and a large jetty, big enough for an Austin Parker, 42-foot superyacht tender. It had seven bedroom suites, four living rooms, a professional kitchen, a massive wine cellar, an indoor pool, and an outdoor infinity pool in over three acres of grounds. It was one of the most expensive properties in Athens.

Wolfgang knew all this because Theodor Konstantos fascinated him. He had become his focus. That had led to the most recent real estate deal for the property, which included the building's floorplan.

Luxury was clearly on tap. But, flicking through the cameras Wolfgang had at his disposal, you wouldn't necessarily have thought so. The place needed tending to. There was fast food packaging discarded all over the cinema room. The kitchen was piled high with dishes. He'd counted twenty-three empty bottles of alcohol, mostly wine but some beer, strewn about in five rooms, including the bathroom. And there were two, out of a likely six, unused lines of cocaine on a side table in the main living room. Wolfgang couldn't be sure of the denomination, but he was fairly sure that next to it was a rolled up 100 euro note.

It was worse than that.

Theodor Konstantos liked his men. He liked his men in most of the rooms, and in the pornography which seemed to be on a loop in the cinema. Wolfgang had counted four young men in the house. One of them looked no more than an adolescent – but Wolfgang gave the Greek the benefit of the doubt.

It was sex, drugs and don't bother with the dishes at Theodor Konstantos's place. He had to assume a cleaner would be in later to tidy up. He hoped so. His German fastidiousness made watching the Greek's mansion a very twitchy experience.

The good news was, the choice for Sam to get a closer look at the Greek looked more and more inspired. If the man were this careless with his security, was subject to a government court case, and had a penchant for boys, it was just possible that Sam might be able to find some cracks.

What was her catchphrase?

Lift some rocks and see what's under them.

Wolfgang had already lifted a couple of rocks. And he hadn't liked what he had found.

Doubtless Sam would find plenty more.

He rolled his shoulders from left to right. Then he pushed his head back and counted to five. He arched his back, lifting his chin to the ceiling.

Eins, zwei, drei, vier, fünf ...

And back again.

He breathed out through his mouth ... all the way out. And back in through his nose.

He checked the timer which he'd set up on the board. It read 22.35. It was still counting down.

That hadn't helped.

He flicked and prodded at the screen. A map of Central Europe hovered and then steadied in front of him. On it were highlighted two routes from Mannheim, Germany, to Athens by car. The shorter took the driver through Austria, Slovenia, Croatia, Serbia, North Macedonia, and then Greece. Just over 2,000 kilometres. Twenty hours if you drove at the speed limit without stopping. The longer kept you in the EU: Austria, Hungary, Romania, Bulgaria and then Greece, but it added 600 kilometres to the journey. Romania and Bulgaria weren't in the Schengen Area and Sam and Jane would need to show passports. But the borders were much more relaxed between EU countries.

Currently, using the computer's best guess of the quickest route, a car-icon was flashing on the Austrian/Slovenian border.

Wolfgang touched the northern, EU only route. The icon joined the route; Graz, southeast Austria, about 120 kilometres short of the Hungarian border.

Whichever they had chosen, they should be in Athens mid-to-late-afternoon tomorrow.

He didn't know which route, because of a lack of secure comms.

Sam had bought six burner phones in Mannheim. And had then purchased, in the quickest forecourt deal in German history, a twenty-one-year-old 1.6 Golf. For cash. She'd messaged him just before they'd set off. Wolfgang had replied, pinging through a data dump. With that she now had access to a highly secure drop box where they could chat and exchange info. But it wasn't instantaneous. Not unless they broke protocol and literally called each other.

They might cross non-EU borders, which would throw up an alert.

And they had to buy fuel. And use an ATM.

It wouldn't take long for a determined intelligence organisation to track them down.

Sam had plenty of aliases, including his cousin's ID, which would throw some smoke. But he guessed Jane had none. And there was an international arrest warrant out for her.

That was his next job then.

Where in Athens could you buy new identities?

He was rapping his fingers against the board as he checked the timer: 18.51.

Scheisse!

He pulled his wheelchair towards him, twisted his body round and sat down. The relief was instant.

Sorry, Sam.

But he had more pressing things than a new exercise regime.

A4 Autobahn, Austrian/Hungarian Border

'Sam! Sam!'

Jane's bark immediately broke into Sam's unconscious. Her eyes opened and she blinked, her pupils already wide and accepting.

They were still moving and, by the look of things, were coming to the Hungarian border. Sam, who had driven from Mannheim to Salzburg before they'd switched drivers, had told Jane to wake her at the first sign of trouble, and at international borders. Hungary was the first border since they'd crossed into Austria at Salzburg.

They'd agreed that they would drive the long road to Greece, keeping within the EU. That route would take them

203

through the non-Schengen borders into Romania and Bulgaria, and that might be problematic. But Sam had argued that Serbia and North Macedonia were more complex, waiting times would be longer, and …

… she didn't actually know. She only had a feeling, especially as the counter argument was the police from EU states would be more 'together'. Driving through Serbia and North Macedonia would possibly be more incognito.

It was a balance. And who knew whether she'd made the right choice? They might find out soon enough.

The old TomTom satnav which she'd managed to blag from the German on the garage forecourt, gave an 'arrival time' of 16.53. Between now and then they had five borders to cross. This one should be a breeze.

'Did you sleep well?' Jane asked.

Sam was busy checking out the oncoming international frontier, which in the past might have been much better protected than it was now. In 400 metres they'd be crossing the old Iron Curtain, a 7,000 kilometre long, impregnable barrier which used to run from the Arctic Ocean to the Black Sea. Before 1991 they'd have been watchtowers, guns, mines, lots of wire, patrols and the odd tank. Crossing between Austria and Hungary would have been nigh-on impossible without special visas, rigorous checks and a political mentor for your onward journey.

And … *right now* … they had just driven across it without applying the brakes. All she saw were signs of a typical border crossing: car parks, shops, fuel stations and a poorly lit customs hut. No barriers. No guards. And no guns.

But there was a police car.
Just there. Off to the left.
Unoccupied.

That was some relief.

If you hadn't lived through it, it was easy to ignore what life must have been like during the Cold War. It was pretty straightforward for those in the West, unless you wished to travel across the Iron Curtain. But it was terrible for most normal people in the East, certainly in terms of freedom. Communism and collectivism might have provided folk with a job, but wages were low, shelves were empty, and travel was non-existent ... whilst the elite still held all of the privileges.

The fact that some of these old Eastern European countries were now reining some freedoms back, such as a politically regulated press and government controlled judiciary, when everyone had worked so hard for so long to break the mould, really frustrated Sam.

But life never stood still, did it? And history was always set to repeat itself ... wasn't it?

And other clichés.

She hadn't replied to Jane. Sam knew that. She was alert. Focused. Her eyes darted left, right, forward, then to the passenger-side mirror, checking behind. It was dark and, therefore, difficult to spot a tail. But she had an eye for headlights. It was what she did.

Whilst her brain ignored Jane's question her right arm was thrust deep inside her daysack. Her hand was on the pistol grip of the policeman's Mauser, her thumb idly playing with the safety catch.

Click, click ... click, click.

She couldn't hear the noise above the Golf's engine, but she could feel it. The momentary rise and fall of the lever as it slid out of one hold and into another, back and forth, was organically satisfying. And it helped relax her.

So she continued the movement.

Click, click, click, click.

As she searched. And checked.

Nothing.

All was clear.

Which was comforting, along with the 9mm pistol in the palm of her hand.

They were five minutes past the border now. Jane had not followed up her question with a supplementary. She knew the score.

'Fine, thanks,' Sam eventually said. 'We should pull over. I need to speak with Wolfgang, and we can swop drivers.' Sam had taken her hand off the pistol and had turned her shoulder. She was reaching for the mobile she'd unwrapped in Mannheim and had used to contact Wolfgang. She'd use it once more and bin it.

'There.' Sam pointed. There was parking off to one side. Jane indicated, pulled into a carpark which had a loo block, and parked up.

'Not here,' Sam ordered. 'There.' She was pointing to a corner of the tarmac which was less exposed. Jane manoeuvred the car whilst Sam worked the small screen on the cheap phone. It was taking some time.

'I'm popping to the loo,' Jane said. If she were exasperated with Sam's brusqueness, she didn't show it.

Sam barely nodded in return. She had Wolfgang's illicit website with the drop box open. The address was a link on the dark web. It had the usual *http* lead but – and this is when Sam had zoned out as Wolfgang had explained it to her – there was an extra layer of software which gave access to a completely separate network. Wolfgang applied some sort of electronic proxy thing which meant she was able to access a one-to-one, Sam-to-Wolfgang chat room, which was as secure as you could get.

Apparently.

She checked the time.

It was 2.57 am.

He might not be awake.

She typed in the chat box: *Hi Wolfgang. X into Hungary.*

She pressed return.

There was a minute when nothing happened. Sam got bored and searched the car park for possible rogue vehicles. There were six articulated lorries, two vans and five cars. It seemed everyone was getting their head down. Apart from Jane, who was jogging back to the Golf. She was breathing steam.

It must be cold out there.

Sam checked the temperature on the Golf's ancient computer: 2 degrees. It was only going to get colder.

Jane got in the car just as the mobile's screen blinked a reply.

Hi, Sam. Glad you're OK. Link below to a summary of what I've uncovered so far ref our man. Of note, I have hacked his video surv system and have eyes on internals.

'What's he say?' Jane asked.

Sam ignored her. She would engage with Jane at some point. She would have to. But just now she wanted to get off this system as soon as possible.

She typed: *Thanks. Should be at loc at the end of the day. Will think of a plan, but if you have any ideas? We need an 'in' and a cover. That shld be pri one 4 u.*

Her thumbs hovered over the keyboard.

She typed some more: *main effort though is linking nine together. What drives them? What's their purpose? Get Frank on that.* She typed another instruction, deleted it and then added: *How is he?*

She then pressed send.

Jane's head was in Sam's personal space, looking at the tiny screen. Sam closed her eyes, and then opened them. She turned the phone so Jane could see the screen. It was the least she could do. Just now it was also the most.

Wolfgang's reply came through: *He should be here by evening. Tomas, do you remember him? He's bringing him. Like old times.*

Of course Sam remembered him. Wolfgang had been shot, a flesh wound, and Tomas had almost killed the man who had done the damage.

He also made exceptionally good boiled eggs.

She replied: *sure. I'll get Jane to look at the docs now. I'm driving. Will chat in daylight. Anything else?*

Sam again pushed the screen closer to Jane. As she did she looked at her friend studying the message thread, the screen's small LED square reflecting in Jane's pupils.

Sam recognised intensity. A sharpness.

Sure, there had been dithering at the port which had given Frank the fright of his life. And then the bouts of sleepiness, such as the nap at the hospital and then a good three hours on the Bavarian motorways. But, in terms of focus, Sam thought Jane might be back in the zone.

Could she guarantee to stay that way?

Sam didn't know. And that meant she couldn't trust Jane with anything other than the most straightforward of tasks. Something which was sequential. One thing happened. Then another. And another one after that. No deviation. No change to H-hour.

It was a bother. But hopefully things would improve over time.

There was a new message from Wolfgang: *I'm onto someone at the location who can offer new identities. I'm going for 2 x English?*

Sam made sure Jane had seen the message.

'English, Jane. Yes? Your language skills are good, especially German?' Sam asked.

Jane looked at Sam. Their faces were no more than 30 centimetres apart.

She nodded, with half a smile.

Sam typed: *good plan. Gotta go.* She moved the cursor to the web link at the bottom of the chat and opened it. There were about two pages of A4's worth of information which turned into what felt like a thousand scrolls of the screen. Sam didn't have the head for it at the moment. She wanted to get on. So she handed the phone to Jane.

'This is what Wolfgang has from his research.' Sam pointed at the screen. 'Download it, turn off the internet and then read it. And get us a summary. Wolfgang has eyes on Konstantos's villa. So let's get there ASAP, and then we'll see if we can get an in. Happy?' Sam had gripped the door handle. It was time to change seats.

Jane was studying the phone.

'Come on,' Sam encouraged.

Jane looked up – she was sucking on her bottom lip. Then she nodded, and reached for the door.

They almost bumped into each other in front of the bonnet of the car, and they did a silly dance as they both moved the same way to make room for each other. When Sam had found space, Jane caught her by the elbow.

Sam stopped and turned.

'What?' Sam asked. She knew there was too much impatience in her voice. Athens wasn't built in a day. It would still be waiting for them tomorrow.

'You don't trust me at the moment, Sam, do you?' Jane's tone was matter-of-fact, but kind.

Sam opened her mouth to say something and then closed it again.

It was cold. Her fingers were already itching. Hopefully southern Greece would be a lot warmer. They could certainly do without having to think about the weather.

Jane still had her hand on Sam's elbow.

'No.' Sam looked down and kicked at a piece of dirt. She then met Jane's gaze. 'I don't. You've been indecisive and sleepy. There is no latitude for either at the moment. Not at the pointy end.' Sam checked Jane's face for recognition. Was she accepting Sam's criticism? It was hard to say.

Sam tried a more passive approach. 'If you want to break clean, that's fine. We can get you a new identity in Athens and you can lay low for a while.' She tilted her head on one side.

There was a moment.

One of the HGV's engine's started, its lights illuminating a set of scraggy trees in the middle distance.

A couple of vehicles sped past on the motorway behind them.

'The Chief handed the baton to me.' Jane's voice was quiet but determined. 'I accepted it. I know I'm not fully fit, Sam. I wasn't in Sarajevo. You knew that.' She paused. It was her turn to look beyond Sam to some distant object. Her gaze returned. 'But I'm getting there. And … I need to do this.' She was squeezing Sam's elbow a little harder. 'After Lao Chai, things have been complicated. I let some people down.' She was looking directly into Sam's eyes. 'So, this is my time now. Help me make it so. Please.'

Jane had not let anyone down. Jane had survived the most horrendous of ordeals in a way which would have broken anyone. The fact that she wasn't in a padded room wearing a turtle suit was testament to huge reserves of inner strength. Sam admired her. She always had.

It would have been a natural thing for Sam to explain that to Jane. To pour it all out. To make the woman feel better. To offer encouragement and support. Empathy, even.

But that wasn't one of Sam's programmes. So instead she replied, 'Sure.' And nodded curtly.

It was the best she could do.

Chapter 9

Costa, Eastgate Shopping Centre, Inverness, Scotland

Heather nursed her Americano in both hands. It was cold in Inverness and the ten-minute walk from the Mercure to the Eastgate Shopping Centre had been necessarily brisk. She'd brought a decent coat, hat and gloves with her, but maybe her blood hadn't thickened enough yet? She'd need to think about it if she were to stay longer. Currently she was out of the hotel tomorrow, with no additional plans, other than back to work next Monday. Anything beyond that depended on what the woman from Downy Birch had to say.

And this was her?

A middle-aged woman wearing slacks, rugged shoes, a heavy outdoor coat and a scarf had just walked into the café. Heather had found a table by the window which looked out onto the newish, but very unbusy shopping centre. There was room for a second person at her table, but no one else.

She waited for the woman, who Heather remembered was called Louise, to look in her direction ... which she had just done. Heather raised a hand in response. The woman grimaced a smile and headed for the counter.

Costa, the UK's ubiquitous and very standard coffee shop, had more people in it than were walking the shopping centre's clean, cream-coloured thoroughfare. And the café still had plenty of room. As a result Louise spent no more than a couple of minutes at the counter before approached Heather's table. She placed a small espresso in front of her chair, grimaced another smile, and sat down without taking off her coat.

'I don't have long, I'm afraid,' Louise said, opening a sachet of sweetener.

Heather took a swig of her coffee and placed the heavy white cup onto its saucer.

'Louise?' she asked, waiting for a response.

'Yes,' the woman nodded. She was now stirring in the sweetener with such vigour some of the coffee had escaped.

'What happened to Peter Lynch's book?' Heather asked. If the woman didn't have much time, Heather thought she'd better get on with it.

Louise scratched her neck just below her hairline. She then looked directly back at Heather, taking a deep breath in through her nose.

'I think you need to appreciate that we may be talking about something quite sensitive. A book which some ...' she paused, finding the right word, '... *dangerous* people didn't want published.' Louis had finished scratching. She now had her hands clasped in front of her.

Heather was nodding, short, sharp nods.

'Tell me more. Please.'

It all came out. Louise, at first tentative, possibly frightened, started at a jog and, by the end was sprinting.

'Downy Birch were fascinated by Peter Lynch's story. I was fascinated by it. We initially gave him a small advance and, six months and two edits later, we were ready to publish. We got Peter in to do some publicity photos and arranged publication – an initial print run of 5,000 books, which was a fair number for a small company. And we'd pulled together a marketing plan. That included a number of guest slots on local radio. There was also a blog book tour, and a Saturday signing in Inverness's Waterstones. It was going to be quite a big deal.' Louise still hadn't touched her coffee.

She continued. 'And then Peter got an offer from another publisher. He didn't tell us how much, but we all sensed it was a *lot* of money.'

'Who from?' Heather asked.

'Not one of the big five. It was a company called "Mainstream Books".' She used her fingers to signify quotation marks. 'I'd never heard of them, and neither had my colleagues. We implored Peter not to take the offer. In fact we offered him better royalties than we had previously. But, it seemed that the money was everything. And he left us. Just like that.' Louise tentatively took hold of her cup, but didn't lift it. Instead she continued.

'Which, in itself, wasn't an issue. Not once we reconciled that we had lost the author.'

'What was the issue then?' Heather asked, a question she assumed was behind why Louis hadn't wanted to meet at the publisher's offices.

Louise looked briefly out of the window, and then back to Heather.

'It was what happened next.' She leant forward slightly. 'Mainstream Books wanted everything we had. On Peter's work ... on Peter. Everything. There were already 1,000 books in a warehouse down south somewhere. We had to surrender them. We had to hand over every copy of the script we had, and destroy all the marketing. We were told to expunge anything to do with Peter and his book from our website and any social media. In short, we were to make it look like Peter had never been a client of ours.'

There was a pause. Heather thought about what Louise had said. She knew nothing of publishing, but thought that Mainstream Books' approach seemed heavy-handed, but hardly threatening. She was about to ask something when Louise started up again.

'We were told to sign an NDA. All of us. For which the company would be paid £5,000. Deborah, our previous boss, wasn't having any of it and turned them down flat. That was over the phone. The next day a guy from Mainstream Books flew up from London and had a long chat with Deborah with the office door closed. He left straight after apparently with an agreement that we would all sign the NDA ...'

But you're breaking the NDA by talking to me?

'... Deborah was shaking when she came out of the office. We tried to talk to her, but she clammed up. She left that night and didn't come back in. Apparently she moved away. The last I heard, she was down south somewhere.'

Heather noticed a couple of beads of sweat on Louise's forehead – and she still hadn't started her coffee.

'But you're breaking the NDA? By talking to me?' Heather asked in a hushed tone.

Louise was nodding, lots of small vigorous nods. The woman was carrying a little more weight than she should and Heather was worried that, if she went on like this, she might have an episode of some sort.

'And then Peter Lynch died. And, I guess, the book has never been published?' Heather asked.

Louise looked down at her coffee. She picked it up with her left hand, but it was shaking so much it spilt. She put it down again.

'I have to go,' Louise said in a rush, grabbing at her handbag and pushing back her chair so that it screeched. But she hadn't yet got up.

'Peter phoned me the day before he died,' she said softly as she furtively glanced out of the window. Heather followed her gaze. The place was filling up a little. 'He sounded scared and frustrated. He told me that Mainstream weren't going to do anything with his book. And that if he attempted to publish it elsewhere there would be consequences.' She was talking so quietly her words were almost lost against the window.

'What consequences?' Heather pressed.

Louise turned back again. She put her hands out and raised her shoulders in a shrug. She then reached into a pocket and pulled out a small white hanky. It was folded on itself. She dabbed at her forehead and then placed the cloth on the table next to her espresso, which had more in the saucer than in the cup.

'I have to go. I resigned from my job last night. My sister lives in Canada. I'm going to see her for a couple of months.' Louise forced a smile. She then patted her hanky, stood, turned and walked quickly out of the café.

Heather watched her go. And then she took out her phone and typed 'Mainstream Books' into Google. The search gave up nothing. There was no such firm. She then put her phone down and straightened her back, her eyes straying to the hanky.

How odd.

Inquisitively she reached for the cloth which Louise had left behind. She picked it up and an object fell out.

It was a key-drive.

Heather stared at it for a second. Then she looked around to see if anyone else was paying attention to her. No, everyone else seemed engrossed in their own conversations.

She reached forward, hanky in hand, and collected the key-drive into its original white cloth ... which she placed in her handbag.

It seemed that she had two options. First was to buy a laptop which had a USB slot in it. She reckoned on £300, which was money she wasn't prepared to spend.

Second was a trip to the local library.

She googled it. It was a 300-metre walk from where she was.

She could do that, even in this weather.

Chequers (Prime Minister's Official Country Residence), Missenden Road, Aylesbury Buckinghamshire, UK

Dominic was using a yellow duster to remove the Silvo polish from a silver candelabra which was bigger than a small bush. It was beautiful. And heavy. And it was standing proud on the floor on top of a green gingham kitchen tablecloth next to the huge sixteen-seater antique table. He wasn't allowed to clean it on the table, for fear of scratching the wooden surface. But it was a two-man lift. And that meant it had got as far as the parquet floor. Apparently, staff had been polishing it this way for over a century.

He didn't mind. In fact there was something therapeutic about cleaning. And something very cathartic about cleaning an ancient silver centrepiece on the floor of the house set aside for the country's leading statesman.

It also gave him some time to think over what, yesterday, he had signed up for – with his new friend Jack Downing. He absolutely recognised where this put him. That he was working for the prime minister whilst

217

concurrently reporting to the security services. That made his position pivotal, in a way.

Didn't it?

Or was he being naive?

If he thought he could help the prime minister by having this connection, then he would. If he could spot something for Jack Downing which might prevent World War III, then he'd do that. And he'd been specific about not wanting to get paid. It was a nice thought, but that sullied what he was trying to achieve. He wasn't stupid enough not to realise that payment meant commitment. And wasn't having any of that.

As Jack Downing was pointing out the things they might be interested in – particularly off-book meetings, changes of moods, telephone calls taken outside of the building in a furtive way – Dominic had almost retold the Bentley episode.

Almost.

But he hadn't.

It was, of course, all of those things Jack Downing had mentioned. There had been a telephone call which the boss had received and taken outside on the patio. The meeting in the lay-by was definitely off-book. And the prime minister's mood thereafter was markedly different from when he'd originally got out of Dominic's Audi.

It was exactly what Jack Downing was looking for.

But he didn't tell.

Mum's the word.

It had crossed Dominic's mind that the whole thing had been a test. That they already knew about the meeting and hoped Dominic would open up and show himself to be a reliable informant.

But he hadn't. And he had looked at the man with the photo ID's face long and hard, trying to work out whether or not he was expecting Dominic to divulge the information. Instead they had shaken hands and Jack Downing had gone on his way.

Did that mean he was one-up on the security service?

Had he protected his boss when someone else was trying to do a dirty on him?

Possibly?

Dominic was finishing off the candelabra's base. He needed a toothpick to get into the grooves around the bottom. He reached for one from a pack just as James walked in.

'How's it going?' James asked. Dominic looked up. He thought James seemed disconcerted. Was it something Dominic had done?

'Fine, thanks, James. You OK?' he replied.

James had stopped short of the tablecloth. White-gloved, he had started to inspect one of the candelabra's arms.

'Yes. Yes. I think so.' He paused as he moved on to the next arm. 'I have some news which will be of interest to you.' He glanced down at Dominic, who had stopped cleaning for a second.

'Go on,' Dominic replied.

'The prime minister wants you to accompany him to Edinburgh. For the climate conference. He leaves tomorrow afternoon. Can you make that?' James's face was unanimated.

Was he jealous?

Dominic wasn't sure.

'Of course. Wow, that's great. I'd really look forward to that.' Dominic was, of course, delighted.

'Good. That's sorted.' James had moved on to the third of the five arms. 'There's a list of clothes he needs. It's been sent through by email. And there's instructions on how you will travel. It's all in the instruction.'

Dominic was still looking at James. The man was inspecting one of the candleholders at the top of an arm. It seemed cursory. As though he were distracted.

'Have I done anything wrong?' Dominic wanted to clear the air, just in case there was any air that needed clearing.

'No. No.' James lifted his head as he replied.

There is obviously *something wrong.*

Oh well. There was little he could do about it. If the prime minister had taken a fancy to Dominic, rather than the more experienced and probably less flexible older man, then that wasn't his fault.

'OK,' Dominic replied.

Scotland. Tomorrow.

In the thick of it.

Fabulous.

Alimos, Athens, Greece

Jane's knee was bouncing up and down, nineteen to the dozen. Her hands were strangling the steering wheel at ten-to-two, and the late afternoon sun was streaming in through the Golf's driver's window, warming her face and prickling at the skin on her forearm. She was awake, though. Which was a plus.

220

It had been a bit of a day. They'd had no problem at the 'proper' borders getting into Romania, then into Bulgaria, and finally into Greece. Their passports had been stamped without delay. They'd both used British ones, the outcome of which was that Sam was convinced the YCA, or their intelligence acolytes, knew the pair of them were in Greece. And that, as a result, Frank wasn't with them. She reckoned they had less than forty-eight hours before they'd be swarmed over by the *Ellinikí Astynomía*, the Greek police. Jane hadn't minded admitting she had got a little more anxious every time they'd spotted a police car. Sam, as ever, was as cool as a cucumber.

They'd communicated with Wolfgang twice. The focus had mainly been on the layout of Theodor Konstantos's villa and what approach they should take to get across the threshold. In the end they'd agreed that Sam would knock on the front door and ask to see Konstantos under the guise of a Russian informant who worked for Baltic Freight, a bona fide shipping company based in St Petersburg. Baltic Freight was, according to their story, looking to put in a hostile bid for Konstantos's European inland shipping business.

Jane thought the proposition was viable. Wolfgang had studied the company accounts and established that the Greek had his business separated into five independent affairs. By far the biggest was his international freight shipping company. The second was outright ownership and some substantial shares in the lucrative cruise industry. The fourth and fifth were a road haulage company, which was mostly based in Greece, and a burgeoning airfreight company which linked Greece and southern Cyprus. The third in value, *Fortigídas Konstantos* – which translated to 'Konstantos Barges' – was the one Wolfgang suggested they

221

focus on. The company managed seventy-five barges and assorted inland boats on the Rhine/Danube waterway and its subsidiaries. Baltic freight, a Russian-owned company, worked the Odessa/Kyiv/Warsaw/Berlin link. It seemed to make business sense that one should acquire the other. As such, they'd agreed that Sam was to approach Konstantos asking for money in exchange for information.

It had taken Sam just fifteen minutes to scroll through the reams of detail in Wolfgang's suggestion. She'd posted a couple of supplementaries, mostly to do with cash flow and some ship/barge names, so she would appear on top of her brief. When she was finished she'd told Wolfgang to put together a company press release and post it on Baltic Freight's website to add credence to their approach. Wolfgang had subsequently sent a link through to the drop box. The title was 'Baltic Freight looks to expand eastwards'. It all seemed very convincing.

Where it went once Sam had got a foot in the door was anyone's guess. Sam had her ways.

Wolfgang had continued to make other, broader documents available, and Jane had scanned most of them when she hadn't been driving. But the reading conditions were appalling. The screen was small, the car gave her motion sickness, and she was tired and often hungry. Looking at the bigger picture would have to wait for Frank's intervention – he'd be good at that, even with a hole in his neck. The good news was that Wolfgang had found someone in Athens who could provide new papers for both her and Sam. They should be ready tomorrow morning.

First though, they had to get through today.

Sam was out of the car at a light blue metal gate which protected a gap in a high white wall, behind which was Konstantos's villa. The two-metre-high wall and the tough-looking gate was all Jane could see, other than some villa-side pine trees, the tops of which waved at her in the brisk onshore wind. Jane had parked on the road about 50 metres from the gate. She could be at the entrance in under a minute, should Sam need to get away in a hurry. And then they could nip onto the main coast road, which ran parallel with the seafront villas. That should allow them to quickly get lost in a crowd.

Wolfgang had sent stills through from the villa's video system coverage, along with a floorplan. By then she and Sam had bought a cheap tablet and a pair of small high-end walkie-talkies from an electronics shop on the outskirts of northern Athens. The tablet had allowed them to get better resolution on the images.

It seemed that the villa's front boundary was only covered by a single fixed gate-camera – the one Sam was looking at now. There were twelve others, covering most of the villa and its grounds. Wolfgang would have those on his screens now.

For the operation Wolfgang would be their eyes, and he would pass the detail to Jane via a burner phone. Jane would then act on what he told her. If she needed to get to Sam in an emergency, she would pip her on the walkie-talkie. Sam also had one of the mobiles with her – backup and all that.

There had been a brief discussion about the pistol, but they'd eventually agreed that it should stay in the car. Jane had it tucked under one leg.

The operation was straightforward enough. Jane was to wait where she was until Sam reappeared. If there was a crisis, they would make it up as they went along. Or, if nothing happened at the gate, they'd give up, find a hotel and think of a Plan B.

At the moment Sam was still standing like a wally by the blue gate. Plan B might be the order of the day.

Ping.

There was a text from Wolfgang.

A man has left the villa and is heading for the gate.

Jane looked toward Sam. She was still waiting idly by the entrance, her hands thrust deep into the pockets of a lightweight hoodie.

A minute passed.

And then the gate rolled back, half a metre. A man appeared and beckoned to Sam. There was a conversation. He asked to look into her backpack. He rummaged around and pulled out the walkie-talkie. There was a conversation, small remonstrations from Sam, and then he hung it off his belt. *One-nil to the Greeks.* He then motioned for her to raise her arms, which she did. He frisked her, spending far too long on Sam's backside than was necessary.

Next he escorted her through the gap in the gate, which rolled closed behind them.

Ping.

She's in, was the message from Wolfgang.

…

Ping.

The messages came thick and fast.

She's in the villa.

Ping.

Waiting in the hall.

Then …

Ping.

K is coming out of the bedroom. He's wearing a dressing gown. Don't have a camera in that room. Probably a man in there.

And then, as quick as a game of professional ping-pong.

Ping.

Sam's meeting with K now.

Ping.

She's been asked to sit down.

Ping.

K and two other men, workers not lovers, in the big sitting room.

Ping.

Pretty sure one has a gun.

Ping.

Still in conversation.

In an instant Jane's concentration on the small screen was broken. A truck and three cars sped past her in the direction of the villa. The truck was like a bullion lorry, big and black, with meshed windows and heavy tyres. And it was motoring.

There was a *screech*. The truck had turned quickly as it approached the villa, skidding and almost toppling ...

... and then it all became clear.

The truck smashed through the gate as if it were cardboard, bits of light blue metal twisting and lifting over its bonnet. Jane was sure it had taken out some of the wall as well. The cars, all dark-windowed and menacing, followed on.

There was a *ping* from Wolfgang, but Jane ignored it. Instead she did two things.

She picked up the walkie-talkie, pressed the 'call' button, which would make a loud *brrr* sound at the other handset, and then she pressed the pressel.

Jane shouted.

225

'Get out of there now, Sam. The villa is under attack!'

And she repeated herself.

'Get out, Sam. Out! Out! Out!' at the same time as she reached for her mobile. Sam's new number was on speed dial. She connected.

It started to ring just as the sound of gunfire cracked through the dense, Athens commuter traffic running on the main coast road.

Oh, Christ.

Sam heard the squawk of the walkie-talkie hanging from the thug's belt across the room. Her hearing was excellent and, even though Jane's cry was a high-pitched shrill, she heard every word.

Sam rose, mid-sentence. She was halfway through her diatribe about the shenanigans of Baltic Freight's ambitions on the Greek's *Fortigídas Konstantos*. She was speaking in broken English, syruped with a Russian accent. Konstantos was in his dressing gown, unshaven and very likely drunk – or on drugs. But he had been patient and interested so far. Jane's walkie-talkie alert confused him. He looked around, his chin in the air.

Sam was already on her feet, backpack in hand.

She knew the layout of the villa, exactly. She knew where the doors were, which way they opened, where the knife drawer in the kitchen was, should she need it, and the quickest ways out of the building. She knew where the light switches were, she knew which door led to a cellar, and she had a good idea of what the grounds looked like. One way in, the way she had been escorted. And two ways out: back the way she had come, or down to the quay and into the

226

water. The villa was surrounded by a two-metre-high wall with accompanying glass shards on the top. That was option three, if the first two alternatives were fruitless.

Along with Konstantos there were two other goons in the room. The first had frisked her at the gate, using far too many fingers to search her nether regions. She didn't think he was armed. The second was resting his backside on a windowsill, between her and the opened patio doors which led to the pool and then, after about 30 metres, through a garden of lawn, bushes and pines, to the big tender. She thought he was armed, his jacket raised about pistol width on one side.

Wolfgang's stills had shown one man in the back garden. Sam was convinced it wasn't either of the two men in the room. Garden man had a short-barrelled, H&K MP5 machine gun, fitted with a curved magazine. That gave him fifteen rounds, about three bursts, before he ran out. If Sam ran and weaved, and unless he was hopeless, she'd be downed with the second burst. A couple of rounds of 9mm would be enough. She'd be dead.

But, garden man would have to want to shoot an unarmed woman. Greek men were old-fashioned. And Sam was good at distraction.

All of those thoughts played out in her mind in a split second it had taken her to stand and start to move.

The guy on the sill with the pistol was now on his feet. The thug with the wandering hands – and her walkie-talkie – was fishing at his belt. She guessed he was trying to get hold of the device to establish what the bloody hell was going on.

The lounge lizard Konstantos's reactions were slow, like that of a man who had drunk or snorted too much, too often. He was the least of her worries.

227

And she must be the least of his.

Whoever was attacking the house – and a loud, metallic crash from somewhere near the front of the villa demonstrated that they were serious – wasn't looking for her. Of course she might end up as collateral. That was still very possible. But, if they were after her, they were after Jane too. And Jane had announced the attack. She had been free to do that from a very vulnerable position outside of the villa. If Jane and she were targets, that wouldn't have been allowed to happen.

They were after Konstantos. Sam was sure of it. And she had absolutely no idea why.

It's definitely time to leave.

She darted for the patio doors. That meant running between an occasional sofa, covered in a remarkably gauche cream leather, and the man with the pistol. She was on him before he realised what was going on; before he'd had chance to reach for his weapon although, glancing at his face, it was about to become an option.

Sam had picked up a vase as she ran. Blue and white. Dresden. Probably pricey.

The guy with the pistol took the vase in the mouth. It shattered on impact, Sam's small frame compensated by the speed at which her limbs moved when she ordered them to. The guy would live, easily. But, just now, he would be dazed and confused. Sore. And possibly a bit bloody. It didn't matter, because she was beyond him now ...

... and through the patio doors as the gunfire started.

It was from behind her. Possibly another guard having a ding-dong with the attackers.

And then more gunfire. Much more. Heavy stuff. Lots of it. It felt as though considerably more of it was incoming than being returned. There was going to be a massacre. And she didn't want to be part of it.

She was by the pool now. In front of her there was a gap between two hedges, as she remembered. A path snaked between them to a large patch of lawn decorated with a folly and a wooden hut, probably a sauna. She'd be there in a second.

More gunfire. And screams now. Windows smashing. The odd round flying over her head. It wasn't aimed, it was a consequence of a battle behind her.

She hoped.

And there he was.

The guard with the MP5.

She had reached the lawn bounded by pines, a wide open space ideal for shooting and being shot. He was 30 metres from her. It was nothing. The MP5 was in one hand, hanging by his side, but he was already fidgety. In fact every millisecond was a fraction of time closer to man getting the weapon into some form of firing position, safety catch off and finger on the trigger.

And still the war waged behind her.

She glanced sideward. Bushes. They were too dense to wade through.

Behind her was a gangster movie.

Forwards was the only way.

She thrust up her hands. And dropped to her knees, her backpack now resting on the floor.

'Don't shoot. I am not the enemy. They are behind me.' English. Loud and clear. There was no reaction. She then said the same thing in Russian. She knew both Greek and Russian were Indo-European languages and were vaguely similar. She also knew that many Greeks spoke Russian.

229

Had that registered?

I dunno?

Come on ,fella!

She would try German next. And then French. She could do that.

The man – actually Sam now reckoned he wasn't much more than an elderly adolescent – was standing stock-still, both hands on the weapon. Which was pointed at her. But more than that. He was thrusting it in her direction.

He looked petrified.

And then he was distracted.

The gunfire, which had been going on for a couple of minutes, had subsided. Now there was shouting – in Greek. Clear orders, the sort you'd expect from battle-hardened soldiers or Special Forces. It was coming from behind her. And it was getting close.

Sam rolled, instinctively. To her left. Quickly. Efficiently. Out of the line of sight of the snaking path. Away, at least initially, from anyone heading down from the villa. Then she was on her feet just as the kid pulled the trigger, shot from the hip.

Could go anywhere.

It did.

Brrrrrrrrrrrrrrrrr!

All fifteen rounds in one burst.

The long spray of rounds lifted as the weapon's recoil pivoted the barrel upwards on the young guard's hip bone. If she hadn't moved the first couple of rounds would have killed her outright. The remainder. No, they were hopeless. They probably broke a couple of bedroom windows and took out a squadron of seagulls.

The poor lad needed some coaching.

Then ...

Brrr!

What?

Sam was ducking away now, into the trees off to one side. She darted behind a wide trunk of pine and pushed her back against the red and brown, knobbly bark.

Shouting. More orders. Greek. She picked up the odd word: 'check' and 'boat'.

Her heart was pounding, but she had control. She knelt, lowering her head away from the sightline of others and then looked around the tree, quayside.

Slowly.

The teenager was dead. His legs and arms a mess of angles and distortions. The MP5 was by his side. A man, all in black, had jogged past him heading towards the sea. He was carrying a machine pistol. Sam couldn't see what make it was.

She edged forward, trying to see who else she might have to contend with.

There.

She pulled back sharply.

A second man. Bigger. Stockier. Sunglasses. He was looking away, back towards the villa. He was carrying an American M16, fitted with a decent sight and curved 30-round magazine, which might be a few rounds short of its maximum.

Brrring!

Her phone rang.

Sam thrust her hand into her daysack and caught it before the third ring. But that was *way* too late. The guy with the M16 would have heard it.

Simple.

There were no choices. But she had to choose one.

She closed her eyes.

And started to whimper.

Then cry.

Not loudly, so the man, if he hadn't heard the phone ring, wouldn't necessarily hear her. But it had to be authentic.

She continued to whimper, and snort, her head in the crook of her elbow.

In some ways it was a fateful action. If the man in black and sunglasses with the M16 had orders to kill everyone in the villa and its grounds, then she wouldn't have to face the barrel of his American rifle. A single round of 5.56 mm to her buried head would kill her instantly. It would be over, as it should have been – as she'd previously longed for – so many times before. Death was a state beyond life. No more than that. If today was the day, just as it had been for the teenager with the MP5, then so be it.

At least with her head hidden she wouldn't have to face the actual moment. It would be immediate. And unknown.

Bang.

Dead.

She'd take that.

But that didn't happen.

'*Poios eísai?*' The man was beside her. She didn't look up.

She kept sobbing.

He kicked her with the side of a boot, like he was nudging a dog to get off his shag pile carpet.

She looked up then.

God, he was big.

'*Russkiy?*' she asked.

The man shook his head disdainfully. He was a man in a rush. And she was an unnecessary distraction. Sam could see that.

'English?' she asked with a Russian accent.

'Yes, of course. What are you doing here?' he barked in Greco-English.

'I had a meeting ... with Konstantos. A business meeting.' Sam tried to sound as petrified as she could. She pushed her shoulders down and made herself shiver. 'Please don't kill me. I am Russian. I can go home now. I have never seen you,' she pleaded.

The man tutted. His face continuing to tell a story that this was not going to end well.

'Get to your feet,' he ordered, stabbing the barrel of the rifle into her cheek

That fucking hurt.

She almost went for him then. It was a split-second decision which she didn't take. It would have been a fight, for sure, but she would have lost it.

Instead she stood, shakily.

'With me,' he motioned with his head in the direction of the quay. She led, he followed and, when she wasn't going quick enough, he barrel-poked her in the neck ...

... which really infuriated her, the red mist ever present.

It took them less than a minute to reach the quay. It was a glorious view. Grey and pink craggy rocks led to a sea which had lost its light blue calmness due to the swell of a busy late afternoon wind. It was peppered in the distance with boats and ships of all sizes and types heading from and to Piraeus, Athens' port, out into the Aegean. The wood and concrete quay stretched out 40 metres into the sea. Beside it

233

was the sleekest of boats, a blue-hulled and white-decked, Austin Parker, 42-foot superyacht tender.

Sam squinted her eyes against a lowering sun.

On the boat was the man who Sam had seen earlier jogging away from the dead kid with the gun. And he was intent on no good. In his hand was a large jerrycan. And he was pouring fuel everywhere.

Sam stopped, mostly in fascination. But not for long. The thug with the M16 stabbed her in the neck again …

What the fuck!

She had to bite her lip *so* tight. An altercation with him would be lose-lose. She had to find her moment. Now wasn't it.

She stumbled on. They were by the boat a minute later.

Her thug barked some Greek at the man with the canister. And then, with a barrel to the neck, he ordered her up a short ramp and onto the boat. She reluctantly did as she was told.

'Bye, bye, Russkiy.' From behind her.

Smack.

And then there was blackness.

Jane was late to the party. And it was already haunting her.

But was she too late?

She'd snuck in on foot, behind the third car, pistol in hand, safety catch off.

There was plenty of vegetation and so many other things to distract Konstantos, his guards and their visitors. She had kept the wall on her right shoulder and moved down the edge of the grounds until she had the side of the villa, which included the entrance, in front of her. The gunfire had started to subside. The tinkling of glass as it fell was over. And the final scream of a man from somewhere in the building was silenced by a single gunshot.

Where are you, Sam?

The two windows she could see gave nothing away.

Her phone buzzed in her pocket. She'd had the sense to stick it on mute before she got out of the car.

Of course ... Wolfgang.

She opened the SMS.

Sam is in the grounds, beyond the pool. I can't see her now.

There was a long spray of gunfire from that direction ... and then a short burst, seemingly in return.

Sod it.

She thrust her phone back in her pocket and pushed quickly past bushes which scratched at her exposed skin and pulled at her clothes. Her breath was raspy and short. Her legs already more tired than they should be. Her heart pounding away.

She had to get beyond the pool.

It had been two minutes. Maybe three.

There.

An open area. Pine trees to her right, following the boundary and ...

Oh my God.

There was a man lying on the floor in the distance. The picnic-soft grass at odds with his contorted position.

Shit.

She knelt down and reached for her phone.

Nothing.

She looked up.

No Sam. But ...

How could she have missed him? A block of a man, just off to her left carrying a military rifle. He was 15 metres away, maybe a bit more, looking back towards the villa. *Shit!* She was exposed. She pulled back into the vegetation, right back ...

... and dialled Sam's number.

Which was a mistake.

Bugger!

She knew as soon as she heard the ring. Loud and clear. Forward left.

The big man turned his head in the direction of the noise.

What have I done?

Jane could have gone one of two ways then. To her subconscious, one was far more attractive than the other. Her bottom lip wobbled. And, as her world fell apart and the tears rose, she was back in the small washroom in the Vietnam villa. The one with the broken mirror and a shard in her hand large enough to do permanent damage. She had been ready then. As she was now.

To end it all.

There she had let two agents down. Exposed them. Given away names, when what she should have done was taken more beatings. She had been faced with the option of offering state secrets for the protection of her family. The photographs she'd been shown were clear: their lives for the intelligence she held.

In a moment of madness – *or was it genius?* – she had found another way. The pink ridges on her forearm an indelible memory to the choice she had made.

Just as she could do now.

She had a pistol ... and she had no hope.

None at all.

Except.

I do have a pistol.

She smeared away the tears with the back of her hand, shook her head and crawled forward. Quickly, but quietly.

Stop.

They were both there now. Sam was on her feet. The man with the rifle behind her. He was hitting her. Prodding her forward with the barrel of his weapon.

Jane's arm sprang up to the firing position, her shooting fist in the palm of her other hand. She was looking over the short barrel, the foresight, rearsight and the broad shoulders of the man in a line.

Sort of.

It was too far.

30 metres?

What if she missed him and hit Sam? She'd already done enough damage. She'd have to get a better shot.

Chase after them?

She could. He'd hear her and turn. She'd shoot … but the odds and outcomes were likely the same. But this time the man would be alert. He'd be turning with a gun, possibly crouching. A smaller target.

No.

There must be a more certain way.

She followed them, staying in the treeline and then through the bushes. It was tough and prickly, but she pushed and stretched and found a way.

Out.

There!

That beautiful tender. The huge man. And the small Sam. Her friend was being forced to the boat. Where there was a second man …

... with a canister of fuel?

Jane knew where this was going. And she knew she had to stop it. Even if that meant she would lose her life, as sure as Sam was going to lose hers if Jane did nothing.

Sam was up the ramp and onto the boat.

In some organic, indescribable way, Jane felt the *smack* of the man's rifle on Sam's head. She sensed the weightlessness of Sam's body as her friend's brain shut down and her legs gave way. And Jane *so* wanted to copy her friend, to crawl into a ball as Sam looked now.

To escape from this madness.

To hide, not to seek.

But she didn't.

She watched.

She watched as the big man left the boat and walked back down the quay. And she watched as the man on the tender continued to pour fuel over the deck, including the final drips onto Sam's lifeless body.

And she watched as the man on the boat descended the short gangplank and retrieved the machine pistol from his belt, just as the big man disappeared into the bushes off to her left, back up to the villa.

Now.

Jane was on her feet. She ran as fast as she ever had. Her knees lifted and her arms pumped.

But she kept an eye on the prize.

The guy with the machine pistol. The one lifting it to aim – two hands, to make sure he controlled the fire. The man who was about to set an expensive boat alight, which had her very dear and very unconscious, petrol-doused friend on its deck.

Jane was on the quay. 20 metres from the end of the boat. 25 metres from the man with the machine-pistol.

238

15 metres … and closing.

Bang!

He had taken a shot at the boat.

'Oiiii!' she shouted just as there was a further *bang*.

A second shot by the man to ensure the heat of the bullet caught the petrol, the smell of which was pervading everything.

He turned towards Jane just as the fuel caught, his long-barrelled pistol following the arc of his movement. But she was quicker than him. And she had surprise. She hadn't needed to waste a second or two setting the boat ablaze.

Bang! Bang! Bang!

On the run. Her shooting was erratic. Confused. It was from a pistol at the end of a long arm which was rushing headlong for a mid-sized man, dressed in black, holding a machine pistol which was now intent on killing her.

His shoulder twisted, high and left, and then he went down in a pile. Jane was six running steps from him – and from the plank to the deck which was starting to catch, flames licking here and there. Spreading. Racing for Sam.

She screeched to a halt, her flatties woman enough for the job, her shoulders turning to launch herself up the gangplank. As she turned, as if in some superheroes movie, the barrel of her pistol remained trained on the body on the quay. And she was still looking at him, her head purposefully remaining on the first task.

Bang! Bang!

The man's body lifted as the rounds from her pistol smashed into his torso, bouncing it against the wood.

You can never be too sure, can you?

Jane's focus changed.

Task two.

She was up the plank, onto the deck. The flames were high, and everywhere. But Sam's body was currently clear. There was a short slick of fire heading to her friend's shoulder. It would be there …

Jane scooped her up just as the flames caught Sam's hoodie. And just as the fire and heat of the deck snagged at her own jeans, the pain of the flames registering immediately.

It was all about momentum.

She was two people now. Probably 140 kilogrammes. Moving through the wall of fire to the far side of the deck. It was five paces, maybe less. Jane wasn't counting. She was too busy moving.

The chrome handrail, which was no more than 50 centimetres tall, caught Jane's knees and propelled her over the side of the boat. But she didn't let go of Sam. She didn't. As they both tumbled into the water and descended towards the seabed, Jane held on to her as if she were her own child. Two women – one unconscious – both probably slightly burnt. One backpack. A pistol. Wet clothes, including two pairs of jeans, a hoodie and two pairs of sodden shoes. It was a swimming test for senior lifeguards.

And there was a dead man with a machine pistol.

On the quay.

And a big man with an M16.

Who might be coming back to see what the fuss was about.

Come on, Jane.

Chapter 10

What the fuck?

A million things raced through Sam's mind.

Water? Can't breathe! What's that pulling me? Where's the big guy with the M16?

She was in the sea. It was cold, but bearable.

Jane?

Was it?

She could see her colleague's backside above her, her legs kicking and twisting, catching on Sam's outstretched arm which Jane had hold of.

And it was lighter. Ahead of them. A long way ahead of them?

How deep are we?

As her senses kicked in and she found her gears, she suppressed the panic of knowing she had lungs full of water.

That she was drowning. That would be the technical term.

Think.

But her head. It was spinning. Out of control. Had she taken a smack to the back of the skull? Or was it a lack of oxygen?

Come on!

Jane was tiring. Sam could feel it. Her arm was going slack. Jane's legs losing intensity as her feet banged against Sam's shoulder

It was Sam's turn now.

She just had to overcome the dizziness.

Sam had been here before. Sinking in seawater, off the coast of Italy. Then Holly, an American senator's daughter and a very strong swimmer, had pulled her from the sea. Sam had been completely out of it. Mouth-to-mouth had brought her back.

This time was different. She was awake.

And Jane was a rubbish swimmer.

Push.

Sam broke her grip from Jane's hand and kicked with her legs. Once, Twice. Three times. She was beside Jane now. And they were both making some progress. But, having neared the surface, the wash of the waves and the heaviness of their clothes was slowing both of them.

Get on!

Jane was behind her now, just. Her face at Sam's chest height. With her lungs burning, Sam grabbed at Jane's hair – it was the first thing that came to hand – and pulled … as she pushed. And pushed. And kicked.

As she pulled.

The surface was just …

Sam was coughing now. Lungfuls of water came up and out as torrents of air replaced it. And Jane. She was at the surface, also coughing and spluttering. More coughing from both of them. And then a sense of overwhelming tiredness. Success was ripped from them as a wave broke over their heads and they were separated.

Sam swallowed some more water. And coughed and spat.

And breathed.

She spotted the shore …

… *shit!*

It came to her then.

Where was the villa? Were they safe from the men – the one with the pistol, and the one with the MI6?

Sam turned her head and looked.

Fuck! The boat was ablaze. Maybe 30 metres away.

But that wasn't anywhere near far enough.

She coughed some more and looked around for Jane.

There. In between the tops of waves.

She was OK. She was pointing away from the boat.

Swim, Sam, swim.

She did. As fast as she could.

It took them twenty minutes to cover not a great deal. The waves dragging and pushing. The sea finding her mouth when she was trying to breathe. They got close enough to shout at each other, and managed to stay within encouraging distance. Soon there was a small beach forward right. It looked far enough away from where they started to belong to the next door villa. Sam pointed, her arm wobbling against the relentless water. They headed for that, the waves and their sodden clothes continuing to make any swimming a high-end gym session with a bastard of an instructor ... and the beach landing, which tossed them about and dragged them back into the water, was one of Sam's most unpleasant experiences.

They both eventually lay ragged on the beach, the ends of the waves washing at their legs, enticing them back into the sea.

They had a brief conversation from their prostate positions.

Jane wanted to rest. She needed to rest.

But Sam wouldn't let them.

Not yet. Not now.

There was little left of the boat, the remaining flames making it look as though the sea was on fire. Any hint of a previous firefight at the villa had been replaced with a multitude of police sirens. Sam reckoned the thugs had been, killed everyone, left some collateral behind – she could pick out a body on the quay which Jane said was the guy who had torched the boat – and gone.

All on a workday afternoon in a very upmarket and busy part of Athens.

A broad daylight massacre. That doesn't happen without the support of someone in authority.

And they had come for Konstantos. Definitely not her. Nor Jane. Behind the pine tree, the big guy with the MI6 had shown no recognition. Sam was not on his radar.

But she had escaped. And they would probably know that by now.

The jigsaw would come together.

So they had to get away from here.

Fast.

She gathered herself. Stood. Bent down to stop herself from toppling. And stood again.

Oh, my effing head.

And where was her backpack?

In the water.

Which was fine. Everything precious was in plastic bags in her waist-belt.

Her legs felt woozy. But she'd live. A very wet Jane, who was also on her feet, grabbed Sam by the arm to steady herself. Sam studied her face. It was etched with concern – sisterly concern. As it always was.

'Thanks, by the way,' Sam said.

Jane smiled.

'One-all, I think,' she replied.

Sam got it, and the maths was wrong.

'No. Two-one to you, if you count Kenema.' Sam knew she was in Jane's debt.

Jane nodded, drips from her hair making their escape in every direction.

'We should go now. Let's try and salvage the car, or at least what's in it.' It sounded like a suggestion from Sam, but it wasn't. It was an order.

Jane nodded.

'Are you sure you're OK?' Jane asked, still with her hand on Sam's arm.

'Yeah. I think I might have a bit of a headache for a while.'

And with that, she turned and strode off as best she could into the garden of another villa.

Let's hope they don't have a dog.

Clactoll Bed and Breakfast, Wick, Scotland

Heather was sitting on her bed, laptop on her thighs, and a glass of red wine on the bedside table of the basic, but very welcoming B&B. It had been a long day and she reckoned it might be a longer night – if she could stay awake. There was a lot to do.

Inverness library had had no issue with her plugging Louise from Downy Birch's flash drive into a USB slot on one of the public computer towers. A couple of mouse clicks later and she had it. There was one file: *The Unsolved Mystery of the North Coast's Abductions – final.*

Heather double-clicked on it. Typical of an old, slower computer struggling with a large, Microsoft Word document full of images, it took an age before the thing

245

settled down. But she was patient. She had the rest of the week.

But she didn't though. Not really. Not here. The book was 186 A4 pages long. And there was no way she was going to be able to read all of it, at her leisure, in Inverness's library.

So she scanned the opening chapter. Looked at the images. And then read the conclusions. When she'd finished the last line – after which was a whole load of references – she placed her chin on her folded hands and stared around the room.

How many young people were there in this large, book-filled place?

Not many.

One of the women behind the counter looked twenty-ish.

Heather continued to add them up. There was a young family – a man, a woman and a baby – in the soft toy area. The lad was reading a pop-up book to an infant. His partner (she guessed) was asleep in a comfy chair off to one side. And there was another young man looking for a book in the thriller section.

Two young men and two young women.

That was it.

According to Peter Lynch, from what she'd read so far all four of them were targets for an unknown abductor or, more likely, abductors. Women *and* men. The author was convinced of it. Heather hadn't had the time to investigate the detail, but the conclusion was clear. The abductions were of both genders.

She'd pressed Ctrl-F and typed in the two names she'd noted from her search at home: Wendy McFort, who had been abducted over a weekend in mid-December in

2003; and Steph Landown, who had gone missing not far from here in Thurso, again in December, this time in 2009. Her body had been washed up on a beach on Sanday, on the Orkney isles.

Result?

Both of those names were in the book. But from what she could see, there wasn't a great deal more in the text than she had found herself.

Heather wanted to cross-reference all the names in Peter Lynch's tome with associated dates, to see if December was significant. And she wanted to pore over every word. To establish if the journalist had discovered a pattern. A connection. Or was his work just a series of random events ... which didn't include her story. And why should it?

The young guy from the thriller section was at the counter. An older woman had come into the library. She was carrying three paperbacks. They looked like a Mills & Boon trilogy.

Heather was scrolling, and quietly muttering.

'Come on, Peter.'

She found a name. She checked the date.

She moved on.

What?

Wow.

A significant revelation had hit her about halfway through the book.

Peter Lynch had noted three foreign sounding names: two Dutch women and a French man. All three had failed to complete university and college courses in Scotland: St Andrews, Dundee and Robert Gordon – all since 2000, but all in different years. They had, according to the author, 'gone home' without telling their colleges, midyear, before Christmas. The universities had raised a query and the missing person police reports had shown that their passports had been stamped leaving the country soon after their disappearance. Exit points were different: Aberdeen airport; Glasgow airport; and cross-channel between Dover and Calais.

But Peter Lynch hadn't been satisfied.

He had travelled to both Holland and France and pressed the local police. As far as anyone could tell, none of the three had actually made it home. And all of the families had filed their own missing persons enquiries. The young people had left the UK and disappeared ... somewhere on continental Europe.

The revelation had been too much for Heather.

That, and the four, very much alive young people in the library – in her mind, potential victims. She felt sick to her stomach. She was tired. And nauseously hungry. And she couldn't do the book justice. Not there. So, she googled a car hire firm and a local PC World and closed the library machine down. With a pretty hefty bite out of her savings, she had then headed north. All the way to Wick, where she had run out of steam.

A quick pop to the local Tesco for some cold meat, bread, salad and a bottle of red wine, and she was soon ensconced in her B&B ... sitting on her bed with her new laptop open on her thighs.

She was onto Chapter 4 of fifteen chapters. And her notebook was filling up.

She had it landscape orientated and had sketched a table with six columns: date; name; gender; where abducted/missing; where dropped; book page ref. Separately she had pulled out a page and had sketched a map of northern Scotland. On it she was annotating initials and dates of the poor young people who had made it onto the pages of Peter Lynch's book. So far she had five.

Why hadn't Peter Lynch made a table?

Whatever sells, she guessed.

As she worked, and ate and drank, she left the muted TV on in the background.

Another name.

Another entry into her notebook.

She checked her watch. It was just gone ten. A glance at the telly and she saw that the evening news was on. She absently reached for the remote and turned up the volume.

Currently they were talking about the upcoming climate conference in Edinburgh. Someone was on discussing the likely outcomes, and whether or not the global delegates would be able to sign their countries up for zero-carbon by 2050. And, even if they did, would that actually restrict global temperatures from rising 1.5 degrees above pre-industrial levels? No one sounded hopeful.

After that there was a separate, but associated few minutes about the security situation. The news showed a clip of activists climbing the Forth railway bridge. They had banners with them, declaring that 'This Is An Emergency', and 'The System Needs to Change.' The report then switched to a senior policeman who went on to condemn the activists' actions, saying that they'd had to close the bridge to railway traffic until the protestors could be removed.

The interviewer then asked a question which seemed to throw the policeman.

'We understand that there is a credible threat to the conference itself. Wider than just activism. And that your force has asked for more resources?' The interviewer was a young woman. She looked very pleased with herself.

After a pause, the policeman was quickly back on message.

'There are always threats to public safety at events which are as high profile as this. We take them all very seriously.'

And that was that.

OK?

Heather realised that she was drinking her wine by the gulp, and not really letting it register. Her mind was a little foggy and her eyes were dry. Future research might have to wait until the North Sea's wind had blown through her ears tomorrow, on a pre-breakfast stroll.

That sounded like a plan.

She was just about to turn the TV off when the next article transported her back forty-eight hours.

It was a follow-on from what she had picked up at home two nights ago; the business of Wi-Fi home assistants listening to everything that's going on in the household, even when you think they are turned off.

Apparently there had been a rally in London. It wasn't a huge one, the talking head reckoned maybe up to 5,000 people, but what was interesting was that nearly all of the attendees were women. Actually, most appeared to be mums.

The raft of protestors were energised under two, repeating banners: 'Stop Listening To Us!' and 'Stop Listening To Our Children!' The march had finished outside a tall new office block ... the caption read: 'Amazon's New Shoreditch HQ'. There, a number of women had placed maybe fifty home assistants of various makes on the beautifully paved entrance area.

And set fire to them.

The police initially seemed to be caught out, but the fire service had quickly been called and then, according to the presenter, five women had been arrested. There was one shot of a mother being grappled to the ground by the police, her arms outstretched passing a baby to another bystander.

It was all pretty shocking, but Heather guessed that was the point.

And there were a number of soundbites. Heather was listening to one of the protestors when she realised she desperately needed a pee ... which would have to be her curtain call.

Pee followed by putting the cork in the bottle, cleaning her teeth and then bed.

But the woman being interviewed fixated Heather.

'These firms need to understand the power of us mums. We know they're listening. We know they're perverts. And we're not having it. This is just the start.' She was pointing at the ground. She was probably thirty, well dressed, angry and ... she was wearing a badge. It was similar to a 'happy 50th birthday' affair which often arrived pinned to a card. The background was a light paisley, a bit Cath Kidston. In the centre was a large letter 'Q', beautifully decorated, like a green and red branch which curved around to meet itself. It was adorned with multicoloured flowers. It seemed like an odd thing to be wearing to a demonstration.

Goodness.

And perverts?

Heather wasn't sure about that. But, just in case, she quickly checked the room for smart speakers.

Flemingstraße, Munich, Germany

251

Frank had managed to calm down. Just. There had been absolutely nothing normal about the past two days, and when he'd arrived at Wolfgang's cellar – well, not quite Wolfgang's, it was actually next door's – the intensity in the room was as heavy as a tractor tyre. Frank wanted to rest. He wanted to recuperate. He had been told to take it easy for at least a week. His neck was as sore as hell, but healing.

But he also wanted to press Wolfgang on the info board. And the equipment. And ...

... he already had so many questions.

He wanted to ask why he was being escorted around the place by a midget R2D2. And, how was Wolfgang – who looked just as he remembered him, but thinner? And where was Tomas going to sleep tonight?

And Frank had nearly forgotten to take his antibiotics. And where was the loo? In fact, where was he going to kip?

So many questions.

But they all had to wait.

Because when he arrived – having been dropped off at an oblique entrance to the house next door and led through some circuitous route, between hedges, then a fake door in a wall, down some stairs to an old musty cellar, to a door which wasn't a door, it was a wall until it decided to open automatically – things were not well in Wolfgang's new and very e-sexy lair.

'Sit here,' Wolfgang had barked, pointing at a chair next to his. He hadn't even turned around to shake Frank's hand.

Frank had done as he had been ordered.

'We've lost them.' Wolfgang was staring at three large screens, waving his right hand about in a dismissive fashion.

Frank leant forward.

From the fifteen or so video-insets on the three screens, he realised they were looking at a white villa. Greece, he reckoned. Konstantos's empire.

God.

He was zoned in now.

There were upturned tables and smashed windows.

And there were dead people. Frank was particularly interested in the man in a dressing gown, whose body was flopped out on a sofa, what was left of his head trying its best to topple over the back of the headrest and onto the floor. There was blood *everywhere*.

You could easily describe it as a massacre.

'That's Konstantos?' Frank asked, pointing vaguely at one of the smaller screens. You couldn't tell. Not exactly. But he was an analyst. He was trained to make very reasoned deductions.

Wolfgang nodded absently. He was focused directly to his front. On the large central monitor were three camera shots of a garden. Two showed images of the pool area. And a third was ...

Bloody hell.

More carnage.

There was a quay. And a big boat. It was ablaze. Next to it was another dead man. He was dressed in black. There was a gun at his side.

'They went into the water. Here.' Wolfgang was pointing to the right of the fiery boat, which was bobbing about a bit. The sea were pretty choppy. It was hardly a serene day on the Aegean.

Who?

'Who?'

Frank still had his satchel pressed close to his chest. He was hoping that he'd be able to unburden himself of its contents soon. Just now, however, looking at the devastation on the screens, he held it tighter still.

'Sam. And Jane.' Wolfgang still wasn't looking at Frank. 'Sam was picked up by a man in the garden and taken to a second man on the boat. This one.' He was pointing at the lifeless body on the quay. 'The first man knocked Sam unconscious on the deck just as the second guy set fire to it. I thought it was all over then. I could see the ...' Wolfgang's voice had tailed off at that point. Frank could sense his pain. If anyone knew anything about being burnt alive, it was him. Frank reached to his right and put his hand on Wolfgang's forearm.

'And then Jane appeared. From nowhere.' Wolfgang was animated now. 'She shot this guy ... twice,' he was pointing again, 'and then pulled Sam from the flames and they both went overboard, away from the fire.' Wolfgang's finger had moved again and was pressing hard against the screen, the pixels changing hue against the pressure.

There was silence. Frank still had his hand on Wolfgang's forearm.

'How long ago was that?' Frank eventually asked, desperation now rising in his own voice. He was heading to the same place Wolfgang was. If Sam and Jane had been involved in a fire and then into difficult water, who knew what had become of them?

'Twenty minutes.' Wolfgang flicked his screens around and, once they'd settled, in prime position was a live image of a busy road. 'I've just hacked into the Athens' department of transport CCTV. This is ...' he flipped at his

254

screen again, an enlarged map appeared above the CCTV footage, '... the dual carriageway next to Konstantos's villa. You can just see its boundary.' He was pointing to a long, white wall, in the far distance. It was obscured by palm trees, but you couldn't miss it. It was lit up by a score of red and blue flashing lights.

'This car ...' Wolfgang had moved his finger, '... the small silver car, here. I think it's a Golf. And I think it's the car Sam and Jane bought in Mannheim.' He used a finger and thumb to enlarge the picture. It pixelated. He then played with the keyboard, which was set into the desk, and some clever image correction software sharpened the picture.

It's definitely a Golf.

Wolfgang left the image as it was for a couple of seconds, and he then flicked it away and dragged back the quayside inferno. The boat, sea and the flames were now indistinguishable from each other.

Nothing.

Frank searched all the screens.

Nothing.

Hang on.

Not nothing.

'Bring back to centre the government CCTV,' Frank ordered. Wolfgang did as he was asked. It appeared in front of them. 'There.' It was Frank's turn to point.

Two people, just better than grey stickmen, were walking furtively through a palm tree punctuated strip of land between the dual carriageway and a parallel access road which led to the villa. Wolfgang was on it immediately. He enlarged and sharpened.

Sam and Jane.

Sam leading. Jane a tree behind.

255

For sure.

Neither Wolfgang nor Frank said anything for the ten minutes it took the two women to slowly, and carefully, make it to the car. And another few minutes as they watched the car back out of its space, turn away from the villa and drive down the access road until the CCTV lost them.

Both Frank and Wolfgang collectively sat back in their chairs and sighed. And then the German count turned to him, stuck out his hand and said, 'It's so good to have you back, Frank.'

Frank took his hand and shook it. And smiled.

It was great to be back.

It was.

That was then.

Now, almost two hours later, they were all back on track. They'd spoken, via a chat room, to Sam and Jane. Both women had minor burns, but were OK. Frank wanted to dwell more on their health, but Sam had dismissed him with a typed *WE'RE FINE*, in a shouty, internet way. At that point he'd let Wolfgang get on with it.

Sam was convinced the attack was designed solely for Konstantos and not for them. As such she felt they still had some latitude in Athens. For now. Wolfgang reminded them that they had new identities to collect tomorrow, and maybe then they should get the hell out of Greece?

The cursor on the chat box had hovered for a few seconds and then Sam continued.

Your brief said Konstantos has a daughter. Lives in Athens.

Father and brother (eldest son) killed in a car accident.

Konstantos has estranged wife.

The screen was rattling away with Sam's comment. Wolfgang wasn't getting a typed word in edgeways.

Daughter in Athens?

We should pay the woman a visit. Tomorrow morning.

Yes, that's the plan.

Then … after a pause.

Check to see if the woman is in.

If clever enough, hack security system.

'Clever enough?' Wolfgang had chuckled under his breath as he had typed a single-word, *OK*, reply.

More instructions followed. Frank imagined Jane sitting in the passenger seat of the Golf twiddling her thumbs.

Sam made it clear that Frank's job was to establish the YCA's purpose. At that point he'd asked Wolfgang to type that he had been working on that in Vauxhall, would look at Wolfgang's output and put together a briefing note as soon as possible.

The cursor hovered.

Good.

And choose our next target. One who is unlikely to die on us, Sam had replied.

And that had been it.

Sam and Jane would pay Selene Konstantos a surprise visit tomorrow morning and then collect their identities.

He and Wolfgang had been given a list of other jobs.

Once the link had closed, Wolfgang told Frank what he knew. The Greek's daughter was unmarried, in her forties, and lived in a pretty swanky apartment in central Athens. In among a ream of hacked information, and with the time available, it was all he had managed to extract.

Sam and Jane needed more.

Frank stood, instinctively reaching for the bandage on his neck.

'Send what you have on the Greek to the board,' Frank said.

Wolfgang did some magic on his keyboard and a couple of folders appeared on the large glass screen. Frank opened them with a dab. There were 300 pages' worth of information. He needed to turn that into usable intelligence.

Which is what he'd started doing, even though he was tired, hungry and in need of a shower.

Selene turned out to be the brains behind the Konstantos empire – her father the ruthless driver. The fact that there was a daughter at all was a surprise. Konstantos was known to favour men. Ten years ago he had been charged with abusing a male prostitute, but the case never made it to court. The view was the victim had settled with a seven-figure sum.

But he *had* married, and they'd had a child before his wife left him.

Every empire needs an heir?

Frank scribbled some notes on the board which were immediately translated into text. Then some more. He worked intently for about thirty minutes. And then stood back, his eyes still fixed on the information he had and the intelligence he was delivering.

His tummy rumbled loudly.

I've got to eat.

He looked across at Wolfgang who was staring at one of his screens with a flat, do-not-disturb hand raised. After a few seconds the hand dropped and he turned to Frank.

'Supper, I think, Frank. Before your stomach eats its lining.'

They'd eaten quickly, chatted about anything other than the current operation, and then got straight back to work. After all, Sam had given them a list.

Frank downloaded his Babylon work onto Wolfgang's system, pinged it to the board and worked away on a document he had entitled, *'YCA – Purpose'*. Behind him, all fingers and thumbs, Wolfgang was hacking away at who knew what.

And Frank's satchel was no longer clinging to him like a limpet. Instead it was in the kitchen-cum-whatever it was, by the chair he'd sat at for dinner. Abandoned.

However, on a spare bit of desktop just behind him was a twin-aspect, solid silver picture frame, about the size of a small child's book. Under one pane of glass was a photo of his mum. Under the second was a picture of Sam Green. The latter had been taken un-posed. A snapshot in his back garden when Sam had stayed with him after Switzerland. When she had been at her most vulnerable. When he had been responsible for her.

When they had been at their closest.

The frame normally sat by his bed, pride of place.

Now, and 1,000 kilometres distant, it was at his workspace.

His new, temporary, home. Two and a half years after the last time he had been here – when they had been taking down the Church of the White Cross, once and for all. And before the attack. And the fire.

He stopped fiddling on the screen and looked around, taking in the large electronics-filled room.

Would this place survive an attack similar to last time?

He had to assume that Wolfgang was as good a bunker architect as he was a hacker. If that were the case, they'd be as safe as houses.

Police Scotland, Tulliallan Castle, Kincardine-on-Forth, Scotland

It was quite a command centre. Lewis was impressed. They'd set up Gold Command, as it was called, in a bespoke room which was separate from the Police Scotland's main operations hub. The room was permanently furnished as an independent Gold Command, with a fully functioning police network, a bank of screens with links into Scotland-wide CCTV, transport-hub passenger databases and, when activated, mobile and BMVs (*body worn videos*) cameras from police on the ground. To the left of the main bank of screens were two more desks; fire and ambulance liaison. And to the right, imported from the SBS's (*Special Boat Service*) headquarters in Poole, a mobile ops team and all their equipment.

The military numbers in the command centre fluctuated, but minimum manning was a Royal Marine's captain and two radio/data, Green Beret operators. The cell had three LED screens, a small bank of computers, and four HCDR (*high capacity data radios*) Bowman sets, the UK military's top-level secure communications. Laid about the desk the Marines also had two landlines, and Lewis counted three mobiles and one satphone – recognisable by its stubby aerial – along with traditional log books and other operational paraphernalia.

DSF (*Director Special Forces*) and COMOPS (*Commander Operations*), the senior naval officer at PJHQ

(*Permanent Joint Headquarters*), had assigned two troops of Special Boat Service's Z Squadron, to the two-week operation. They were on standby, with land, sea and air transport options, at MoD Caledonian, a Royal Navy Reserve base on the north bank of the Forth. In addition, an unknown-nomenclatured Astute-class nuclear-powered submarine was fishing about off the North Sea coast. And three Archer-class coastal vessels were patrolling the estuary. Not to be outdone, the RAF had deployed their latest counter-drone ORCUS technology to roof-top locations throughout the city. This system was brand new – and top secret. As a result he had no idea how many, or where the machines had been deployed. Lewis had seen a short video on the system a couple of months ago. A single unit consisted of three man-sized tripods. One held a swivelling, chunky day/night sight; the second a radar, which not only detected the drones, but also jammed their comms; the third a double-barrelled machine gun. The video showed a drone flying in at around 800 metres from the setup. The day/night sight moved and jerked. The radar spun and spun, and then the machine gun traversed left until it had acquired the target. The rest was history.

And that wasn't the end of the military involvement.

The 2nd Battalion, the Royal Scottish Regiment, had a company of soldiers on thirty minutes' notice move at Glencorse Barracks, in Edinburgh. They had spent the last two weeks training in the counter-riot role. But they could be used for any purposes, the most likely at the moment being to empty the bins near the conference centre, as the local refuge collectors had gone on strike. In addition Balaclava Company, previously the prestigious Argyll and Sutherland Highlanders battalion, was Scotland's ceremonial unit. They had a platoon's worth of soldiers providing some regimental colour at key locations on site. Technically they were on 'public duties', as the army called them. Looking straight and smart. However, few people would appreciate that their SA80 rifles were loaded with live ammunition, often the case when threat levels rose, even at Buckingham Palace.

And, of course, there were a number of SRR (*Special Reconnaissance Regiment*) teams on location – hidden from view – providing eyes on. Exactly where, or how many, was directed by DSF. Lewis wasn't party to that info either. Suffice to say that should HQSF identify a threat, that information would be passed to the Gold Command in an instant. At that point the DCC would make a decision as to which forces to deploy. Lewis's job, as JRLO, was to help interpret his decision back to the military chain of command if any were necessary.

Of course the police had primacy.

And they weren't short of assets. In particular the OSD (*Operational Support Division*) had their hands on their own AFOs (*authorised firearms officers*), marine and air operations, lots and lots of dogs, and 2,500 officers, who had all recently undergone riot control training. Significantly, every police officer was issued with a BMV which was both Wi-Fi'd and Bluetooth'd into the system, so that the Gold Command could single out any camera at any time. It was a helluva setup.

Lewis reckoned they were as ready as they could be.

And the delegates had started to arrive.

The conference centre would be open this morning (it was currently 1.17 am, and didn't Lewis know it), and the major speeches by the greatest and the best would follow tomorrow. POTUS (*President of the US*) was due to speak at 9.15 am. The British PM at 11.45. In between and around

262

them the stage was set for all manner of dignitaries, political and environmental. Lewis hoped that sometime those two would overlap.

A joint operation such as this wasn't uncomplicated. There was a single point of command, the DCC, but the troops to task were wide-ranging, spoke different operational languages, used different operational communications, and followed different SOPs.

But they'd manage. They had before.

And that was the point of this command centre.

However, there were two major outliers.

First was the US's Secret Service, or more colloquially, the President's security detail. There were hundreds of them, and one or two had been in and out of the building in the past couple of days. They had made it clear that they worked alone. Lewis had tried hard to get them to position an LO in the command centre, but that had been curtly declined. As a result, Gold Command had absolutely no idea who and how many there were, where they were positioned, or what they looked like. This wasn't unusual. But it never helped.

Second, the UN had its own police. Multinational, and dressed in dark blue with light blue berets, they would argue that they ultimately held the responsibility for security of the conference site. And, particularly, the safety of the UN Secretary General. They had forty officers in Edinburgh – nowhere near enough. But, unlike the Americans, they were more than happy to accept help. And, unlike the Americans, they had provided an LO to the command centre. She was due to turn up tomorrow lunchtime ... sorry, this lunchtime.

And that was that.

Lewis yawned.

263

He needed to get his head down. He had thought about trudging back to his hotel but decided that he'd take up the DCC's offer of a couch in the headquarters' main staffroom. There was a shower and he had a change of clothes. It would do.

The rest of the day should be straightforward. POTUS was flying into 'Lossie' (*RAF Lossiemouth*) late this evening, and then hopping down by helicopter. And Fordingly was coming up in one of the government's two A321 Airbuses, painted in 'Global Britain' colours, late this afternoon. He was attending a pre-conference shindig at the Edinburgh Grand, after which he was staying in the Duke of Nairnshire's Edinburgh home. Lewis would see that through and, hopefully, get back to his hotel before midnight.

Hopefully.

Chapter 11

Ploutacchou, Kolonaki, Athens, Greece

Sam was surprised by the overcrowding. The street where Selene Konstantos lived was in the very upmarket suburb of Kolonaki. But rather than wide tree-lined boulevards, the roads were narrow, the kerbs packed with cars, and the four- and five-storey buildings ordinary looking, their persistent balconies slim with views of 'over the road' and someone else's washing. It was hardly the accommodation she'd associate with the now CEO of a £21 billion shipping empire. Maybe her mother was the frugal one?

It was 9.35 am and, even as final leaves fell from the few pavement-planted trees, it was already getting hot. Between them, she and Jane hadn't yet got their wardrobe sorted. Jane had left the UK dressed for late autumn; she was in heavy slacks with small turn-ups, a long-sleeved blouse, flatties and too much hair. She was carrying a mid-sized backpack which now held everything they owned. Which wasn't much: some toiletries, two changes of underwear, Jane's coat, Sam's slightly charred hoodie, which had dried overnight in their shabby 'boutique' hotel, a further, Jane-sized change of clothes (winter, of course) and two burner phones.

Sam, who had lost her day sack in a fight with Poseidon, was wearing jeans, an unlogoed t-shirt and a pair of pumps. Her waist-belt pouch, which contained her wallet, five passports and a German ID card, was in the small of her back, covered by her t-shirt. She was in the same clothes she had worn to Konstantos's villa, but without the hoodie. She had rinsed everything through last night to remove the smell of the salt and the seaweed, and it was almost dry when she had put it on this morning.

But it was rubbing. Which wasn't pleasant.

Once they were finished with Konstantos's daughter they'd have to shop. Then they'd go and meet with Wolfgang's Greek forger – something which wasn't without risk. That worried Sam, but they had little choice.

And then they'd get the hell out of Athens.

They were on their feet because they'd ditched the Golf. Yesterday afternoon it had allowed them to escape from the villa, but it was probably compromised. She was convinced the YCA knew they were in Greece. As a result it was only a matter of time before she or Jane made a mistake, or the enemy had a breakthrough.

First thing this morning they'd managed to speak to Wolfgang and Frank, rather than message them. There was an internet café just down from the hotel. Wolfgang had rigged up some secure link which allowed voice comms (apparently, Wolfgang had said, it was all about bandwidth. The more you use, the more conspicuous you are). And, having borrowed a couple of sets of headphones from the guy who owned the café, the four of them had chatted for twenty minutes or so.

They wasted some time checking on everyone's health – which bored Sam, although she tried not to show it. She and Jane both had very minor burns from the boat fire, but the dowsing and sanitising in cold sea water seemed to have saved them from major injury. Frank's neck was, apparently, sore – but he'd live. *Of course you will.* And Wolfgang, who had eventually got over the shock of the villa escapade, was fine. Apparently he had fifty cases of the

Piesporter in the cellar, among many other bottles. If things got really bad, he and Frank would drown their sorrows.

Most of the constructive chat had been about Selene Konstantos. Wolfgang thought she was in residence, although it was difficult to say because there were no internal cameras. He had, however, hacked the entrance lobby CCTV and booked an appointment for the pair of them to see the daughter at 10 am. He had access to the concierge's electronic calendar which recorded visitor traffic.

'That doesn't mean Selene will know you're coming. But the concierge will think it's prearranged. You should be able to get in the front door,' Wolfgang had said.

'Who are we? And why are we visiting?' Sam had asked.

'I made up two English names. Jan Tipner and Sarah Ogilvy. I know you don't have IDs, but I thought it better than using your real names,' Wolfgang had replied.

They'd then spoken about how they'd approach the meet, should Selene be in and let them through her apartment's front door. Frank had added some further useful background on the daughter. And then Wolfgang had given them a time and address to meet the forger.

Frank had wanted to talk about the YCA's purpose, but Sam stopped him and told him to send a document through to the drop box – they had a city to cross. However, before they closed down the conversation he had managed to blurt out that he'd found a tenth – technically now ninth with the death of Konstantos – member of the YCA. Sam had lifted her hands from the keyboard.

'Go on,' she said.

'A Russian. Living in Berlin. His name is Kirill Semenov. I was onto him in London, but without

267

corroboration. Wolfgang's research showed financial linkages. And I then spent an hour last night looking at photos ...'

'And you found a watch?' Sam interrupted him.

'Yes. An **Elias Bosshart, YCA monogrammed watch,**' **Frank had replied.**

Sam heart gave a little flutter. And not a good flutter. The last Russian oligarch she had dealings with was Sokolov. And he was a monster. She wasn't sure how she would cope with another.

'What does he do?' Sam asked, expecting a reply which included a lengthy list of oil assets, mineral mines, shopping complexes and Premier League teams.

'He's a White Russian. A Cossack. I can't find any linkages to industry or companies. But he does own a wealth of real estate, stretching from Moscow through Belarus into Poland. And he has land in the Baltic States. The family goes back generations and has links to the Tsars.'

'And the YCA's CEO, the Duke of Nairnshire, is he a friend?' Sam pressed.

'Sorry. I'm not there yet,' Frank had replied.

'He might be our next stop. We're more appropriately dressed for a continental winter,' Sam had replied, before making a couple of keystrokes and closing down the link.

A White Russian?

And a dead Greek.

What *was* this organisation about?

They needed to find out. Only then might they have some way of exposing it and possibly bringing it down.

She and Jane were a corner short of the street where Selene Konstantos had her apartment. They'd be there in five minutes.

According to Frank, Selene Konstantos was forty-two, divorced, no children. A recent *Time* magazine article said she was one of the most influential women in Southeastern Europe. As the de facto COO – now, highly likely, CEO – of the Konstantos empire, *Time* had reported that she ran the many businesses like clockwork. Whilst she did that, her addled father looked for acquisitions and mergers ... and lived 'the high life'. *Time* hadn't expanded on that phrase, but Frank had found enough other material to confirm that Theodor Konstantos was an alcoholic, drug user and into young men. Sam had sensed all of that yesterday in her short one-to-one with the man before the walls had literally fallen down.

In any case, all the responsibilities had changed since yesterday. There would be a new top dog of the Konstantos empire.

Yesterday.

Whenever that was.

CNN had reported the attack on Konstantos's villa as gangland murders. The Greek news – Sam had managed to pick out the odd word – had little to add, except some discussion about his ongoing trial.

But Konstantos's murder had amended the ground rules, hadn't it? One of the YCA had been assassinated. In his own home. That meant they weren't untouchable. They might be billionaires and belong to an exclusive club that influenced world events, but they weren't out of reach.

In broad daylight, though?

Konstantos hadn't been taken out by a sniper rifle. Or his car discreetly booby-trapped.

A very efficient and deadly gang of thugs, all dressed in black, had routed his home – and set fire to his very smart tender.

269

In the afternoon.

And they had killed everyone there.

Almost everyone.

It was a message.

Sam was sure of it.

It was a message from a group of people who operated with absolute power. Wolfgang had said that the police cars had only arrived on the scene after the truck and three cars had left. There was daylight between the two. No chance of a mix-up. Sure, the traffic was tough on the dual carriageway, but the chances of no overlap seemed slim.

Konstantos had been murdered by his own.

And Sam had no idea why.

But it did change everything ... because that meant there were fissures. The YCA wasn't so tight a circle that you couldn't find a gap.

Maybe Selene was the opening?

Or, unless there was something unconventional about her father's will, Selene Konstantos was now the magnate. As a result, had she inherited her father's watch?

Did the YCA take women members?

Sam thought it unlikely.

...

They were on Selene's street now. Her apartment was halfway down, on the other side of the road. 30 metres away.

Sam glanced behind.

Jane was with her. She grimaced a smile. Sam nodded back.

They had a plan.

Of sorts.

And then Sam spotted something.

Maybe nothing.

The road, a narrow one-way street, was blocked by a couple of cars. There were four vehicles in the queue. Two black: an Audi A6 estate and a BMW X5. And behind them were a yellow Fiat Panda and a red Ford Focus. The black cars were creating the blockage. The two behind, closest to Sam and Jane, making a fuss.

Sam stopped and put her hand out. Jane came to her shoulder. She also stopped.

'Get down.' Sam's voice was quiet. And calm.

They both dropped below the height of the parked cars.

They were maybe seven vehicle lengths from the red Focus. Sam did the maths.

The black cars are outside of Selene's apartment?

It was a guess. A good one.

She needed to get closer.

Crouching, she jogged beside the line of parked cars on her side of the road until she was alongside the Focus. It was a Mark 2. Probably 2006. 1.4. She couldn't stop herself.

She popped her head up.

Both black cars had drivers. Both had their engines running ...

... and she now had the registration of the X5.

Gotcha.

She ducked down.

Three men, all dressed in black, were coming down a set of steps that led up to a double glass doorway. She recognised one immediately.

The thug with the M16.

This time, though, there were no signs of weapons. She glanced up at the apartment block – according to Frank, Selene owned the whole of the top floor.

Nothing.

And then back down to the black cars.

The Fiat Panda hooted its feeble horn.

The men in black ignored it, got into the two cars, and then both vehicles took off.

Sam was on her toes now, trying to get the registration of the Audi. But it was hopeless.

They were gone.

She turned. Jane was with her.

'Was that ...?' Jane didn't finish her sentence.

Sam nodded, turned to face the apartment and then, squeezing between two parked cars, dashed across the road.

She was up the steps two at a time. The double glass doors slid apart and she bounded into the small lobby. It was marble and tile. And cool. A lift, a set of stairs, two side doors that looked as if they opened into apartments – and a concierge's desk.

Jane was already at the desk.

'Sam!' she called.

She was beside Jane in an instant.

The concierge, thankfully, was alive. But he was effectively trussed with grey gaffer tape. Legs, arms and mouth.

'Help him get free. But don't let him call the police. I'll be as quick as I can,' Sam snapped.

'Where are you ...?' It was another unfinished sentence from Jane.

Sam didn't know why, but she took the stairs. It was something about the uncertainty of a lift. And the wait, whilst it did its thing at its own pace. And the music.

Stairs were better.

She took the steps – two at a time.

Fifth floor.

One set, two ... five.

Here.

She opened the door. It led into a small, elegantly decorated atrium with an antique side table on top of which was a vase. There were three doors: the one that led to the stairs, the lift's, and a heavy wooden one, directly in front of her.

It was slightly ajar.

Sam picked up the vase – she was getting used to this – and tentatively pushed at the door with her elbow. It moved soundlessly.

She pushed it some more.

And then she put her head around its edge and peered in.

A lobby. Four more doors. More money in the pictures and ornaments in this small room than in a high street bank.

There was smart wallpaper, another antique table with another vase, marble flooring, a rug which looked as if it might have been bought in Persia 300 years ago, and paintings. Lots of them. Too many for Sam to catalogue, although she really liked the oil of the Corinth Canal. It had been painted from one end of the waterway, with a steamer emerging from the canal's tall, straight limestone walls.

'It's by a lesser known Greek artist from between the wars. It's one of my favourites, too.'

Selene Konstantos was standing by the furthest door. She was tall, taller than Sam. A long face, with shoulder-length dark hair and equally dark eyebrows. She was slender, but curvy – a Marilyn Monroe body. And she wore pale green slacks which finished above the ankles, and a white, open neck blouse, which showed off the biggest emerald Sam had ever seen. And a simple black ribbon, tied in a knot, hanging from her wrist.

273

'You can put down the vase. I am not armed.'

Sam looked at her weapon, lifted it so she could see the base. There was a Japanese character which she couldn't decipher.

'It's Satsuma. It's not that valuable.' Selene continued in her unnervingly casual manner. 'We've had things stolen from the elevator lobby before, so I don't tend to put the family's best out there. That one ...' There was only one other vase, and it was on the walnut veneered, half-moon table beside where Sam was standing, '... now that *is* valuable. So please be careful when you put the lobby-bling down.'

Sam placed the vase next to its much more expensive cousin and, now a little unsure as to where to put her hands, let her arms hang down straight. She wasn't comfortable. There was something unnerving, something disarming about Selene Konstantos's confidence, which made Sam feel quite small. As though she was being told off by the headmistress.

That was a new feeling for her.

'Which one are you? Tipner or Ogilvy?' Selene Konstantos continued. 'Your names magically appeared on my schedule this morning. I've no idea how, or why?' The woman's English was excellent, her accent only spoiled by her 's's', which were more rounded than you'd find in Surrey.

'Jan Tipner.' It was the first words Sam had spoken.

'What do you want?' It seemed unlikely that Selene Konstantos was going to ask Sam in for a cup of coffee. But she hadn't yet ordered her out of the apartment. There was still a chance.

'I was with your father yesterday.' That was the opening line they had all agreed.

274

Silence.

Then Selene Konstantos mouthed an 'Oh', followed by, 'Come in. Please'. And then she opened the door and motioned for Sam to follow her.

Jane was getting impatient. The concierge, who was well into his sixties and liked his beer, was fidgety. He was clear that Jane was no threat, unlike the three men who had assaulted him, but she wasn't allowing him to do his job.

'Please stay calm,' Jane said. She had motioning 'down' with both hands. 'Please.'

She didn't speak a word of Greek and the man, she guessed, little English.

'My friend will be here in a second and then you can call the police.'

The word 'police' was something he recognised. He immediately reached for the landline.

Jane was ahead of him and pulled the phone to one side, out of his reach. The concierge spluttered, his face red and his eyes bulging more than they should. But he didn't make any more of a fuss. Instead, he sat insolently on his stool, reached for a bag and pulled out a sandwich.

He chewed away, at one point offering Jane a bite.

She declined.

Outside the block life went on as usual. Cars and vans tracked down the narrow road, left to right. A few, but not many, pedestrians walked by on both sides of the road. After ten minutes a police car drove slowly past, but it didn't have its lights flashing and there was no recognition that they'd just missed the assault of an elderly man at a front desk – and who knew what else on the fifth floor.

A few minutes more passed …

... and then Jane was beginning to worry.

The most likely outcome was that Sam had found Selene Konstantos in a pool of her own blood, and she was currently searching the flat for clues. If that were the case, Jane really wished she'd blooming well hurry up.

Twenty minutes now.

Come on, Sam.

What if someone came in? She'd have to let the concierge do his thing. But she'd have no idea what they'd be talking about and all manner of messages could get passed. The visitor could then call the police.

It would be two versus one.

So ... if that happened, she'd be straight upstairs and get Sam out of the building. Wolfgang had identified a couple of back exits. They both knew where they were.

There was a *clump* from behind her.

The stairs door was open and Sam came out just as the front desk's phone rang.

'Let Phoenix answer the phone. Selene will put him straight. We're out of here.' Sam walked briskly past Jane, stopping only to let the glass doors open.

Phoenix?

Jane shot a short wave at 'Phoenix' as she chased after Sam, who was already down the steps.

'Sam, Sam ...' She was bored with playing catch up today.

'Yes?' Sam barked over her shoulder.

They were walking fast in the direction of traffic.

'Stop and tell me what happened!' Jane knew she sounded desperate, but that was how she felt. She couldn't go on like this – playing second fiddle.

Sam stopped abruptly. And turned. Jane almost bumped into her.

276

Sam forced a smile. But it was brief.

'She doesn't know anything. Not really. The thugs this morning were a warning, nothing more. But she's not fazed. She's a strong, contained woman. It's about the court case. Apparently her father phoned her yesterday morning to say that his lawyer had arranged a plea bargain. He knew some damning stuff about people – international people. And if he sold them out, the case would be dropped.' Sam then figuratively cut her neck with a flick of her hand.

'The YCA?' Jane asked.

'She doesn't know. She really has no idea. And I believe her. She told me her father belonged to a "club".' Sam used her fingers for quotation marks. 'She knows everything about the business, but not everything about her father. He used to disappear. Sometimes for days on end. She gave me some dates. And ...' Sam was looking around. 'Let's talk as we walk?'

'Why?' Jane was still sounding exasperated.

Sam was already off. Jane jogged to catch up.

'Because Selene was given strict instructions by her visitors that she was to tell them of anything unusual. Particularly if she was visited by someone who matched my description.'

'They know?' Jane asked incredulously.

'Maybe only from yesterday. Or maybe they've caught up with us from one of the border crossings,' Sam replied as she strode.

'And is she going to tell them?'

'Yes. In half an hour. She has no choice. She knows that these people are ruthless. She can't fight them.'

'Oh.'

How far can we get in half an hour?

Jane now didn't think they were moving quickly enough.

The lounge was comfy. There was a vending machine which dispensed free coffee, and a woman in an RAF uniform had recently brought in a tray of biscuits which she'd left on a table. Dominic had arrived an hour and a half early for the flight. For the most part he'd been scrolling through his phone and watching the news, which was being relayed to the lounge's four occupants via a TV hanging in the corner. But time was marching on. The flight to Edinburgh was due to take off in forty minutes.

It was all going to be a bit of an adventure.

He could see the runway from where he was sitting. He was surprised at the number of small private jets taking off and landing at the airfield. It was pretty busy. A poster on the wall told the story: Northolt was as much a government-run private airfield, raking in the cash (it didn't actually say that), as it was a secure hub for various official organisations. The Queen's Colour Squadron, the central band of the RAF, various reserve forces, the military's post office, and the London Air Ambulance were the main ones. However, in addition to its more formal business, the runway accepted 12,000 private flights a year.

Why not? It was as close to London as Heathrow and, as a rich dignitary, why would you want to mix with the plebs when Northolt was close by?

It also appeared to be the preferred base for a pretty big, red, white and blue-liveried passenger plane which was on the apron nearby. He'd checked his boarding pass and

278

then looked at the plane. The big Union Jack with wings was his ride.

How many of them were travelling? Did they really need a jet that big to go to a climate conference?

Who knew? And who was he to judge?

It didn't matter. He was accompanying the UK's prime minister to a meeting. And they weren't flying with a load of tourists. After only a week on the job, that was something else.

The news on the TV was the same dull stuff. There was a section about the current Brazilian leader. He was due to turn up at the conference tomorrow, but only to stay for a day as there was a snap general election scheduled for the following weekend. Like Prime Minister Fordingly, the Brazilian guy fell into the 'popularist' column – although that wasn't a term Dominic approved of. He much preferred 'libertarian', which was the way his boss was often described: small government with minimal intervention in both the markets and people's lives.

Folk needed to look after themselves, didn't they? Dominic had shown that was possible. All that was required was some brains, hard work and tenacity.

Dominic had to agree, however, that the Brazilian chap was a bit extreme. He had clearly allowed business to run unchecked over the Amazon rainforest with scant regard to the indigenous population, or the planet. But, on the other hand, places like Brazil were poor. And why wouldn't any country's leader want what was best for their people? And if that meant raising money by doing what first-world countries had done for almost two centuries, who could blame them?

The news was now showing the Brazilian opposition leader. The caption underneath read, 'Sanchez faces multiple death threats in the run-up to Saturday's election'.

Banana republic.

And then the news moved on.

He checked his watch. Half an hour to lift off.

He looked around.

I wonder where the boss is?

Then he knew.

The double swing doors burst open and a troupe of dark-suited and grey-skirted staff and advisors surged into the room. In the middle of the melee was the boss. He looked a little hassled. His communications director (Dominic recognised the woman, which pleased him) was at his side, iPad open, pointing at something. In the crowd Dominic recognised at least one minister, one of prime minister's SPADs (*special advisors*) and a couple of other staff he'd bumped into in Downing Street the day before yesterday.

The team fanned out around the room, all of them ignoring Dominic. The boss took a seat a couple of rows away. A small multitude sat around him. One young girl – she was probably an intern – had already visited the vending machine and was ferrying a hot drink to a small table in front of the prime minister.

And then the most extraordinary thing happened.

The prime minister spotted Dominic and pointed at him as he rose to his feet.

The small lounge was full of people now, save some seats which had been left empty around Dominic. He clearly had no friends.

Except ...

... the prime minister wasn't having any of it.

The boss stepped around the table with the coffee on and navigated the rows of chairs until he was in Dominic's personal space. By then Dominic was on his feet, bolt upright.

The prime minister thrust out his hand. Dominic took it – the boss's grip was, as always, tight and strong.

'Hi, Dom. So glad you could make it. Hey? How are you?' The prime minister did that thing again where he dropped his shoulders briefly and looked up at you.

'Fine, sir. Thank you. I'm so glad you asked for me. I'm really looking forward to it. I hope I don't let you down.' Dominic regretted the final sentence as soon as he said it.

'Of course not,' the prime minister snapped back dismissively. 'You'll be fine.' And then he leant forward as if he were going to give Dominic a hug. But he didn't. He just whispered to him.

'I have a job for you later. Stay close. Hey?'

The prime minister then stepped back, released Dominic's hand and stuck up both thumbs.

He mouthed, 'Mum's the word?' followed by a big smile.

Dominic nodded. And smiled back.

What was that about?

He'd have to wait and see. The boss had turned and was heading back to his entourage.

Flemingstraße, Munich, Germany

Frank had slid his chair back to his own station. He'd been sitting beside Wolfgang after they'd taken the most recent call from Sam and Jane. The news was rather good all round.

281

Sam and Jane had made it out of Greece. They'd taken a coach to Bitola in North Macedonia, alighted, found an internet café and made the call. Between them they were getting slick at this.

'Your man in Athens was as good as his word,' Sam had said. 'We have new IDs and a bank card which, the Greek told me, you have guaranteed with indefinite credit. Jane and I are thinking about an all-inclusive world cruise, if that's OK?'

At least she has retained her humour.

'That's fine by me, Sam. Though I think you might get bored,' Wolfgang had replied.

Wolfgang let Sam continue.

'We're going to hole up here for the night whilst we look through all of your latest drops. Do we have enough on the White Russian to get a foot in the door?' Sam asked.

Wolfgang had looked at Frank at that point.

'Wolfgang will have to give you chapter and verse on his location and what CCTV opportunities we have, but I'm some way from building a decent file on him,' Frank had replied. 'Wolfgang's work is excellent, but it's broad. And I don't have Cynthia, Babylon's mainframe, to act as a coarse filter. But, if I focus on him overnight, I reckon I should have a couple of pages for you tomorrow.' Frank had finished with, 'If that's to be my priority.'

Wolfgang chirped up.

'He has numerous residences. There's a dacha in St Petersburg, a castle in Lithuanian, a number of minor houses in Poland and Belarus and a pretty swish penthouse in Berlin. Which is where we believe he is. He's on the jury at "Berlinale", the Berlin international film festival, which is on this week. I have a script running on one of my mainframes just now. That should let me know if I can access the man's penthouse in the next hour or so. I'm feeling pretty positive.'

'What about his itinerary? During the film festival, is he out in the open enough for me to proposition him?' Sam butted in.

'I'm on that too,' Wolfgang replied. 'But you'll need to be careful, whatever you do. Every photo of him, apart from those which are posed for magazine articles, show him surrounded by minders. And if you're already on their radar ...'

'Fine.' Sam's response had been dismissive. 'If we can't find an opening, then I have two new offers. First, Selene Konstantos made it clear that she didn't always know where her father was. He'd leave the country without letting her know. These were often random trips. Except ...' Sam paused briefly, '... he was always away just before Christmas. Every second year. For as long as she could remember. Mid-December. For a week. She had pressed him on it a couple of years ago and he had bitten back. That it was absolutely none of her business, and that she should leave well alone.' Sam paused again. 'I think we should follow up on that lead. Can you do that?'

Frank had looked at Wolfgang. They had both nodded. Frank replied, 'Sure,' on behalf of both of them.

'And, second, and probably more important,' Sam continued. 'Being a member of the YCA doesn't come with a bulletproof vest. We know that because Konstantos crossed a line. He was about to do a deal with the Greek prosecutor where he would give, and I quote Selene pretty much verbatim, "some damning stuff about international people".'

'The YCA?' Frank pressed.

There was a beat. Frank didn't know if Sam thought his question stupid, or she was forming a reply which answered his question more accurately.

'I'd say 75%. Which, as you know, is good enough for us to turn information into intelligence. But that's not my point.' Sam paused again, as though she was waiting for someone to fill the gap.

Frank obliged.

'Dead people. Better still, the relatives and dependants of dead people.'

Wolfgang shot him a curious glance.

Frank elucidated.

'I think Sam's point is that we will always struggle to get audiences with members of the YCA, even though we know who they are and where they might be. And anyone who tries will be putting themselves in danger. But ... Sam's intervention with Selene Konstantos has proven that those close to deceased YCA members – murdered, possibly because they were likely to break, or had broken, some sort of code – those relatives might have an axe to grind. And they will almost certainly be easier to access?'

'Exactly,' Sam confirmed Frank's presumption. 'So let's see if we can find at least one more dead, preferably murdered, YCA billionaire. And then build a family tree. It's got to be our best approach, don't you think?'

'Sounds good to me,' Wolfgang had replied.

And then there was a different voice from Bitola. It was Jane's.

'Where are we with the YCA's purpose?' she asked.

The question didn't surprise Frank. Sam had pretty much always been tactical, or operational. She saw the bigger picture, sure. But she uncovered intelligence by prospecting for it – a physical approach to fieldwork.

Jane, on the other hand, was a strategist. She used a bigger canvas. She let the intelligence do the work, rather than fight for it. She stepped back and looked at the forest whilst Sam was felling the trees.

In that respect they were a good team. Even though Frank sensed that Sam would be frustrated at having help, especially if Jane were still dithering, like she had in Rotterdam.

'I've still only got conjecture. That's all,' Frank had said. 'I'll drop a link to the paper I'm writing. So far I cannot find a manifesto. Why would there be? But what I have done is drag out the themes which are familiar between the ten, now nine members.'

'And what are the themes?' Jane asked.

Frank leant to his side and turned his right-hand monitor so it was facing him. His purpose document was up on the screen.

'In no order,' he started. 'Right wing, bordering on fascist. This leads to the obvious strap lines of: small government, low taxes and personal responsibility.' He paused. 'Massive wealth. All of them run their businesses through offshore accounts.' A beat followed, then, 'Power. Four already have biographies. Two others have long articles written about them. All of the writers make the point about power. There is charm, but there is also control. There are, that is were, thirty-six separate lawsuits against them as individuals. Most are for bullying, sexual assault, harassment, etc. None of those cases have made it to court. And, notably, there is no encompassing religious affiliation. Four Protestants, two Catholics, two Muslims and one abstention.' He paused again. 'That's all I have.'

There was silence.

Frank's stomach rumbled. He and Wolfgang hadn't stopped. He looked down at the digital clock on his screen. It was 17.40. They needed to eat.

Then ... 'So no unifying purpose, other than greed?' Sam chirped up.

It clearly wasn't good enough for her.

'No. Not yet,' Frank replied.

'Not good enough. There is something.' Sam was adamant. 'Something that brought this group together – who knows when – and keeps it together now. Narcissists are solitary figures. They don't work in packs. They attack others, buy them out, sink them somehow. There *has* to be some central tenet which pulls this lot together. And from which Konstantos was ejected. It's a shame it's not religion. Some sort of grand wizard, or wizards, affair. That would do.'

'I think Sam's right,' Jane added. 'Otherwise it just doesn't hang together.'

Frank clearly had to work harder. But he knew that.

They closed the call then and agreed to talk again tomorrow morning.

That was at least two mealtimes and a short nap away. Frank could manage that.

'What's on the menu?' Frank asked Wolfgang. He thought 'eat now, work later' was a sensible call.

The German pushed back in his chair, turned and smiled at Frank.

'I don't know!' he exclaimed, putting both hands up. 'Matilda is my first attempt at AI. So this morning I asked her to prepare something vegetarian for you, Frank. It'll be ready by six. She's particularly good,' he added.

Frank nodded at Wolfgang just as the German's machine made the noise of an incoming call. Wolfgang turned back to his screen.

'It's David,' he said, with caution.

Frank was across at Wolfgang's side in no time. The German opened the call.

'Wolfgang?' David's bite could be heard across the airways.

'Yes, David?' Wolfgang replied.

'Why haven't you called me? I can't get hold of Sam. I have no idea where Jane and Frank are. Put my mind at rest. Please.' David was struggling to hide his frustration. 'And I have some information,' he added in a more conciliatory tone.

Frank quickly put out a hand and mouthed, 'Mute', to stop Wolfgang from replying.

The German shook his head. 'I get it,' he replied quietly to Frank, before continuing his conversation.

'All's well, David. With all of us. I can't say any more than that, you understand?'

'What? Just in case the line isn't secure? You assured me it was.' David initially sounded affronted, but he then seemed to realise what the issue was. 'No. Of course. You don't know who's in the room with me. Whether I'm talking to you under duress. Sorry, too much time tending my roses. OK, I get it.'

Frank relaxed. Wolfgang was ahead of him.

'What do you have, David?' Wolfgang asked.

It took Frank's old senior manager fifteen minutes to update them.

There was nothing helpful from his American contact.

'He's a staunch Republican. They're onto the YCA. But I sensed that, in many ways, their philosophies, if you could call them that, coincide. The power of money. Freedom of the individual. The Second Amendment ... all that sort of nonsense. And they still have at least one Forever War to deal with in Iraq. Plus the inconvenience of white supremacy delivering home-grown terrorism, which is providing them with some irony issues. I think, therefore, we can draw a line under that avenue, certainly from my perspective.'

That had all made sense to Frank.

David continued.

'The French, though, they're more concerned about the YCA's influence on the Republic. They're clear that Louis Belmonte, the leader of the charge against the billionaire sect, was murdered. But there is factional fighting within DGSI as to how to proceed. Bizarrely, Belmonte's wine-growing billionaire brother and YCA member, Marc, has secured himself an advisory position on the reforming programme of the French security services. The committee is made up of government ministers, senior officers from the *Gendarmerie Nationale, Armée de Terre*, DGSI and DGSE, the equivalents of MI5 and SIS, and a handful of select civilians. Belmonte is one of those.' David hadn't drawn breath.

He continued.

'My contact in DGSI senses that Belmonte, plus a handful of officers on the YCA's payroll, may be looking at a power grab. The issue the YCA have in France is that, unlike the UK and the US where the media influences politics – rather than reporting on it – they are not able to pull strings at the highest level in the Republic. In the UK we recognise that Fordingly is a Michael Connock, the Australian media baron's stooge. In France, the president is much more independent. So the YCA is looking for an opportunity to work *within* the French security network, not to direct it. Apparently they already have some influence, hence the death of Louis, but not enough.

'The problem is ...' David paused for a beat, '... this is taking the French intelligence service's eye off the ball. The YCA, with its wider-than-the-Republic's reach, isn't considered as important as, say, the French's military effort in Burkina Faso, Chad and Niger, as well as overseas intelligence operations in, along with others, Algeria. And not forgetting domestic terrorism, which continues to haunt the DGSI.'

David paused again. There was a lot there. Frank didn't quite know what to say, and as he had vowed to be schtum on this call, he let Wolfgang break the silence.

'So, what they're saying is they know it's a problem, but it's not as big as other problems they have. As a result, they're leaving it in the pending tray.'

There was a further pause.

'The impression I got was that they'd like to get a grip of the issue, especially their clear understanding that some intelligence officers are on the YCA's payroll, but they haven't got the resources to police themselves. In short, because the YCA is international, they're hoping someone else will pop the balloon for them.'

Which was depressing.

'Thanks, David,' Wolfgang said. 'I'll make sure that is passed around the team. Are you safe?'

There was more silence.

'I think so,' David eventually added. 'We have relatives in Wales. We're going away for a while – tomorrow. I'll keep in touch, but I think that's all you're going to get from me at the moment. I'm sure "my visitors" will understand when you next speak to them.'

Wolfgang looked at Frank. Who nodded in return.

'Thanks, David. And safe travels.' And with that, Wolfgang hung up.

Chapter 12

The trip was going to take an hour. When Heather had driven her hire car onto the belly of the red and white liveried Pentland Ferry, she felt as though she was leaving one world and heading off to another. Orkney wasn't Scotland – was it? It was more a mystical place of stone circles, ritualistic behaviour … and secrets. It was more Celtic, more extreme, and even more wild than the deserted moorlands of the mainland's far north.

It was a step closer to nowhere.

Sure, it wasn't Shetland, which was another level of weirdness. At least you could see the Orkney Islands from the north coast – on a bright day. Shetland, on the other hand, was halfway to Norway. She'd looked at photos and could see more sheep than people. More sea than land.

She sensed the supernatural, which was unlike her. Something altogether new. Out of the ordinary.

She'd never been to Orkney … or Shetland.

Have I?

There was an uncomfortable familiarity about the slapping of the waves on the hull of the boat. Her shoulders rocked very slowly with the yaw. It was all so distant, so strange.

But, at the same time, there was a nudge of recognition.

Had she done this journey before?

She was standing on one of the ferry's side decks. On her left was the sea; her right a drop into an open-topped vehicle platform. There were two campers. Numerous cars. An articulated lorry. And a panel van. A Ford something-or-other. It looked old and battered. It was an off-white, its edges attacked by rust. Could there be a young woman – or man – held captive in there, their feet and hands tied, a gag in their mouth, and their brain awash with chloroform?

How long had her journey taken all those years ago? Was it longer than an hour? Was it *much* longer than an hour? Hadn't she tried to make some noise on the journey back? If someone was in the white and rust van, and they were making a noise – banging, maybe – wouldn't she be able to hear them now?

She listened.

There was a car alarm bleating away. And the wind. And the heavy *thud, thud, thud* of the ferry's diesel engines.

But no banging. No knocking from a young person being taken to a distant cellar to be repeatedly abused.

And never seen again?

Heather had got to the end of Peter Lynch's book. She had filled her notebook. Completed her table. Finished the map, although she had had to redo it as it had got very scruffy, very quickly.

Peter Lynch had listed seventeen unsolved abductions – or unsolved missing persons – stretching back to the early 80s. Fourteen young women and three men.

Fifteen young women, if you included her. Eighteen overall.

The writer had told their stories. In nearly all of the cases the people, sometimes two in the same year, had just disappeared. They had gone out and never returned. If you included Heather, only four were available to tell their tale. They had reported being kidnapped and then raped, two of them repeatedly, and one of those was a man. The rest had no reason to leave home, or give up their studies. They had just disappeared.

Three were the foreigners Peter Lynch had investigated, from Holland and France. They'd left for home, but never arrived. The rest, they were either locals or students/seasonal workers.

Eighteen unsolved cases.

If you include me.

Peter Lynch's book read well. And it expertly told the stories of the young people on the north coast of Scotland who had disappeared in mysterious circumstances. He wrote with jeopardy and atmosphere. The book showed off his skills as a writer.

But he had failed to find the glue which held these poor souls together. Maybe he'd got so caught up in the emotion of it all that he'd forgotten his journalistic credentials? Maybe he had been writing about *their* stories, not *the* story.

Because Heather thought she was ahead of him. She had insight where he hadn't. She was one of the victims and had the whole disgraceful episode in her head. It didn't need to be interpreted by the writer.

As a result she had done something with the evidence which Peter Lynch had failed to do. And, on the face of it, his failure seemed like a rookie mistake.

Heather's table had ended up on three sheets of notebook; landscape. This morning, over a cup of coffee as she was trying to work out what to do next, she had laid them out on the Formica table, side by side.

She had sipped her *latte*.

293

And looked.

And sipped some more.

And there it was.

A pattern.

Wasn't it?

She had counted with her fingers.

Eighteen disappearances.

Fifteen of them in the month of December, two of which were a pair.

Fifteen abductions in the same month. Starting in 1981; only three assaults occurred in non-December months.

That isn't a coincidence?

She'd sipped some more.

That wasn't all.

There were gaps. Some Decembers had no assaults. No abductions. She counted again.

The first recorded was 1981. Then 1985, 1987, 1989, 1991, 1995 and 2003. Then 2007, 2009, 2013 and 2017. Finally, 2019.

And 1999 ... *that one is me.*

She ran along the line, the names and numbers a struggle to keep balanced in her mind.

And then she had it.

Every second December.

People go missing, sometimes in pairs, in December.

But only in the odd years.

According to Peter Lynch the last disappearances were in 2019: one of the Dutch girls, and a guy on a singleton holiday, trekking across the moors.

There were gaps. She was able to fill one of the gaps where Peter Lynch had a hole. *How could he have known*? There could well be more like her.

But, with what she had, if you focused solely on December – the odd years – there was a pattern.

Wasn't there?

Heather had pushed back in her chair at that point.

Where are we now?

Just turned December.

In an odd year.

Heather couldn't cope with the revelation. She scooped up all her work, thrust it into her handbag, grabbed her small wheelie suitcase, and ran out into the street for some fresh air.

It was too much to contemplate.

She had to keep moving. She had to do something.

And that something was, it turned out, a ferry journey across to Orkney.

Why?

Why not?

She had nothing else to go on. She sensed her own abduction had included a trip on water. And the only other account where the sea was part of the story was Steph Landown's.

2009.

A body washed up on the beach on the Orkney island of Sanday.

That's where Heather was heading.

Because?

Her phone rang before she had chance to rehearse that argument.

It was Fi. Heather connected immediately.

'Hi, love. Are you OK?'

'Sure, Mum. You? Where are you? I'm worried.' There were no gaps between Fi's sentences.

Heather was looking out across the grey and blue dank sea to the grey and green dank island which was being oppressed by a heavy, grey dank sky. It had started to rain. The sort of rain which fools you. More mist than rain, but easily wet enough to soak. She reached behind her to pull out the hood on her jacket.

'I'm fine, love. I really am.' It was all she could find. 'Tell me about your day,' she deflected.

'Where are you, Mum?' Fi pressed. 'Are you out walking?'

Heather smiled to herself.

Out walking? Not really.

'I'm on a ferry, love. To the Orkney Islands.'

'What?! That's in Scotland, isn't it?' Fi's voice had raised a pitch.

'It is, love. It is. It's a long story. Everything's fine. I should be back at the weekend and I'll tell you all about it then. Now, what's going on with you?'

Hotel Titar, 35 Stiv Naomov, Bitola, North Macedonia

It was just gone ten. She and Sam had eaten in a tiny but clean pizzeria, and then made their way back to the £35 a night, small but very workable hotel-cum-hostel. They were sharing a twin-bedded room, which had a shower across the corridor. The beds were comfortable and the sheets clean. There wasn't much more they could ask for.

Conversation at supper had been muted. Sam was never a great talker; she only spoke when there was something to say. Jane had pushed a couple of questions at her because she wasn't a woman who liked to live in silence. And she had many things on her mind from which she needed distraction.

'Are you happy with Wolfgang's man in Athens?' she'd asked.

Sam had finished chewing on a slice of pizza. Her plate had arrived and the chef had cut the segments in a way so that they weren't even. It had taken Sam five minutes to re-slice the pizza so that each slice looked the same. At that point she'd grimaced at Jane and then only eaten three of the now many segments. The rest was going cold as she sipped at her beer.

'Yeah, sort of,' Sam had replied absently.

And then she'd looked straight at Jane.

'We have to assume the man is compromised, or will be compromised at some point. We should use the new IDs at borders only. I know we have Wolfgang's new wonder-card with unlimited credit, but I'll continue to use the German card and account he gave me. Or I'll mix it up. We have to sow as much confusion as possible.'

That had made sense.

'And tomorrow?' Jane has asked.

'Train to Berlin. Hopefully Frank and Wolfgang will have more details on the Russian and we can think of a suitable mining expedition. Maybe I'll just go up to him and ask him a question about the YCA. Straight out?'

Sam wasn't asking Jane for her opinion; Jane knew her well enough. It was more a question to herself. Jane would offer something tomorrow, once they had the new intelligence.

Jane had finished her own meal and drained the wine from her glass.

'Do you want to talk any more about the Konstantos's villa?' Jane tentatively asked. She had both hands on the table. If Sam's hadn't been by her side, she would have reached for them.

'No.' Sam's response was immediate.

Which was a huge shame. Because Jane *desperately* wanted to talk about it.

And she'd wanted to talk about it as they walked back to their hotel. As they showered and undressed. And particularly now, as she lay curled up in her bed, her knees held tightly to her chest and tears running down her cheeks.

She knew she had messed up in Rotterdam. That her inaction had given the policeman time to get a couple of rounds off, one of which had found Frank's neck. And she knew that her phone call to Sam in the villa grounds had alerted the man with the military rifle and, as a result, he had found Sam, which had almost got her killed.

And Jane knew that just before then, for a split moment, she had been close to giving up ...

... everything.

But since then she thought she had been on point. She had ripped Sam from the deck of the burning boat and then helped drag her to safety. She had followed Sam's orders ... to the letter. She had prevented the concierge from calling the police. And she had helped Sam with the document exchange.

Since then Jane had felt much better. Much more on form. Much more of a help than a distraction.

That's what she thought.

And Sam's responses had become less dismissive. She had used the 'we' word more. And 'us'. In the last twenty-four hours Jane felt they had become more of a team. That Sam had started to trust her again.

Which was good.

But that wasn't why she wanted to talk about the villa.

It wasn't why she was currently curled in the foetal position, her head lying on a wet pillow.

It was because she had killed a man.

Jane had never done that before. She had been in firefights in Iraq and, recently, in the Hanoi embassy and outside Sarajevo.

And she had seen plenty of death.

But not by her own hand.

Not with a pistol as she had run headfirst to the man from the boat, her arm outstretched, the weapon thrusting at the man's torso.

Bang, bang.

They were small noises in her head just now. They had been small noises then, the exploding cordite in the pistol's chamber no match for the banshees running riot in her brain as she had driven relentlessly forward.

The man had fallen. He was probably dead before he'd hit the floor.

But that hadn't stopped her from firing two more rounds into his chest as she turned to launch herself up the gangplank to lift her friend to safety.

Two more rounds.

Had that really been necessary?

More important … had she really meant to feel so good about it?

That was the cause of the pain; the point of the tears.

Not that she had killed a man.

No.

But, that some demon had taken over her soul, fired the shots, killed the man, and then double-tapped him just to be sure.

And enjoyed it.

Jane Baker.

Murderer without remorse.

Sam was tired. She thought that maybe she hadn't fully recovered from the cold dip in the sea, from the exertions of the swim in wet, heavy clothing, and then helping Jane to the bank. They'd had some sleep, but it had been fitful and interrupted by a multitude of plans and ideas. She was always thinking. Always noticing. And always remembering. The passport exchange this afternoon. The Athens man's features as he handed over the IDs. His face. His workshop. The registrations of the cars in the street. Everything. It was like her visit to Selene Konstantos. If you created the same sized space, and had a heap-load of cash, Sam could have refurnished an empty room to make it look *exactly* like Selene's sitting room. Vases, pictures, photos, rugs, lamps, the location of the light switches – everything. It was all uselessly stored in her head. And, when she wasn't concentrating, random bits of it came back to visit.

Just now she was recalling the roof of the satellite complex in Venezuela. Just before the Americans came. Before the cannon fire.

She knew so much – it hurt.

But it probably wasn't that which was making her feel so dog tired. Doubtless a sizable chunk of it was her body's reaction to shock. It happened. You can't survive a firefight, get clubbed on the head, break out of a burning boat, drown and then come to life again, without your body struggling with the enormity of it all. Shock was dangerous. She knew that.

So was a club to the back of the head.

There was a bruise the size of a plum just above her hairline. It was too painful to touch. There was likely some internal bleeding. She should probably rest.

Which she was trying to do.

But the pathetic bleating coming from Jane's bed was an earworm. It was cutting through her usual nonsense – stuff she could normally cope with. And it was wearing her down.

Sam knew why Jane was crying. And it wasn't to do with the stress of recent events. Sam knew Jane well. Very well. She also understood what she had been through. Sam had undergone the same case office training which Jane had. Sam had served in the field with SIS in Russia. She understood Jane's experiences. Some of them they had gone through together.

Like Jane, Sam had even tried to kill herself.

A bottle of vodka and more paracetamol than you need to put down a horse.

She knew what it was all like.

She understood.

She did.

It had never made Sam weep, though.

It had just strengthened her resolve.

But there was *something* which had constantly plagued her. Brought her close to tears. Which had, at times, subsumed her – in a more damaging way than the cool waters of the Aegean Sea.

And Jane was suffering with that now.

Sam should do something. If nothing else it might stop Jane from bleating and allow them both to find some precious sleep.

She snorted. And then turned so she was facing Jane, her bed arm's length from her friend's, Jane's back to hers.

She reached out and put her hand on Jane's bare shoulder. Just gently. She didn't stroke her, nor offer words of comfort. She just touched her. Sam didn't feel comfortable with it. It wasn't her way. But it was the right thing.

There.

It was the best she could do.

Jane didn't move. She just sniffed, her shoulders part of that action.

'Will I ever get over it?' Jane asked between sniffs.

'No,' Sam replied quietly.

There was silence for a good while. Jane was still on her side. Sam's outstretched arm was not in the most comfortable of positions. She needed to get on with this.

'You saved my life, Jane. If you hadn't killed the man, he would have taken both of us. I wasn't conscious, but the distance you must have covered in the open to get close enough to shoot accurately was a helluva thing. A brave thing.' Sam tried to sound compassionate. She wasn't really pulling it off.

Jane sniffed again.

'It was instinctive.' Jane's reply was almost lost in her pillow. 'I created the mess by calling your phone.' *Sniff.* 'There was no other option.' Jane lifted her head and turned her shoulders so she was facing her friend. Sam pulled her arm back and rested it by her side, her head lying on her other elbow.

They stared at each other. It was dark, but not so much that Sam couldn't make out Jane's face. It was a splodge of skin and tears.

'I shot him twice,' Jane offered.

'That's good, Jane. A double-tap. You know that.'

Two shots in rapid succession was industry standard for taking out the opposition with a pistol. A low-velocity, 9mm round was as lethal as a spud-gun, unless it ripped through your heart, cut a major artery or smashed through your skull. Two shots. Twice the effect and twice the chance of hitting the target.

'No. I don't mean that. That is, I did double-tap.' A beat. 'And then I shot him again. When he was on the ground. Twice,' Jane said quietly.

I'd have saved ammunition, myself.

But Sam could understand it. You don't want the man getting up again.

'That's fine, Jane. You know ... you can never be too sure.'

There was a pause.

Jane seemed to be thinking about what Sam had just said.

Then ...

'That's what I thought. As I turned the corner. And fired again. "You can never be too sure".' Jane was nodding, small, thoughtful nods.

'Good.' That's all Sam could think of adding.

There was silence again. Sam was hoping her short counselling session had been enough and they could both get some sleep. But no ...

'I enjoyed it.'

What?

303

'Sorry?' Sam's forehead was etched with lines that tightened the skin over the back of her head and highlighted the pain of her bruise.

'I enjoyed it. It was as if I were in a film. *Bang, bang*. Like a movie where lots of people die, but there's no blood ... and afterwards they all go to the canteen for tea.'

It was all getting a bit too much for Sam. She needed to close the conversation down. She had been through enough therapy to know that talking about it worked for some people. For others it just extended the pain when what they should be doing was dropping all of it in a trench and covering it with earth.

'That's OK,' Sam said. 'That's so much better than despising yourself for it.'

She thought she really meant that.

Jane's mouth opened to say something, but Sam raised a finger and stopped her.

'You have to understand that here, in Bitola, North Macedonia, your pain is my pain, Jane. I have the same memories too. The same tragic experiences. You may want to talk about them, but I don't. I can't. You have to understand that. And, for now, we have something much more important to focus on. And pity and remorse and any self-analysing is going to distract us from the mission. You have to understand that too.'

Sam looked for recognition in Jane's face. She thought she saw something, but she couldn't be sure.

'Now please go to sleep. We've got a Russian to photobomb tomorrow.'

Police Scotland, Tulliallan Castle, Kincardine-on-Forth, Scotland

It had been a quiet day. The conference centre had opened, some delegates had meandered about looking at the various stands, there'd been a couple of fringe presentations and meetings, the world press and their satellite dishes had turned up in their thousands, but all in all, it had been incident-free. Well, apart from the lack of wheelchair access into the main auditorium, which to Lewis seemed like a pretty big oversight. It wasn't exactly a security issue, so it was someone else's problem. And it had been sorted by lunchtime.

If that was the biggest issue over the next seven days, they'd all be delighted.

Oh, he'd almost forgotten. POTUS had arrived. 'Telegraph has landed' was the call the Command Centre had received from Lossie ninety minutes ago when Air Force One was 'wheels down'. Telegraph was the current president's Secret Service code name. As with tradition, his family were all given nicknames, starting with a 'T'. For the conference Telegraph was travelling with Tweenie, his wife. Lewis had no idea what the Secret Service called the president's three children, but they'd certainly begin with a 'T'.

And Prime Minister Fordingly was also in the building, so to speak. He was currently having a hearty meal with some Commonwealth delegates at the Edinburgh Grand. Lewis wasn't sure what he felt about the current bloke. As an army officer he was trained to look over all of the detail – not to dismiss a thing. He wasn't a big hand, small map man. Fordingly, though. He wasn't always on his brief, was he? He said things which pleased people, even if sometimes it was bollocks. Lewis felt the man had no political instinct other than keeping his job. He was a

305

popularist. He did what he thought people wanted, not necessarily the right thing for the country.

That was Lewis's view. Although he tried to remain as apolitical as he could ... as a military man.

Whatever, the top man was in Edinburgh. Hopefully he would be out of the dinner in an hour and a half's time so that Lewis could get back to his hotel for a kip before it all kicked off with the speeches tomorrow.

He counted the staff in the room.

The ACC (*Assistant Chief Constable*) was the current Gold Commander. If there were an incident, he would hold the fort until the DCC came rushing in. There were: three police officers attending to the screens; a fire and an ambulance LO; a Canadian, UN-badged police officer; and, on the military desk, a Royal Marine captain, a boot-neck corporal and an RAF sergeant. Eleven, including him.

The latest threat warning hadn't changed. The level was still 'severe', which translated into 'an attack was highly likely'. The DCC had thought it appropriate to beam the current threat onto the main Command Centre screen – and leave it there. Lewis glanced at it, although he knew it off by heart:

- Attack window: D-1, D Day and D+1.
- Attack ambition: discrete targeting of world leader(s).
- Attack methodology: seaborne.

The good news was they were nearly through D-1.

One down, two to go.

They knew pretty much where all the world leaders and the 'official' senior dignitaries were staying. Many were in Edinburgh, but their locations stretched all across the central region. The police had a map with over 150 red dots on it. The diameters of the circles indicating the importance of the delegate. State leaders – presidents and prime ministers – were a certain size. Ministers, slightly smaller. Etcetera. It all made sense to someone.

There were two gatherings this evening. Fordingly and the Commonwealth delegates were at the Grand. And POTUS was holding a small get-together at the Dalmahoy Hotel and Country Club in West Lothian, his not-so-secret-conference location. That guest list included various EU leaders and the Canadian Prime Minister, who was also staying at the Club.

They were less sure where the unofficial dignitaries and celebs were housed. The conference had attracted all manner of high-profile climate activists, pop and film stars, and celeb hangers on. Other than the world-renowned young Swedish activist, HQ Scotland's G2 cell (*military intelligence*) had all but discounted the 'unofficials' as targets. They were being afforded no special treatment. The view was that general policing would mop up any threat and, as always, they'd be prepared for the unexpected.

G2's IPB (*intelligence preparation of the battlefield*) had discounted this evening's POTUS event as a likely target, as the threat remained very firmly 'seaborne' and the club was ten clicks from the Firth of Forth. The Commonwealth meet, however, was considered 'viable'. The Grand, in central Edinburgh, was 1,500 metres from the sea and whilst there had been lots of modelling done on 'terrorists delivered by small boat and attack various locations', the most novel was considered to be an armed drone attack on the conference centre, or a secondary location where dignitaries congregated. Interestingly, but not surprisingly, a drone attack was still firmly second to a MANPAD (*man portable air defence system*), from the deck of a boat, taking a pot-shot at a plane full of important people.

They knew the threat. And they had everything covered.

The estuary was awash with police boats. Beyond that, the sea was full of grey ships, surface and subsurface. The SBS, in support of the police, had three RIB-borne teams at immediate notice to move. The local plod were on every street corner, and a football stadium's worth of them were hanging about in riot gear. The RAF were on drone watch. And the SRR were hiding in bushes and down drains – Lewis knew not where.

Everything was covered.

'Sir!' It was the RAF operator.

The Marine captain was immediately on his shoulder. Lewis was all ears.

'ACC!' the captain shouted, and then, 'Get this on the main screen, Corporal King!'

The ACC had his feet up on a table and an 'nth' coffee in his hand. He was upright just as the main screen flipped to a muddle of mostly greens and blacks. The only thing that was clear was the outline of the Firth of Forth, which had been superimposed on the image as a thick yellow line.

'What the blazes are those?' the ACC asked, the incredulity in his voice unmistakable.

'Multiple drones,' the captain said.

'What the hell are they doing?' the ACC continued …

… but the Marine captain was ahead of him.

'Get the locstat of the point of disembarkation. And, ACC, get this across the police airwaves. Multiple drone attack. Targets, not yet known but ...' there was a pause as the captain studied the myriad of moving dots, '... direction of threat is from the east, heading for the conference centre. Time on target. It's bloody minutes.'

Lewis had done that assessment.

He'd also worked out, in principle, where the drones had been launched from. There was a holding quay 5 miles east of Leith docks where a number of larger craft, including a Greenpeace ship, had been ordered to moor for the duration of the conference. The spew of dull red dots was emanating from there.

There were so many of them, and they were moving so fast, he couldn't keep up. Yesterday the RAF sergeant had given everyone a short presentation on what and how a terror cell could pull off a drone attack ... and what ORCUS, the military's new anti-drone equipment, would do about it.

It was a well put together presentation. Lewis remembered most of it, but one thing remained vivid. It was a photo of an Amazon-bought drone, currently used in remote locations. Its spider-like body was held up by six propellers, under which was a box big enough to hold a small fridge – a payload in the order of 20 kilogrammes. As an aside, the sergeant had explained that the latest professional drones could carry ten times as much, up to 220 kilogrammes.

The smaller Amazon drone in the RAF sergeant's photo could travel at 100 kph.

Which they were.

It was like watching an outpouring from an ants' nest which had been flooded with boiling water.

As the captain said, they were heading west. And whilst a number of the flashing dots blinked and then went

309

silent, which Lewis hoped meant ORCUS was doing its job, a good number were already over the city centre.

We're going to lose some people.

Cheval, The Edinburgh Grand, Edinburgh, Scotland

Dominic was standing outside of the main dining room. He wasn't alone. There were maybe ten 'flunkies' in the wide corridor of the Grand which ran the length of the frontage of the building. The corridor was accessed by two lifts and an imposing staircase, the balcony of which he was resting his backside against. Like the rest of the hotel, the corridor was ornately decorated with a long, unbroken carpet. It was furnished with a number of side tables and plenty of old Scottish landscapes painted in oil and hung in big gold frames which probably took two men to lift them off the wall.

He hadn't eaten. Which he thought was an oversight on behalf of the organisers. He could smell food. And he had seen it being delivered via a couple of catering lifts just down from him, and then served to the guests through two wooden double doors, which were ornately carved and sported the biggest brass doorknobs he had ever seen.

And he was interested in the multi-nationalism of it all. The prime minister had given him a couple of sheets of A4 entitled, *The Commonwealth of Nations' Climate Dinner*. There was a date and a list of twenty-four attendees from countries across the world. On the second page was the menu: Scottish beetroot-cured salmon with watercress, followed by Aberdeen Angus sirloin steak with new potatoes, buttered carrots and spinach. Any moment now they would be served triple chocolate mousse cakes, followed by a Scottish cheeseboard and Kenyan coffee.

Dominic hadn't remembered which wine was to be offered with which course, but he had kept the menu. He would buy one of the bottles this weekend and give it a go.

If he could afford it.

He was, of course, sober – he wasn't so sure that was true of all of the motley crew which had congregated on the corridor/landing with him. He was the only one formally dressed: black tails, white shirt, black bowtie – but no white gloves. Not today. He wasn't serving. The rest of the men wore suits. The women, dresses and jackets. One or two had struck up conversations. But not him. He had a particular job which the boss had asked him to do ... at 22.13.

He checked his watch.

22.11.

Two minutes.

The boss had been very, *very* particular about the time.

Now it was ... 22.12.

One minute.

A train of waiters and waitresses arrived with empty silver trays. They queued up at either door.

Time to collect the debris that once was the main course.

22.13.

Move.

It was a bit of a scrum. A minute earlier and he would have had the double doors on the left to himself. Now he was entering with six penguins. They were marching efficiently to their places. Dominic stopped briefly at the door to find his man.

There.

Prime Minister Fordingly was, of course, in the centre of a long table, off to Dominic's right. His seat was square on to one of the room's six grand windows. The boss was already looking over his shoulder. He caught Dominic's eye, and nodded a sharp nod.

Which is a bit odd.

Dominic made his way down the table, eventually brushing past a waiter who was standing to attention on the prime minister's left, silver tray by his side. Dominic worked his way around the man to the prime minister's right.

Some people might have felt uncomfortable about crashing a formal dinner. Conspicuous. Unsure of their place in such a grand and formal setting. Dominic didn't. This was his job. He just had to look smart and efficient. Which he was good at.

He bent forward and presented the boss with a small slip of paper. Dominic had penned it earlier.

It read: *Emergency telephone call. Foreign Office.*

The prime minister all but snatched the paper from him, glanced at it and, as he stood – for which both the waiter and Dominic had to move quickly to make room for a sliding heavy chair – passed some pleasantry to his neighbour on his right. Dominic didn't hear what he said, but he assumed the boss was making his excuses.

I have to make a call. Now. Please excuse me.

And then he was off.

At a lick.

So much so he caught Dominic off guard – just a little. But the prime minister's second valet wasn't going to appear rushed. Nobody was on fire. And he was a dignified manservant. With a straight back and tight lips, he walked quickly but purposefully out the way he had come, the

312

double door to the corridor already closed behind the prime minister by the time Dominic had got there.

Which was a little frustrating.

He hoped nobody had noticed.

As Dominic made it into the corridor he was surprised to see the prime minister was already halfway down the staircase. His boss glanced up and threw Dominic a quick thumbs up, but it was fleeting …

… and lost on Dominic.

Because his mind was diverted by what can only be described as a train crash.

It came from the dining room. There were multiple *smashes* as, he thought, many of panes of glass from the six big windows broke into pieces. That was followed by an almighty explosion. And then another, so loud and so fierce, a painting by his shoulder catapulted from the wall and landed with a *thud* just behind him, missing him by centimetres. The walls shook. The landing also. And then another explosion. And two more. More damage in the hallway. A candelabra which hung from the high ceiling to light the curving staircase fell like a seasoned apple from a tree. He didn't hear it land.

There was so much more noise now. Screams and cries. Shouts in a multitude of languages from the staff in the corridor.

And a final explosion.

It might as well have been meant for him.

Dominic had made it past the bewildered and panicked staff, as far as the right of the two double doors, just where the stairs rose to the corridor. He was thinking he should probably have gone to ground as soon as the war had started.

Lain flat, maybe?

But he was doing his job. Chasing his boss.

The *bang* was as loud as anything he had ever heard. And whilst it was still in the room where all the poor dignitaries and waiters were currently, almost certainly fighting for their lives, it didn't stay there.

One of the double doors by his left shoulder blew off its hinges. Outwards.

Dominic didn't see it.

He was turning and taking the first step on the stairs.

But it found him.

He had no idea what the door weighed, but it was one massive chunk of wood. As it smacked against his back with all its force, Dominic was lucky not to be killed instantly. In that moment the well of the staircase saved his life. The door hit him square on, broke his back and, as it flew onwards towards the far wall, he spun down a short flight of steps onto a small landing, where the stairs pivoted right before a final turn down to the lobby.

Clump.

He hit the far wall shoulder first, the pain not yet a viable sensation in Dominic's mind. The door bounced above him and fell into the well, smashing one of Dominic's tibias into several pieces. It would have finished him off if it had fallen onto him, rather than toppling down the next set of stairs, an action which would frustrate ambulance crews twenty minutes later.

He was dazed. And he knew he was injured. But he couldn't feel anything.

I can't feel anything.

He moved his head and his arms. They worked. But below his waist was hopeless.

The noise around him was furious. There had been no more explosions, but the cacophony of screams and shouts and cries were too much.

So he blocked those out.

In fact he blocked everything out.

Because he only had one thought in his mind. It was a recurring one.

Had Fordingly known about the attack?

Was that why he'd asked him to come into the dining room at an exact time, literally just before the explosions, and offer him an excuse to leave the dinner?

An emergency call from the Foreign Office.

But there hadn't been one, had there? Because Dominic had made that up. All Fordingly had told him to do was come and whisper something in his ear. Something which made it look as if he had to leave the room, 'pronto'.

'A phone call. I don't know. Use your brains?' The prime minister's usual *bonhomie* had deserted him as he'd given his instructions just before dinner. Dominic had accepted the directions with good grace. But he couldn't help noticing that Fordingly had looked distracted and pale. Just like he had when he'd got back in Dominic's Audi the other night.

Had he known about the attack?

Dominic couldn't hold his thoughts. They had been broken. The pain had started.

Oh God.

He was feeling delirious. He was lying in a heap, one leg at an angle which didn't look right, and there was a red patch on his shirt.

Christ, that hurts.

But his brain still cantered.

Had Fordingly used him as a mule? Had he set Dominic up for this?

The man had survived.

And looking at the angles of Dominic's torso and legs, he wasn't sure he was going to.

Police sirens now. And more shouting. More screaming. More crying. It was all now breaking into his consciousness.

There was movement to his right, in the corridor at the top of the stairs. Someone was thinking about coming down, but hesitated.

Think again, kiddo.

The pain.

The blood.

Fordingly?

The man had known, hadn't he?

He had.

Dominic found his phone. His initial thought was to call his mum. That's what any decent son would do.

But instead, slowly and God knew how painfully, he scrolled through his address book.

Downing.

He pressed the green call button.

It rang three times and connected.

'Hi, Dominic. How can I help?' There was a beat. 'More important. What the fuck is all that noise?'

Dominic had forgotten about the noise. He was ignoring the group of people at the top of the stairs looking down at him. Looking beyond him for an escape route.

'Fordingly ...' Dominic started. Then he raised his spare hand to his lips. He touched them and looked at his index finger. It was red.

Blood.

316

'What about Fordingly?' Jack Downing asked.

'There's been an explosion ... at the ... hotel.' This was a monumental effort. Blood and pain and dizziness.

Christ. Can I do this?

'What? Is the prime minister dead?' The man's words were a shrill.

He had to get this done. He didn't know how much time he had left.

'Listen ... Fordingly used me to get him ... away from the explosion. I was to ...' He took a deep breath. Everything hurt now. Everything from his waist upwards. 'He told me to get him out. Just before the explosion ... he knew it was coming. The timing was perfect ...'

'What? The PM knew of an attack? And used you to get him out beforehand?'

Was this guy listening? It was blurred sarcasm.

'Yes. Exactly ... me. He brought me up to Scotland ... especially. So I could ...'

'Fuck. Are you OK? You don't sound OK?' the man with the ID barked.

'No. But ... also. Last Saturday night. We drove out of Chequers ... stopped in a layby.' He drew breath. *Shit, that hurt.* 'He was picked up by a Blue Bentley. ...' Dominic knew this would likely be his last hurrah. 'Registration DG 55 ... 5. That's it.' The phone fell away from his hand as his heart gave up the fight against the multiple traumas it was being asked to cope with.

And then the Prime Minister's second valet slumped to the floor.

Chapter 13

Wolfgang was as good as his word.

To kick off they had taken a taxi from the hotel to Skopje, a nightmare of a journey where the reckless driver had overtaken a coach on a blind corner in the mountains. Remarkably it had been Sam who had held her knees together and kept closing her eyes – Jane seemed to be enjoying the ride. *Whatever.* The flight from Skopje had been unremarkable and Sam and Jane had arrived at Berlin BER airport at 15.05. From there the X7 bus had taken a further ten minutes to whisk them into Berlin's centre.

Where Wolfgang had been as good as his word.

He had organised a short itinerary which took them via two shops.

First was a heavy duty electronics bazaar where – already paid for – they collected some very sexy looking journalistic recording equipment. There was a case with a strap, a Canon XA11 professional video camera, a series of microphones, one of which was a mini-boom mic, and a decent iPad and stylus. Sam had noticed the bill – it was an eye-watering 4,500 euros. Next was a bit of a hike (they were against the clock) to a poorly-lit, backstreet stationery shop, which was a muddle of copiers, printers, paper and card. Here the exchange was more 'under the counter'. They showed their fake passports to an elderly Einstein-lookalike local who handed over an A5 brown envelope. In it were two forged *Berlinale* name badges: reporter and cameraman from the fictitious *Film ADX* magazine. Sam had no idea what the ADX stood for. Wolfgang would have thought of some witticism or other.

They then had to dress appropriately. Well, one of them did.

They'd decided that Jane would be the reporter, with Sam number one on the camera and mic. Jane spoke German pretty fluently and, whilst she wouldn't pass as a native, she could do a good job. Sure, she didn't speak Russian – and they were hoping to meet a white one – and Sam did. But what she had over Sam was the look. Jane was mid-forties, but she could easily pass as younger. And she had the air of a well-educated, middle-class woman. She looked like someone who had been in journalism, especially reporting on the red carpet, all her life.

Sam couldn't do that. Even if she tried. She was a couple of centimetres shorter than Jane, her hair was at best unkempt, and she had a pretty masculine demeanour – until she smiled, which she didn't do often. So, she was easily the technician of the two.

Tonight, Mathew, I am going to be a cameraman. You had to be her mum's age to get the joke.

And, as important, whilst Jane was doing her red carpet thing Sam would be on guard. Assuming they got to the White Russian, Kirill Semenov, Sam reckoned they were going to need every angle covered.

This was not going to be easy.

Sam had been to the Potsdamer Platz once before on a city break during her Russian immersion training in Latvia. Not much had changed, other than tonight's imposition of the extravaganza that was the *Berlinale*, the Berlin International Film Festival. It had smothered the square with tentage, stages, red carpet and journos, with

319

their accompanying vans and satellite dishes. And there were plenty of fans.

Good. They might need to get lost in the crowd.

The additional news was that between Frank and Wolfgang they had a good deal more on the Russian. In fact they had a good deal more on a lot.

In the short gap waiting at Skopje for their flight, she and Jane had purloined an airport 'pay-as-you-use' computer and had had a longish chat with Munich.

Kirill Semenov was fifty-seven and, if you believed the hype, a minor royal. His family – along with the family gold – had escaped Russia to Poland in 1917, just before the House of Romanov had fallen. His father had returned in 1991, once the Wall had come down. Whilst the business oligarchs had risen through the ranks by buying and selling industries and mines, the Semenov family had reclaimed their land – some of which they paid for, much of which they had coerced from sitting tenants. Apparently it hadn't been pretty. On occasions Sememov's father was known to administer punishment using one of the ancestral Cossack sabres.

The family land had been quickly re-administered into the fold. It was then re-let to tenants, a few of whom were oligarchs in their own right, raping the land for oil and minerals – always for a handsome profit. Daddy Semenov had died in 1999 leaving an empire to Kirill, his only son. Frank reckoned the man was worth £56 billion with a rental turnover in excess of £750 million a year. He owned real estate in fourteen countries, including a pretty sizable chunk of Mayfair, where it was assumed much of the cash was laundered.

Semenov was a household name in Belarus, much of western Russia and Poland. He played on his Cossack

320

history, the likely fictional resistance his wider family played out against the Bolsheviks, his uncle's role (and death) as a Spitfire pilot in the Second World War, and the family hereditary title: Baron Kirill Semenov of Byelorussia. Which was a little amusing as Frank had been unable to find any noble history. Nor was there anything which noted resistance against the Russian revolution.

'But his uncle *did* die in the Battle of Britain.' Frank had been excited and had wanted to tell the whole story. Sam had stopped him in his tracks.

But ... there was no doubt. The family did own a great deal of land.

Semenov was still married to his first wife, Tatiana. There were two children, both of whom, having been educated in the UK, were now working in the US. They all had German citizenship. Wolfgang said the grandfather had bought that opportunity for cash, straight after World War II, during which the family had lodged with friends in Switzerland. Semenov's primary residence was Berlin, where he and his wife spent most of their time supporting the arts, hence a place on the jury at the *Berlinale*.

That's what they had on Semenov. It was something.

And it was enough for now.

Frank had then brought them up to speed on a number of other developments.

He'd recounted David Jennings' telephone conversation: that the US weren't that interested in the YCA, and the French knew it was a problem, were clear that Louis Belmonte had been assassinated, and that the DGSI were worried about a power grab within the security services. But they were too busy to deal with it. Could someone help please?

Frank had then amplified on Selene Konstantos's comment that her father was always away every other year, in mid-December. Looking wider he reckoned there was a pattern emerging. Sort of. To begin with he had checked Konstantos's passport usage. Sure enough, the Greek was never in the country between – and the dates varied a little – 10 and 18 December, every odd year since as far back as Wolfgang had been able to hack the system.

'Where did he go?' Sam had interrupted, her impatience getting the better of her. They had a plane to catch.

'I'm working on it. His flights around that time are mostly, but not exclusively, from Athens. So it's complicated. However, out of fourteen years – that's odd years; my earliest is 1987 – it seems he's been heading to northern Europe, predominantly the UK. There are interconnecting flights, so the search is huge. But ...'

Sam had been about to interrupt again, but Frank ploughed on.

'... I've managed to cross-reference that time period with two other YCA members: the Swiss, Bosshart; and the American, Jimmy Johnson Jr. Both of those men were away from their place of domicile in mid-December. Odd years.'

'UK?' Sam had managed to get a word in then.

'Yeah ... well, possibly. Certainly northern Europe. There are issues. Of course there are.' He'd 'huffed' at that point. 'For example, I know for a fact that Johnson flew into Paris Charles de Gaulle on 9th December 2001 – and didn't transit. His next flight was out of Schiphol on the 20th, back to Austin, Texas.'

There had been a short silence.

Sam had filled it.

'There are plenty of ways he might have travelled onwards to the UK. Either illegally by aircraft, or by Eurostar, or even ferry. Let's keep on this, Frank ... Wolfgang ... whoever.'

'Sure,' Wolfgang had replied.

'What else?' Sam asked.

'I've found another dead YCA member,' Frank replied.

'What? Brilliant,' Sam and Jane had replied together.

'Well, maybe. I searched for "billionaires who met an untimely death", my most fun Google search ever. There are only a few. And I was lucky. In 1977 a Norwegian oil tycoon died in a plane crash on the way to one of his company's newly commissioned North Sea oil rigs. His name was Eirik Pedeson. I don't have much more at the moment, save a photo of him taken at a family home two years previously.'

'Is he wearing an Elias Bosshart, YCA watch?' Jane had asked.

'That's how I found him,' Frank had replied.

'No sons who may have taken his place?' Sam asked.

'One daughter,' Frank had replied.

1977?

'1977 is a long time ago, and memories fade. But it's an option. Press on with that, Frank,' Sam had added.

That hadn't been it. Clearly Frank and Wolfgang had been very busy.

'Two more things from us,' Frank had continued. 'Have you got time?'

Sam had checked the large clock on the Skopje terminal's wall. They had twenty minutes.

'We've a few minutes,' she'd replied.

323

'First, all those years ago when I was working in Vauxhall ...' Frank's sarcasm was lost in the ether, 'I've been keeping an eye on QAnon pages, from Facebook and similar. On the assumption that the YCA are manipulating elements of the population, albeit obliquely. There's so much going on, but the tops in terms of activity and plain weirdness is a huge groundswell against home assistants ...' Frank had paused, just in case someone had wanted to ask the obvious question, 'What is a home assistant?' No one said anything.

'A second is the xenophobic uprising in Germany against what is seen to be an orchestrated stampede of Syrian migrants from, interestingly, Belarus into Poland.' Again, he paused to let pennies drop.

That is interesting.

But neither Sam nor Jane said anything.

'And third is a pretty muddy campaign against the Brazilian opposition leader. There's a national election this weekend.'

Sam had thought for a moment.

'Who gains, Frank, in these? Anyone?' she asked. If there was a link to the YCA there had to be a reason.

'Keeping a popularist leader in power for a third term,' Jane answered first.

That is a possibility.

Sam didn't want to contribute. She needed time to reflect on Frank's briefing. But she did add, 'Always ask the question, Frank. *Cui bono?* Who gains? If you can't find an obvious link which benefits the YCA, then park it. It seems like you have a lot of other things to do.'

Sam was about to cancel the call when Wolfgang asked a question.

'You've heard about the Edinburgh drone attack?'

324

They had. They'd missed it first thing. But, once they'd got their boarding passes and before they'd connected this call, Jane and Sam had spent ten minutes staring at an airport TV screen with their mouths hung open. Twelve dead, three of whom were Commonwealth leaders – and a fourth major dignitary, the leader of the Scottish Independence Party. Fordingly was at the banquet, but was not one of the dead, or the injured. It hadn't yet been confirmed but it seemed he had miraculously escaped, but most of the details were missing.

As a result, there was a lot of media coverage giving little detail.

But one thing was clear: the climate conference was still going ahead.

And that's what had surprised Sam about such an attack.

If you're a climate terror organisation – and there was the slightest hint that the attack might have been launched from a Greenpeace ship (someone had seen something who had told someone else) – what on earth could you expect to gain from killing the very world leaders who were trying to solve the crisis? If anything, a terror attack would strengthen resolve.

It was that question again.

Who gains?

Maybe a strengthening of resolve was the point?

But was it?

It really, *really* bothered her.

And it reminded her of a madcap theory which Wolfgang had put to Sam when they had first met. He had explained it excitely over a glass of wine whilst she cooked chilli in her shabby outer-London apartment. He'd put together a spreadsheet on a number of major 'non-natural' disasters, most of them aircraft falling from the sky. His uncorroborated view was along the lines of: kill hundreds, murder one.

You cover up the death of a key individual, by killing a large group of other people in a major disaster.

'Kill hundreds, murder one?' Sam asked rhetorically.

There was another silence. Wolfgang would get it. She was sure she'd mentioned it to Jane and Frank at the time, but they'd possibly forgotten.

'One of the twelve dead was the target. But the terrorists wanted it hidden?' Frank was on it.

'Who?' Sam had asked. 'And that's definitely rhetorical. We have a plane to catch. But think about it.'

After that she quickly closed down the link before the conversation spiralled into a lengthy discussion as to who might want whom dead.

And now, seven hours later, the beautifully woollen-coated Jane Baker stood just off the red carpet which led to CinemaxX Berlin, where Baron Kirill Semenov of Byelorussia was about to watch *'Eine verrückte Angelegenheit'*, a German film of unrequited love between a teenage boy and his football coach. It was, apparently, a major contender in the 'Panorama' section of the festival, where the films had to be 'sexy, edgy and daring'. She and Jane had spent much of their flight from Skopje becoming film buffs. It was a new diversion to Sam although, now she was better informed, she didn't think the film would be high on her 'to-watch' list. Not that such a list existed.

That didn't matter. She was just a camera person.

It was Jane who had the gift of the gab.

...

And Kirill Semenov was on his way up the red carpet.

He had a beauty with him; not his wife. Sam had seen her photo. But she instantly recognised the woman by the Russian's side. It was the actress who played the young mother of the film's principal lad. She looked striking in the marketing bumf. She looked just as beautiful in the cold air of Berlin's early evening, the route between limousine and cinema entrance lit with multiple arc-lights, which threw competing shadows.

What she and Jane had very quickly appreciated was that, as they were one of the many crews on the carpet, they were expected to speak to anyone who stopped by. Which, at one of the more minor international film festivals, meant pretty much everyone.

Jane, bless her, was doing really well – with a little help. Sam had to nudge her as to who was who. But, once she had a name, the rest came naturally. And her interviewing seamlessly switched from German to English, depending which language suited the guest.

Currently it was English.

'Werner Köhler. The director,' Sam had whispered to Jane as the man arrived in front of the camera.

'Herr Köhler, do you think this is your best film?' had been Jane's opening line.

It was the perfect question, which elicited a long, flurrysome answer,

A few questions later it seemed that the man was now completely engrossed.

'I zink Bertie played ze role of ze elderly lover with real dignity, *richtig*?' Köhler had asked of Jane. His English was excellent, his accent strong.

Jane, of course, hadn't seen the film. But it didn't stop her offering an opinion.

'Yes. I think you're right. He's a very *atmospheric* actor.'

Köhler seemed confused by Jane's answer, as if it wasn't something he'd thought of Bertie before.

'*Jawohl*, I can see zat now. I would say, perhaps, more deep ... thoughtful? *Nein?*'

Jane needed to get her answer out now as Kirill Semenov was on the director's heels and, as they had learnt, if there's a bottleneck a guest can slip past and on to the next waiting journalist without pausing.

Jane, thankfully, had spotted the problem and didn't need Sam's interruption.

'Yes, of course ... Herr Semenov?' Jane had put out a hand and was waving frantically at the White Russian. The director, a key man in any production, looked confused, especially as Sam had switched the camera to ensure their next victim knew he would be on film. The director shook his head, raising his hands in a shrug, and walked on.

Semenov was heading their way.

And, *bloody hell*, a minder had appeared behind Sam, on her shoulder. And there was another, looking similarly menacing, beyond Semenov and the beautiful actress.

'Herr Semenov, or should I call you *Baron* Semenov?' It was a sterling start from Jane.

The White Russian, 1.85 tall, slim built, attractive in an angular way, and dressed in expensive clothes, smiled at Jane. He showed a thin line of teeth which could convey many messages. Sam thought he looked downright menacing. Or, maybe it was the presence of the minder on her shoulder? Or the guy across the carpet, who was currently assessing potential threats.

With one eye permanently on the camera's screen and with her new friend on her shoulder watching every move, Sam couldn't spend too long doing her own security review. But, after a quick scan, if the man across from her was armed, it was in the small of his back.

Let's hope we don't have to find out.

'My friends call me Kiri.' Semenov's mouth showed more of a smile.

He still looked threatening.

And he hadn't answered Jane's question.

'May I introduce the leading lady?' Semenov offered the actress to Jane. She was wearing an unfussy, shimmering blue, off-the-shoulder evening gown. And not much else.

She must be cold.

'Yes, of course.' Jane's response showed the first hint of lack of confidence. Sam had not had time to remind her of the woman's name.

But it didn't matter.

'At such a tender age, how did you manage to play the role of mother to a young teenage boy?' Jane's form returned.

The actress answered in English. And then Jane, still clearly unable to remember the woman's name, asked a couple of other intelligent questions which the woman was only too pleased to answer.

By then the steam of the interview was running out, and it was time for Semenov, who was looking beyond them to the next journalist, to move on.

Jane seized the moment.

'Baron Semenov?' Jane asked to the side of the man's face.

'Hmm?' He turned his head. And flashed another smile which would scare any child.

'How long have you been a member of the YCA, the Young Crofters' Association?' Jane had thrust the microphone as close to the man as she could.

The smile broke. No, it shattered. The recognition from Semenov was instantaneous. His anger immediate.

He opened his mouth. And then shut it again.

Jane didn't wait for a response.

'Is it possible to have a private interview to discuss your role in that organisation? Maybe after the performance?' She rushed out the question as the White Russian looked set to move on, his composure only just holding – as if it were held together with chewing gum.

Semenov then turned square on to Jane, as though he was about to throw a punch.

He didn't. Instead he replied, 'No.' And nodded at the minder on Sam's shoulder, who recognised the sign immediately.

It was a combination of the minder's lunge plus the speed of Sam's elbow which created the maximum amount of pain. His large bulk was moving one way, the pointing end of Sam's elbow the other.

He went down on the floor like a heavy wet towel.

Semenov was instantaneously lost. His charge had screamed, both hands lifting to her mouth in a movement she would have rehearsed endlessly at drama college. Anyone close by had stopped what they were doing. The action was no longer in the cinema. It was happening on the red carpet.

And Jane was in her stride.

330

'Can you comment on the murder of Theodor Konstantos, another YCA member, who was brutally killed in Athens yesterday?'

Sam had to hand it to both interviewer *and* interviewee.

Jane was deadpan. As if the melee, which was only going to get worse, wasn't happening. She was the steadfast, upright reporter commenting on a hurricane, when her competitors were leaning at 45 degrees to remain standing in the worst weather to hit the coast in a century.

Semenov was cool. In fact he was smiling again. There was confidence there. Smugness. Untouchability.

And Sam was still recording it all.

'You have absolutely no idea what or who you are dealing with. I suggest you think very carefully about what you say, and what you do ... next. ' The man's voice had lost all of its charm.

Without a flinch Jane then asked a question they had not rehearsed.

'Why are the YCA orchestrating a surge of refugees across the Belarusian border into Poland?'

Semenov closed his eyes briefly. And Sam saw his jaw tighten. But he didn't respond. Instead, as he turned away from them, he reached for the arm of the lead actress and grabbed it. Sam felt the woman flinch. He then threw a nod to the minder who wasn't groaning on the floor and started to move up the red carpet towards the cinema ...

... but he was immediately stopped by a second reporter who had moved to get a better shot of the action. Sam spotted the sign on the mic. It was *Arte*, the very influential German arts channel.

Semenov, who was still gripping the arm of the actress, snorted and nodded at the same time. And then he bowed his head deferentially.

'We have a performance to see. The one here is finished. Please.' Some of his charm had returned.

The *Arte* reporter then began to ask a question, but Semenov interrupted her.

'*Keine weiteren Fragen, bitte.*'

And he navigated the lady in shimmering blue around the obstacle, still holding her arm.

The next few seconds were a blur.

The man on the ground was regaining his composure. He had one hand tight on Sam's ankle. The second minder was halfway across the red carpet. He had his hands at waist level, outstretched ready for action.

And all this surprised Sam.

Berlin was known to be 'arty'. To be left wing. It was a place to paint, to write poetry. To be environmental. It wasn't Sofia. Or Moscow. Mega-rich men, escorted by a lorry-load of well-dressed thugs, didn't crash the streets at night. Berlin was relaxed and metropolitan.

So Sam didn't expect a gangster reaction to their interview bombing.

How did Semenov expect to get away with it?

Entitlement.

In the split second before she needed to act, it was the only answer she could find.

And so, here they were. One thug coming round on the ground, his hand gripping her ankle ever tighter. The second now in full flight across the red carpet.

Sam dealt with both in a single movement.

Out of the corner of her eye she could see that Jane was already moving to one side, to deflect any attack. The momentum of the man was probably enough to miss Jane's feint and topple him to the ground. But you couldn't be sure.

And if Sam didn't do something now, she'd have her legs taken from under her.

She lifted her spare foot, stamping it down onto the wrist of the man on the ground. The one holding her leg. There was a *snap,* which might have been the sound of some part of Sam's shoe breaking, but was probably a bone.

As she then launched forward she turned the stocky camera – one hand on its base allowing the pivot, the second grabbing the lens.

Sam pushed her hands forward as hard as she could. The back end of the camera met the man's face. Now moving at speed and altogether surprised, he must have seen a black object coming and instinctively turned his head away. But it was too little, too late. The camera cracked, a slither of sharp plastic cutting into Sam's palm. But most of the damage was done at the flat end. Sam reckoned there'd be a broken cheek and nose. Certainly a black eye. Whatever, the man's outstretched hands missed Jane's throat as they found themselves lost and confused between two actions: attack, or defend?

The second minder joined his colleague on the floor.

Sam was sore, her shoulder in pain from the attack, her hand already losing a steady stream of blood and the red mist was down. And her blood pressure was up, adrenaline was running amok, and her breath was short and spasmodic.

What now?

Thankfully Jane was ahead of her.

Her friend had already grabbed Sam by the wrist, pulling her onto the red carpet, away from the thugs who would be too professional and too hardened to be on the floor for long.

Jane led, first at a jog and then at a sprint. They pushed past incredulous celebrities, journalists and fans, before they made it out into the less dense centre of the Potsdamer Platz. Jane dithered, but only for a second.

And then they ran, side by side, for the U-Bahn.

Northwall, Sanday, Orkney Islands, Scotland

It was dark. And lonely. Heather was standing on a wooden picnic bench which was perched on a thin sand dune. In daylight she would be looking over a white, sandy beach beyond which was, who knew?

Norway? Denmark?

She'd made it to the far eastern edge of Sanday, one of the Orkney Islands' northernmost blobs of land. Wikipedia told her that the Orkneys were an archipelago of seventy islands, only twenty of which were inhabited. Sanday was one of those. Just.

The ferry from Kirkwall, the capital of Orkney, to Sanday, had taken twice as long as the one from the mainland ... and it had been a little rougher, the sea angry and restless. She'd booked into a guest house on the island before she'd caught the ferry. But rather than do the obvious and head to the place and book in, she'd driven straight to Northwall, a hamlet not a great deal short of the beach where the body of Steph Landown had been found.

Heather couldn't work out why she had to go to this beach. Or why she had to go to this beach before she went to the guest house.

Something was driving her. An unknown force.

334

She needed to make a connection. There was absolutely no guarantee that this woman who had gone missing in mid-December 2009, her body washed up on these remote shores, had been abducted by the same awful men who had taken her ten years earlier.

But, to Heather, there *was* a symmetry.

1999 and *2009*.

In December.

And it was the only mention in Peter Lynch's book which had any association with water.

Here.

On this beach, if she could see it.

The poor woman.

Heather looked into the distance. There was no horizon, just a grey black sea meeting a grey black sky – somewhere. The clouds were low and there was no ambient light, other than the sweep of the Star Point lighthouse: a double flash and then an extended break.

She'd read somewhere that each lighthouse has its own distinctive code. Had Steph Landown seen the double flash? Had she witnessed what Heather was witnessing now?

Had she experienced everything Heather had?

How would she ever know?

The wind was lifting the bottom of Heather's jacket and the cold was having a go at her waist. There was damp in the air and her cheeks and nose, the only things sticking out from under her hood, were unhappy with the exposure.

She needed to get back into the car.

She needed to go to the guest house.

She needed …

What was it, though?

Come on! Her frustration merged into anger.

What *was* the point of all this? What the flippin' hell was she up to?

And yet, she still needed ... *what exactly*?

To find some answers?

How was that even going to be possible?

The police had investigated each disappearance. A journalist, not a forty-something clerk with absolutely no experience of anything other than office work, had travelled everywhere, including overseas. He'd spent an age, had written it all down ... and still he hadn't come to anything.

She was bumbling about aimlessly. Her emotions leading her to the edge of nowhere. It was pointless.

But was it?

I can't even decide that.

She was doing something, though.

She was out of Bristol, her mind free from the shackles which had previously tied her. She loved her daughter more than anything. But she knew, deep down inside, that with that unconditional love came responsibility. The responsibility to let Fi go. To free her from her maternal bonds.

Heather knew that.

And this thing, the thing which had plagued her, was eventually losing its control. Wasn't it? Here in the cold, windy and wet islands off the north coast of Scotland.

If nothing else, her past, was now – here on Sanday – being unpicked by her present. Which might just free her for her future.

That was fanciful. Wasn't it?

There?

A light.

In the distance.

A ship?

Probably.

It was an intermittent blip. As though a distant swell was rising above it, and then dropping.

A ship.

It was.

Her mind wouldn't settle. She didn't want to leave this place – Steph's place – even though the wind and the damp now stung her face.

A ship.

She knew that she had been on a ship. That certainty had settled. And she thought she had been on a ship for longer than an hour. Longer than the short ferry from the mainland to Orkney.

It *was* longer. She was sure of it.

How much longer?

Was it an age? Was it hours longer?

Maybe.

Had Steph taken the same route? Had she been on the same ship?

Had she been on the ship ... and then thrown off it?

Was that the ship? That one there?

Of course not, you fool.

But ...

... if it was that ship, or one like it, would the current bring Steph to this shore?

Heather didn't know.

But she intended to find out.

Flemingstraße, Munich, Germany

Wolfgang was doing the standing thing again, his right hand on his wheelchair, his back not quite straight. Frank was

337

asleep at his desk, his head resting on his arms. It was 3.16 am. Wolfgang knew this because he was timing himself. He was standing for fifteen minutes at a time. An hour's worth of standing in two. That was the plan. So far he was managing it. Just.

He'd slept an hour, either side of midnight. That was enough for now. Frank had eaten a couple of chomps of whatever the veggie stuff Matilda had delivered, drank a beer and was back at his desk in no time. Wolfgang had savoured a steak and *pommes mit mayo*, at a slightly slower pace. They'd had the call from Sam and Jane just before they'd eaten. Both were alive, which was a relief. Sam had cut her hand and, 'by the way', there was a video in the drop box they might want to look at. The call had been short. The pair were getting out of Berlin as quickly as possible. Jane said that they had just poked a stick into a hornet's nest and weren't going to hang around and wait for the swarm.

'Which direction?' Sam had asked.

'Head to Kiel – as a launch point for Norway – if you want to catch up with Pedeson's daughter. She lives in Trondheim. She's a doctor, we know where she works, and we know her shift pattern. You'll need some warm clothes.' Frank's direction had come out in a splurge.

'Got it. We're off.' And with that Sam had closed the call.

Wolfgang and Frank had watched the video. Twice.

The imagery was all completely clear until the camera had twisted in Sam's hand at the end, and then all you saw was a whirl of Sam's contorted face as the lens moved through the air … and then all went blank. It was obvious what Sam had done. And, as always, Wolfgang was amazed at her tenacity and courage.

Hence the standing regime.

He could do it.

He would do it for her.

But what had the intervention with Semenov achieved? Wouldn't it have been better to arrange a meeting with him, somewhere? Wolfgang could have accessed diaries, faked some more IDs and put something together.

Sam had her ways, though.

It was what it was.

Once the second showing was over, he'd asked Frank what he thought they'd achieved.

'I think there are three things in Sam's favour,' Frank replied after a pause. He had been sitting at his desk, his chair turned to the briefing wall. Wolfgang was on his feet for the second fifteen minutes of the night.

'First, this is what she does. She's a disrupter. She lifts rocks. Second, she and Jane were relatively safe out in the open. You saw what the Russian's apes had intended. In an office, which would have had walls and security, Sam and Jane might well have been overcome. Third, she got some results. We know from the encounter that the YCA were behind Konstantos's murder and – and this is a surprise, isn't it? – they also have something to gain from the Belarusian refugee situation. I'd say they are influencing what's happening. So, I think it's a good result.'

Wolfgang had nodded. Frank was right.

Overall, though, were they actually making progress?

Maybe.

The video proved, for the first time, that the YCA actually existed. Sure they had photos of the men with watches, but hitherto there had been nothing concrete. Nobody had ever asked any of them. Not directly. And it was now clear that both Semenov and Konstantos were/had been members.

That meant the YCA-embossed watch link was key. Have a watch; be a member.

But what else did they have?

Wolfgang was now resting his frame by placing his free hand on the display board. His face was now too close to it to focus.

Think.

He closed his eyes.

His hacking had produced a mind map and a wiring diagram for every YCA member. The mind maps focused on YCA businesses and real estate. And, accessed by a click, underneath every business he had uncovered three years' worth of accounts. It had taken a long time and a good dose of computing power.

But it was unlikely to be *everything*.

If YCA member 'X' wanted to hide a cash-only business, which required no electronic bookkeeping, that would be beyond his sightline.

The wiring diagram showed lineage: fathers, mothers, brothers, wives, etc. Where possible he had provided a one-pager on every relative, which included email addresses and telephone numbers where he had them. He had highlighted the relatives he thought 'important' by opening the backdoors he had previously accessed into Interpol and national police forces. There he searched for arrest warrants and cautions. Out of the 167 family names currently attributed to the eleven YCA members, seven had a police entry. Which was quite a hit rate. He had brought those, and their misdemeanours, forward in a single document.

And, for the nine known surviving YCA members, he had their travel records now stretching back over the past five years. To top that he had hacked the servers of the YCA members' main companies. It was more than one mine of information.

There was so much. Too much.

Frank was taking a wider view.

He was still looking for 'purpose', and trying hard to follow Sam's leading question: 'who gains?' Wolfgang had marked off a section of the board specifically for his English friend. He had looked over it earlier. In the middle, in its own goose egg, was the acronym: YCA. From there the spokes led to eight more goose eggs: fascism; small government; wealth; power; religion(?), media; comms(?); and QAnon.

Some of those spokes had their own diversions; their own mini-goose eggs on spokes. QAnon, for example, spawned: home assist; Belarus migrants; and Brazilian election. There were plenty of others.

It was a piece of art. For sure.

Aber ... '*Was sollte ich jetzt tun?*' Wolfgang asked of himself out loud.

'We should ...' Frank's stilted interruption startled him a little. He was awake and standing on Wolfgang's shoulder. His friend was yawning, with a mouth large enough to lose a *Hofbräuhaus stein*.

'We should ...' Frank started again. And yawned again, his hands outstretched, his tummy-button making an appearance below his grey t-shirt which was emblazoned with, 'Destroy the patriarch, not the planet'.

'... focus on two things.' He finished both his sentence and his yawn at the same time.

'*Was? Kaffee?*' Wolfgang replied with some sarcasm.

'No.' Frank chuckled. 'We need to know how they decide to do things. If, as Sam thinks, there's some unifying purpose, then there has to be a meeting, somewhere, where this is all discussed. Don't you think?'

'But that assumes leadership?' Wolfgang asked.

'The Duke of Nairnshire. He's the man. Until we have anything else, it's as good as it's going to get.' Frank paused, his mood contemplative. 'But ... how do they talk to each other?' He was now pointing at the board. 'You sent me the Swiss, Bosshart's, private and public email and WhatsApp threads last night. There is nothing there which connects him to any of the other YCA members, or their businesses. Nothing. It's as though a Chinese wall has been erected around each member.' Frank dropped his hand. 'But they must talk?'

'Why?' Wolfgang pressed. 'Maybe it's like being superfans of, I don't know ... ABBA?'

That seemed to confuse the hell out of Frank.

'What?'

'If you're a superfan, you get a super badge making it clear that you and your other superfans like ABBA an awful lot. You buy all their records. Attend all their gigs. But you don't actually have to meet?' Wolfgang offered.

Frank thought for a second.

'No, no, no, Wolfgang. And we now know that's not true.' Frank had now thrust his hands deep into his jeans pockets.

'Why, Frank? You just said you've checked one of the team and there is no sign of any contamination between him and the others?'

342

Frank turned to Wolfgang, his hands still in his pockets. He was a slight man. A man who you might think would get blown over in a stiff wind. But Wolfgang knew differently. Frank was wiry. He was tough. And Wolfgang could see that his friend was wide awake now. Firing on all cylinders.

'Because who ordered Konstantos's hit? That can only have come from a member or members of the YCA. And, if they're just superfans, then why would any of them be bothered that their Greek member has fallen out of love with ABBA and now likes, I dunno, David Hasselhoff?' Frank smiled ...

... and Wolfgang laughed. So much so he almost lost his balance. Frank offered a hand to steady him. His friend clearly knew that, to the amusement of every other non-German, 'The Hoff' was huge in his country. Although, not quite Wolfgang's thing.

He snorted once more. And then suggested, 'If that's the case, then someone will be talking after the events in Berlin last night? Using an, unknown to us, comms channel?'

'Yes. That's good ... hang on.' Frank had a finger raised. He looked about to issue instructions. Which was good. Because Wolfgang needed to be told what to do next.

Frank continued. 'Before we start, have you sorted the meet for Sam and Jane tomorrow in Trondheim?'

Of course. Whilst you were sleeping.

'Sure. At three tomorrow afternoon. It's in the doctor's diary.'

'Good,' Frank replied. 'Then I think we need to focus on the following.' Frank kept a finger raised. 'First, let's put our heads together and establish if there is anything behind this rush to northern Europe, maybe the UK, by the

343

members of the YCA? We pick a random, odd year in December, draw a map, add some times, and see if it comes into focus.'

Wolfgang had a lot of that information.

'Second,' Frank had raised a second finger, 'Let's focus on Semenov's outfit in Berlin. If he needs to speak to someone about last night, maybe to cool people's nerves in case he's due to get the Konstantos treatment, let's try and find out how he does that.'

'And third?' Wolfgang asked.

Frank shot him a quizzical look.

'*Kaffee*. And, I think, *ein Berliner*?' Wolfgang smiled as he said it.

'What do you mean?'

Wolfgang could sense Frank's wheels turning to no effect.

'It's an urban myth. JFK came to Berlin in 1963 and said in a speech – possibly his greatest during the Cold War – *ich bin ein Berliner*. Which means both, "I am a citizen of Berlin", and "I am a doughnut".' Wolfgang paused, searching for his friend's reaction.

'I hope,' Frank replied, 'that Matilda has doughnuts for us.'

'She does. And they will be freshly baked and scrumptious.'

Chapter 14

Newgale Beach, Wales, UK

'I feel hopeless,' David Jennings said, the offshore wind rising to a gust, lifting a clump of his wife's hair from her shoulder before it fell back to a place not far from where it had left.

They were sitting on a bench, high on a cliff.

Sally Jennings reached for his hand and held it tight.

'I know, darling. I know.' Her softness always surprised him.

'It's Sam and Jane – and Frank, you know, working on their own with Wolfgang. That doesn't feel right. There's something going on, bigger than just the usual nonsense. The Chief, that's another example. On paedophile charges? None of it makes sense. And yet, here ...' He didn't finish his sentence. Instead he stared out across the choppy grey sea.

Next stop, Cork.

The wind played a tune on a metal bin beside the bench.

'Do something, then. Make yourself useful.'

He was gazing aimlessly at the horizon. As he did, he knew she was looking at him.

He turned to her so their eyes met.

'Are you sure?' His wife had originally been firm with him. They had family. Grandchildren. He had risked his life for his job on a number of occasions. She had said goodbye to him once – when he had been in a coma having been spiked with a poisonous umbrella on Westminster

Bridge. Four days ago she had said she wasn't prepared to do that again.

But things had changed, hadn't they? Even in those short few days. The news was bleak. Migrants on the borders. A climate change conference almost derailed by the most horrendous of terror attacks.

And he had changed.

At first he had been resolute. This had been someone else's problem. He was too old. Too out of touch. There were younger and brighter pups than him.

But the US's lack of concern and the Republican Party's acquiescence to the YCA's existence? That worried him. And the French's realisation that there was a problem, but there was little they could do about it. That was unnerving.

And his old staff: Jane, Frank and Sam. Putting their heads above the parapet whilst he languished in the relative safety of the Pembrokeshire coast.

Pipe and slippers.

The very thought annoyed him.

And now his dear wife, the mother of his children, was suggesting that he 'do something'. Had he been that obvious? A post-hibernation bear. Had his mood been so low that she had had enough?

Get out of the house and stop sulking.

Was that where they were?

She was smiling at him, her hand still holding his.

'I think you must. The world is facing the existential threat of climate change. We know that. And we know our grandchildren will never forgive us if we don't do something about it. That's not your problem. You're not trained to fight that. But if there are unholy forces playing with the truth, forcing their own priorities on us, incarcerating the good and influencing the decisions of government, then people like you have no choice.' Her hair did its parascending thing again.

'For good men to do nothing?' he suggested.

'Does that sound too dramatic?' she asked.

David looked back out across the sea. A gull of some description was hovering on the wind just by them. It looked at him and then twisted away, the wind catapulting it to some other, far-off location.

'And what about the children? Their safety? It's unlikely, but if I get involved they, whoever *they* are, might need leverage?' David's voice lost its intensity as his words were blown towards the beach.

'They'll have to get past me first.' His wife's reply was a combination of strength and humour.

As he turned back to her, he was nodding.

'I'm going to make a call ... now. Is that OK? And then I might have to go to London?' he asked.

She let go of his hand but kept her smile.

'Of course, darling.'

He grimaced in return and picked his mobile from his pocket. As he dialled, it was his wife's turn to look at the view.

The phone connected.

'Hello, David. This is a surprise.'

The voice was that of Joe Ledbetter, previously one of his opposite numbers in Thames House (*the headquarters location and one of the colloquial terms for Security Service/MI5*). David kept in touch irregularly, mostly meeting at a club in London – as and when. Last David had heard, Joe was still serving. Above all, though, he trusted him implicitly.

'Hello, Joe. Can you talk?'

'Sure, David. I'm in a Faraday cage. You're not. But you know that.'

Most of the inner workings of Thames House (and SIS's headquarters in Vauxhall) were constructed within metal mesh cages. This prevented radiation leakages which made eavesdropping of the UK's security services home base almost impossible. However, away from the buildings the signals to and from towers could be intercepted. If someone were interested, David's phone would be triangulated. An enemy would know where he was to within a few metres. That was a risk he was prepared to take. For now.

They could find him. But they couldn't hear him. As a retired SIS officer his phone had additional encryption beyond the standard A5 GSM algorithm. As a result, David felt confident he could talk freely.

'I want back in the game.'

He was going to add something about 'feeling fit and sharp', but decided against it. He *was* feeling fit and sharp. But that was his view against how he felt yesterday, not how he might have been feeling ten years ago.

And who was he to judge?

There was a pause.

'Why now?'

'Because I have some people working at a distance. They're doing good work. And ... sod it. I don't trust this government. And, frankly, if my old organisation can let their boss go down without a fight, then they've been influenced. And that's a bloody dangerous place to find ourselves.' David was on his feet now. He was pacing and turning.

There was another pause.

348

Then, 'How can I be sure you and your operatives are on my side?' Joe Ledbetter asked.

David picked up another couple of gulls in the distance.

'Whose side are you on, Joe?' David shot back.

The wind blew away the pause. His wife was with him now. She had her hand through the crook in his elbow.

'Good point. Look … we have an extraordinary lead here. Something huge. But it's on very close hold as, like you point out, we don't know whom to trust.'

There was a further beat. David imagined his old pal Joe Ledbetter on his feet, his free hand rubbing his forehead.

'I have to guess that one of your "team" is Jane Baker? Because …' Joe Ledbetter didn't let David answer the question, '… if she is, and she had access to reliable comms, we could do with a non-attributable third party. Someone away from the building.'

It was David's turn to wait now. His lips found his wife's forehead, and he kissed it.

'We should meet,' he replied eventually. He then put one hand on his wife's shoulder and pushed himself gently away. 'I'll come to London. Tonight. You pick a place and time. I'll be there.'

He was looking directly at his wife now. And she was gently nodding at him.

Kirkwall Ferry Port, Kirkwall, Orkney, Scotland

Heather had bought fish and chips from a chippy-cum-Chinese in Kirkwall, the capital of Orkney – a small, rugged red-brown-bricked fishing port looking out over the Bay of

Carness. She'd then driven the short distance to the inconsequential looking ferry terminal to the west of the town. No bigger than a Cornish seaside resort, Kirkwall was still much more of a port than St Margaret's Hope, where she had landed just yesterday.

Another day, another ferry.

She'd slept well overnight, eaten a cooked breakfast big enough for two Scotsmen, and asked her landlady if she knew anything about the shipping lanes and currents around the islands.

'Why's that, dearie?'

The woman's accent was a delicious combination of Gaelic and honey.

'I'm doing some rather macabre research. Which includes dropping bodies at sea.' Heather plumped for the truth. She beamed her biggest smile, with a hope that the woman didn't think she was working out how to commit the perfect crime.

'Ach, no. But Jimmy does. He knows these waters like the back of his hand.'

The conversation then stopped. Heather had hoped her landlady might tell her who Jimmy was, or maybe even make an introduction. Instead she cleared the table next to hers. Only once she had all the crockery balancing in her hands had she restarted the conversation.

'Ach. He owns the croft just up from here. He may be out with his sheep, but he's never far away. Shall I call him for you?' she asked kindly.

'Yes, please. If you don't mind,' Heather had replied.

It had taken her landlady a couple of minutes to deposit the dishes into the kitchen and then call 'Jimmy'. Heather had to assume it was via a mobile, but the woman was so loud she might well have been shouting out of the kitchen window at the poor man.

'Get your carcass down here now, Jimmy lad. There's a wee lass here who needs your help.' There had been a beat during which Jimmy may well have been offering some very plausible excuse. 'I don't care. Get here now, you hear?!'

After that the landlady had come into the small dining room brushing her hands against her apron.

'Jimmy's on his way. May I get you some more coffee, lassie?'

The answer to that question had been, 'Yes, please,' and it hadn't taken long before a quad bike had roared up outside the guesthouse and a white-bearded, elderly man wearing rough farm clothing had burst in and stood bewildered for a second before making the connection that there was only one 'wee lassie' in the room. And that would be Heather.

And he was lovely. And *really* knowledgeable.

It seemed that up to 1,000 ships sailed in between Orkney and Shetland each year. It was the main route from northern Europe to the Faroes, Iceland and then Greenland. Most of the traffic was fishing boats, but there were plenty of cargo ships and freighters, and a weekly ferry from northern Denmark to Reykjavik.

'And, let's assume I dropped a package from one of these boats, where would the currents take it?' Heather had asked.

Jimmy had asked for a pen and paper. Heather's landlady, who was busying herself with more coffee than Heather could drink, delivered a scruffy A4 pad and two coloured pens.

It then all became clear.

The movement of the sea around the islands was dictated by the Gulf Stream, which was still strong this far north. It swirled clockwise around the top of the UK, cutting between Orkney and Shetland, forging into the North Sea. But there was the tide. It wasn't as strong, but when it peaked it either increased the northwest to southeast flow into the North Sea, or decreased it.

'So, if I were to drop, say, a body into the water here ...' Heather was pointing at the midpoint between Orkney and Shetland, around the location of the Fair Isle, 'it would drift into the North Sea, here.' She was now pointing at the middle of the expanse of water which separated the UK from Denmark and Norway.

Jimmy had pulled back at that point. He touched his nose with the non-writing end of the red pen he was holding.

'You're talking about Miss Landown in 2009?' Jimmy's question didn't come over as accusatory. But Heather sensed she might be asking him to break a bond of silence.

She nodded hesitantly.

He put the pen on the table. And said nothing.

Maybe I have crossed a line?

'Hmmm,' he eventually said. 'Nobody asked me when they found the body. I would have told them if they had.'

'Told them what?' Heather's voice was still hesitant.

'She had been in the water for a day. No more. The fish hadn't yet got to her. And she had been bound. I saw the marks on her wrists where she had been tied.' He held his hands together in front of him.

'But the coroner put the death down to misadventure? The body was meant to be decomposed?' Heather offered. She'd read nothing about tie marks.

'Pah!' Jimmy's retort was loud and dismissive. 'She had been tied.' He leaned towards her. 'I saw it. And she may have been alive when she was dropped in the water. The sea is so cold. In December a wee slip of a lass like her wouldn't have survived for more twenty minutes. She was as good as dead. No matter.' Jimmy was nodding sagely.

Heather thought about the burn marks on her wrists which had remained there for weeks.

She offered a pen to Jimmy.

'Where might she have been dropped? If she washed up here?' She nodded at the scribbly map.

Jimmy didn't waste a second. He put a cross off the sea, next to Sanday.

'Five miles. No further.' He then placed the pen back down.

'And what sort of boat might have sailed through here?' She was now pointing at the cross. 'This close. No, hang on ...' Heather stopped herself, before restarting. 'If we assume that Steph Landown had been abducted in a van which was being transported in a boat, what sort of vessel would have sailed past here?'

Jimmy thought for a second. Heather could see that he was cleaning his front teeth with his tongue.

His tongue stopped as he picked up the red pen. He drew a long, flowing line. It started at Kirkwall and cut close to the island of Sanday before sailing past the Fair Isle and ending up in Lerwick, in Shetland. He then turned the pad so that it was landscape .... and wrote out three words under the line.

Northlink Car Ferry.

'Are you sure?' Heather asked.

He nodded. And then said, 'Tuesday, Friday and Saturday nights. Leaves Kirkwall at just before midnight. Arrives in Lerwick the following morning.'

'And when does it return?' she pressed.

'Tea time from Lerwick. Wednesday, Saturday, Sunday. Arrives back at Kirkwall late in the evening. The girl was found on a Monday morning. Could have been dropped from the Sunday night return ferry.' Jimmy was looking solemn. 'I reckon.'

'And nobody asked you?'

'No. I went to the police station in Kirkwall the following week. I saw the sergeant there. My father knew his pappa, a long time ago. And do you know what the policeman said?'

No.

'No, Jimmy. What did he say?' Heather asked.

'He told me to leave it well alone. That the girl wasn't worth it.'

If it were possible, the sadness in Jimmy's face had deepened. It was as though he was somehow responsible for the girl's death.

'That was an odd thing to say ...' Heather added.

And so was the fact that if Heather had followed the same route as Steph Landown, she would have had to take two ferries. One from the mainland to Orkney. And a second from Kirkwall to Lerwick. And back again. And she didn't think she had done that.

'Are there any other ferries to Shetland? From the mainland?' Heather asked.

'Yes. Every day.' Jimmy was nodding again.

'Where from?'

'Aberdeen.'

That was all she needed to know. Heather now had a thesis. It was a poor one. But it would do for her.

Steph Landown had taken the long route to be abused in Shetland. She had been abducted at Thurso, on the north coast, on a Friday night. It would have been pointless driving all the way south to Aberdeen just to sail back up again when there was a short-hop ferry to Orkney which did the trick. Shortest route; quickest time.

Heather had been abducted in Aberdeen … where there had been a ferry waiting for her.

That was it, wasn't it?

It was enough. Jimmy's revelations had given her added momentum to carry on with her journey. But timing was now an issue.

She was due back to work.

And the weekend closest to 'mid-December' in this, an odd year - the date she now associated with the abductions - was next Friday.

She was dipping a chip into a sachet of tomato sauce.

The chips were still warm. Their heat was transferring nicely into her thighs.

It was cold outside. Proper cold. And the sea, even here in the bay, looked untidy and miserable. It was going to be a bit of a journey.

To where?

She didn't know.

For how long?

That was also part of the mystery.

First get on to Shetland.

And then she'd make a decision.

It had taken them an age to find Janne Pedeson's office. St Olav's was a monster of a hospital spread over a couple of blocks, the other side of the Nidelva River from the city centre. And, even though Sam was a competent linguist, the language was incomprehensible. There were too many letters with lines drawn through them. She would have to work on it when she found the time. Which was a joke. They were struggling to stay ahead of themselves at the moment, let alone find the space to do something extracurricular. But, eventually, they had found the waiting room down from Doctor Janne Pedeson's office. Sam was sure of that. She had seen a sign on the door. And she'd been able to check escape routes, which she hoped was an unnecessary piece of detail.

You never know.

She and Jane had landed at Værnes, Trondheim's airport, with enough time to take a taxi to the street where all the multicoloured, riverside merchant houses were. They had found a café, used an airport-purchased iPad to log on to the local Wi-Fi, and talked strategy.

There was a lot to discuss.

Too much – which was why time seemed such a precious resource at the moment.

They'd both agreed the interview with Pedeson would be much more straightforward than the red carpet one with Semenov. Jane, again, would lead; Sam would observe. It should be a simple question and answer affair ... until the doctor called hospital security. Whether any gen came from it, would have to remain a moot point, for now.

The big issue was much more about what to do next? Frank's latest drop (they hadn't spoken to Munich directly; after Berlin, Sam was really worried about being compromised) was a five-pager. It was an update based on three themes.

They now had more than just a feel that the YCA gathered together in the December of odd years. Frank had chosen 2013 at random. In that year the then ten YCA members had congregated in the UK over the weekend 14/15 December. The earliest arrival was the Emiratis, Sheik Rashid bin Nahzan. He'd landed in London on Tuesday 3rd December, and flown out again on the 18th. The man with the shortest window was the South African, Edouard Freemantle. He had flown from Cape Town to Glasgow, via Schiphol, landing in Scotland on Friday 13th. He had flown out again on Monday 16th, using the same route.

Leaving aside Edward Grinstead, the Duke of Nairnshire, the remaining seven non-Brits – the Australian, Michael Connock; the Swiss, Elias Bosshart; the American, Jimmy Johnson; the Frenchman, Marc Belmonte; the now dead Greek, Theodor Konstantos; the Nigerian, Chibuike Grandom; and the German/Russian, Kirill Semenov – had arrived in and left the UK either side of the weekend. Bosshart had crossed the Channel on Eurostar. Marc Belmonte had taken the ferry between Cherbourg and Portsmouth. Everyone else had flown. But there was no pattern of airfields. In fact, the only pattern was that there was no pattern.

Fact: they now knew there had been at least one gathering of the YCA in the UK. Frank's report had made the point that it seemed likely that that meeting was Scotland-based. Otherwise why would the man spending the least time in the UK end his flight plan in Glasgow?

That narrowed the obvious location for the meet: the Duke of Nairnshire's, YCA's likely CEO, estate in Fife. Frank and Wolfgang were now trying to pin that down.

Frank had two other avenues of research worth reporting. First was about how the YCA communicated with each other. First he'd tried to answer the question, how was the hit on Konstantos orchestrated? There was no evidence of phone or email connectivity – Frank had included a couple of paragraphs penned by Wolfgang which explained, in too much detail for Sam, why he thought that unlikely. No matter what security protocols you employ, phones can be tapped and emails intercepted.

Because of that Frank's view was, like the European terror cells of the 70s and 80s, the YCA interacted physically, either by couriers – with dead letter boxes, passing written words using paper codes – or by 'trusted lieutenants', who met one-to-one and had the authority to make decisions.

Frank preferred the latter. Having come to a dead end with the hit on Konstantos, he and Wolfgang had looked at the fallout of the Berlin red carpet operation. They focused on Semenov's inner circle: his senior lawyer, his accountant, and a couple of other colleagues close to the centre of his business. At the time of writing the brief, none of them had 'left the building'.

But Semenov's daughter had.

The timeline looked something like this: Jane had started her interview with Semenov at 18.17, Central European Time. It was over at 18.29. The following morning the daughter had caught a Lufthansa flight out of BER to Birmingham, UK, at 07.35. It had been booked the previous night at 19.47. Having disembarked, she'd hired an Avis rental. From then onwards there was no detailed record.

Outside of Babylon Frank couldn't run ANPR (*automatic number plate recognition*). But Wolfgang could access the motorway cameras. So far, all they knew was the daughter had headed north on the M6 – toward Scotland. It wasn't proof that Semenov's daughter was a courier and was heading for Scotland. But it was a strong possibility.

Finally Frank had listed nine YCA family members with police records; standard SIS coercion practice, find a weakness and exploit it. If nothing came of their meeting with Dr Pedeson, pursuing one of the family members might be an option. The list looked interesting. The geographically closest was someone Sam already knew: Daniel Grinstead, the Duke of Nairnshire's son and a nasty piece of work. He was London based, but would probably be heavily protected and arrogant enough not to engage with them.

A further post-Trondheim alternative was to make the Duke of Nairnshire and his Scottish pile the main effort. She and Jane could do some physical stakeout, whilst Frank and Wolfgang hacked the systems and worked the electronics. If the pattern was as obvious as it looked, nine YCA members would be heading to the UK in the next week or so. Perhaps they should crash that party?

That was as far as their discussions over an eye-wateringly expensive cup of coffee in downtown Trondheim had reached. Fly to Scotland and camp out – that thought sent a shiver of cold down Sam's spine – and then crash the YCA's party.

'We wouldn't make it through the front door,' Jane had offered.

She was right, of course. The Duke of Nairnshire's castle was probably impregnable, as it had been for 500 years. And the grounds were big enough for some large dogs to rip an intruder apart, before one of the gamekeepers buried them in a peat bog on one of their grouse moors.

She, Jane and the two men in Munich would need to be cleverer than that.

And, as Sam looked out of the waiting room's window at the snow-covered roofs of the quite beautiful fjord-side Norwegian city, she didn't think they were cleverer than that.

In fact, she didn't think they were clever at all.

They had expended a huge amount of effort on three catch and grab interviews: Konstantos, his daughter, and then Semenov.

And what had that actually achieved?

Konstantos. Nothing, other than a near-death experience. Oh, maybe not nothing. She was now certain you weren't a YCA member for life. There were rules. And there was a code. Konstantos had broken that code and paid the ultimate price.

His daughter? She had told Sam about the December meeting regime. That was something.

Semenov?

They now knew for certain that the YCA actually existed. And this grouping of billionaires were instrumental in Konstantos's murder and, and Frank's report had agreed with her on this, the YCA were behind the Belarusian border rush of Syrian migrants trying to make it into the EU.

They knew that.

And Frank reckoned the YCA communicated via trusted lieutenants.

That was it.

So, what resources did the fabulous four have at their disposal, against a world class, billionaire-funded criminal network?

One of the best hackers in the world.

Tick.

A very decent analyst.

Tick.

And two has-been SIS case-officers, who were fast running out of spare identities.

Tick, tick.

They were depressingly overmatched.

And unarmed.

I wonder what Trondheim's like to live in?

Expensive, for sure.

Cold.

Nice people, though.

Lots of smoked fish.

Decent but expensive coffee.

But away from prying eyes.

As safe as a northern Brazilian beach?

Possibly.

Probably better. Trondheim had an international airport. A decent rail network. And fabulous roads.

And enough people to get lost among.

Isn't that what they should be doing, the four of them? Splitting up and finding somewhere to retire to?

Sam's thoughts were interrupted by the woman who had shown them to the waiting area ten minutes previously.

'Doctor Pedeson will see you now.'

Jane was away with the fairies. Her eyes had settled on a newspaper on the table. It was called the *Aftenposten*, which she assumed meant, 'Afternoon Post', or something similar. The front page was dominated by a photo of an electronic home speaker. It had been made into a cartoon, the egg-shaped contraption now had massive Dumbo-esque wings. The title read, '*Høyttalere har ører*'. She had no idea what that meant, but she got the gist.

'Doctor Pedeson will see you now.'

The call from Pedeson's secretary broke through her lack of concentration. She lifted her head, nodded, looked to Sam who frowned at her, and then Jane stood, picking up her backpack. This was her lead. They had spoken about it.

Pedeson was a vascular surgeon, which was impressive. Jane didn't know whether to expect her office to be a mess of books and periodicals, accompanied by a full-size poster of the body's organs and the arteries and veins which connect them, or ...

... as she found it.

Norwegian.

Immaculate and minimalist. Lots of dark, carved wood and brushed metal. The coffee table and the four chairs around it were works of art.

'Please sit down, Miss Wild. English?' The doctor was pointing at one of the four chairs. Jane sat. Sam helped herself to a second chair without being asked.

'You are from the British Heart Research Group? It's a new company. Your website is a little, how do you say in English, perfunctory?' The doctor's English was unsurprisingly excellent. Her accent, straight from *The Bridge*. She had walked around her desk and collected an iPad.

Jane didn't reply to begin with. She waited for Doctor Pedeson to join them.

The woman, who was older than Jane, but in very good *langlaufing* shape, took a seat and placed the iPad in front of her.

She looked at Jane, tilting her head on one side, waiting for a response.

Come on.

They'd rehearsed this.

'We're not here from the BHRC, Doctor Pedeson ...' Jane waited for a reaction from the Norwegian. She didn't reply. Instead she shifted in her seat, displaying a little discomfort.

'We've come about your father,' Jane continued.

Still no visible or verbal response from the doctor.

'My friend and I are British Secret Service. We are investigating a group who call themselves the Young Crofters' Association. We believe your father was a member ... until he died.' Jane's questioning was deadpan. Professional. That's the message she wanted to convey. And she had a lot of experience at this.

The woman looked at the window which, through the gaps in the blinds, showed nothing but the city's ambient light breaking through an almost-Arctic blackness. And then back at Jane. She hadn't looked at Sam once.

'You should leave,' the doctor said. There was a hint of a threat in the woman's voice.

'No.' Jane's response was immediate and strong. 'We're not going anywhere until you answer, to the best of your knowledge, some questions about your father's role in the YCA.'

The woman was having none of it.

'You should leave. And I don't mean, because I don't want to talk to you.' She fidgeted again. Then she looked down.

There was a long pause. Jane had been here before. A number of times. In the business this phase of the interview was called 'realisation'.

Something broke inside of the doctor.

'You should go now. Because they will be here soon.' Any stiffness was gone. It had been replaced by alarm in the doctor's voice. She started to rise from her chair.

Jane beat her to it. She put a hand on the Norwegian's shoulder and firmly pushed her back into her seat.

'Did the YCA murder your father?' It was Sam's turn.

Doctor Pedeson shot a glance at Sam.

'Yes. For sure. But you don't get it, do you.' The words were speeding up. 'They will be here. Soon. They watch me *all* the time.' Desperation now. A sense of real panic. 'They will kill me. They will kill you.' She looked to Jane, then back to Sam. 'You *must* go now. Take my car.' She reached into a pocket in her slacks. She pulled out a car fob and threw it on the table.

Jane looked to Sam. And then back at the woman.

'What is the YCA? What is its point?' Jane kept pressing.

The woman looked to the window again, breathing in through her nose. She turned back to Jane. Her eyes were damp. Her shoulders had dropped. She was defeated.

'I don't know. I don't. I wish I did. I was too young. My mother told me a little of what she knew just before she died. In the 70s it was a rich man's club. Papa was asked to join. They talked about world politics. How to get richer. Who could support whom. And then ...' She stalled. Sam was on her feet. She had walked to one side of the window and had lifted the blind.

'Then what?' Jane pressed.

'Then Papa told my mother that they were no longer discussing politics. They were *playing* it.' Doctor Pedeson leaned forward. She rested her forehead on an open hand, an elbow on her knee.

'What do you mean?' Jane asked.

'Apparently Papa was told to lower the price of his oil. We owned multiple rigs in the Norwegian Sea. It was a game ... against OPEC. The YCA apparently wanted to bankrupt some Middle Eastern countries. It was complicated and involved the breadth of Russian influence in the region. That's as much as I know.' She was shaking her head. Jane couldn't really see the doctor's eyes under her hand, but she sounded as though she was crying.

'And he didn't. And they murdered him?'

The doctor looked up at Jane. There were tears in her eyes. She nodded.

'What else can you tell us? Do you remember any other detail about your father's business? Or something which was completely out of place?' It was Jane's turn to lean forward. Her face was close to the doctor's.

The doctor looked to the ceiling. She sniffed.

'I don't know. It was all such a long time ago.' She dithered, and then looked to Sam and back to Jane. 'He went away before Christmas once. And he came back with a present for me. A floppy doll. It was a big issue for my mother.'

'Why?' Jane pushed.

'I don't know. There was a huge argument. My mother said that if he went "there" again, she would leave him. She threw the doll onto the fire. That's all I know.'

Jane was about to continue her questioning when Sam darted across to the table. She picked up the key fob and asked, 'Where's the car?'

Jane's mouth opened. And quickly shut.

'There's a carpark in the basement.' The doctor was staring at Sam. 'I'm bay 135. It's a ...'

'Volvo,' Sam interrupted as she grabbed Jane's hand.

'Describe the doll.' Jane wasn't finished.

The woman's eyes darted between a seated Jane and a standing Sam.

'It was ... dressed in a checked material. You call it tartan?'

That's enough.

Jane rose.

'They're outside. We have to go.' Sam's direction to Jane lacked impact. It was as though she had been caught off guard. Sam then asked, 'What colour was the check?'

The woman looked confused, as though Sam had asked her the square root of some incredibly long number.

'It was dark. Too dark for a doll. Greys and blues.' The doctor's face was a contortion of angst and tears. Jane *so* wanted to reach forward and hug her, but Sam was now pulling at her. Dragging her away.

'Come with us?' Jane said as Sam opened the office door.

'It's no use. There is nowhere to hide.' The doctor's response was feeble. The tears rolling down her cheeks.

And then the pair of them were gone.

They had broken into someone's life and within a few minutes had, likely, destroyed it.

'This way,' Sam said, still holding Jane's wrist. She was striding, close to a run.

And then she stopped abruptly as she reached a corner.

'Shit.' Sam turned quickly and, still with Jane's arm, dragged her back the way they had come, jogging past the doctor's office. They turned another corner. Ahead of them was a short corridor which led to a push-bar exit, beyond which was probably an external fire escape.

Sam stopped again, let go of Jane's wrist and then looked back the way they had come. She pulled back sharply.

'Two men. Long coats. They're heading for the doctor's office. When they don't find us there, they'll be all over this place.' Sam, slightly shorter, was looking up at Jane.

Was she after ideas?

'We hit the fire escape running. It will be alarmed, possibly linked to the desk at the main entrance. If I were the assault party I'd have a man down there. They'll know which door has been sprung.'

No, she's not after ideas.

'I'm going to lead: down the fire escape, right and then away from the hospital, through the car park and across the main road. They arrived in a dark VW transporter. They left a driver with the van. I'm going to make sure that he sees me. Then I'll make it away.' Sam handed Jane the doctor's key fob.

'Bay 135. Follow me down the steps,' Sam continued. 'Turn left. Go round the building to the A&E entrance. Go in, down – there's stairs on the right – and find the car. Meet me at the café in half an hour.'

Jane dithered momentarily, but only for as long as it took for her to hear the *thud* of what she thought was probably a silenced pistol being fired a few offices down from where they were.

It was followed by Sam crashing through the fire door and a screech of alarm.

Jane lost her in the darkness.

She didn't need any further motivation.

Let's go, Jane.

Sam sprinted around the corner of the building, and almost stumbled off the pavement onto the tarmac which lined the 200-or-so space car park. Unlike a UK hospital, where there wasn't room to squeeze in a scooter, St Olav's was half full. And the black VW transporter was as obvious as a cherry tomato in a green salad. She had to get the registration number – and she wanted to see the driver's face. Sure, she had no sketch artist on hand, nor did she have access to Cynthia's facial recognition programme. But she'd have his face. And she would remember it forever.

Half-paused, she looked up at Doctor Pedeson's window. The light was on, but the blinds were still drawn. And there was no movement. She had heard a low velocity shot and she could picture the scene. That was under a minute ago. The attackers would probably be out of the office and on the fire escape by now.

Oh well.

Sam picked her way quickly through gaps between the parked cars on a straight route to the black VW. It was a long wheelbase T6, registered sometime between 2016 and yesterday. Kerb-side sliding door, which had a blacked out window. She could have run through the available engine sizes if anyone had been bothered to ask.

From her view out of the doctor's window, only the driver was left with the vehicle. She had to hope that was the case – and that he'd want to stay with the van. Because she was about to run in front of it.

Right in front of it.

The VW was side on to her. The left-hand bay of two. In the right-hand bay was a fourth generation Ford Mondeo. Eco boost. Probably 2019. Bonnet closest to the veedub. The gap between the two vehicles was narrow.

It didn't matter. She was committed.

Sam slowed to a jog, then a fast walk.

She was in the gap. The VW's bonnet was high. She had to twist her shoulders to find space ... she overdid it, so she was facing the windscreen. The car park lights lit up the cab and gave the driver's face some relief.

Gotcha.

There was a moment.

His face scrunched up. Their gaze fixed for no more than a split second.

He had it then. He knew who she was.

And he had absolutely no idea what to do about it.

Should he stay – make a call? Or chase after her?

It didn't matter to Sam. She was beyond the bonnet now and had turned immediately left, between the van and a BMW X3 – her brain ignoring age, nomenclature and a spectacular list of extras which she'd read about somewhere. Instead she jogged to the back of the Transporter, clocked the registration ... and then ran as if her life depended on it.

Sam was still an athlete, albeit with a stomach wound which had yet to fully recover from surgery undergone in an Israeli hospital all those weeks ago. Her recovery on the beach in Greece had included a daily run, and whilst she wasn't anywhere near her best, she reckoned she could push out a three-and-a-half minute kilometre – maybe quicker. After that she would need to slow. But if you combined her military and SIS case officer training with her cadence, she'd be difficult to catch.

She was also excellent in the dark. She knew where to hide. Where to draw breath. Her route selection was text book. It was about surprise. It was a well-worn argument, but if you surprise yourself with your route choices, that sure as hell was going to surprise any tail.

And she was fitter than most men.

Definitely.

But the attackers wouldn't be far behind. If they hadn't followed Jane – and Sam hoped her diversion would mean they hadn't. She imagined them stopping very briefly with the VW driver, getting directions and then rejoining the chase.

The wrong way.

Sam had shown the driver her route: across the road, left to the end of an apartment block, and then right. But it was a show. Nothing more. As soon as she had turned the corner, she had crossed the street, snuck low and jogged behind parked cars until she was back at the corner. And then, using a dawdling car as cover, she had cleared the gap.

It was a feint.

A good one.

The attackers would head down the street she had just exited.

She was convinced of it.

But ...

These people were good. Somehow within half an hour of her and Jane arriving at the hospital, an armed and well trained group – one of whom was an assassin – had arrived at the hospital.

How is that even possible?

Sam didn't know.

Come on.

She was well beyond the hospital now. She had made a couple of unscheduled turns and was as far off course to the café as she could be. But, she had given herself thirty minutes to meet up with Jane. And she had seen a map of Trondheim – and remembered it. She would be at the RV in time.

As she ran she couldn't ignore her previous thoughts. How could the YCA pull this off? It was like Dick Cuthbert's murder in Copenhagen, earlier in the year. Two skateboarders with a knife, and a fucking barge fitted out with a half-inch sniper rifle?

How does that work?

Did they really have a team on standby in every city there was likely to be trouble? Doctor Pedeson – *bless her* – had said they were watching. Here, in far-off Trondheim, *for Chrissake*.

Sam dropped her run to a jog. She'd been on her feet for over twenty minutes. She was getting close to the pick-up point.

Just around the corner.

She checked her watch.

Twenty-eight minutes since she'd left Jane.

She got to the corner and peered round so she could pick out the entrance to the café.

Nothing.

Sam jogged away until she came across a darkened alcove. She slid into it.

And waited.

Four cars drove past. No VW transporter.

No Jane.

She jogged back down to the corner.

And peeked again.

No Jane.

Nothing.

She waited.

It was thirty-five minutes now.

What the hell was Jane up to?

Nothing.

And then a car. An old Saab 900i. Red. Not the turbo. The wheels were wrong.

Stop it.

The car drove past.

Nothing.

Another car.

A Volvo.

It slowed by the café. And stopped. There was nowhere to park. Its four-way flashers came on.

Sam waited.

And waited.

It if moved on, it would have to pass her.

She waited.

Nothing.

Thirty seconds.

A minute.

Should be clear.

Sam darted across the road to the passenger's side of the car.

It was Jane.

Thank God.

Sam sprung the door, jumped in and shouted, 'Let's go!'

Nothing happened. Sam looked at her. Jane's face was a picture of grief.

'Did we just get that woman killed?' Jane asked, her voice little more than a whimper.

I don't need this.

'Just drive. And if you can't, get out and I will.' There wasn't the time for a therapy session.

Jane looked ahead, selected a gear and the Volvo moved off.

Chapter 15

Vauxhall Pleasure Gardens, Vauxhall, London

There were a number of places where, over the years, spies had met. The Black Dog, which was within walking distance of Babylon, was a suitable location for a low-level cascon over a pint. So were the foyer and street tables of The Tea House, a small bespoke theatre which put on minor plays, monologues, debates and choirs. As unlikely as it sounded, case and intelligence officers felt safe at both locations. Sure, you didn't do Top Secret, as there was always a chance that someone who shouldn't be was listening. But the succession of landlords and patrons knew that an SIS technical team would debug both places once a month, and they, the owners, would report anything suspicious.

However, David didn't want to meet Joe Ledbetter, his MI5 buddy, at either location. He didn't want to bump into anyone he knew. Even if they were on his side – if there were sides – he didn't want anyone to think he was hoping to be back in the game.

But he also knew it would be late by the time he'd get to London. And he wanted to be somewhere familiar. The back end of Vauxhall Pleasure Gardens, a fishing cast from the Black Dog, was as good a place as any.

And both men knew the place.

Sure enough, as David approached the chosen spot – a bench by the kiosk – he picked out Joe. It was dark, but there was enough light to make out his face.

David stopped short. He glanced around and then looked back to the bench. His old buddy was sipping from a Styrofoam cup.

All was clear.

A minute and a half later they had all but caught up with the pleasantries. It was time to get down to business.

'Where are your team?' Joe asked.

David was still unsure about this revitalised relationship. Joe was an excellent operator, one of the best in MI5 for a generation. It was sacrilege that he hadn't been given the top job. He was a team player. He looked after his folk. And they needed that. Both Services needed that. Especially now, when you couldn't distinguish Judas from Saul.

'I can't tell you that.' David put up both hands. 'Actually, I really can't. Not with any certainty. But, in any case ...'

'You can't tell me that.' Joe completed David's sentence.

'Indeed.'

'But you have contact with Jane Baker, Britain's most wanted spy?' Joe asked with a touch of humour.

'Yes. Again, sort of. Via a third party.'

'Whose name or location you can't disclose.' Joe was still ahead of him.

David nodded. 'However.' He had to give something. He needed to bolster his credibility otherwise he wouldn't get anywhere. 'I can tell you that Jane Baker has teamed up with Sam Green.'

Joe Grant didn't say anything. Instead he sipped his drink.

Joe eventually asked, 'She's the girl with the Israeli connections? Sarajevo? Seoul and the train, among others?'

375

David knew his friend well and he would know if his Sam/Jane revelation had been a surprise – or if Joe already knew and was throwing smoke.

Joe didn't know.

Which was some relief.

David nodded.

Joe continued. 'And if the analyst chap of yours, Frank, is with them – The Box know of him after the death of one of ours under a train – then you have quite a competent outfit on the loose. With no ties.'

It was.

Jane, providing she was well.

Sam and Frank ...

... and Wolfgang.

It was the sort of unaffiliated agent-grouping any SIS case-officer would have sold their mother for. The four were very competent, agile and they knew each other well. They had a well-balanced basket of skills, and the doggedness to see any operation through.

It was the A-Team.

And Joe Ledbetter didn't know about Wolfgang. He was the icing. Wolfgang had to be kept out of any discussion. The German would tie the team to a location. It was a key piece of intel which must not be shared.

'That's correct,' David replied. 'Sam Green does have a tendency to do her own thing. But she has skin in this game and, goodness, does she have tenacity.'

'And they are, to all intents and purposes, agents? No longer government employees? Do you feel at liberty to use them as such?' Joe asked. His friend had finished his coffee. He reached across and threw the cup in the bin.

David took a long breath in through his nose. He held it ... and then breathed out.

It was *the* big question. Of course there was no guarantee that any of them would take directions from him. He suspected, provided he could nurture their confidence, and offer them support which they couldn't get elsewhere – even with Wolfgang's hacking skills – they might.

But could he deliberately cross SIS's very well defined risk-threshold and put them in harm's way? He would if he were dealing with an agent of his. But not a member of his staff. Where would he draw the line here for the benefit of the Service?

He wasn't sure.

He leant back onto the metal slatted bench and gently stretched his back. The orthopaedic surgeon who had fused the two discs in his spine wouldn't be happy that he'd sat all afternoon on a train and was now letting the cold of the steel bench soak into his crumbling bones.

'Yes, of course,' he lied. 'But first we need to give them something. They currently trust no one. I wouldn't if I were in their position. So I have to offer two things. First is support. A secure connection to the run-of-the-mill intelligence services, such as police records – here and abroad – mug shots, vehicle registrations, mapping, satellite imagery, the usual niff-naff.' He looked at his friend's face to see if he could register any pushback.

There was none.

'And second?' Joe asked.

'We need to offer them a piece of intelligence which demonstrates goodwill. Something hot. Something connected to the YCA. Something timely.' David leant forward. 'Something I don't have.' He offered a hand as if he was expecting Joe to put something in it.

His friend nodded again.

'This is a challenging time, David. A dangerous time. The Director is caught between two feuding cabals. It's as though there's a schism between right and left – and it's almost an ideological break. There are those who believe our values are in danger, the literal colour of our nation is changing. That wokeness is allowing, no *encouraging*, the wrong sort of socialism. It's all unwritten, but one side believes that the majority is in danger of being overwhelmed by a sea of minorities. That this country's fabric is being attacked by an ideological left, which is using any play, any group – activists for climate change, black lives matter, immigrants, even the "do-gooders" in the church and the judiciary – to undermine what used to be.' Joe sighed, the air colder than it was when they'd arrived, his breath a puff of steam. 'They, and they are mostly older white people, are disquieted. They worry for the foundation of the Union. For the future of the monarchy.'

'And the YCA are on that side of the argument?' David asked.

Joe screwed up his face.

'My view is the YCA has no political foundation. I can't confirm that – and we are a long way from adding to that canvas. But I sense that the YCA's only concern is the YCA. Money and power is everything. That means capitalism is king. Free markets, offshore accounts, tax havens – they are all central to the economic survival of these disruptors.'

They had both leaned forward, their elbows on their knees, their tones hushed.

'But they naturally support the right,' David added. 'The left is all wrong for them. That ideology sees the redistribution of wealth, net-zero and the immediate cap on fossil fuels to tackle climate change, and the removal of borders. Migration becomes unchecked?' It was sort of a question. But David had rehearsed the arguments a number of times to himself.

'I think that's spot on. But I do think the YCA, with their hold on much of the world media, probably a sizable number of bot farms delivering some expert perversion via social media platforms ...', Joe paused, just for a second.

'... are widening the trench. They are purposely playing to everyone's concerns. Fordingly for example – and more about him in a second. We are close to nailing him as a Michael Connock implant. You and I both know that Connock, with his video, internet and print media, has been all over the political discourse for years. That for almost three generations he has backed the winning prime minister. Some would argue, *picked* the winner.' Joe took another deep breath and expelled another cloud of steam. 'But, this time ...' He paused, as though he was deciding whether he was going to say something that might be better left unsaid.

'This time, what, Joe?' David asked.

Joe, still forward, his chin now resting on his hands, was staring across the park.

'We think it's deeper than that. Much deeper, and much more unpleasant.' His head turned so that he and David were eye to eye.

'Go on?' David asked. And then he added ... 'Is this the big revelation I can share with my team?'

Joe nodded again.

'Yes.' And then he added, 'You have to guarantee that you can control your team. I'm about to hand you the nuclear codes. In exchange I want access. I need to be able to manipulate them. They might just be the operational freedom we need.'

379

It was David's turn to nod.

'Who are *we*, Joe?'

'Me, three intelligence officers, two analysts and my secretary. It's called Operation Hullabaloo. It's on the tightest of holds. The boss knows of its existence, but doesn't have access to the files. It's the way he wants it.'

'OK, you've got it,' David said, although he knew there was no way he could guarantee that Sam Green would be manipulable. 'It's a good place to start. Count me and the team in.'

Joes took another breath.

This is taking a lot of effort.

'We recruited Fordingly's second valet. It was a long shot,' Joe said.

'That old game – it's a bit hit and miss, isn't it?' David replied.

'Sometimes. We've always been careful. Normally we give the staff a year to settle in. We look for themes, openings. As you do. And we're rarely successful. But, with Fordingly, we were in a rush.' Joe's face was earnest.

'Because you don't trust him?' David asked.

'Yep. Never have. We've been following his career for a decade or so. There's not much good to say about it. And he's not been harmless, either. As Foreign Secretary we're pretty sure he slipped intelligence to the Russians for cash. But we've never been able to get to him … until now.'

David didn't say anything. He had absolutely no idea what was coming. And he was fascinated.

Joe continued.

'I guess you know he escaped the attack on the Grand. The official line was that he was called out of the dinner by a call from the FCO.' Joe paused for effect. Which was a good job, because David was struggling to believe where this was probably going.

'Except, there was no call?' David asked, his voice unable to hide its horror.

His friend shook his head,

'How do you know?' David followed up.

'The valet. He'd given us nothing up until then. He'd only been on our books for a week, so we weren't expecting anything. But he reached out, if that's what you want to call it. He pulled Fordingly out of the dinner. Which, apparently, Fordingly had instructed him to do. At an exact time. Just before the drone attack.' Joe's voice had an edge. There was anger, and some residual disbelief.

'Why don't you … what can you … ' David's line of questioning didn't complete itself.

'The valet phoned his handler – one of my three IOs. He had been caught up in the blast. So much so he didn't make it, bless him. But he found the energy to have a conversation.'

'The man needs a bloody posthumous medal!' David blurted the words out.

'That's not all,' Joe continued.

'What, there's more?'

His friend nodded.

'Fordingly's contact prior to the Grand was, highly likely, Daniel Grinstead.' Joe's voice still had an edge.

Who's he?

'Sorry, Joe. Who?'

'Daniel Grinstead is the son of the Duke of Nairnshire, one Edward Grinstead.'

David had it then. Jane had told much of the story. Edward Grinstead was number one at the YCA.

'This is blood dynamite, Joe. Can you actually piece this together? In a legally tight way?' David asked.

'Last Saturday night the valet took Fordingly to a clandestine meeting, away from Chequers. The valet drove his own car. Fordingly transferred to a Blue Bentley, registration DG 555. The car and private plate belongs to Daniel Grinstead.' There was a beat. 'It's not bulletproof, but it's as good as we're going to get it.'

'The YCA warned Fordingly of the drone attack. They wanted him alive and, with no need for logic, the others are dead? Why?' David asked.

Joe shook his head again.

'That's why I need your team's help to find out.'

E6, South of Trondheim, Norway

They hadn't spoken for twenty minutes. Sam had barked a few orders at her, Jane had obeyed, and they were out of the small city's limits in ten minutes. Fifteen minutes later they were one of a few cars heading south towards Oslo which, Sam had told her in a monosyllabic response, was 500 kilometres away. An eight-hour journey, give or take.

Jane wasn't sure she was going to make it.

She wasn't sure she should be driving.

Leaving aside her stay in the Villa in Lao Chai, it had easily been the worst few days of her life. The killing of that poor man on the quay. The second double-tap had left the barrel of her pistol with no small amount of glee.

And now the death of Doctor Pedeson, whose life had likely been on an even keel until she and Sam had burst into her office. They might as well have pulled the trigger themselves.

382

Should they have known?

Should they have been more careful? Maybe arranged to meet her away from the office, somewhere less conspicuous?

If they had, though, would the Norwegian have come?

And, what had they *actually* learnt?

That the YCA were as ruthless as they were omnipresent?

For sure.

And there was more confirmation that the group met in December, even in the early years. But they knew that already. One woman's life wasn't worth the confirmation. What about the tartan piece? Didn't they also know that? The Duke of Nairnshire was a Scottish laird. He was the top man. They came to his house every couple of years for a shindig. They had that already.

Jane was mouthing the questions to herself as she drove.

Should they have gone to Scotland rather than expose the doctor? Put *their* lives in danger, rather than that of some other hapless individual?

Jane was shaking now. It wasn't cold. The Volvo's heating was excellent.

It was shock, or fear … or remorse. Or all of those.

She needed a hot drink. Some food.

Sleep.

A holiday.

Anything but this.

'Sam?' she asked.

'Mmm?' Sam's answer was dismissive.

'I need to stop. I need something to drink. Tea, or coffee. Sleep, probably.' Jane was surprised her teeth weren't chattering.

'OK.' Sam glanced over her shoulder. There was a car behind them. Jane didn't think it had been there for long. 'We need to lose the Volvo. Find another way to get out of Norway. I'm not confident our IDs have survived contact with the enemy. We might have run out of options there.' Sam's tone was lifeless. Jane struggled to find any empathy. She hardly had enough for herself.

'There,' Sam continued. 'Those lights ahead. Looks like it's a town. Turn right here.'

Jane slowed, and then turned right into what appeared to be an off-the-main-road village.

As the Volvo managed the corner, Sam kept checking behind. Jane spotted what she was looking for. The headlights of the car behind had stayed on the main road.

The village was called Småvollan. It was unremarkable, especially at night, caught between two rising hills which squeezed in a pretty big river, the main road to Oslo, and a smattering of buildings ...

... and a bloody big hotel.

It was a large rectangular block of a building, wood clad, but not in an attractive way. Jane knew it was a hotel because there was a large neon sign on the front wall: Støren Hotel. She pulled into its car park, found a slot among other cars as far from the main road as possible, and rested her head on the headrest.

She closed her eyes.

'Get inside,' Sam said, surprisingly with some softness. 'Use the cash, and if that's not enough, the Athens card. See if they'll take some fake names. And then get a drink from the minibar and get into the bath – something way too hot for a toddler. I'll be up in a bit.'

'What are you going to do?' Jane had lifted her head. She felt marginally more comforted by Sam's instructions.

'I'm going to change the plates. If I'm not with you in thirty minutes, come and pay my bail.'

Jane snorted a small laugh and she didn't wait for anything more.

Fifteen minutes later she had a cold coke in one hand whilst the other tested the temperature of the water coming out of the bath's tap.

It was wonderfully hot.

She was naked. Not even a towel.

She caught sight of herself in the mirror above the sink.

The image was skeletal. You could easily make out her ribs. Her eyes were sunken and her hair was greasy and unshapen. She felt as attractive as a prison inmate.

But it wasn't about her, was it?

No, I'm not going there again.

She wasn't.

The bath was now hot and full, almost to overflowing.

She tentatively got in, lay down, closed her eyes, and was fast asleep in seconds.

Sam was cold. The outside temperature must have been below zero; she'd almost slipped on a patch of ice on the path into the hotel lobby. There was a woman behind the front desk. She was blonde, tall and wore her uniform a little too tightly for Sam's taste. But that was probably jealousy on her part.

'My friend has just booked in.' Sam was at the desk. The blonde woman was pouting.

Give it a rest, girl. I'm really not your type.

'Ah, yes, the English lady. She told me to expect you.' Another pout. And a toothy smile. Sam didn't have the energy for this.

'What room is she in?' Sam scowled a little in the hope it would stop the woman from flirting.

'325, that's ...'

'Third floor.' Sam made an unnecessary pointy-upstairs gesture. 'I'll need a key.'

The blonde pouty woman now realised her charms were missing the mark. She stopped smiling, reached down for a key-card, did that special thing in a machine which recodes it for your room, and then handed it to Sam.

'*Takk skal du ha.*' Sam hoped that meant 'thank you' in Norwegian. And she even tried an accent. She had picked the phrase up at the hospital. And a few other words. She'd soon be able to order a beer.

The receptionist was caught out by Sam's thanks. Her chin dropped a centimetre and she smiled again.

Sam couldn't prevent her own smile. But it was accompanied by the smallest of shakes of the head.

She used the stairs, because that's what she did, found the room, entered quietly, dropped her bag on the bed which wasn't covered with Jane's clothes, and opened the mini bar.

She checked the prices. And immediately declined the limited choice of alcohol. She closed the small fridge's door.

What now?

She really didn't know. Whatever they chose to do next, and she wasn't sure if 'they' was in fact just a 'she',

386

they were running out of lives. Their IDs and bank cards were shot. And there was little chance of Wolfgang pulling an iron from the fire, not here. Oslo wasn't an Athens-esque 20-million-person metropolis where, if you weren't avoiding paying your taxes, you were dealing in something, or running something else. Sam didn't think all Greeks were crooks, but corruption was a way of life for some and, with much of society generally impoverished, making money illicitly was one way to survive.

Norway didn't have those issues. Hence finding a forger would be a tricky task.

So they, or she, were in the red column of the risk register. And anything they did from now would increase that risk.

But she recognised that 'what now' wasn't her most pressing question.

First she had to find out what Jane's plans were.

She took off her hoodie and walked into the steamy bathroom …

… and it was good to see that Jane had followed her instructions.

There she was.

A bath full of piping hot water, a submerged waif of a body, and a head which was dead to this world.

Sam sat on the edge of the bath. She stared at Jane.

One part of her wanted to get back into the Volvo, drive as fast as she could to Dunkirk, jump on a ferry, drive north until she hit the Duke of Nairnshire's fucking estate, grab a rock in one hand and a club in the other, and knock on his door.

Leave Jane here.

Her friend would think of something.

Something safe. Maybe she'd get Wolfgang to send through some other cousin's ID card. Norway was in the Schengen zone. Jane would be welcome. She would learn the tongue quickly. She'd be teaching English as a foreign language before you knew it. Two years and she'd be shacked up with some handsome Norwegian arborist – cross-country skiing in the morning, smorgasbord for lunch, two junior ginger Vikings to pick up from playgroup, an afternoon sauna, followed by an evening of dark police thrillers and bootleg beer.

She smiled to herself. It wasn't a bad option. And it would suit Jane.

And that would suit Sam ... Jane morphing into the Norwegian countryside.

Sam would be back on her own.

With only herself to look after.

One woman, one mission.

...

She lost herself in wistful options.

'Are you OK, Sam?'

Jane was awake, making no attempt to cover her modesty. It was a sister thing.

'Sure. You?'

Jane shook her head.

'Not really. I'm fazed. Upset. Angry. Disappointed.' She paused. And then added, 'Frustrated.'

Jane had wanted to say something else, but Sam raised a hand.

'I don't care, Jane. I don't care how you feel, that you're fazed, upset, angry, disappointed and frustrated.' Sam rattled off Jane's sentiments back at her. 'How you feel is irrelevant. How *I* feel is irrelevant.' She paused. Just for a second.

Jane was looking straight at her, her friend's face emotionless.

Sam continued.

'The only thing I care about is whether or not you are effective. Are you competent? And can you stay that way? Because ...' Sam stood. She looked at herself in the bathroom mirror. She was all tatty t-shirt and mousy curls. Her pointy nose the only good thing going on in the mirror. How on earth did the blonde pouty woman find her remotely attractive? Or did she flirt with everyone?

Probably

'... because, we're at the top of the rollercoaster. And the only way is down. And I'm staying on that train.' She pointed at her chest. 'I have the motivation. It comes from those teenagers in Bosnia. From the abject disaster I witnessed in Abuja. I'm fired up ...' Her tone had shifted. There was anger now. '... after the assault in Athens. Of the speed, reach and ruthlessness of these people.'

She slowed then.

'I'm in this for Doctor Janne Pedeson.'

Sam turned to the bathroom door. And without looking back, she finished her monologue with, 'Think about it. But make one decision. And then stick with it.'

She walked out of the bathroom.

Muness Castle, Unst, Shetland

Heather caressed one of the slabs of rock which was the top layer of a dry stone wall that surrounded the castle. It was cold to the touch. Everything was cold. She had bought a thick woollen hat from 'The Final Checkout Café', a warehouse-sized metal lock-up which sold everything from cereal to socks. And woollen hats.

She had done nearly all of Unst, the northernmost island of Shetland, by car and had arrived here. Her masterplan was to drive every available road and track on the islands ... looking.

Searching.

For what?

She didn't know. And she was pretty certain she wouldn't recognise it even if she found it. But she had to try.

Something old.

With a cellar.

Like Muness Castle.

Except, nothing like Muness Castle.

Sure, it was a helluva fortification. It was castle-shaped, built with thick, two-storey high stone walls. It had turrets, and slits for windows. And a moat.

And the view from where she was now, even in the dark, was breathtaking. The sea was 500 metres away, but the wind was in the direction where she could hear the waves arguing with an unseen shore, the twinkle of a distant lighthouse the only hope for those lost at sea. It was perfect castle territory.

It was also perfect dungeon territory. A far-off, very distant place where young men and women could be trussed and dragged to ... and then abused. It was exactly what she was looking for.

But it wasn't.

Because Muness Castle was a shell. And it was a shell which you could walk around, explore every nook.

She was loving Shetland for that reason. Everyone was charming. The place had a welcoming 'please join us; our island is your island' feel. Here, at the edge of the earth, a once mighty castle, perched on a high cliff, was open for anyone to walk around. There was no health and safety. There was just access.

And that made her happy.

But it also made her feel depressed.

If all of Shetland – she had only done the northern island, there was plenty more to explore – was this congenial, was she really expecting to discover a centre of terror? Some hideous, monstrous dwelling among all of this pleasantness?

Certainly not at Muness Castle.

Heather had booked a B&B on Yell, the Old Post Office, the next island down. Searching that island and its smaller neighbour, Fetlar, which only had one short road, was tomorrow's job. And then she'd be onto the main island, which had a good number of roads and tracks. That would probably be a two-day expedition.

Four days in total. Four days before the Friday of the middle weekend in December.

Four days.

She needed more time.

Time she'd not secured.

She headed off to her car, taking out her phone as she walked.

She opened her messages and found the latest thread with her boss.

She typed: *Thanks for letting me go at short notice. I need another couple of days, maybe more. It's a long story, but it would be great if you could give me the time. Happy to be off, unpaid. Heather.*

She pressed send.

What would happen if he said yes and a week later she was no further forward? Could she cope with that level of failure? Had she opened a wound which, if she wasn't able to suture it, would bleed and bleed?

Her tummy did a thing.

No, she wasn't going to think about it.

Onwards.

Flemingstraße, Munich, Germany

Frank looked to Wolfgang who was sitting an arm's width from him. His German friend was staring back.

Had they really just heard that?

'I think I need a coffee,' Wolfgang said without emotion. 'I guess it's herbal tea for you?'

Frank nodded a series of nods, which after time developed into a shake of his head.

This is not real.

Wolfgang's electric wheelchair purred backwards, spun and headed to Matilda's place. Frank looked at the digital clock on the screen. It was 01.43. Well past his bedtime. But could he sleep? He wasn't sure.

David had just been in touch. It was a clunky connection which Wolfgang had set up over a web address attributed to the RAC Club in London. After some work it eventually allowed David to talk via his smartphone. Apparently he was staying there the night having met a friend from 'The Box'. He had news.

And what news.

In short, the UK's prime minister had purposely avoided the Edinburgh drone attack. He'd been given the nod by none other than Daniel Grinstead, the Duke of Nairnshire's son. Grinstead was a man Frank already knew to be a hard-right-supporting, nasty piece of work. He mixed in the upper echelons of society and was married to a British princess. She had benefited from the now defunct (thanks mostly to Sam Green) YCA owned, illegal liver-transplant hub in Minden, Germany. Frank didn't like him at all.

David's senior connection in MI5 strongly suspected that Prime Minister Fordingly was in the YCA's employ and that Fordingly had been shoe-horned into power with the explicit support of Michael Connock's media empire. And he had survived a fatal terrorist attack on the banquet for Commonwealth leaders because that's what the YCA wanted.

As David talked Frank had opened up the front pages of yesterday's right-leaning newspapers. They all ran the story, of course. But those owned by Connock were much more focused on Fordingly's escape, rather than those who had died. The most right-wing tabloid, which wasn't short of readers at almost three million a month, had the headline: *Thank God! The PM is alive!*

It was all incredibly shocking.

But that wasn't all.

David's MI5 chum – no name offered – wanted their help. He was heading up a small six-strong team, which was leading on the YCA. It was semi-autonomous, but lacked the independence a group like theirs could add. David's view was that they could share intelligence and advice, with the MI5 team offering additional horsepower and, importantly, the usual gamut of resources which Sam *et al* could only dream of. David trusted his pal, and added that between them they had a real chance of making something happen.

'We'll need to speak to Sam and Jane,' Wolfgang had said.

'They're not with you?' David had come straight back.

Realising his mistake, Wolfgang had shaken his head. He'd made a mistake by unnecessarily placing Frank with him, and Sam and Jane away. Frank trusted David, so it was hardly a major issue. But the less everyone knew about everything else, the less chance there was that intelligence would spill. That's the world they were in.

'I need to make some calls.' Wolfgang had made an attempt to correct his error.

And now he was making them both a hot drink.

Frank was too tired to think about it all. In fact he was struggling to cope with the enormity of it all. If MI5 didn't have the horsepower or reach to prevent an Australian media tycoon from running the country by proxy, and the UK's intelligence organisation was so divided that they had to set up a semi-autonomous cell to look into something this big, what chance did the four of them have?

Weren't they in danger of poking at a monster with a toothpick?

Hadn't that always been the case?

And why hadn't they heard from Jane and Sam?

If they lost those two, what would he and Wolfgang do? Frank wasn't a field agent. And Wolfgang was home schooling.

What on earth were they playing at?

The smell of camomile tea arrived well before Wolfgang did. His pal handed it to him. It was in a lovely, blue calico, Meissen bone china mug – Frank had checked its base. And he had fallen in love with it.

'You can take that with you. When you leave,' Wolfgang said, raising his demitasse of coffee by way of salute.

'Thanks, Wolfgang. That means a lot,' Frank replied.

'*If* you leave,' Wolfgang then added. 'Let's face it. I'm not sure you're welcome anywhere else at the moment?' The German smiled.

Frank nodded. He hadn't got that far. But it was a good point. How long would he remain here? Surely he couldn't stay in the cellar? He needed to get out. In fact, Wolfgang's comment immediately made him feel trapped. Not in Munich. Not really. Munich was a lovely city.

But in the cellar.

Then there was the whole sleeping and bathing arrangements. They could share Wolfgang's huge bed, as they currently were. That didn't bother him. But that couldn't last for much longer, could it?

How long can I do this for?

He was about to ask Wolfgang how he might break out, even for just a couple of hours, when the German's screen bleeped.

He had a call.

'It's Sam.' Wolfgang put his coffee cup down. And tapped on his keyboard.

'Hi, Sam,' he said.

'Hi.' A single word reply from the ether.

Frank filled the void.

'How was Doctor Pedeson?' he asked.

'Dead,' Sam replied without emotion.

'We think,' Jane quickly added sombrely.

What?

'How?' Wolfgang spluttered. 'She was with us yesterday ... when I made the appointment?'

'She wasn't when we left the building,' Sam replied, again without feeling.

'Are you both OK?' Frank interjected, his voice higher pitched than he would have liked.

There was a long silence from Norway.

Wolfgang shot a glance at Frank. He shrugged his shoulders in return.

'You better have some options for us. We're out of ideas here. And, to be fair, we're struggling to hold it all together.' It was Sam.

There was a further beat.

Then, 'What Sam means is that I'm not sure I can go on with this. Pedeson's death has hit me much harder than anything I've been through previously,' Jane said, her voice hardly audible.

'She died because of the meeting? Were you ambushed?' Frank asked as sensitively as he could.

'Yes. Look ...' Sam's tone was more businesslike now. 'We need a plan, noting that these people are everywhere. Quickly. If it were left up to me I'd be tempted to walk onto his fucking Lordship's estate and put a brick through his window.'

'Wait.' Frank found himself raising his hands. 'We have a lot to tell you, some of it ghastly, some of which might be helpful. Let's get everything out there and then we can work out what to do next?' He found himself, unusually, taking control. Things must be really bad in Norway.

There was another pause.

'Go on,' Sam eventually said.

Frank led. He left the MI5 revelation to end. He didn't want them to become preoccupied with that. First, he updated them on what Wolfgang and he had pulled together since they'd last spoken.

'Our 2013 search now guarantees that the nine travelling YCA members were in Scotland for the weekend in December. We can't access the ANPR cameras for that year, so we're going on bank card and passport usage only. But they're all there. Interestingly one of the group used his Amex as far north as Wick, which is 120 kilometres from the Nairnshire estate. We're assuming that was a day trip of some sort.'

'Where was it used – specifically?' Sam asked.

'An ATM,' Frank replied.

Sam didn't add anything.

'Moving on. We can confirm that yesterday Semenov's daughter picked up a hire car from Birmingham airport – Wolfgang can access a rolling twenty-eight-days' worth of CCTV and she was easy to find. She took the car north and the last guaranteed sighting is near Aviemore, on the A9.'

'That's not far from Nairnshire's estate,' Sam butted in.

'Correct,' Frank replied. 'And I'm not finished with the trusted lieutenant's approach. We did a search on Daniel Grinstead's movements over the past two months. He's been abroad recently ...' Frank deliberately didn't finish his sentence.

'Athens?' Jane chipped in.

'Exactly. He flew in three weeks ago and stayed for five days,' Frank said.

'Arranging the Konstantos murder,' Wolfgang added. 'I think we can assume that.'

There was a beat.

'Useful. But not really helping. What else?' Sam asked. There was a resigned tiredness in her voice.

Frank didn't take offence.

'We can confirm that Semenov flew to Moscow six weeks ago. A couple of days later he connected to Minsk,

Belarus, where we know he visited the House of Government on Independence Square. Wolfgang did his CCTV thing again. Semenov was in the building for five hours. He left with the Belarusian interior minister.'

'To arrange the influx of Syrian migrants on the Polish border?' Jane asked.

'It's a possibility,' Frank concluded.

'What else?' Sam now sounded tired *and* impatient.

Frank looked at Wolfgang. He pointed his finger at him, and then back to himself. Wolfgang got the message. He pointed back to Frank and mouthed, 'You'.

'OK. This is pretty big and it may well change the complexion of how we go forward,' Frank kicked off.

It took him just a few minutes to relay the conversation they'd had with David. At the end he leaned back in his chair and put his hands behind his head.

There was nothing.

Eventually Jane said, 'Bloody hell.'

But Sam was silent.

Frank knew that Sam would have a problem with accepting help from MI5. It would be a twofold objection. First, she didn't want to be moribund by association with the British government, no matter how 'independent' David had made the team out to be. Second, she wouldn't trust them, no matter the assurances.

So it surprised the hell out of him when she eventually replied.

'Jane goes to the UK. She works alongside the MI5 team. Becomes our LO in their place. Acts as a go between. The problem we have is that our IDs are shot. All of them. These people were in the hospital within half an hour. They knew we were there. And if they've got six brain cells between them, our Athens passports will be shot too.' She

398

paused for a second. Frank imagined Sam looking at Jane just to make sure there were no violent objections. 'So, get back onto David now. Jane needs a route out of here. MI5 should be able to charter a private plane and fly her incognito into the UK. Make that happen.'

Frank glanced at Wolfgang. He was scribbling notes on a bit of spare paper.

There was another pause.

'What, Sam?' Frank asked.

'Shut up. I'm thinking.'

Frank briefly raised his eyes to the ceiling.

Sam started again.

'I need to get to the US. As soon as possible. But not from here. Throw the scent. Wolfgang, you know my IDs, pick one and plan a route. I need to go to Atlanta. And I need to be there yesterday.'

As Wolfgang made a further note, Frank asked, 'Why?'

'Never mind. Again, best to keep this cellular. But the principle is, the only way we can expose these people is to beat them at their own game. And I know some people.'

Frank screwed up his face. He had no idea what Sam meant.

'And when you're all moving, what do you want us to do?' Frank asked.

There was another beat. Sam was obviously making this up as she went along.

'We need as much factual information as we can get on the YCA's interference on the world stage. We've got the Fordingly survival debacle, although nobody has asked the question, "who gains?" That's the first question. Who died, and why? The second could well be the Belarus thing. Third is the Sarajevo facility, and – and I'm going to need to speak to my pal in Mossad – Abuja is the fourth. Last time we spoke you mentioned the death threats against the Brazilian opposition leader. We need a YCA link there, if there is one. We could add that to the list. And others. I want fact-checked examples of how these fuckers are making everyone else's life a misery ...' Sam's list of orders tailed off.

'What about the upcoming weekend, Sam?' Wolfgang asked. 'Excluding the Duke of Nairnshore who is currently hosting a shooting party on his land, we already have three YCA members in the country. It all looks set for another biennial meeting.'

'Who's here?' Sam asked.

'Sheik Rashid bin Nahzan is in his Park Lane apartment. The South African, Edouard Freemantle, is a guest speaker at an Oxford College tomorrow night. And Chibuike Grandom is at his UK lithium-ion battery manufacturer, Inux Power, which has its base in the Welsh Valleys. I've got alerts on the rest of them, but it seems likely that the pattern is being followed. I am running every programme I can, and probably using half of Munich's power bank as a result, but I am close to hacking the Nairnshires' estate security.' Wolfgang exhaled, his cheeks expanding as he did. He added, 'All of this takes time and power. Your priorities are helpful.'

Frank reached over and touched Wolfgang's forearm. He reckoned they'd had no more than eight hours' sleep each in the past three days.

'I'll find time to help here, Wolfgang.' It was Jane's turn. 'As soon as I've liaised with the MI5 team, we'll get eyes on the estate. If nothing else, the main entrance. I'm sure they'd be up for that.'

'OK.' Sam brought everyone up short. 'Get Jane to the UK, safely. Share what we need with MI5. Let's get eyes on the Fordingly estate whilst we monitor the YCA's incoming movement. And let's get a tirade of awfulness to use against them. The MI5 team might be able to add to the list. And, Wolfgang?' Sam asked.

'*Ja!*' he replied.

'We're just outside Trondheim. I want to be in Atlanta by teatime tomorrow. They won't be expecting that, so take whatever risks you need. Questions?'

Kismet

Chapter 16

Gloup, Yell, Shetland, Scotland

The Shetland island of Yell, about 30 kilometres long and 10 kilometres wide, was serviced by one major road, south to north, the A968. Off it was a loopy B-road, the B9081, which covered a wide bit of the island which the A-road ignored, including the wonderfully sounding hamlets of Otter Wick and Burravoe. Heather aimed to cover both of those places this afternoon. Now, though, she was at the end of the only other road, the B9082, which led to the northern tip of the island, the Ness of Houlland.

Which was beautiful.

She had been blessed with a cold but clear day, the long grass along the edge of the small and very narrow sea loch, the Easter Lee of Gloup, frosted white. There was no wind, and whilst the sun was up it was idling about just above the horizon, casting long shadows and offering little by way of warmth.

That didn't bother Heather. Under multiple layers she was toasty and, if the route continued to be this taxing, she might have to discard some clothes to cool down – her gloves were already stuffed into her handbag. Wearing trainers, jeans, a t-shirt, a blouse, a cardigan, a decent winter coat and her recently acquired hat, she might not look as if she was dressed for hill walking, but she was determined to be warm. That was unless she mis-stepped and toppled into the freezing loch, which was a fairly steep 5 metres down, off to her right.

She repeated to herself – it *was* beautiful.

The loch was as clear as glass, its bottom a combination of white sand, rock and seaweed. She could see hundreds of fish which might soon be bait for a lazy seal. It was sleeping on a boulder, just across the loch at the bottom of what looked like an even steeper slope than the one she was on. Her OS map – she was really pleased that she hadn't forgotten the skills she'd learnt at Brownies – told her the loch was a mile long and the stumbly path, which was no more than one shoe wide, followed the loch to its end at Mare's pool, and then came back on itself, along the far shore.

She'd borrowed the map from her B&B. It showed a hut at the end of the track on the other side of the loch. She could already see it from where she was. It was a roofless stone building, barely bigger than half a single garage. Beyond that the track headed up the hillside, away from her. The map identified two more structures over the top of the hill. She'd cross-checked with Google Earth. The closest looked derelict. The furthest, only a kilometre from the loch, appeared to have a new roof. It seemed the only way to access the two buildings was on foot, which probably disqualified either as places of interest. But, for completeness, she thought she'd give it a go.

That had been her approach thus far, and she thought she was doing a fair job. She driven the roads and tracks to get places. And then she'd used a map/Google Earth combination to check out buildings on foot that she couldn't reach by car. So far this was the furthest trek she'd attempted. Heather hadn't yet started on the main island. Hopefully there she'd be able to tick everything off from the warmth of her hire car.

Whatever ... she had a sandwich and a can of coke with her. And so far, she was making sensible progress. She reckoned she'd be able to see the furthest building in an hour or so. And, if it didn't look like a place where they raped young people, she'd turn round and head back.

Next stop, Otter Wick.

Next stop?

If she had the energy.

The walk was tougher than she originally thought it might be. The track underfoot was stony. The frozen mud, slippery. And the relief, hardly flat. But, she could see the end of the loch now. There ... where the track turned back on itself.

There was a river.

But no bridge.

Sod it.

I can do this.

Twenty minutes later, and with one wet trainer, she was over the river and mountaineering along the track on the other side, heading back the way she had come. It took a further half an hour to get to the building without a roof. And by the time she'd reached the top of the hill and made it to the skeleton of a building, she was pretty exhausted.

But determined.

She paused. And caught her breath.

There it was. Exactly as Google Earth had predicted. In the distance. The second, small building – about the size of a one-bedroomed bungalow. It was brick built, but had a corrugated metal roof. And there was smoke rising from a wood burner's chimney.

Occupied?

Heather stepped off.

And then she stopped.

Occupied?

All of a sudden the courage she thought she had dissipated. The notion of finding where she'd been incarcerated for the weekend seemed like a really stupid idea. The house in front of her was no larger than a hut. And it wasn't made of stone and didn't, in any way, appear large enough to have a room where you could sit four for tea, let alone have a cellar with a fireplace and ...

She dismissed her thoughts with a shake of her head.

It's probably a farmer's hut.

But this was moorland. There was no farm. And no sheep.

And it was occupied.

She remained still. Her lack of movement and a slight wind on the top of this boggy plain very quickly took the edge off any heat she'd generated coming up the hill.

What's that?

About 10 metres in front of her was a short, black, metallic stalk, about half a metre high. She had no idea how she'd missed it until now. On top of it was a small black dome, the size of a large tennis ball. It looked like a mini-Belisha beacon, like you get marking the ends of a zebra crossing by a school. Except this one didn't blink yellow.

She took out her phone and clicked an image. And then she changed the angle and took a photo of the house, its thin stream of grey smoke struggling to mark a very blue sky.

What?!

There was a man. By the house. He was heading round the back.

In a hurry.

Noise now. The sound of an engine starting up.

Heather was rooted to the spot.

Oh shit.

It was all unravelling.

Twenty-two years of latent anxiety exploded in her mind.

The man was on a quad bike.

And he was racing towards her.

A man.

Someone she didn't know.

In the wild.

Speeding … chasing her way.

She wanted to run. She needed to run.

But running didn't come.

The man was going to get her. There was no escape.

She was going to be captured again. Taken. Humiliated.

Attacked.

Heather looked at her mobile. She tapped and swiped, hoping to open the phone keypad. Dial 999.

Shit!

The device slipped through her fingers onto the floor. She bent over quickly, fumbling for it among the damp, tufty grass.

'What do you want?' The man's shout was easily heard above the approaching bike's engine.

The quad bike was on her quicker than she could ever have expected. But that made sense now. There was a track of sorts from the house to the beacon. He'd covered the couple of hundred metres in no time.

'What are you doing here?' The man's accent was as English as hers. He was forthright. And he was right there. In front of her, sitting on the bike. Mid-forties, probably bulky under his green waxed coat. He wore a flat cap. And he needed a shave.

And … *shit* … there was a rifle sticking out from a holder on the quad bike.

Heather struggled to find words.

'I'm just walking.' She sounded as scared as she felt.

'There was a sign. At the path. It said "no trespassers". Didn't you see it?' The man barked out his words.

Did I?

Was there?

There were some signs on the gate. But she couldn't remember anything specific.

'No, sorry,' she bleated.

'Have you been taking photographs?' The man was pointing at her phone.

'No, well … yes.'

'Give it to me,' he ordered, his hand out straight.

Heather didn't even think about what she was being asked to do. She handed over her phone.

The man prodded and swiped, and then handed it back to her.

'This is private property. Go back the way you came. Don't take any more photos. And don't come back. I won't be so generous next time.' He slapped the fat end of the gun.

Heather shook her head, tears forming.

And then she turned away from the small metal-roofed hut, the strange black beacon, and the angry man with the gun, and quickly took off.

Schiphol Airport, Amsterdam, The Netherlands

408

Sam had missed her flight. It was due to take off at 4.35 pm. She'd arrived at Schiphol at 4.05. There had just been enough time – if she had run. But she hadn't. At first it was about her legs not wanting to go any quicker than a walk, having been sitting on her backside for an age. But it very quickly became part of the plan.

They were onto her. They must be. Athens, Berlin and then Trondheim – the latter being a question as to who could run quickly enough. And that had been her. She'd changed the plates on the car, which had given them a bit of a buffer. And they hadn't rushed headlong down the spine of Norway to make their escape, which was the obvious thing to do. Instead, they had stopped just outside of Trondheim, hidden the car and paid in cash. The YCA might be most places, but they weren't the Stasi.

But both of them were spent. For sure. And there was nowhere they could hide for long.

A plan had come together and she thought Jane would be OK.

She'd dropped her off at Notodden airport, 100 klicks southwest of Oslo. It was a local hub that probably couldn't take a 747. But it was perfect for a MI5-booked, UK-registered Eclipse 500 – a tiny two-engine jet which could take an extended family, but not much baggage. Via Wolfgang, David had told them that the aircraft would be on Notodden's apron by 10.30. They had made it there just after. Sam hadn't hung about to see Jane take off – she had her own plane to catch half a continent away. But a recent message from Wolfgang had confirmed that Jane had made it to the UK and had met up with the MI5 team. Apparently the operation was codenamed Hullabaloo, *which is nice for it*.

So Jane was OK.

409

Good.

She had been worried about her. Not that she had shown it.

And hopefully, the YCA thought Sam had caught the 16.35 to Atlanta. They'd be surprised when they found out that she wasn't on the plane. Or, as Wolfgang had booked multiple flights from multiple European locations to different destinations, using all her aliases, there was too much to keep track of.

That would keep them busy for a while. But only for a while.

The next flight to Atlanta was at 8.10 pm. It would get her in before midnight. She had arranged a meeting for breakfast the following day. She needed that to go well, and then she had to get back for the weekend. If history repeated itself, the YCA would meet to do whatever they did this Saturday, maybe into Sunday. She hoped the location was as plain as her nose ... the Nairnshire estate. That wasn't yet confirmed. But Frank and Wolfgang would be doing their thing, and then Jane would get eyes on.

And then?

Who knew?

Her plan was threadbare, knitted together with luck and goodwill.

She needed tomorrow's meeting to work. She needed some belief. They all needed some dominos to fall. And then she thought they had a chance.

Just now, though, she had to stay safe ... and get in touch with her Mossad pal, Micah.

And that might be problematic.

Sam had used Wolfgang's cousin's card to take out cash from an ATM at Notodden and, with the same card, bought four more burner phones and a cheap tablet. She had the latter open now, next to a long cup of coffee. Sleep was moments away. It would have to wait, although that wasn't always her choice.

She had found a quiet corner in Café Rembrandt, had her back to the pedestrian traffic, and had logged on to the airport's Wi-Fi. It was hardly secure, but it was as good as she was going to get.

Sam opened the website link the Mossad officer had used to communicate with her previously. A couple of months ago when she was recovering at the IDF's Tel Nof airbase south of Tel Aviv, he'd said, 'that URL will always be available'. She hoped he was as good as his word.

It was a black screen with an orange double forward-slash, followed by a 'greater than' symbol. Just as she remembered it.

She typed in '*Hi*'. And pressed return.

Nothing.

She sipped at her coffee ...

... and looked around the bit of the departure lounge she had eyes on.

All clear.

And still nothing from the screen. Just a blinking cursor.

She sipped some more coffee. She'd need the loo soon.

Nothing.

An earnest looking man, tall, mid-thirties, jeans and a black leather jacket, walked slowly past the café, left to right, taking everything in. Sam watched him. He was bag-less, which was a little odd. No obvious security paraphernalia. No ear-mic. But they were so small nowadays.

And still nothing from the screen.

411

She sipped some more coffee. Craned her neck to get a better view of bag-less man, but he'd gone. It was a concern.

And then the cursor moved.

What's my partner's name?

Sam immediately replied: *Hannah*.

The cursor hovered.

What was the name of the Serbian girl?

Sam's fingers were all over the keyboard.

Medeni.

The cursory blinked.

How's Schiphol?

Sam snorted. Of course they knew where she was. The e-link went both ways. They'd have immediately worked out which Wi-Fi she was using. Her only hope was that the enemy weren't yet keeping up.

She typed.

Good. I need your help.

Sam pressed return. And then she added,

Please.

Undisclosed airfield, Norfolk, UK

Jane already felt part of the team. The lead was David's friend, Joe Ledbetter. He'd met her with a smile on a tatty runway which didn't look sound enough to land a Cessna, let alone a pretty smart executive jet. Travelling with her from Norway was the pilot – and Nadia Bashir, an MI5 intelligence officer. Jane had tried to answer the woman's sensible questions, but she was exhausted … and flat out by the time they reached 41,000 feet.

Having slept for the rest of the flight, and after a quick bath in her Nissen hut accommodation followed by a cup of tea, she felt much more human. An hour in the small conference room later, between her and the MI5 team they were close to sharing the sum of all knowledge.

They were sitting around four Formica-topped tables, which were pushed together to form a square – of sorts. The tables were old and chipped, and their legs weren't quite at the same height so where they met in the middle looked dysfunctional and untidy. There was a beamer, a pull-down screen reminiscent of her school days, and a couple of white boards with plenty of pens. The plaster on the walls of what she thought was probably an old RAF headquarters, was chipped, the paint no longer happy sharing the space with anyone else, falling in chunks onto the floor.

But it was warm, even if the ancient finned radiators juddered every so often. The chairs were comfortable. And there were plenty of hot drinks ... and some biscuits.

It was dark outside. Joe had pulled the blinds but, just before he had, Jane could see nothing but black through the glass. They were in the darkest bit of countryside she'd been in for a while. That made her feel reasonably safe. Certainly safer than the Støren Hotel, which was too close to Trondheim for comfort. As soon as the place entered her consciousness, she dismissed it. Any thought which took her back to the doctor's office was wholly unwelcome.

Not here.

Not now.

'And your friend, Sam Green. She wants us in overwatch on the Duke of Nairnshire's estate?' It was a male analyst, sitting next door to Nadia.

Jane looked around the team.

Joe was older than her and clearly experienced. You don't get to become a Deputy in the Secret Service without a slab of history. Nadia – her age – seemed competent. The two other IOs, both men, were more Sam's age. She hadn't yet put them in a box, but they were making all the right noises. The two analysts were a spectrum apart. The one who had just asked the question was older than Frank, by quite some margin. The second, a girl, looked as though she was just out of university. She hadn't said a word so far.

'Yes. That's correct. I'm guessing we don't have any assets, SRR or similar, who can do the job for us?' Jane replied.

'I think, first,' Joe interrupted, 'we need to work out the aim of the overwatch.'

Joe was right, of course. But then he'd never worked with Sam Green. And Sam had been clear: she had a plan, but wasn't prepared to share it. Not yet.

'I don't know what's in my colleague's mind. She's working in a cellular way which, considering we're sitting at the backend of some godforsaken airfield, working incognito, is something you clearly chime with. All I can say is this ...' Jane stood and walked over to the whiteboard and picked up a pen.

She drew a diagram of words, lines and circles as she spoke.

'Our view is that historically the YCA meet every second year – the middle weekend in December. Odd years. We reckon that's three days away. They get together in Scotland, almost certainly the Nairnshire estate.' She'd double-underlined '3 days'. 'My team, although I'm not using "my" in a possessive manner, have three known YCA members – four if you include the Duke, who is currently shooting on his estate – already in the country. I will talk

414

with my people once we've done with this. More may have arrived today.' Jane was now pointing at a flipchart sheet she had scribbled on earlier and just about managed to Blu-tack to the wall, which had been reluctant to accept any decoration. It showed the eleven YCA names her team were aware of. She had drawn a line through the very deceased Eirik Pedeson and the recently murdered Theodor Konstantos. The list of names had sparked an earlier debate from which they'd now moved on. From that she was clear that much of this was new to the MI5 team, whose files were, understandably, UK focused.

'One of the team, let's call him W, is a world-class hacker. He is close to breaking into the estate's security infrastructure. But we need eyes on. To be confident, for example, that we're not being led astray with a fake feed.' Jane finished and put the lid on the pen.

'So we make sure they're meeting. And then what? We're not a SWAT team. And the meeting of a group of businessmen is neither illegal, nor is it worthy of a warrant. Not without due cause,' Nadia said.

Jane bit into the top of the pen.

'Nadia has a point, Jane. What's the outcome?' It was Joe again.

Jane took the pen out of her mouth and put it back on the table.

'I don't know. But Sam does. As I said earlier, as well as getting eyes on the estate, she's asked us to pull together the widest and deepest YCA resume. You have the shocking Fordingly intelligence. We have unequivocal evidence from Sarajevo. I was there. Sam is hoping to free up whatever happened in Abuja. That's not known to me, but I believe it's pretty damning stuff. There's Belarus ... and there must be more. W and F,' she'd introduced Frank as F earlier, 'the two of them are working together in Germany. They are on the case. But so should we be. Deep and wide. And somehow, I know not how, Sam believes the timing is right. Her line was "to take them on at their own game". And she's in the US making that happen.'

There was quiet for a moment. One of the male IOs stood up and took his teacup to the table on the side of the room where he refilled it.

'We don't have access to any assets, Jane,' Joe said. 'Not without the risk of this spilling. If we're to get eyes on the estate, it's just us. I can magic up plenty of resources from The Box, but no people. What do you think we need?'

Flemingstraße, Munich, Germany

Wolfgang was worried, like a father whose late teenage son had said he'd be back from the *Gasthaus* and was now running late.

Frank had gone out. He needed some space and, like a reluctant father, Wolfgang had said 'yes'. There was a back route: Frank's original way in. It was lit when needed and should give his friend the opportunity to stretch his legs across to the *Englischer Garten* in relative safety. He'd provided a map. They'd agreed on a time. And Frank was now five minutes late. Wolfgang thought that unusual for Frank. He was efficient with his time, and keen never to disappoint.

Wolfgang had handed Frank a German mobile, which was set up in a way which made it untraceable. And there was a panic button on it. That hadn't been pressed. Not yet.

But ...

How long should he give his friend before he called him?

Is this what parenthood is like?

Sam – and Jane – knew how sharp the YCA were. They'd been in the thick of it. 'Everywhere, but not quite omnipresent.' Wasn't that how Sam had described them? The current approach to Sam's safety was to blanket-book travel options to give those interested a headache. Her missing the flight to Atlanta was a minor act of genius, although she did say she had given up the chase by the time she'd reached the airport.

It all helped.

He hoped.

But airports were pinch points. Venturis. If you wanted to travel across continents, you couldn't avoid them. And there were only so many to choose from. He wouldn't be happy until she was through Atlanta Hartsfield-Jackson International and lost in a crowd.

Sooner still ... he wouldn't be happy until Frank got back.

Where was he?

Get busy, Wolfgang. That's the tonic.

They were continuing to make progress. They would soon have the Nairnshire estate wrapped up. He had hacked into the security mainframe and had access to all of the CCTV footage. It was real time, and covered much of the huge stately home's interior, and a lot of the close-to gardens. With that, earlier he and Frank had managed to put together a floorplan, camera positions and a vague understanding of the number of staff and their itineraries.

What was unclear was what physical security the Duke had in place. It certainly wasn't a Colombian drug cartel's headquarters. There were no roving guards with machine guns. No lookout towers.

But there must be something?

Frank had worked hard to establish alternative routes in and out. There was the main, tree-lined drive, accessed by an electric gate which was serviced by a camera. Wolfgang had that. And there were two other lesser routes. Both led to lodges with big wooden gates that fed onto public roads. A camera on each. Wolfgang had those too.

Frank had pressed Jane before he'd gone out. They could share the live CCTV footage. In return, did the MI5 team have recent satellite imagery? The answer to that question was yes. Jane had tasked one of the team to send the imagery over. Between Wolfgang and a young female analyst, they had set up a secure link which allowed video and large file transfer. The images had appeared half an hour later. That would be Frank's next job.

'We're hoping to be in position tomorrow evening,' Jane had said. 'Anything you can give us on the location that we haven't picked up, wing it over. We're going to leave two people here. The rest of us are heading out in the morning.'

The three of them then had a chat about what they thought Sam's plan was. That conversation had come to nought.

'Is she alive?' Jane had asked.

'We believe she's in the air. That's all I have,' Frank had replied.

'Atlanta?'

'I couldn't possibly say,' he'd said.

They'd had a chance to skim through the MI5 files. Frank hadn't needed to explain to Wolfgang that MI5 kept an eye on the UK; SIS internationally. But he had anyway. It hadn't been a surprise, therefore, that the files the team had shared were focused on the Duke of Nairnshire, his son Daniel Grinstead, various politicians, including the now – in Wolfgang's mind – wholly discredited prime minister, and a number of senior military and intelligence staff who they thought were working with, or being coerced by, the YCA. It was interesting, but not earth-shattering stuff.

Wolfgang had also made progress. The Swiss, Elias Bosshart, was now in the UK – that made four; five if you included the grouse-murdering Duke. Bosshart had travelled by Eurostar and was staying at the Chewton Glen hotel, a six-star country estate in the south of England. Wolfgang also knew that the Australian media baron, Michael Connock, had a flight booked from Adelaide to London, arriving at Heathrow tomorrow.

There was definitely a quorum gathering.

In addition, the Nairnshire estate's CCTV cameras had given them the earlier arrival of Semenov's daughter. The Duke, still dressed in heavy outdoor tweed, had met her in what Wolfgang thought was the Duke's office. The meeting – there was no audio – lasted twenty minutes and concluded with a hug. Semenov's daughter was attractive. And the Duke of Nairnshire, a bit 'handy'. She had pulled away from him quite sharply, but it was difficult to see if any offence had been taken by either side.

She'd left ten minutes later. The job, the message, or whatever it was, had been done. No paper trail. No interceptible data stream. Just a plain old conversation. It was bombproof.

The MI5 team had a lot on the second known trusted lieutenant, Daniel Grinstead. In the past forty-eight hours they had managed to place a tracker on his Bentley and had been given a warrant to tap his phone. Jane had said the warrant came with a clear caveat. His wife Princess Emma, the one with the relatively new liver, was off limits. It was an unbreakable rule. And the team were sticking to it. So far there had been nothing of note to report.

In addition, Wolfgang had also been trawling bank accounts and sifting through business emails. There was so much stuff. Thankfully he'd given access to one of his servers to the MI5 team. One of the two staff, the young female analyst, was on the case. She was called Trish, and he liked her already.

And finally, Frank had spent a couple of hours trying to establish the intent behind the drone attack in Edinburgh. He'd explained his findings to Wolfgang on the info board just before he'd headed out for air.

Which reminds me, where is he?

Wolfgang checked the time. He would give him five more minutes. And then he'd phone.

The drones had killed twelve and injured seven more. Frank had discounted 'staff', for obvious reasons. That left the deaths of five very prominent people: the prime ministers of Uganda and Sri Lanka; the equivalent of the foreign secretaries of Pakistan and Grenada; and the leader of the Scottish Independence party. The seven injured included two more prime ministers, a further foreign secretary and four treasury/business ministers.

'For now, I've ignored these seven.' Frank had pointed at the list of injured dignitaries. 'We have to assume that if these people are capable of pulling off a multiple drone attack, then they're going to finish the job. So it's the dead I'm working on.'

'And what do you have?' Wolfgang had asked.

'Leaving aside the Scotswoman, and Grenada's foreign secretary – who is well loved across the board – lots of people would benefit from the death of Uganda's and Sri Lanka's prime ministers. Their demise has sent both countries into a maelstrom of uncertainty, but clear replacements are already emerging. The likely new chiefs signal a changing of the guard. And the same can be said for Pakistan's foreign secretary. I have a list.' Frank had tapped on the board and a splurge of words had appeared in three columns, each headed by a dead dignitary.

Wolfgang had put up both hands.

'I need a coffee. And you need some fresh air. Talk me through this when you get back.' Wolfgang's wheelchair was already on the move. Frank loved his lists. And Wolfgang needed to wake himself up before his friend launched into the detail.

And now Frank was twenty minutes late.

Which was not a good sign.

Wolfgang dabbed at the numbers on his keyboard and waited for the phone to connect ... just as a night-vision image flashed onto his screen. It was Frank. At the back door. He looked fine. And he was carrying a plastic bag.

Wolfgang tapped at the keyboard again, opening the side gate and illuminating the path to the trap door. As he did he flicked at his screen to expose the remaining cameras which provided imagery around the outside of both houses. As the cameras searched, jilting, green-lined boxes appeared on the screen, highlighting movement.

Concerns.

There was one.

Just there.

Wolfgang dabbed. The screen enlarged.

There was nothing. Not now.

But the camera had sensed movement. It was, therefore, something.

421

He kept looking.

A flash of black, quickly framed by a green box.

A cat. Jumping from a wall.

That was all.

Wasn't it?

He kept watching the screens.

Nothing.

The door into the cellar opened. Wolfgang smelt the curry wurst instantly.

'I'm back. And I come bearing gifts!' Frank shouted.

Wolfgang turned to look for his friend.

The returning hero.

With curry wurst.

His favourite.

As he smiled in his friend's direction, he missed a further green box which followed the hunched shadow of a man moving quickly down the road, away from where Frank had just entered.

Hartsfield–Jackson Atlanta International Airport, Atlanta, USA

They knew she was here. They had to. Wolfgang's multi-flight approach was imaginative – unaffordable to most intelligence services – but it wasn't unbeatable. They just had to constantly check the flight manifests. A team of three and a decent computer was all they needed. She had to assume the YCA had a Sam-shaped pin in Atlanta.

So that meant spotting and then avoiding the tail. She was good at that, providing she wasn't swamped.

There was no one on the flight who fitted the bill – and the earnest looking man at Schiphol hadn't resurfaced.

Next was passport control.

Because this was the US, Wolfgang had used her real name and set her up for a UK/US visa waiver. Other than her Israeli passport, at short notice any other choice would have been much more problematic, maybe impossible.

She had made it as far as one of the APC (*automated passport control*) terminals, which had let her down before. This time …

She was through.

Next was customs. With only her day sack she hoped she wouldn't be stopped.

There was a wait. Five or six people. One black woman with a large suitcase was pulled from the queue and taken somewhere. Sam didn't rate her chances. The queue shortened. Then it was her. She showed her passport, which contained her customs declaration form.

'How long are you staying in the US for Miss … Green?' The customs official was a large white woman with a lot of badges. She had a name tag. Just in case she forgot.

'A couple of days,' Sam replied. There was a simple rule at airports. Never joke with anyone in uniform.

'Business or pleasure?' The woman shuffled a little so she could get a better look at Sam's rucksack. She had thrown one of the phones away having used it at Schiphol, had one in her pocket, and a third was unpacked, but SIM-less, in her bag. And a fourth was still in its packaging. She hoped being over-phoned wasn't going to be a problem.

'Pleasure. I'm meeting a friend.' She smiled.

The woman was still looking at Sam's backpack.

Sam knew she looked too scruffy for a mid-thirties tourist. She was neither in Hawaiian shirt, holiday mode, nor was she wearing a businesslike skirt and blouse. Her

423

jeans needed a wash, her t-shirt likewise, and her un-logoed hoodie was better suited to a local rapper. Everything was a little off colour. And her trainers were typical of someone who had just finished an ultramarathon.

She was a state.

Possibly too much of a state for the heavily-badged customs officer.

That was another rule when entering the US. Don't break the mould.

Sam smiled again.

The woman handed Sam her passport back. And squeezed out her own smile.

'Have a good day, ma'am,' the woman said, without any conviction.

Sam nodded, and moved along quickly.

She had decided that speed would be her approach. She had carried out a map recce and had chosen to use the MARTA train to get to the city centre. That meant walking to the domestic terminal (there was a skytrain, which she would ignore), buying a train ticket and getting on a multi-carriage train which might, or might not, be busy – whilst keeping an eye out for unwanted company.

A taxi would have been easier but every taxi had a number, and whilst she could get out at any point, she worried about being boxed in. At her pace, the walk to the train would stretch any tail, and she could get off the train at a number of stations, swop to a taxi, walk, maybe run some ... she had options.

Sam knew where to go. She had rehearsed the route. She knew the subsidiary choices. She had alternatives.

Go.

It was an 800-metre trek through the terminal. A few jigs left and right, but pretty much straight. There were

424

all manner of shops and eateries. Plenty of people, some with massive loads on trolleys, others with bags smaller than hers. And there were armed cops, a smattering of airport security, and a number of uniformed soldiers – unarmed, travellers just like her.

Sam didn't look behind her.

It was cool in the building. And probably just about the same temperature outside. The sun was up in a cloudless sky but, even this far south in the States, the late fall weather was crisp. A good day for sightseeing. If you had the time.

Not her.

She was on a schedule.

Even though the building was cool, it didn't take long before she felt the prickle of dampness under her arms. Ideally she'd take off her hoodie, but she didn't want to waste a second.

Ticket machine.

She had her own bank card out. They were all compromised. It didn't matter now.

She feinted left … and then right, squeezing through a group of Pacific Rim tourists. She found the machine furthest from the main atrium and looked around.

No one.

The machine got her attention. She prodded on the buttons and then tapped on the pad with her card, which issued a ticket.

She looked again.

No one.

That was, no one obvious.

Go.

The trains were below ground. She took the escalator, squeezing between two big lads who were surprised by the attention. Sam looked back up the moving stairs. The lad up from her – defensive-tackle-sized, and now more than a foot taller than her – looked down his nose and smiled.

Sam grimaced in return. And then she pushed his big arm to one side so she could look back the way she had come from.

Fuck it.

There.

Mid-thirties, mid-height, cargo pants and a leather gilet. Sunglasses.

Fuck it.

How do they keep doing this?

He was pushing his way down the line. Bumping people about. He'd be on her in a matter of seconds.

She looked back at the big guy. He smiled again. And nodded, a knowing nod.

Oh, please.

'There's a guy pushing his way down the escalator.' She glanced around him again. 'Sunglasses. He's after me. Can you stop him? Please.' It was a splurge of words, followed by her best smile.

The big man looked confused, as though English wasn't his first language. But then he turned his shoulders just before the man with the sunglasses arrived.

'Now, hold on, buddy ...' the big man said as he put an arm out to stop Sam's might-be assailant in his tracks.

Sam didn't catch the rest, nor the small melee which followed. She was already nipping past the queue and making some headway. As she reached the bottom of the escalator she turned to catch the altercation between the two men. The big man had his hand round the throat of gilet man, whose sunglasses were now hanging from one ear.

426

Of course it wasn't a result. The MARTA train terminated at the station. There would be only one option and, unless it departed in very quick order, her tail would make it and she'd have made no progress. It would be her and broken sunglasses man, all over again.

So Sam turned at the bottom. Quickly. And dropped to her haunches.

'Excuse me,' she said, as she slipped between two very confused soon-to-be fliers, on their way up to departures.

She remained crouched, the woman in front of her doing her absolute best to ignore the stranger whose head was too close to her backside.

The escalator trundled on – and up.

And then Sam was all but catapulted from the top. Still crouching, she moved away from the entrance to the MARTA station before standing. Ignoring what might be following her, she got to her feet, snuck into another crowd, weaved and turned, before popping out of the terminal into the sunny but cool Georgian morning.

Taxi.

She knew where they were. She knew where everything was. She had to assume she had lost at least one of her tails. And, hopefully, given herself an opportunity to break clean.

A taxi was no longer a poor option. There was a bank of white and yellow cars off to her right. She moved quickly. Ordinarily she would have taken the third, but these people were too organised for that and she wouldn't be able to jump the queue. This wasn't Liberia. There would be no messing with the system.

Sam looked behind.

And stared.

No one.

A taxi driver put up his hand.

Sam acknowledged him, jogged forward and got into the back of the white and yellow Prius.

'Four Seasons, 14th Street northeast, please,' Sam asked.

Her driver was olive-skinned, slim and smartly dressed.

'Yes, ma'am.' He had a mild Spanish accent.

Sam looked at her watch.

'How long?' she asked.

'Thirty minutes, maybe a little longer,' the man replied, his warm smile connecting via the rear-view mirror.

She nodded and searched the concourse for trouble.

Nothing.

The incident with gilet man concerned her. What was he going to do? Murder her on the spot? On the platform? Were they that desperate? Why weren't they just monitoring her? Connecting her connections? That's what she would be doing.

Unless he had spotted her, thought he was going to lose her and was making up the distance and had inadvertently bumped into the big man?

Sam shook her head.

She didn't get that line.

No, he was going to kill me.

That's what they had done in Athens. And in Trondheim. That's what they would have done in Berlin. These people had no regard for the law. They were above it. Kill someone, maybe get arrested, and then a high-powered lawyer releases you. No harm done.

It was all pretty extraordinary.

428

Chapter 17

Heather was sitting up on her bed, still in her day clothes but with her socks off. She had her phone in one hand and a cup of tea, which she'd made from the complimentary drinks tray, in the other. It was just after lunch. She'd asked her landlady if she minded if she spent the afternoon back in her room. The woman had said, 'of course not, it's your room, silly,' in a lilt which Heather could listen to all day.

She was done for. A cup of tea and a lie down was all she was worth at the moment. Her nerves had been sandpapered and her energy levels in need of a recharge. She had tried to continue the motion after yesterday's incident on Yell, with the man with the gruff tones and the gun. But she hadn't been able to face it. Yesterday afternoon had been a washout, in more ways than one. It had taken her almost an hour to get back to her hire car. She had slipped off a rock in the river and bruised her knee – which still hurt like hell. And as the damp from the water and the whipping wind did its best to chill her extremities, clouds formed on the horizon that had raced across the sea. Heather had made it to her car before the deluge, but it was a close-run thing.

She had still managed to drive the remaining miles on Yell, keeping an eye out for likely locations, but the conditions were poor and visibility negligible. She had given up before tea, crossed the sound between Bigga and Booth of Toft, which only hours earlier she would have found amusing, and headed for her next guesthouse.

The weather had improved this morning, and she had driven to the north of the main island on the A970, before heading west to Hillswick, and on to the lighthouse at Esha Ness. It was all lovely, and at another time she would have been wowed by the fabulous views. But that wasn't possible. There was little about her current disposition which she was finding fabulous and, if she'd had the energy, she probably would have driven back to Lerwick and caught the ferry south. Home comforts, undisturbed by a man on a quad bike, were calling her.

She had tried.

Had it made a difference, though?

Last night, after a cold meat pie and a can of beer from the local shop, she was so shattered she had bathed, fallen into her bed and slept soundly through to the Northern Isles alarm clock of late daylight and the smell of another cooked breakfast, which had been beautifully presented but offered exactly the wrong levels of saturated fat for her taste.

She had slept, though.

Sleep.

There had been no residual anxiety about whether or not Fi was safe. Of course she worried for her. She would gladly give her own life for that of her daughter. That was usual mother-level anxiety, wasn't it?

But she had none of the previously consistent levels of desperation which ordinarily made sleep an elusive commodity.

Maybe she was fixed?

I hope so.

She wouldn't know until she got home.

Would she?

How long would 'getting home' take?

430

Heather put her cup down on the bedside table and tapped at her phone ... just as it rang.

It was Fi.

Heather connected.

'Hello, love,' Heather said with as much enthusiasm as she could muster.

I'm so tired.

'Hi, Mum. Where are you now?' Fi asked.

Heather breathed in deeply. She unconsciously smiled to herself.

'Shetland.'

'Where the hell is that?' Fi asked. It wasn't an accusatory question. It was just the language she used.

'Geography's not your best subject, hey?' Heather said.

There was a snort from the other end of the phone.

'Yeah. Duh,' her daughter replied.

'It's an island. Off the north coast of Scotland. Pretty close to Norway.'

'What?!' Fi's tone had now changed. 'What on earth are you up to?'

Heather looked around the room. There were two windows with far-reaching views of a treeless, yellow moorland, above which was a greying and miserable sky. Inside, the walls were decorated incongruously with chintzy prints of Paris. There was a potted plant on top of a small desk. It was a perfect 1960s guesthouse.

I can't keep at this.

'I've got something to tell you ...' Heather started.

It took them an hour to get through it. All of it. There were tears on both ends of the phone and, at one point, Heather had to take her mobile away from her ear and place it on her chest. Once the story had been told and all the questions spent, her daughter had, between sniffs, asked, 'What are you going to do now?'

Come home.

That was what Heather wanted to do.

'I don't know, love. Come home?'

'No!' Fi's response had been immediate. 'If these people are who you say they are, then this weekend is it. You *must* see this through. Warn people. Speak to the police, at least.' Fi was insistent.

'But ...'

'No, Mum. No buts!'

There was quiet for a couple of seconds. Heather sensed that Fi was tapping at a keyboard. Then ...

'Stay where you are. I'm coming up. I can catch a flight to Shetland tomorrow. Loganair into ... Sumburgh, wherever the hell that is. I can get there just before teatime. Do you know where the airport is? Is it far from you? You should go to the police tomorrow morning.' Fi was excited. Her words tumbled out.

'But, I don't ... isn't it expensive? And what about your studies?' Heather knew it was a typical mum reply. But she was enthused as Fi. When had they last been away together?

'I have tutor on Friday. And a dull lecture tomorrow. I'll survive. Do we have a deal?' Fi said.

Of course we do.

'Of course, love.' There were tears forming again in Heather's eyes. 'I can't wait to see you.'

The Nook on Piedmont Park, 1144 Piedmont Ave NE, Atlanta, USA

Holly Mickelson paused outside the brick façade of the diner. She sensed a tingle down her spine.

This is going to be interesting.

She'd never been to the place before, which wasn't a surprise. It was a good ten-minute taxi ride from her office, and there were many more local places to grab an early lunch.

She checked her watch. It was 10.59. She was exactly on time.

She took a breath, opened the door and walked into a typical American bar-cum-diner. There was a lot of wood and numerous TV screens. Football and baseball. She could cope with that.

Holly looked around. It wasn't a small place, but it wasn't so big she couldn't pick out every table by turning her head.

No sign.

Oh well. She spotted an empty table by a window and made her way across to it …

… just as someone gently touched her shoulder.

She spun.

It was Sam Green.

Almost exactly as she remembered her.

Holly opened her arms and threw them around Sam.

Who grunted in return, her arms dangling limply beside her.

'Oh, Sam. Why so long?' Holly's accent was hardly Deep South, but neither was it smooth East Coast. She let go of Sam and stepped back, her hands still resting on Sam's shoulders.

Sam nodded imperceptibly.

'We should sit. Follow me.' Sam issued her orders without emotion.

Holly smiled, then frowned, and then shook her head at the bizarreness of their introduction, or lack of it ...

... and then read the room.

'OK, Sam, you lead.' Her tone now much more serious. She should have known better.

Holly was led to a corner booth which was probably the darkest in the joint. Sam sat one side, she the other. By the time they had taken their seats, a waitress had appeared. She placed a paper menu in front of both women. Holly showed a hand to Sam, and nodded.

'Coffee please,' Sam said without looking at the woman.

'Will you be eating?' the waitress asked with no particular grace.

Sam glanced to Holly.

'I'm famished,' Sam said, still without enthusiasm.

'Me too,' Holly replied. And then to the waitress, 'Two coffees, please. We'll have decided what to eat by the time you come back.' She finished with a smile.

The waitress nodded curtly, turned and disappeared.

The pair of them sat in silence for a short while, their eyes not quite meeting. Sam had her hands on the table in front of her. Her rucksack beside her on the bench seat. She looked the same, but different. When they'd met on that godforsaken yacht four years ago, they had been flung together, their paths heading towards death in the clutches of one of the world's most evil and vile men.

Sam had saved her life.

And, very soon afterwards, she hers.

They had then driven to Rome in an old sports car which didn't want to go as fast as they needed it to. And, with the police chasing them, Sam had broken away and saved the city from a terrible ordeal.

It had been no more than a day. Maybe less.

And yet, she felt as close to Sam as she did her sister.

Sam Green.

Who now looked shorter. Maybe stockier? Certainly less well-kempt.

But – *what is it?* – resolute.

Just as she had in Rome.

Holly opened her mouth to say something.

Sam raised a hand.

The waitress was heading over with two mugs and a jug of coffee.

'You choose the food,' Sam said blankly.

An unflustered Holly scanned the menu and ordered two burgers and rings.

The waitress nodded, chewed a little, and then disappeared.

'How much influence have you got at CNN?' Sam asked without any explanation.

We're getting on with it.

It was an interesting starter and Holly was wholly unsure where this might be going.

'Well. Good to see you, Sam.' She smiled. It was the only nicety needed. And it wasn't replayed back to her. 'I'm a production assistant with *One Wor*ld, a lunchtime show. I have some influence as to what goes into the programme. But not all. Why do you ask?'

Sam was sipping at her coffee. Both hands on her cup.

'I've got a big story for you. It requires, or will require, little or no further investigation. It's backed with both MI5 and MI6 credentials.'

Wow.

If this was anything like the Rome thing …

'It's bigger than Rome.' Sam was reading her mind.

Bigger than Rome?

Bigger than a nuclear suitcase?

'Well, great. That's great.' It was all Holly could find to say. What else was there?

'It needs to go out this weekend.' Sam was focusing on Holly over the brim of her cup. Her eyes managing a perfect balance of steel … and tiredness. She'd obviously been on a journey.

'That's not possible.' It was the only sensible response. 'Not without the authority of the board.'

Sam put her coffee down.

Holly could see it then.

They'd not seen each other for four years. Four years for them both to get a little older. Holly was mid-twenties. Sam – she'd never asked – probably mid-thirties, maybe older. In those four years Holly thought she had done well. She'd graduated and, after a short internship with arguably the greatest TV news show on earth, been offered a minor but important post on the midday programme.

She thought she had blossomed. People liked her. More important, they trusted her work ethic and her judgement. She was doing what she had always wanted to do. And she was doing it well.

And she loved it.

Sam, on the other hand, looked as though she had spent the last four years on the frontline of a major war. The lines around her eyes told a story of hurt and suffering. The way she dressed, the way she held herself, was a reflection of someone who had burnt more fuel than the tank could hold. She had the demeanour of a woman who had fought too many battles, and won too few of them.

But those eyes.

Those eyes.

They told a different story.

'I need you,' Sam pointed at Holly, 'or whoever your friendly anchor is, to tell a story. Probably this Saturday. And I will act as a correspondent on the ground – live feed. I will also deliver a background of images and intelligence which will provide absolute certainty to the message your network will be broadcasting.' Sam paused, then seemed to think she had missed something. 'It's in Europe.'

No.

That's not possible – on so many levels.

'A lot of the slots are pre-recorded, Sam. The live slots, all EST, are mostly morning based. Except for a single afternoon newsreel, which is live. And finally, live again at midnight. You'd need to pick your slot.' Holly was shaking her head as she spoke. 'But, sorry, Sam. This is ridiculous. There's no way. And we'd want our own anchor on the ground, with a dish and the usual backup.'

Holly stopped talking. Sam was staring at her. Her face was completely still. Her mouth a slit of mild pink in a face which had been to places where memories shouldn't be retold.

'You haven't heard the story yet.'

Sam had two same-length fries in her hand. She had got through most of them and, as she talked, she had nibbled at a bit of her burger. Holly hadn't touched her food. But she had asked for two refills of coffee.

'That's what we have,' Sam said matter-of-factly. 'I can get the team to share the detail with you, but only if you are prepared to run the story. And that means you have less than thirty-six hours to set it up.' Sam finished her fries.

'And if CNN doesn't run the story, what will you do?' Holly had asked very few questions up until now. This was the most obvious and the biggest one.

Sam didn't want to think about the answer.

'We'll put something together after the weekend and see who wants it. It won't be a bidding war. It will be more of a case of who has the guts to put it out there. Knowing your organisation, I assumed it would be you. But if not, we'll find someone.'

Sam wasn't anywhere near as confident as she sounded. Not at all.

It was a helluva story, especially if they could add some live video to the arc. But it was also explosive and, for the safety of those doing the posting, potentially *extremely dangerous*.

She was confident that if it were left up to Holly Mickelson, CNN would be all over this like a well-wrapped Christmas present. She'd only met Holly briefly, with much of the hideous details expunged from Sam's memory. But she clearly remembered watching her swim off into the distance as they escaped Sokolov's yacht. Holly was a semi-professional swimmer. Sam wasn't; and she was injured, her shoulder having earlier been ripped from its socket. She had started to flail. And then went under. She had popped up again, but she was weak. Wretched. And then she went under for the last time.

Sam had woken in an old Italian villa. Holly had dragged her from the sea and then hauled her up the beach until she had found refuge.

She had saved her life, but it was much more than that. The shared horrors of their ordeal had provided an unbreakable bond between them. Sam had rescued her; Holly had reciprocated in a manner which spoke to depths of reserve and commitment which Sam had seen in very few people. Wolfgang was probably in the same league. He had that unswerving commitment to do the right thing, no matter the cost. Jane and Frank were there somewhere. But Holly was different. There was fire. And it burnt strong. Like Sam, that didn't necessarily make her a good person or, indeed, great company.

But it did make her devastatingly resourceful … if she believed in something.

That's why Sam had come.

She had kept an eye on Holly. She knew what job she had at CNN. And she knew, with everything else, she was the only person Sam knew who had the courage and the facilities to help her pull this off.

Holly pushed her untouched food away. She stared into Sam's eyes. Sam blinked. Holly forced a smile.

'I'll go straight to my anchor. And I know of an appropriate board member who is friends with my dad. The QAnon angle is big with us. As is Michael Connock's reach into US media – and I think that's what's going to sell this. I know the company has been after him forever. Other than Jimmy Johnson Jr, the other YCA members are news to me. We'll need to check our own history with them. If we go ahead, the company will have its backside sued until they run out of money. But we're used to that.'

Holly smiled again, a businesswoman's smile.

439

'I guess you haven't got time to come with me to run an elevator pitch?' she asked.

Sam shook her head.

'How do I get in touch with you?' Holly followed up.

Sam had prepared a scrappy piece of paper with Wolfgang's circuitous internet contact details. She took out a pen from her waist wallet and jotted down two Norwegian mobile numbers.

'These are burners. I might or might not use them. Give me a couple of hours to get in touch with him,' Sam pointed at Wolfgang's name, 'so he knows who you are and what you want ...'

Sam spotted something through one of the diner's windows. A police car. It hadn't parked. It had thrown its front wheels onto the pavement. No flashing lights ... but they weren't coming here for food.

They're coming after me.

'Cops.' Sam flicked her head at the window. 'I'm going. You're in the clear – for now. But the moment you mention any of this, your life is in danger.'

Sam didn't wait for a reply. She picked up her bag, slung it and headed for the cloakroom. She had checked it earlier. There was a window.

The police had made it through the front door as she reached the washroom. She caught sight of them. Two officers: large white male; slim black female. Blue/black uniforms. They were City of Atlanta police. Both armed. Both pistols holstered.

They'd had a tip-off. But nothing more. There was no SWAT team. No snipers on the roof.

I hope.

The female restroom door closed behind her.

It was as she'd left it. Four cubicles, four basins, and a Sam-sized window at the end.

She reached for the latch, pushed the window open and pulled herself up onto the sill. She stuck her head through. A fenced rear yard. Bins, bottle bank, a couple of bicycles. Over the wooden fence was an apartment block; maybe fifteen windows. Sam checked them all.

Nothing.

She squeezed out through the gap, turned on the outside sill, pulled the window to, and lowered herself slowly to the floor.

Ouch.

That wasn't great for her stomach.

She'd survive.

How did the city police know I was here?

It wasn't Holly. Sam was sure about that.

But how?

She shook her head. It wasn't important. Not now. All that mattered was that she got to the airport, contacted Wolfgang and flew back to the UK. She had the same length of time Holly had. Thirty-six hours. It was tight. But it was doable.

She carefully pulled open the gate.

An alley. A brick wall in front of her, a fence to her side.

Two choices.

Left, after a jink, led back to the main road. That's where the police car was. Right headed into a communal park which serviced the apartment block. She knew. She'd recced the area using Google Maps.

Right.

'Police! Stop where you are!' An Americanised yell from behind her. The yell would be accompanied by a gun. That was how things worked in the States.

She ran.

It was 10 metres to the park. There were trees and a playground. That would give her options. And if the shouts had come from the big policeman, she had the legs on him.

One, two, three ...

She had no idea why she was counting. Was she checking how long it would take for the policeman to get off a shot?

Or counting to something more deadly?

BANG!

The shot was from a pistol. She had 15 metres on the man and Sam was weaving as she ran. Just enough. The round squeezed past her, creating its own perceptible bow wave.

Four, five, six ...

She wouldn't be so lucky next time.

The second round exploded out of the barrel of the policeman's 9mm Glock 17 just as Sam entered the park. She was turning, pivoting left around the corner of the wall. She had a plan. The park had a series of bushes, or some sort of foliage. It would provide limited cover between her and another alley which ran along the side of the apartment block. After 20 metres, that spilled out onto a street which was perpendicular to the one by the diner.

It was a chance.

That is, it would have been a chance if the 9mm slug hadn't sliced through the sleeve of her hoodie and taken a chunk out of her upper arm, nicking the bone.

The shock – the instantaneous pain – was too much for her. Her arm flew forward, which, as she turned at speed, unbalanced her. The searing heat of a bullet's slash took up all of her brain's capacity.

She tumbled, her damaged arm hitting the ground first, her torso compounding the problem by landing on the wound.

'Fuck off!' she shouted spontaneously.

And then stars. Lots of them.

Had she hit her head?

Had the round snuck an artery and was she already losing too much blood?

No. That's not right.

She scrambled to her feet, but her legs immediately gave way.

What is wrong with you?

She took three deep breaths, trying to force sanity back into her lungs. A second later the stars dimmed and the green of the park, the form of the trees and the red of the bricks behind them began to take charge.

She got up on all fours ... just as a blue/black uniformed policeman kicked her in the stomach.

What the ...?!

'Stay down! Stay. Down,' she heard, the accent tunefully Deep South.

Sam snorted. And shook the remaining stars from her consciousness.

There was a lot of pain going on. Too much for any resistance.

Still on all fours, she looked up at the policeman.

It wasn't either the big white man or the black woman from the diner. But it was still a city policeman. Same arm badge. No SWAT team. Just a few old boys doing their job. Directed by the YCA.

Fuck.

443

There were two now.

'Face on the floor. Hands behind your back,' the guy who had shot her ordered.

Sam obliged. The 'hands behind your back' bit was excruciating.

A set of cuffs was clumsily applied. And that hurt. Then she was lifted by the cuffs to the vertical ... which hurt so much that she momentarily lost consciousness.

And then she was on the floor again. In a heap. One side of her face slapping against the grass, her open mouth contorting and her tongue sticking out.

What the hell is happening?

A face. Opposite hers. On the grass. Eyes wide open. But no sign of life.

The policeman who had shot her.

A man-sized *thud* on the other side of her.

What?

She couldn't easily turn to see what was happening. Not without a great deal of pain.

And then someone was un-cuffing her.

'Up, Sam. Come on.'

She recognised the voice immediately. She knew then she was in the safest of hands.

North of Drynachan Lodge, Nairnshire, Scotland

It was a bugger's muddle, for sure. This was not Jane's area of expertise and, having spoken with them, nor was it Joe's – or Nadia's. Using aerial photographs and other mapping, and having checked with Frank, who was carrying out the same work, they were sure there were only three vehicular entrances to the estate. The main one, where she was now, was a confluence of two very minor roads. One led south from the coastal town of Nairn. The second came in from the east. It branched from the B9007, which ran north-south and was the eastern border of the Duke of Nairnshire's pile. The two roads met at the main lodge to the estate, on the River Findhorn. Even in the blurriness of dusk, she had eyes on the junction now.

Joe had let Jane lead, and she had split the team into two. She was heading up the main overwatch on the junction at Drynachan Lodge. With her was Nadia and the older male analyst, Nigel. Joe was on mobile patrol with the other male IO, a Jack Downing. They were covering two gated lodge locations: one on the A9 – which formed the estate's southern boundary; the other, to the east, on the B9007, south of the road which led back to Jane's overwatch.

We've got it covered?

She didn't know.

It wasn't her area of expertise.

They had two white, unmarked Nissan vans, decent binos, night vision equipment, cameras, secure two-way radios, and encrypted, data-enabled satphones and relays which linked back to the airfield. They had blow-up mattresses, army ration packs, plenty of water, heaters, small gas cookers and, incongruous against that list, a Sig Sauer MCX short-barrelled rifle, in each team. Like SIS, MI5 intelligence officers have to undertake regular weapons training, but don't carry unless the circumstances were exceptional.

Jane had no idea how Joe had green-lighted that decision, but it didn't matter. Both teams were adequately armed with a NATO 5.56mm submachine gun capable of winning a firefight. It wasn't in any way to her taste. And recent events had spelled out that the last thing she wanted to do was to carry a firearm ...

... just in case she had to use it. And what feelings that might generate.

But.

She couldn't say no. Not when she was asking the MI5 team to do something ordinarily left for Security Service specialists. Or, more likely in heavily rural locations such as this, handed over to the SRR or the police experts, such as the Met's SC&O10.

So she had a Sig, as did Joe.

It had taken Jane a few seconds to remember how to make the rifle safe and then reload it. She'd handed it over to Nadia who, in one movement, had checked the safety, removed the magazine, pulled back the working parts, made sure the chamber was clear, released the mechanism, fired off the action, and reattached the magazine, as though the weapon was a fifth limb. Which was, in its own way, reassuring.

They had pulled the white Nissan off the barely tarmacked road into a clearing in the forest. Jane had asked Nigel to check to see if the van was visible from the track whilst she and Nadia had gone forward to ensure that they had a well-hidden but uninterrupted view of the junction. They had. The main house was a further 5 kilometres away, up the heavily wooded Findhorn valley. Wolfgang had confirmed that Semenov's daughter had used the route earlier on the way to the house. And, not long after, come back out the same way. He'd also confirmed that currently none of the YCA had made it this far, but the money was on them arriving soon for their biennial get-together.

446

That meant that the three of them had to get comfortable. And in temperatures dropping below zero, that wasn't going to be easy.

Jane had asked Nadia to work out a roster. If they took four hours each they'd cover darkness. It would be easier once the sun was up.

It would all be easier still if we had an inkling of Sam's plan.

Tomorrow was Friday.

Then it was the weekend, at the end of which history dictated that the YCA would disperse.

So Sam needed to articulate her plan. Soon. Otherwise they were endangering themselves and freezing their extremities for no reason.

Jane and Nadia were sitting on a bed of very comfortable and relatively warm pine needles. They were 10 metres short of the junction, in heavy trees. The only light came from the Lodge, which was set below where they were and on the other side of the road. They had a clear line of sight of where the two roads met, and from there the gravel track which led deeper into the forest and onwards to the main house.

Since they'd arrived they'd only seen one car. It had driven in from the north and over the lip into the Lodge's carpark. Their image intensifier had picked out a man getting out of the vehicle – identified as a BMW 4 series – and using the Lodge's front door. Nadia had taken some shots with a low-light camera and pinged the detail, via the satphone, back to their airfield base.

Since then, absolutely nothing had happened. And whilst they were sitting in the ever worsening cold, warmed only by a flask of sweet tea which Nigel had brought forward

447

earlier, the smell of woodsmoke from the Lodge reminded Jane of the periodic futility of her job.

Its unnecessary asks.

She had a history of uncomfortable nights, either working too long in the office, or roughing it in military style accommodation in far-off places. She had been blown up in Iraq, shot at in South America, and had endured hell in Southeast Asia. More recently she had been in the thick of a firefight in Bosnia and, just days ago, experienced the same in Greece.

And now, against the most complex threat imaginable, with a small team of MI5 officers, supported by a German count, an SIS analyst and a discredited case officer, she was putting herself on the line again ... with a semiautomatic MCX beside her, which was now almost too cold to touch.

She laughed inwardly.

What chance did they have?

Wolfgang had yet to find the main house's defence system, other than a decent suite of cameras. But that gave her little comfort. The YCA had proven themselves to be utterly ruthless. Konstantos was dead. Doctor Pedeson was almost certainly dead. She and Frank had been shot at in Rotterdam. There was a liturgy of savage attacks. There was no compassion.

There was only death.

That's what they brought.

Against six MI5 officers and her.

And Sam and Frank and Wolfgang.

Ten against who knew how many.

There were no odds. There was only certainty.

And so the brutal cold of the Sig was no comfort.

No comfort to her. A woman in emotional turmoil. Unable to hold on to life's railing.

She was on a journey. She had paused at the King's Cross hotel. She had paused again, quayside, in Rotterdam. She had almost lost it, then gone crazy in Athens. Berlin was an aberration. She had felt on top of the world. Unbeatable. Unbreakable.

And then Trondheim.

Where death had stalked them, but in the end taken its chance with someone who hadn't deserved to die.

From there she didn't know where she was. Sam had confronted her. Given her a choice. Which had been easy. She had accepted the lesser of the two evils.

Working in a group. In the relative comfort of like-minded professionals.

The other option had been to stay with Sam. The maverick.

The individual.

That wasn't Jane's way. She was a team player. A systems person, with boundaries and rules.

Boundaries and rules.

That wasn't the way this was going to play out. It was never going to be that easy. She wasn't back at work. Not in any conventional sense.

She, Jane Baker, was skiing off-piste. Night overwatch on a junction in the Scottish Highlands was maybe new ground to her, but it wasn't anathema. It wasn't.

But the avalanche warnings were red.

And, at some point, the whole lot would come tumbling down.

On all of them.

And there would only be one outcome.

She knew that, deep down.

Sam knew that.

This was their current business.

That was the YCA.

A cold spot grew between her shoulders.

She needed to generate some heat.

'I'm going to phone my German base, Nadia. OK?' Jane whispered.

Nadia had the thermal imaging binos pressed against her face.

'Sure. You should get your head down. You're back here at ten.' Nadia hadn't looked up from the binos.

Jane tapped Nadia on the shoulder. And then slid back off the rise they were positioned on.

Food, Wolfgang, sleep.

In that order.

Chapter 18

600 miles west of British airspace

The Gulfstream G280, twin-engined executive jet was as smooth as it was comfortable. Sam was sitting in a sumptuous leather armchair. In front of her was a beautifully veneered, highly polished table, across from which was a chair similar to hers. She was finishing off the vegetarian option offered to her by the male steward. It was accompanied by one of the best cups of coffee she'd had for an awfully long time, served in a delightful, half-sized china coffee cup. It was logo'd with the letters IAI.

She'd learnt something today.

Come on, you learn something every day.

Like the names of the two Atlanta City policemen who were on the floor with her.

Before she'd been dragged from the scene she had checked their badges. At the time the names didn't seem important, but one day they might be. And once she'd seen them she would never forget them, nor the exact time and place. And even with both of them out cold, she could deliver a decent sketch via a mugshot artist if that were ever needed.

However, her 'learnt thing' she was referring to was even less useful than the names, faces and DTG (*date/time/group*) of the two floored policemen.

What she didn't know until today was that the very well-known and ubiquitous executive jets, Gulfstreams, were made by Israeli Aerospace Industries. She knew of IAI. It delivered top-of-the-range military drones, really decent army scout cars and a huge breadth of other high-quality military kit.

But Gulfstream jets?

She hadn't known that.

'I didn't realise IAI made Gulfstream?' she said casually to Micah, who was sitting opposite her finishing off a chunk of steak, served with a cold bottle of Viru Pilsner.

'Mmm.' He nodded, chewing on a mouthful. He finished, patted his lips with a cotton napkin and added, 'We do a lot of stuff really well. For a relatively small country.'

Sam nodded slowly and looked out of the window. There were wispy white clouds decorating a dark blue North Atlantic. She spotted the tiny red hull of a ship. Following it was a scribble of white wake, which ran out of enthusiasm as soon as it started.

'I've got to phone my pals in Germany. Can you set it up?' she asked, without taking her eyes off the insignificant red boat.

'Sure,' Micah replied. 'Have you got a URL?'

Sam turned to face Micah, the man who had saved her – again – from at the very least an uncomfortable stay in an Atlantan jail. More likely, much worse.

He'd followed her. More accurately, he'd followed the YCA-sponsored hoods who had met her at the airport. His view was the guy she'd avoided on the elevator at the MARTA station was just doing his best to keep up with her.

'That was quite a move. Using that man mountain to block the tail was inspired,' Micah had said once they'd made it to a Mossad safe house in uptown Atlanta. She hadn't replied. At that point Sam had been more interested in wolfing down some painkillers than having any conversation about anything. Micah's dressing, which he'd applied in the pick-up car, had stemmed the blood loss, but it hadn't relieved the excruciating pain. She was surprised how much a relatively small, but deep, gash hurt.

As he'd cleaned the wound and then sutured it, he'd continued to talk. She guessed it had been to distract her.

'You knew they'd be onto you?' he'd asked.

Sam, again, hadn't replied. She was biting on her bottom lip whilst frustratingly wiping away pain-tears, which she couldn't prevent from forming.

Micah had continued.

'We knew. That's why I came. There was a second guy. I don't think you spotted him. He got into a white Chevrolet Suburban and followed your taxi.' He'd finished his sewing. He now had a cotton wool pad, dabbed it with alcohol, and added to Sam's discomfort by finishing off his field surgery with a final clean.

'There.' He smiled, looking pleased with his work.

Sam had been sitting on a wooden chair in an almost bare room, decorated only with radio equipment and a small armoury. She was still in her jeans, but only wore a bra on top. It was discolouring at the edges. She had a change of underwear in her daysack. That was her next job.

'Thanks,' she'd managed, drumming up as much feeling as she could muster.

Micah was clearing up around her.

'Don't mention it. We are still very much in your debt.'

Micah was just as Sam remembered him. He had the form of a ballet dancer and the field skills of a man who wouldn't lose a round in a welterweight bout.

'Where were you following me from? Tel Aviv or Abuja?' Sam had finally found the energy to ask a question.

'I was in Lagos. The centre patched you straight through. We want to help. And, as you described it on the webchat, the only way that would work was if you stayed alive long enough to effect your plan. We picked up your flight. I followed. We were lucky with timings. And the rest is a short struggle outside the yard of The Nook diner.' Micah had put everything away. He'd walked across to the small apartment's kitchen and flicked the switch on the kettle.

'How's Hannah?' Sam had asked.

Micah had stopped still, a teaspoon of coffee poised above one of two cups.

He smiled at her, a genuine smile.

'Really well, thank you. She'd love to see you, if you're ever in Nigeria?'

Hannah was Micah's oppo in the small team in Abuja. They'd dragged Sam from the clasps of the YCA's Nigerian thugs. And then, between them, they'd pulled off the Abuja raid. It was another of those short-term relationships which had forged an indelible bond.

Sam had nodded in response. She looked across to the wall opposite her. There were two analogue clocks, side by one. One read EST, the other the time in Tel Aviv.

'I need to get to the airport. I'm against the clock.' Sam stood, the effort of standing forcing her arm to cry out for mercy. She steadied herself.

'If you look in the drawer, over there ...' Micah pointed '... you'll find some clean clothes. Some might be appropriate.' He finished making two coffees. 'I have an aircraft on the pan. It's fueled and ready to take you anywhere you want to go.' Micah's generosity wasn't offered with any grandeur. It was said matter-of-factly.

Sam was at the chest of drawers. She had placed her hand on the top and had taken a deep breath.

'Can you fly me into Inverness ... or Aberdeen, Scotland?' she asked as she opened the bottom drawer.

'No. Mossad still has that thing with your government. But we can land at RAF Lossiemouth, which is closer still to the Nairnshire estate, providing we burn and turn.'

Sam glanced at Micah, a thin, turquoise woollen roll-neck in one hand.

'No Israeli boots on the ground, I'm afraid,' he added with a smile. 'That's your colour, by the way.' He nodded in her direction.

She stared at the jumper. And then back to him.

'Fuck off,' she said.

And now, a few hours later and Sam wearing clean underwear and a turquoise lambswool jumper and her old jeans, they were ninety minutes out from Lossie. Frank and Wolfgang knew she was on her way. And they knew the outline of the plan ... that was, *likely* plan. It depended on whether Holly Mickelson had managed to persuade the board at CNN that this was a story that deserved to break. Sam had relayed that information before they'd left the Mossad safe house. It was now time to fill the gaps, find out how Jane was doing, and tie the next thirty-six hours down as tight as she could.

Flemingstraße, Munich, Germany

They were getting close. Between him and Wolfgang, and the two-person MI5 team, they had been able to squeeze a quart of information into the pint mug of intelligence –

455

without it breaking. When they got the detail of the Abuja operation from Sam's Mossad contact, they had an extraordinary story to tell, with known links and likely connections to a series of events and issues, which was filling up the middle half of Wolfgang's info board.

His German friend was at his computer.

Frank was standing back from the board, marvelling at the quality of intelligence they had put together.

The image looked like a many-legged cartoon monster. Its small body in the centre. Three letters: YCA. In a thick-lined box.

The multitude of legs wound out to rectangles, filled with facts, and goose eggs, uncorroborated intelligence. Many of those shapes had their own tentacles, some of which led to new shapes, others circling around to join the original list. Each was filled with a single line of intelligence. Touch it, and a drop down box linked to a series of emails, notes, and press articles substantiated the claim.

The rectangles included the Bosnia operation and the yet to be detailed Abuja affair. Then there was the original intelligence from Louis Belmonte, which included the links to his brother's diary, the original list of YCA members, the YCA monogram, and the Elias Bosshart watches. Links took you to photos, business details, and other connections.

They had put the drone attack – and Fordingly's escape – in a rectangle: a fact. Trish, the young MI5 analyst (who Frank thought Wolfgang already had a crush on), had confirmed that a day prior to Daniel Grinstead's clandestine Bentley meet-up with the British prime minister, the Duke's son had been to his father's estate. Via GCHQ, MI5 had uncovered an SMS thread between father and son which preceded that meet. The key line in that thread was: *I have a job for you regarding your primary agent. Meet in person in the next 24 hours. He will be at his country estate.* Trish reckoned that was enough to link the Duke, his son's meeting with Fordingly, and the prime minister's 'lucky escape' as a single YCA-backed operation.

They'd also had a result with the Belarus affair – that was also now in a rectangle.

The outcome of Semenov's meeting with the Belarusian interior minister was no longer a mystery to them. Trish had spoken to an SIS case officer in the small Minsk station. Her casual enquiry about a meeting between a White Russian oligarch and a Belarusian minister hadn't raised any flags – and they had come straight back. SIS had an agent in the interior ministry; they knew of Semenov's visit, and whilst there were no minutes from any meeting, the post-meeting verbal instructions from the interior minister were to orchestrate a refugee pile-on at the Polish border. Apparently, and this piece of intelligence was conjecture, the aim was to force Poland to be authoritarian in their response, further weakening their position in the European Union.

Frank had asked of Trish, 'How do the YCA gain from this?'

Trish had stewed for a moment.

'The breakup of the EU is in everyone's interest, apart from the EU,' she had said. 'As a trade and security bloc, they are globally powerful and impressively resolute. Dividing and ruling allows the YCA to exploit countries individually as and when.'

It had been good enough for Frank. Hence, the Belarusian affair – now known to be orchestrated by QAnon-badged militia herding unfortunate refugees to the border to be met by the Polish military with water cannons – was in a rectangle.

To finish the 'certainties', Frank had included the assassination of the Greek shipping tycoon Konstantos, and the murder of the Norwegian doctor Janne Pedeson.

Among a number of goose eggs – which included the death threats to the Brazilian opposition leader – was what Frank thought was a genius bit of intelligence gathering: the home assistant conspiracy.

It was, in principle, an obvious extrapolation of the information presented.

The conspiracy was that all of the home assistants listened to and recorded everything you said. That audio was stored in some massive, central server where it was reviewed and filed. Here your relationships, shopping thoughts, political persuasion, sexual preferences, and all manner of nonsense, was interrogated ... and then exploited.

Apparently.

This was, of course, nonsense.

Sure, GCHQ could target a particular home assistant and use it to listen to and record audio. However, they'd need a warrant and a couple of operators working full-time to turn an epoch of information from a single home assistant into intelligence. Multiply that by the 3.2 billion people across the world using voice-activated software and you have a capacity problem. If, and when, AI was clever enough to duplicate the work of over 6 billion analysts, then you might want to attach some credence to the conspiracy.

But not now.

Especially as that wasn't the point.

In a random search on the dark web Wolfgang had uncovered the real conspiracy. And it was the perfect YCA play.

Michael Connock ran the largest satellite, comms and cable network in the world. In the UK alone, Connock's empire delivered fibre broadband to 13 million customers. His latest home entertainment hub was voice-sensitive. As well as providing TV streaming services, if you owned or rented a Connock system you had a readymade home assistant, from which you could ask for anything, from showing your favourite programme, to dimming the lights or ordering a pizza. It was its own home assistant, but cleverly disguised as a TV remote.

But, if you already owned a home assistant from another company, then you might not activate the Connock hub. Why would you?

Unless you were encouraged to sabotage your own device and use the 'safer' Connock TV.

Wolfgang had found a bot farm based in Kazakhstan. It was running countless QAnon-underpinned memes encouraging revolt against the best known home assistants. As a result there were thousands of protests across the world where ordinary people were destroying their electronic helpers. They were being dropped in buckets of water, thrown onto fires, and stamped on – all with the best possible social media coverage. It was a catalyst of destruction.

Except the Connock entertainment hubs.

Because they aren't the same?

Who ran the bot farm?

It had taken Wolfgang less than an hour to find connections between Kazakhstan and Connock headquarters in New York.

It was a pretty neat way of taking over the world.

Frank particularly liked that piece of work.

And there were others.

Frank had put together a brief which he had made available to Holly Mickleson. That had been Sam's final instruction before she'd got on the plane to fly back to the UK.

He touched one of the rectangles at random just to make sure the drop down box appeared. It did.

He stepped back. And took it all in again.

It was quite a story. And the world needed to know about it.

But ... and it was a niggling but.

He was no further forward on the YCA's purpose. Nor on the rationale behind the drone attack.

Other than Edinburgh, each operation, each event, made sense on its own. The home assistant conspiracy suited Connock. The Bosnian transplant hub spoke for itself – it was a huge medical convenience for anyone in the YCA's inner circle. The destabilising of the EU suited any businessman where working with individual countries was preferred to trading with a bloc.

The deaths of commonwealth leaders?

Kill hundreds, murder one?

He had nothing conclusive on that.

So it all made sense. And yet, it didn't make *any* sense.

And that made the info board story and its accompanying brief interesting in its individual pieces. But there was no holistic outcome. Nothing that he could yet see.

There was a bleep from Wolfgang's computer.

'It's Sam,' Wolfgang called out.

Frank took one last look at the board and then found his seat next to his German pal.

It took Wolfgang a minute to connect Sam, link to Jane's satphone and then open the connection with the MI5 team. There was no video, but the audio was crystal clear. And encrypted.

'Do we have a quorum at the Nairnshire estate?' Sam asked without any further introduction.

'We're just missing Jimmy Johnson.' Jane's voice was delayed slightly as multiple satellites, other linkages and heavy encryption connected her to the basement in Munich. 'We have seven confirmed, either visual here, or picked up by Wolfgang's cameras where the vehicle's occupant was unseen through blacked out windows. It's very close to being a full house. And, interestingly, no other attendees. So it seems likely that our list is pretty tight.'

'Any idea if Johnson is coming?' Sam pushed.

'He's on a flight into Glasgow this evening. He should be on the ground at 8.05,' Wolfgang answered.

'That means, if they need unanimous decision making, then they're going to wait until tomorrow?' Sam asked for confirmation.

'Seems so,' Frank answered.

'With that, anyone got any idea on purpose? And have we shared the summary file with CNN?' Sam asked two questions.

Frank chipped in.

'Yes to the second. Have you read it?'

'Yes,' Sam came straight back. 'The Belarus and home assistant lines are helpful. And my Mossad contact is putting together a few lines on what they're prepared to

461

share from Abuja. He and I have discussed what should be included. It's pretty explosive. You should have that any moment now. Make sure CNN understand the file has been updated.'

Frank leant forward. His shoulder brushed against Wolfgang's.

'Yep. I'll do that. And, as for your first question, no. Sorry. No purpose.' Frank sat back again. Wolfgang looked at him. He wore a resigned look, as though he had failed in some way.

'Anyone?' Sam barked.

'I don't get anything other than money.' It was Trish. 'And creating the conditions for the longevity of their clans. In perpetuity.'

There was silence.

'No. There's some glue,' Sam came back. 'Sure, they can help each other out here and there. Scratch each other's back. But there's no guaranteeing Connock's media success will improve the price of Chibuike Grandom's commodities, or the value of Marc Belmonte's vineyards.' There was a further beat. 'Unless it's all super detailed. Too complex for us to see from a distance. Maybe the aim of the next two days is to agree on a two-year business plan with such intricacy – with every 'what if?' covered – that they all go away *d'accord*. But, if that's the case, where's the supporting staff? Who's been working this up? Three of them, including the CEO, are over eighty. They're hardly in the prime of their cognisant lives.' Sam paused again. 'No. There's something else here. We know it's not religion, which is a shame. But it's something like that. Find it. Someone.'

Wolfgang looked to Frank. They both raised their eyebrows.

'And ... what about the drone attack in Edinburgh? Who gains? As far as I can tell the event has stiffened the resolve of the delegates to tackle climate change. Was that the point?' Sam pressed.

There was more silence.

And then ...

'What if we've missed the target? Been blinded by the Commonwealth angle?" It was Jane.

'What do you mean?' A question in unison from Frank and Sam.

'We think the YCA are looking to facilitate the break-up of the EU. That seems to make sense. But ... the Duke of Nairnshire is an Englishman abroad. Sure there's Scottish heritage there, but originally he's as English as fish and chips. And the last thing he wants is the break-up of the British Union.' Jane didn't finish her chain of thought.

'So they kill the leader of the Scottish Independence Party,' Frank suggested. 'She's a formidable woman. And, as I understand it, after her death the party is already in disarray. One broadsheet has an independence vote put back by maybe as long as five years?'

'Perfect,' Sam offered without praise. 'Now prove it.'

The conversation then changed tack. Next on the agenda was how Sam was going to meet up with Jane. And, if and when they launched a live cinematic recce on the main house, how would that work? Would they use mobile phones' cameras? How would the data be shared among them? Would they get enough information to prove the existence of the YCA in real time? And who would relay the feed to CNN so they could broadcast it live?

Wolfgang was sort of listening.

But only sort of.

Because he'd noticed something on his screenful of security cameras of the Nairnshire estate.

It was nothing.

Was it?

Possibly.

He screen-grabbed a couple of views. Then he deftly tapped away, accessing previously stored videos from exactly the same time the previous day. And then the day before. The screen was full of similar looking shots.

'What are you up to?' Frank asked him quietly so as not to interrupt the conversation between Jane and Sam.

Wolfgang stuck up a hand to gently dismiss Frank.

'Hey, everyone,' Wolfgang said. But he didn't break through. Sam and Jane were still discussing logistics.

'Hey!' Wolfgang raised his voice. Everyone went quiet. 'Jane. Is there anything happening at your end? Any cars? Outward movement?'

'Wait.' Jane's response was immediate.

There was a long pause.

Then ... 'No. Nothing from here, nor the southern team. It's all quiet.'

'Why?' Sam asked.

Wolfgang pointed at the original screen grab from a few seconds ago, and then a second one he'd just recovered from exactly the same time the day before yesterday. They were running in parallel.

'Do you see it, Frank?' Wolfgang's question was loud enough for everyone to hear.

Frank leant forward.

'Bloody hell,' Frank swore quietly. 'We're being played.'

'There's something going down, Sam,' Wolfgang said. 'There's been a smooth transfer of security footage at

464

the main house. What I'm looking at live is a copy of what I saw two days ago, but superimposed with today's date.'

There was a further pause as everyone digested Wolfgang's comment.

'Hang on!' Jane spat the words across the ether.

As they waited Wolfgang could hear Jane talking to someone, probably her southern team.

'Joe – he's down on the B9007, east of here. He's picked up noises,' Jane came back.

'What sort of noises?' Sam's question was sharp.

'Wait …'

'… a helicopter. Just. It's some distance away, but from the direction of the house,' Jane said.

There was a beat.

'Heading where?' Sam pressed.

'Wait …' Jane replied.

There was more walkie-talkie discussion. And then they all heard it. The unmistakable *wokka wokka* of a helicopter blade cutting through the air.

'… just flown nearby. Maybe 100 foot and rising. Heading north-ish …'

'MI5?' Sam's broke into Jane's description. 'Have we got access to friendly radar?'

Silence. Then …

'We'll try. If the chopper disengages its transponder the only thing we can hope for is a pick-up from a civilian airfield, Lossiemouth or, if we're lucky, an early warning station. But engineering any of that takes time. And, noting a helicopter has a fly time of no more than four hours – 250 miles equivalent – then I'm not in any way hopeful we can catch it in the air.'

'Fuck it!' Sam vented all of their feelings.

The tension across the airwaves was electric.

465

Sam broke the impasse.

'If we assume we've lost the helicopter then Jimmy Johnson's it. We need to find him – and then follow him.' Her instructions were authoritative. 'Jane, meet me at Lossie. Bring everything you have. And get Joe to Glasgow to get eyes on Johnson's incoming flight. MI5, see if we can track down this helicopter. Frank and Wolfgang, keep plugging the gaps in the brief. And confirm with CNN how we're going to broadcast this video. We can't afford to lose what little advantage we have.'

Marvis Grind, Shetland, Scotland

They'd parked the hire car off the road and walked the short distance to the shore. The weather was being kind. It was cold and dank, but there was no rain and little wind. There was an infoboard down a short set of steps. It told them that they were in the only place on the planet where you could see both the North Sea and the Atlantic at the same time. Heather showed her paper map to Fi and pointed where they were. Her daughter pored over the map, her finger tracing the shore line out past Turvalds Head and into the ocean.

'It's the Atlantic,' Heather said. 'Next stop Greenland, I think.'

Fi looked up and out across the inlet. It was a palette of muted colours. Greys and fawns and browns and a muddy blue. A seabird flew overhead. Incongruously there were an ancient set of tank traps lining some of the shore, and a concrete plinth where there was once a gun, probably. Heather had learnt that both Orkney and Shetland were coloured by their military past. A Viking longboat here, a sunken battleship there.

'Look, Mum. A seal!' Fi was pointing to what looked like a small rock perched on a larger rock.

'Your eyesight's better than mine, love,' Heather replied, squinting in the direction of what was almost certainly a seal … she'd take Fi's word for it.

'That's fab!' Fi exclaimed. Her daughter reached for her mum's arm and slipped her hand under Heather's elbow and then held it tight.

'I love it here,' Fi continued. 'It's so calming. It's, I dunno, kind – in an inexplicable way. Do you get me?' She had turned to look at Heather. They were the same height. The same shape. Like mother, like daughter.

Heather searched into her daughter's eyes. And she found what she was looking for. What she had been yearning for, after all of these years.

Love.

Tears welled.

'Mum! Aw, Mum.'

There was hugging now. A deep, strong touch which warmed Heather against the cold of the late afternoon.

This was more important than anything which had gone before. This single hug demolished all of the history. The anxiety. The fretting. The late nights longing for a phone call. A text to say that her daughter was safely home.

As the tears found their way down the contours of her face, Heather knew things were different now – since that evening at home which had begun the search for the truth. Since the meeting with the editor in Inverness, the revelation in Orkney, and the fruitless search on Shetland. Since that phone call with Fi – the outpouring of her own youth to the only person who mattered in the world. That had clinched it. It had, once and for all, changed everything. It was still mother and daughter … but it was also now *so* very different. There was a bond. A connection, where before there had been a widening gulf.

Fi understood her mother now. She got it.

And that felt so extraordinarily good.

It brushed aside the events of twenty-two years ago. It even dismissed her experience in Lerwick this morning.

On the phone Fi had told her to go to the police, so she had. The policewoman behind the counter had been interested; aghast, almost. She had been scribbling down notes, but had stopped when it was clear this was no ordinary walk-in. She had called for a sergeant, who had joined them. Heather had started again. She had, in as few words as she could manage, recounted the events of that weekend in December 1999. She had cantered through the revelations of the last couple of weeks up to her altercation with the man, the gun and the quad bike on Yell.

The policewoman's mouth had been ajar. The male sergeant had been standing with his arms crossed. His mouth closed. Heather couldn't work out what was going on there.

'So … it's every second year. Odd year. This weekend. This evening. Tomorrow morning,' Heather had explained. 'If you follow the logic.'

'Mmm.' The police sergeant's acknowledgement had lacked conviction.

'Shall I take a statement?' the policewoman had asked her boss.

The man's head turned slowly to meet the question. He was toying with the idea.

Heather looked at both in turn.

468

'Sure. Take a statement. Put it on my desk,' the sergeant said.

'And?' Heather asked.

The sergeant's reply was sharper than Heather expected.

'I'll look at it.' He frowned. 'I might need to take some advice.'

'What about the ferry? Tonight's ferry?' Heather's voice had raised a pitch.

'I said I'll look at it.'

Heather glanced to the policewoman, who responded with the mildest of shrugs.

She had almost walked out at that point. Fi's plane was landing in a couple of hours and Heather had wanted to get a picnic together. But, she had started something which needed finishing. And Fi would expect her to turn this into something formal.

In the end the interview with the policewoman had taken less than an hour. It had been recorded on a tape machine and, the policewoman had said, Heather was to report back to the station tomorrow where a typed version would be available for her to sign.

'Tomorrow? What about the ferry?' Heather's exasperation had been spent. She was being ignored, or at very best she was being humoured. Nobody was going to do anything about this.

'Tomorrow,' the policewoman had said flatly. 'Sorry. Sergeant McVeigh has made it clear.'

And that had been that.

It had been her daughter's first question after she'd taken the five short steps down off the tiny plane, and having made it through what must be the smallest terminal building in the world – it was no more than a two-bed bungalow.

After a rushed embrace Fi had asked, 'What did the police say, Mum?'

Heather hadn't been able to stop smiling. It was so lovely to see Fi. To be together in a different place, away from home. The dynamic had already changed. The relationship perceptibly altered.

'They took a statement, love.' She had taken her daughter's bag in one hand and was leading her to the hire car, holding the other.

'That's it?' Fi had sounded incredulous.

'That's it.'

They were standing with the boot of the car open, hand in hand.

'What do we do now?' Fi had asked.

'I'm going to take you for a picnic. To where the Atlantic meets the North Sea.'

And that's what Heather had done. It had taken them thirty-five minutes to drive to Marvis Grind and they'd spent a further hour eating their lunch on their laps. Heather had steered them away from the obvious topic of conversation. Instead she'd asked Fi about university, her course, her friends and anything other than an event which had led to the birth of her daughter.

Once Heather had cleared the rubbish away from the dashboard, there had been a pause. A single car had passed them on the road, one of only a few that had travelled this way in the time they had been parked up.

Eventually Heather had broken the ice.

'Does it hurt that your dad is … is, one of them?'

Fi had been staring into space. She hadn't replied to begin with, so Heather reached across and took one of her daughter's hands.

Fi turned her head to her mother.

'I don't know, Mum. I don't feel like a bad person. There's no inner anger, you know. I've never done anything wrong. Never felt the desire to. Maybe I got all the good genes?'

'I'm *so* sorry, love.'

In that moment a little piece of Heather's heart irrevocably broke.

'I'm so sorry that I didn't tell you. And I'm so sorry that I have told you. But this thing has been a dagger in my side for such a long time.'

Heather could have gone on – and on, but words hadn't seemed enough at that moment.

'Let's go and look at the sea.' Fi had perked up. 'Come on, Mum. It's beautiful.'

And now here they were.

Mother and daughter. Lochside. Facing out towards Greenland. Or somewhere.

'North Sea now, Mum!' Fi broke away from their embrace and ran like a child up the bank, across the road and down to the opposite shore. Heather followed her, enjoying watching her grown-up child behave in such a frivolous way.

As she reached the road, Heather stopped. Fi was already on the shore, a foot pushing at a rock on the water's edge. Beyond her the view was the same as she'd just left. Sea and sky and a craggy landscape.

But it was different.

They were now facing east.

And it was getting dark.

471

Over her shoulder was the ebbing of the day. In front of her the advance of night.

Darkness.

A sudden gust of wind pulled at her hair which was exposed below her hat. It flew across her face and she used a finger to push it back where it belonged. Fi was looking across the bay. She cut a lonely figure against such massive terrain. And that thought caught Heather. It sent a spike of fear through her. That she had inadvertently brought her precious cargo to this place. On the surface, a humble, warm island where everyone knew everyone else. Where the welcome extended beyond the porch and into the village.

And yet, Heather had met a grunt of a man with a quad bike and a gun.

Not far from here.

Things were not all they seemed on Shetland.

She jogged down to Fi's side and put her arm around her. Her daughter nestled her head against her mum's ear. The instant seemed to last a lifetime.

'What are we going to do, Mum?' Fi asked without taking her eyes off the encroaching darkness.

'I don't know, love. One part of me wants to go home. One part wants to stay and fight.' She hugged her closer.

A seabird, which was originally flying left to right, was caught unawares by a squall and was diverted directly overhead.

'We should wait by the ferry,' Fi said.

'Sorry?' Heather's response was immediate. She pulled her head away from her daughter's.

Fi followed suit. She broke from her mother's embrace and turned to her.

472

'Get supper in a bar, buy some supplies and then wait for the ferry. See if we can spot a truck which might be shipping in some people. Like happened to you?' There was immediacy in her daughter's voice.

'What? I don't ...' Heather spluttered out an unfinished reply.

'Come on, Mum.' Fi's voice was laced with earnest. 'We need to stop this from happening. And if the police won't, then we should.'

RAF Lossiemouth, Lossiemouth, Scotland

Sam managed to escape a farewell hug from Micah. In the end they'd settled for a handshake.

'Thanks,' she said, her voice raised above the sound of the jet's engines and the gusting wind.

'Got to go,' he replied, and then pointed at a white Nissan NV400 which was heading across the arc-lit apron. 'I think that's your lift?'

Sam looked. In this light it was impossible to see who was in the front of the cab. She had to guess it was Jane. She turned back to Micah and gave a thumbs up. The Mossad agent took the four metal steps back into the belly of the aircraft in two strides. He turned and faked a salute.

'You know where we are!' he shouted.

Sam waved, turned and walked across to the now stationary Nissan.

It was Jane. She was out of the cab. As was a man and another woman. None of them looked particularly comfortable with what the weather was throwing at them.

'Hi, Sam.' It was Jane's turn to shout.

Sam waved nonchalantly in return.

473

'This is Nadia and Nigel.' Jane pointed. 'Can we get in from the wind?' Jane had a hand protecting one side of her face, the other pointing to the van's passenger door.

Sam nodded and jumped onto the bench seat.

Jane followed, forcing Sam along. Nadia took the driver's seat. Sam heard the sliding door open and close. Nigel had clearly been relegated to the back. The women were in charge.

'Anything from anyone?' Sam had put her daysack between her legs and was now using her fingers as a comb. She glanced left at Jane and then right to Nadia.

'Not yet,' Nadia answered. 'We're working with the MoD and NATS (*National Air Traffic Services*) at Prestwick. NATS has no helicopters north of the Great Glen. There are four currently operating in the North Sea, working the rigs. There are only two aircraft across the Highlands. One's an Air Canada 777 heading for home, and the second is an EasyJet A320 off to Reykjavik. Nothing else. Not even a private jet.'

'Can these people turn off transponders?' Sam asked.

'Sure,' Nadia answered. 'And a helicopter can fly nap of the Earth, which makes radar more difficult. The MoD might be our best bet, but they are very touchy about sharing information. The problem we have is that this team doesn't have the clout. And Joe will not reach out to the boss.'

'In case we get compromised?' Sam pressed.

Nadia nodded.

'Any other news?' Sam wanted something. 'Is Joe at Glasgow yet?'

It was Jane's turn. Sam's head was playing tennis.

'He's on his way. And we got a holding reply from Holly. There's an extraordinary board meeting at CNN later this afternoon, EST … about midnight tonight. We should have something then.'

'But, as at now, we can't fulfil our end of the bargain,' Sam replied angrily. 'Sure they have plenty of decent intelligence. But it lacks the impact of a live feed. As it is, it's a slow-burn, *Washington Post* story. If we had video, the presence would be instant and much more effective. CNN will be expecting that. No video and they won't run the story.' She closed her eyes and shook her head.

There was a long pause.

'What now, Sam?' Jane asked. 'The Station Commander wants us off his base as soon as possible.'

Sam kept her eyes closed.

'Where the fuck are they going?' she whispered, between gritted teeth. 'Anyone?'

'North.' It was Nigel, in the cheap seats.

'Why?' Sam opened her eyes and half turned her head.

'Because it's more desolate. We've all seen *Skyfall*. There's a hunting lodge in the middle of nowhere with the Duke of Nairnshire's name all over it. Even more remote than the one we've just left.' There was a beat. 'If nothing else, let's get to Inverness. From there we have a civilian airport on tap, and main roads in most directions. Johnson's flight lands in an hour. We should have more then. It'll take us that long to get to Inverness,' Nigel offered.

He's right.

'Let's go, Nadia,' Sam ordered. 'And, has anyone got any paracetamol?'

Chapter 19

They were parked next to the River Ness. One kilometre north and you'd end up swimming in the Beauly Firth. Ten kilometres southwest and you'd be worried about losing a limb to the Loch Ness monster. Jane had chosen the spot. She'd directed Nadia via Google Maps and, without any communication with Sam, had dispatched Nigel to pick up McDonald's for all of them. That job was done. She now needed a pee and there were no loos nearby, nor bushes to crouch behind. Although there was an unlit, gated carpark 20 metres away which was furnished with a couple of wheelie bins. That would be her in a few minutes.

The last hour had been pretty depressing. Nothing had happened. There'd been no comms with either Joe or Wolfgang. Nadia and Nigel had kept themselves to themselves. And Sam had sat between them with a face which would curdle cream. Sam had shown no hint of wanting to be involved. She had sat there with her arms crossed and her bottom lip stuck out like a diving platform. It was the face of a petulant child who hadn't been allowed to watch the end of a film because it was past their bedtime.

Jane loved Sam Green. She had since the beginning. It was an odd, deep mixture of maternal and sibling affection. It was blood, not water. They had been in so many scrapes together, saved each other, screamed at each other and, although never with any empathy from Sam, hugged each other.

477

Since Rotterdam nothing had changed. Jane's ability to cope had waxed and waned, but she had always been upfront with her friend. Sam had been, as she had since Loa Chai, ruthless. Determined. There was a goal, albeit one that was a million miles away. Between it and them were more obstacles than Harrison Ford managed in a *Raiders* movie. But none of that deterred Sam. There was something clockwork about her.

Jane had a cousin with autism. The lovely lad was uncomfortable in company. He didn't do affection – he wouldn't take a hug without a fight. And he was listless ... until something interested him. And then everything changed. He was incisive, particularly if the something required attention to detail and a bit of maths. Give him a complex Lego toy and, whilst he was no quicker than an average child, he would be absolutely systematic about it. It would be built to perfection. Little pre-constructed blocks of plastic laid out in lines of size and colour.

That was Sam. She was that child. Except ... she had both a physical and intellectual cadence which was faster than anyone Jane knew. And, intellectually, there was a savant quality about her. She missed nothing. And remembered everything.

Jane loved her for that.

But ... she didn't always like her.

And just now, that was an understatement.

If she could move to a different room, she would. A next door county would be good.

Sam made things difficult. She always did.

She didn't mean it. Not really. There was no spite in Sam Green. There was only right ... and wrong. And if your version of the world didn't point in the same direction as Sam's moral compass, then you would be given short shrift.

And don't expect an explanation, unless it suited Sam. She had no energy for that.

Just now, though, what Jane would give for some empathy from the bundle of pent-up energy sitting beside her.

She checked her watch. It was just gone 7 pm. Johnson's aircraft should be landing about now. Nadia had an MI5 tablet linked into the satphone. She was monitoring the website Flightradar24, which displayed all the aircraft in the sky which were pinging.

'Anything?' Jane asked Nadia.

'It's on top of Glasgow. Not circling. It should be down on time,' Nadia replied.

Jane reached for her spent McDonald's wrapping and tidied it and everyone else's into a single bag. Without looking she passed it into the back.

'Nigel ... please,' she asked kindly.

'Got it,' he replied.

There was no doubt that the MI5 team Joe had put together was excellent. They were on everything and, so far, had shown no signs of flagging.

And the weather had calmed. A touch. There was only a smattering of idle rain on the windscreen. Which reminded her ... she needed a pee.

'I'm popping behind the bins for a wee,' she announced casually. And she didn't wait for a response. Two minutes later she was wiping herself and pulling up her slacks.

Sam appeared as Jane came out from her not-so-secret loo.

'You OK?' Jane asked to fill any awkward gap.

'Yep,' Sam answered perfunctorily.

479

'You've been taking quite a few painkillers.' It was more gap filling.

'I've got a headache,' Sam replied as she navigated her friend and found the same spot where Jane had just finished peeing. She continued talking as she undid her belt. 'You understand that if we don't expose these people ... if we don't bring down this cabal of monsters, then we're going to spend the rest of our lives looking over our shoulders. Every day might be our last. We can never rest.' Sam had pulled down her pants and squatted. There was no attempt to hide her bodily functions from Jane.

'I know,' Jane said. 'I want this as much as you do. I've struggled with all the hurt I've caused along the way. So I desperately want some closure. You understand that?'

Sam's face was in shadow, but Jane could still pick out the grey of her eyes. A dribble of urine was snaking towards her shoes. She took a step sideways.

'I do,' Sam said without feeling. She was wiping herself now. She stood up and stepped into the half-light. 'I want you to promise me that you'll keep Nadia and Nigel safe.' Sam was buttoning her jeans. 'They might think they know what they're heading for, but they have no idea. We do. We've faced these people in Bosnia. I have seen their terror in Abuja. This is not your regular Box stakeout. Nadia and Nigel aren't in some building with a long lens and a shotgun microphone. If we find these people, the perimeter's going to be brutal. Step over it and it will be carnage. The more of us there are, the more casualties there will be.'

Sam was close to Jane now. She could now see the intensity in her friend's face.

'Promise me,' Sam said again.

Jane nodded her head. 'I'll do my best.'

'Good. And ...'

'What, Sam?' Jane asked.

'Nothing. Let's go.'

And with that Sam walked around Jane and then broke into a jog, back towards the van.

Sam was not in any way comfortable. She hated uncertainty. It irked her. When it presented itself, she either ran towards the problem, or ignored it and found something else to concentrate on. She didn't do waiting. She just did action. Or sleep.

The lack of intelligence around the location of the helicopter wouldn't have been so much of a problem if there was something else she could be doing. Some other rock to lift. But there wasn't. Everything hinged on finding the YCA's winter hideout. And for the last hour and a bit, that had lodged an apple-sized knot of frustration in her stomach which was spiking her anxiety. And her effing arm hurt as much as any injury she'd had. Pain was draining. It sapped strength and messed with your mind. Hurt revealed who you truly were. She knew she was being unnecessarily grumpy. That if she were a little kinder, everyone else would be in a better place.

But that required effort. Which in itself would be a distraction. And she had enough of those. Even with a close-to-overdose number of paracetamol inside her.

The satphone rang. Nadia connected and then pressed some other buttons which sent the call through to Munich.

'Jane?' It was Joe.

'Yes,' Jane replied.

'He's down. I'm in the police control room with a suite of cameras. We don't yet have eyes on.'

'Wolfgang?' Sam barked at the phone which Nadia had placed on the dashboard.

There was a pause.

'Yes?' Wolfgang replied.

'Anything from you?'

There was a further pause.

'Nothing yet on subsequent passenger manifests with his name on it. Nothing irregular from the hire car companies. Twenty-six pre-booked cars. None of which we can pin on Johnson,' Wolfgang replied.

'Have we got someone at the arrivals gate?' Sam pressed.

'Yes,' Joe replied.

Sam glanced at Jane. She was staring at the satphone.

The phone went quiet – just some mild background noise which, Sam assumed, was coming from the police control room.

Still nothing.

Sam filled the gap.

'Whilst we're waiting. Frank. Anything to add on the drone attack?'

'Yes.' There was a pause, as though Frank were fearful of interrupting the more critical operation.

'Get on with it. Joe will interrupt if he gets anything,' Sam said.

'First, Fordingly was staying at the Duke of Nairnshire's Edinburgh house. He went there straight after the attack. It's a reinforcing connection. Second, and this makes it a wrap in my book ...'

'Wait, Frank … we've got eyes on the United passengers,' Joe interrupted. 'They've reached the first CCTV. Wait.' There was a long pause. 'I've got three images of Johnson on the desk here and none of them yet match any of those alighting the plane.'

'Wolfgang. Did he travel first class?' Sam barked.

'Yes.' A single word reply from Munich.

'He should be first off, then.' Nadia said what everyone else was thinking.

'Can't see him,' Joe added.

'Look harder,' Sam pressed.

'Second CCTV, now … wait … no, nothing.'

'Was he on the manifest?' Sam asked the question, but she knew Wolfgang would be on it.

'Yes.' Another single word reply from Germany.

'They're all past the first camera. I've just seen a stewardess.' Joe sounded infuriated. 'This doesn't make any sense.'

There was an off-call conversation. Sam assumed Joe was pressing some member of staff for more information.

'The view here is that if he was on the flight, we should have visual by now,' Joe said.

'Did he use his own passport from Newark?' Sam asked. She knew the answer.

'Yes.' Wolfgang was getting good at the one-word replies.

'He must offer it here then? Can he avoid Border Force?' Nadia asked.

There was another unheard conversation from the control room.

'There's a fast track passport control. But we have that on CCTV here. We've got eyes on every exit. It's the best

483

we've got. And I can't stop the efflux of passengers. Neither the police nor Border Force are prepared to change their processes, not without authority from the Scottish Office. That's not going to happen at this short …'

A shrill Wolfgang interrupted Joe's explanation.

'No need. I think I know where he's going.'

'Tell us,' Sam snapped back.

'A new flight plan has just been submitted to the NATS, Preswick. It's a Cessna Citation X, tail number: G-657DA. Flight leaves in fifteen minutes. Johnson's on the passenger list of one.'

'Where's it going, Wolfgang?' Sam asked.

'Lerwick. ETA 2315.'

'That's Shetland,' Nigel offered from the back.

'How have we missed him?' Joe's frustration was evident.

'There's always a set of stairs off the walkway. It doesn't matter.' Sam was struggling to hide her frustration. She would have had that option covered. 'When can you get us to Shetland, Wolfgang?'

'Wait … wait … there's 6.40 out of Aberdeen tomorrow morning. Logan Air. You'll be on the ground before 8.00 am. Wait …' Everyone waited. 'There's only two seats.'

Both Nadia and Jane were looking at Sam. Waiting for a decision.

'What other options are there?' Sam wasn't hopeful.

'Wait …'

Two of them could catch the flight. But they'd need a car on arrival. And they would be travelling light. They certainly couldn't carry the Sauers, which Sam thought they would probably need. And all of the visual support equipment. If she had been on her own? She'd swim if she had to.

Fuck it.

Nothing was going right.

'There's a ferry from Kirkwall, Orkney, leaving tonight, just before midnight. It arrives in Lerwick just before 7 am tomorrow. You'd need to catch a short connecting ferry from Scrabster. But ... wait.' They waited again. 'Time is tight. I can book the ferries. You'll need to be at Scrabster in two and a half hours and it's 112 miles. It looks like the last ferry from the mainland is designed to catch the late evening from Kirkwall to Lerwick,' Wolfgang reported efficiently.

'Drive!' Sam threw a pointed finger in Nadia's direction. 'Jane, get the quickest route.'

Nadia had the engine running and was already pulling out of their parking spot.

'Joe!' Sam growled again at the satphone, which she was now holding on to as Nadia was driving with the alacrity of a rally driver.

'Yes, Sam.'

'Get on the Aberdeen flight to Lerwick. And keep in touch,' Sam ordered.

'Yes, ma'am.' There was a touch of sarcasm in Joe's voice.

'And, Frank?' Sam asked.

'Yes?'

'Finish your briefing. The interesting bit.'

'OK. Look, I've spoken with a woman in the Scottish Independence Party leader's outer office. It seems the boss of the SIP wasn't invited to the Commonwealth banquet by the prime minister's office, which is where the original guest list was formulated. Their invite came from the CEO of the

Grand Hotel. Which, according to the outer office, was all a bit odd. It's widely accepted that their leader and the prime minister have no time for each other, for obvious reasons, and are rarely in the same room. One is pro-union, the other fights fiercely for Scottish independence ...'

'Get on with it, Frank,' Sam said. 'We know that.' She was working out what the YCA might do in the seven hours between Johnson joining the cabal and her team's arrival in Lerwick – ferries permitting. Of course that was the least of their worries. Shetland was an archipelago of islands. What chance did they have of finding the right HLS? And, without boots on the ground this evening, how could they possibly track Johnson?

The lack of certainty and the countless options were plaguing her.

'The CEO of the Grand is also the Chief Operations Officer for the Nairnshire estate. They are one and the same,' Frank concluded.

Blimey.

'That's it, then.' Jane filled the void left by Sam's various deliberations. 'The YCA set up the leader of the SIP. Fordingly is warned off a few days earlier, via a meet with Daniel Grinstead. It's out of his hands?'

'Seems so,' Frank replied.

'Put it in the brief. Make sure you let Holly know of the connection. She'll be telling the story to the CNN board as we're throwing up over the side of a ferry. And, somebody ... please.' Sam paused as Nadia overtook a car on a corner where, if a truck had been on the opposite side of the road, there would be nobody left to run the operation. 'Let's scan every inch of Shetland for a suitable lair. One with an HLS. We need to hit the ground tomorrow running.'

486

Wolfgang could smell the coffee before Lukas delivered it. A couple of years ago he'd spent some time idling away, designing an interface between Matilda, the cook, and Lukas, the house elf, so one could make coffee and the other deliver it.

There was a whirr. The noise squeezed past Frank, who was tapping on his keyboard, and stopped short of Wolfgang's chair. He looked to his left. There it was. A full mug of steaming coffee, drip-brewed via a filter and served black, with sugar. It was the way Germans did it. And, just now, as he struggled to break through a duvet of tiredness, coffee was essential.

It was well past midnight, UK time. Sam and the team had made it onto the Kirkwall to Lerwick ferry, just – next stop Shetland. And Joe and his oppo were holing out in a cheap hotel in Aberdeen waiting for their morning's flight to Lerwick.

However, between them they were no clearer as to which part of Shetland should be the focus. Frank and Trish had carried out a review of the most recent satellite imagery that MI5 could get their hands on – it was five weeks out of date. Frank had explained to Wolfgang that their search criteria was blunt: dwellings worthy of a Duke. They had found twelve of interest. And all of them had lawns large enough and flat enough to accommodate a decent-sized helicopter. Frank and Trish had taken six each. They had searched for perimeters, satellite dishes, other comms infrastructure, anything which stood out – and had, without any confidence, reduced the list to seven priority targets.

Five were on the main island, one on the northern island of Unst, and one on Fetlar.

It was something. But Frank had not been convinced.

'This is like picking a stone from a beach, cracking it open and expecting to find a fossil. We've gone for size. But, for all we know, the YCA could have taken over an Airbnb, or a local bar. I'm not comfortable with this approach,' Frank had been talking to Trish on a secure video link, whilst he pointed at a scribbled list of coordinates on the briefing board, 'and I'm not sure we should present it to the mobile team.'

'What else have we got?' Trish had responded. 'The MoD have a decent radar station at Herma Ness, but they're not playing. Not without authority from Main Building. And we can't get that.'

And they were no further now.

The satellite imagery was the best they could do. And that's what Frank was still at; looking back over the stuff, trying to find something.

Wolfgang had to admit that they really needed a break. And Frank had dismissed Wolfgang's offer of a hot drink with a flat hand, as though any disruption to his concentration would be a disaster.

On his side Wolfgang was still working through a myriad of stuff. Forty minutes ago he'd got a message from Holly to say that the board were still in conference, and there would be a delay. Wolfgang hadn't mentioned that they'd lost eyes-on the YCA cabal and that, currently, the mobile team were heading for an island with absolutely no certainty attached. Sam's latest view was that the only option was a cascon with some locals on arrival and hope to trigger some recognition.

Nothing from the images?

Use your tongue.

It was something.

Wolfgang picked his coffee mug up off the small plastic plate which balanced on Lukas's head.

'*Danke*,' Wolfgang said unnecessarily. He raised his mug to the robot in mock salute. '*Jetzt muss ich eine Tür finden.*'

A door.

He needed to find a door.

In among a myriad of work he hadn't forgotten about Sir Clive Morton, the chief of SIS – known colloquially as 'C'. Two weeks ago he had been arrested on paedophile charges. Jane and Frank were convinced it was a setup. The chief had been taken down because, like all of them, he was after upending the YCA. And that, clearly, hadn't been allowed.

The disgraceful images had made it onto the internet. They showed Sir Clive shockingly *in flagrante*, and they were *very* convincing. As was the metadata associated with the photos, which linked conveniently with a number of blanks in the Chief's diary. All of that had also been leaked. With no markers on the photos to show they had been doctored, Wolfgang had turned his attention to hacking the CPS's (*Crown Prosecution Service's*) server. Once in he could explore all of the evidence, in particular, what was the Chief's defence? Where *was* he when these photos were meant to have been taken?

He drummed his fingers on the worktop.

In the middle of his central screen was a time bar counting down. It was the final stage of the CPS hack. He was close.

Sixty seconds.

489

He took another sip of his coffee.

…

Thirty seconds.

His finger drumming continued.

…

Scheisse!

His left-hand screen threw up a grainy image of the front of his house, which showed two green movement boxes. His concentration on the timer was immediately broken.

Polizei!

There was a police car and, behind it, a van. Three policemen had got out of the car. All would be armed – that was the way with police here in Germany. The lead officer was carrying a folder.

A warrant?

And then the van disgorged its occupants.

Eight.

No nine.

And these were not your ordinary state police. They were dressed in dark coveralls, wore sight-mounted helmets and carried long-barrelled weapons. One of them was holding a Halligan bar. It was big and scythe-shaped. Once, a long time ago, he'd seen a video of it being used by the police. It brought down an average door in seconds.

They might well struggle here. All of his doors were wood-covered, metal reinforced. They'd need a battering ram.

'Frank.' Wolfgang's call was no more than a whisper.

'Huh?' Frank didn't look away from his screen.

'We've got company.'

That was all it needed.

They'd been here before. Sure, in the cellar next door and without the metal cages and reinforced concrete. And there were no signs yet of an RPG designed to set the house ablaze.

But a police assault would be much more thorough. The pair of them would be found. Eventually.

Frank was beside him.

'Shit,' he said.

'Indeed.'

Wolfgang had rehearsed this. Not necessarily with the police as the antagonists. But a similar sort of assault. With the same equipment.

He reckoned he could withstand twenty-four hours. If they found the hidden entrance to the underground corridor which led to this cellar, he had enough of a defence between him and the attackers to hold out for a day. Maybe a bit longer. Even if they blocked the venting, he had oxygen on tap. And everything else he needed. And the computer cabling which connected him to the outside world was buried 2 metres lower than him. It was safer than he was.

But it was designed for one man … and two robots.

Just him.

'You must pack, and go,' Wolfgang said.

The first policeman was at the gate. He had rung the bell. One of the now many images on Wolfgang's left-hand screen showed a close-up of his face. There were glasses. And a moustache.

Wolfgang ignored the policeman. He had another job to do.

'No,' Frank replied. 'I'm staying here. Sam and Jane need our support. We have an ongoing operation.'

Frank didn't sound convinced. And Wolfgang couldn't judge him for that. Why should Frank stay and

491

suffer the same fate twice? He wasn't a soldier. He was a civil servant. An extraordinarily good one. But he wasn't trained for a fight.

Wolfgang, on the other hand, was a Neuenburg. His ancestors always fought on the side of right, even if they were more musicians than military.

And this was his home. He would always defend it.

'Go to the castle.' Wolfgang pulled out a drawer, dug around, and handed a business card to Frank. 'Tomas will be expecting you. There is a set-up similar to this. You can work from there. And, should this get a bit crazy, you can act as backup.' Wolfgang smiled, and then glanced back at the screen. The policeman had a letter open and was showing it to the camera. Wolfgang only needed to see one word: *Gewährleistung*.

Warrant.

This wasn't going to end until it was over.

Wolfgang glanced back at Frank. As he did he reached further into the drawer and pulled out an ID card, a thick wedge of euro notes and a bank card. They were held together with a crocodile clip. He handed those to Frank, who accepted them tentatively. Wolfgang then opened a lower drawer and pulled out a 7-inch tablet and charger.

'Go now. Lukas will take you to the garage. Pick a car.'

Frank looked at the haul he'd just been given.

'Another long-lost cousin?' he asked.

'No. This is you.' Wolfgang pointed at the ID. He then sighed. He didn't have time or the energy to be subsumed by emotions. But throwing Frank out was tugging at something deep inside. 'Ever since our last time together, I was determined to be prepared ... just in case it happened again, Frank. You don't need to be here. You can keep in touch with this.' He tapped the tablet. 'And when you get to the castle we can be up and running again. Side by side.' Wolfgang nodded, and kept nodding. 'Go, Frank. Just go.'

There were tears in Frank's eyes, which further disturbed Wolfgang. And, to his right, the policeman with the Halligan bar was through the gate and had now taken prominence on the porch.

Good luck with that.

Whatever resolve Frank had, broke. He lurched forward and hugged his German friend.

'Good luck, Wolfgang,' Frank whispered in his ear. And then he stood up, wiped his eyes with a sleeve, turned and headed for Matilda's room.

Wolfgang watched Frank go, but only for a second. He needed to ensure the back area of the neighbour's house was clear of police, which it currently was. And he was fascinated by what the man with the scythe was up to.

Not much, at the moment.

To add to that, there was a ping on his machine.

It was a call from Holly. Wolfgang connected.

'Hi, Holly,' he said.

'Hi, Wolfgang. Good news. We've got the green light from the board. My anchor, who doesn't work weekends, has been brought in to take the file, the images and whatever else we can find. He's to put together a forty-minute track which we can throw into the schedule at a moment's notice. I'm helping with production. Happy so far?'

Wolfgang was. Although concurrently he was keeping an eye on the back, whilst enjoying the *Polizei's* attempt to break down the main door of the house. They'd go for a downstairs window next. Those were all alarmed to the hilt and would wake everyone in the neighbourhood.

493

Good luck with that too.

He felt Frank's presence beside him. Wolfgang glanced up. Frank had his bag and was ready to go.

'Holly?' Frank asked of Wolfgang, who nodded in return.

'Go on, Holly,' Wolfgang said. As he replied, he turned his head to Frank. 'Go. The back of this property is clear. But it might not be for long. Go!' He ushered him along with wave of his hand.

Unawares, Holly continued.

'We're quite clear here. Unless you can deliver live feed of the YCA doing something collective – preferably something nefarious – then we won't break our usual schedule. Does Sam understand that?'

She certainly does.

'Yes, Holly. She is clear. And we're getting there.'

'Where's there?' Holly asked.

'I can't tell you,' Wolfgang replied, 'Not until the team's on site. Then we'll let you know.'

'When is that?' Holly pressed.

That's a good question.

'My guess is later on this afternoon, UK time.'

'The later the better,' Holly said. 'Midnight UK makes pretty decent primetime here.'

'OK. I'll let Sam know.'

And with that the call went dead.

Wolfgang immediately turned. Frank was at the door. He raised a hand; Wolfgang did the same.

And then his English friend was gone.

Car park, Lerwick Ferry terminal, Lerwick, Shetland

It was quiet. And still dark. The car park was almost empty and, at just before seven on a Saturday morning, the main road into Lerwick was still. Just the odd car. And the squall had blown through, leaving behind the dawning of a cold day with high clouds. Puddles were iced over, and this morning Heather had almost taken a tumble on the way to the car. In the end she and Fi had opted for a B&B, with an early start. No breakfast.

The ferry, a big ro-ro, was the same sort as the one she had travelled over on. It might well be the same boat. They had watched it berth and now, completely and utterly unsure as to what to do next, the pair of them were waiting for the cars and trucks to disembark.

They had discussed what to do. And had come to no conclusion. Heather definitely wanted to go to the police station this morning and sign her statement. In some ways that would bring closure – of sorts. It would be better than nothing. Between now and then they had agreed to watch the traffic, see if they could pick out something which might be transporting some poor young people to a weekend of abuse – maybe worse – and then …

What exactly?

Follow that car? Or van?

And then what?

'We'll phone the police, Mum. Dial 999. Once we're sure we're onto something,' Fi had offered.

'What does "something" look like, love?' Heather had asked without enthusiasm. 'Do we follow the van up a path where there are big signs which say, "no trespassing"?'

Her daughter, who was brimming with confidence – too much, Heather thought – had grabbed her hand, squeezed it and said, 'Let's see, shall we?'

And here they were.

Waiting.

'There,' Fi pointed. 'The first car.'

Sure enough. A dark coloured hatchback was first off the boat. Then another car. Then a motorhome. Another car. A blue truck, like a Transit, although colour was a moot descriptor in the poor light. It had windows in the back that you could see through if you got close enough.

Not that one.

As Heather watched the rattling of vehicles coming off the ferry, the enormity of what they had taken on washed over her. There were too many cars. So many trucks. And ...

'There!' Fi pointed.

'Where?' Heather asked.

'That whitish one. There are three people in the cab. No side windows.'

'What about that one?' Heather was pointing at a reddish van, behind the white one. It was smaller. It looked like the van her window cleaner drove.

'No, Mum. The white one. It's newer. We have to take a chance. Go on, otherwise you'll miss it,' Fi ordered.

Sam's mood had improved. Just a little. She'd had some sleep in one of the Pullman seats on the ferry, eaten a decent but fatty breakfast, and the painkillers were doing a better job on a wound which looked as if it might heal nicely.

Jane had barged into the loos just after they'd boarded. Sam had been inspecting Micah's handiwork.

'Sam!'

Just what I need.

Jane was all over her then. She took charge, demanding the back story, not that there was much to tell.

'You do get yourself into some scrapes,' Jane had said in a motherly tone, as she bathed the wound with warm water and a little soap. She'd then used some toilet paper as gauze and reused a clean bit of Micah's dressing to complete the job. The finished article was solid. All case officers received yearly first aid training; Jane had clearly paid attention to her instructor.

And now, feeling on the better side of middling, they were on the hunt.

Wolfgang's news, that the police were searching his house and as a precaution he had dispatched Frank to the castle, was troubling. But he hadn't sound panicked when they'd spoken to him an hour ago.

'The *Bastarde* are taking apart the house brick by brick,' Wolfgang had said. 'They're nowhere near me at the moment. And Frank has just arrived at the castle. We have comms. In the end it's worked out well as we now have redundancy ... should things go astray here.'

Sam hadn't been happy with Wolfgang's last sentence, but there was nothing she could do. Wolfgang was his own man. He was capable of looking after himself.

In any case, there wasn't time to dwell. They had a needle to find in this particular haystack.

Frank's list of seven large properties was interesting, but hardly helpful – especially as, overnight, the static MI5 team had worked hard to assign owners, none of whom appeared conspiratorial.

So with nothing to go on, the emerging plan was linear ... to begin with.

First stop would be the Lerwick police. Ask questions.

Second, the airport. They'd meet Joe and press the ground crew on helicopter movements.

497

Then they split up. Wolfgang had hired six cars – that would mean all of them would be mobile. Sam had split the islands into zones and each of them would knock on doors and ask questions. If any of them got a hint, they'd converge, compare notes and make a decision. It was due to get dark just after three – that gave them five hours of decent light. If they didn't have an opening by then, they'd scale down the search until dawn broke. Then they'd start again. Or something else. Sam really hadn't made it that far.

Police first then.

Nigel was driving. Jane took the middle and Sam by the passenger door. Nadia was in the back, but she was kneeling behind them, her head between Jane and Nigel. This was their first trip to the northern isles. In any other circumstance it would be quite an excursion.

Story of my life.

The traffic ahead of them had slowed for the junction onto the main road. Nigel had stopped, leaving a gap for a car to pull out of the car park. It was an ugly Nissan Jute. Red. A hire car. The two women in the front hadn't taken down a paper sign which hung from the rear-view mirror. Sam stared at them. A little too long. And a little too hard.

They were looking back at her. Both of them. There was anxiety in their car. Sam could see it in their eyes. Even at this distance, she sensed the driver's tight grip on the steering wheel.

Sam blinked.

The women stared.

Nigel waved his hand, signalling for them to pull in front of them.

The driver, elder of the two and probably late forties, shook her head and motioned for the van to fill the gap.

Sam hadn't taken her eyes off the two women.

'Move it, Nigel,' Sam said, a little bored now. 'We haven't got time for a couple of tourists.'

As the van moved off, Sam kept her eyes on the car.

And then it was out of sight.

Sam shook her head to dismiss what was an odd, but irrelevant distraction ...

... and refocused on the view.

Cars.

Windows into houses. An industrial estate. An old man walking. A dog, not on a lead.

Absence of the normal.

She'd rehearsed this principle with the team earlier, as they were having breakfast in the ship's restaurant. She'd pointed out a couple of men at a table just down from them.

'Like those two blokes. Cropped hair?' she'd said.

'What am I looking for?' Nadia had asked.

'Absence of the normal. You're not always looking for things which shouldn't be there. Better to find things that should, which aren't,' Sam had replied.

Her three companions had looked, in turn, at the table with the two men.

Nadia, who Sam was warming to, was bent forward, her fingers entwined and resting on the Formica top in front of her. She'd started to say something, then stopped. She lifted her head and stared again at the two men. She then returned to her 'speaking in hushed tones' position.

'I've got it!' she whispered.

'What?' Jane exclaimed in a voice much louder than Nadia's. She then turned her shoulders and looked again.

'No, I can't see it,' she said, the ridges on her forehead exposing a frown.

Sam was enjoying herself for the first time in a while. It crossed her mind then that, if she got out of this in one piece, she might take up teaching.

Or something.

'What, then?' Sam was looking at Nadia.

'They're eating cereal. Not a greasy breakfast.' Nadia was shaking her head and smiling, as if that might help her explanation. 'No two blokes, away from home, would eat seeds when they could be stuffing their face with black pudding, bacon, sausage and toast, with lashings of butter. Would they?'

Sam looked at Jane – she was nodding her head, slowly, as though a penny had dropped.

'That's what I had,' Sam replied. 'They're too scruffy to be gay. And they've got bellies, so food is important to them. You might even think one of them would be having a pint with their breakfast. But, no. Muesli all round. It's not normal.' Sam had raised her coffee cup. 'Gold star to Nadia.'

Sam would bet on Nadia spotting something now.

If there's something to spot.

And that made the analyst instincts in Sam work harder still. She wasn't a competitive person. She just didn't like to be beaten.

They were in the heart of the town now.

Three more turns and they would be at the police station. When they got there, they'd agreed Nadia would lead with her recognisable MI5 ID card, with Sam in tow. Nigel would stay with the van – with the Sauers. Jane would walk the perimeter. If the YCA had property here, then they likely had some bent coppers on their books. Jane's job was to look for any triggers.

They turned a corner.

And another ...

... and were about to make the final turn when Sam confirmed that the hire car which had been behind them since they'd left the port – the one with the two women – had turned with them.

What the blazes?

She really didn't have time for this.

'Pull over. Put your flashers on,' Sam barked.

Nigel dithered.

'Now, Nigel!'

The van's ABS juddered as the vehicle came to a sudden halt.

Sam was opening the passenger door as she shouted to the back.

'Nadia, I want to see a Sauer's barrel out of the rear doors. Now!'

Jane said something, which was lost on Sam. She was too busy powering between the side of the van and a couple of parked cars.

'Mum! They've stopped! Can you pull past them?' Fi's voice was a blend of panic and instruction.

But she was too late. The white van had come to a halt, and Heather had reacted slowly and was right on the van's bumper.

What on earth?

Heather was immediately terrified. The intense woman, who had stared at her forever at the terminal, was coming around the back of the white van and ..

Oh no!

'Mum!'

It was all happening too quickly for her. Fi had screamed, the back door of the van had opened and the barrel of a gun had poked through. And now the intense woman was at her door.

Heather tried to find reverse but, before she could, her door was prised open by the intense woman, and there was a rough hand on her forearm.

'LEAVE MY MUM ALONE!' Fi's scream hurt Heather's ears as her daughter pushed her head between her mother's chest and the steering wheel. Fi's reaction had an effect. The intense woman pulled back slightly, but didn't let go of her arm.

'Shut up!' The intense woman's voice was raised, but it wasn't a shout. 'I'm with the police!'

That seemed to do the trick. Some order was established. Fi's face was still in the space in front of Heather, but there was no more shouting.

'Why are you following us?' The intense woman hadn't let go of Heather's forearm, but her grip was looser.

'We're not ... we're not following you.' The lie was obvious, but it was all Heather could manage.

And then the dam broke.

Heather's sobs were immediate and uncontrollable. She had suffered every conceivable emotion since she'd left home. Low lows, and then, over the past day, the most fabulous of connections with a daughter – who was now protecting her. Heather was scared. And elated. Wound up as tight as a child on Christmas Eve. But as free from her emotional turmoil as she ever hoped she might be.

And that combination was too much.

Her tears were unstoppable. Her head was shaking. Her breathing finding an erratic passage through an overwhelming desire to cry.

'What do you want from us?' Fi said angrily. 'Can't you see my mum's upset?'

The intense woman let go of Heather's forearm and stood up. She turned away from the car.

'Fuck's sake. We don't have time for this,' the intense woman said scornfully.

And now there was someone else. Another woman. She was taller – the one from the middle seat of the cab. She seemed kinder. As the intense woman backed away, a hand on her forehead, the kinder woman knelt down beside her mum.

'I'm with British intelligence. My name is Jane. We don't have much time. Why *were* you following us?'

Heather gulped some air. Her anxiety had peaked and some of her fear was dissipating. She was about to tell all when Fi got in before her.

'Show us some ID!' she ordered.

The kind woman sighed. And then reached into a pocket and pulled out an official-looking ID card. It had the letters 'SIS' on it.

'Secret Intelligence Service,' the kind woman said. 'James Bond, in a skirt.' She smiled.

Heather's breathing had begun to regulate, and she was feeling calmer still. Though she still couldn't get her words out.

But Fi managed.

Chapter 20

He could hear them now. The incessant banging. The deep shrill of the cutting machine.

The police had found the hidden back door of his neighbour's house. Once through that they were one more door away from finding him. He reckoned five, maybe six hours. If they resorted to explosives, forty minutes, max.

Six hours might be enough. But it might not be.

The team didn't know that. He hadn't told them. Wolfgang, who was now one of four outstations on a collective call, had recently given his update as though nothing had changed. Sam had asked, 'How's things with you, Wolfgang?' He'd replied, 'Fine. On track.'

And they were.

They all were ... of sorts.

But it had been a long few hours with three fraught collective calls with the team. And the police and their power tools were edging ever closer.

They'd had a frantic half hour just post breakfast, following the revelation that Sam and the Shetland team reckoned they knew of the YCA's cabal location. It had come after the most serendipitous of exchanges with a couple of women who were searching for what they were looking for, but for completely different reasons.

Jane had started to explain.

'We've inadvertently bumped into a woman and her adult daughter. The mother had been kidnapped and serially abused over a mid-December weekend in 1999. I

504

repeat that: she was kidnapped and then serially abused in the December of an odd year. She spoke of hooded men, a cellar and an open fire. She told us that there is a history of young people going missing in northern Scotland. It goes back as far 1981, maybe longer.' Jane let the weight of her announcement sink in before starting again.

'The woman, who lives in England, had parked the abuse in a corner of her mind until she could no longer ignore it. Thirty-three years later, after an unlikely investigation, she thinks she might have stumbled across the location ...'

Sam had interrupted Jane. Things clearly weren't going quick enough for her.

'She came across a manned security outpost on Yell. I read:' Sam paused. Wolfgang guessed it was a military procedure. To alert people to make notes. 'Grid 498042. The woman was approaching from the east when she was stopped by an armed man on a quad bike. He was unapologetically gruff with her. She left feeling threatened. He's housed in a single-storey, metal-roofed building. It's a security outpost. The giveaway for me was when she described something she saw sticking out of the ground: an element of a sonar or seismic array. A small black dome on a single, metre-high pole. I'm fairly sure it was the array which alerted the man to her presence.' She paused. Wolfgang reckoned she was waiting for people to take it in.

Sam continued.

'The problem is there are no buildings on the OS map, or visible on Google Maps, to the west of the encounter. One klick north and one klick west is sea and ocean. So it's a relatively small piece of real estate to hide something which you'd expect to show up somewhere. Interestingly there is a road or decent track coming in from the south. It's on the terrain overlay, but not on the OS map. It stops at, I read:' She paused again. 'Grid, 502004, 3.5 klicks short of the encounter.' She waited.

'I have the latest Langley satellite imagery up now, Sam.' It was Trish. 'Frank, have you got it?'

'Wait,' Frank replied, all the way from a castle on the German/Czechia border. 'Yes.'

'Good.' It was Sam again. 'We're still with the women. They were going to the police to sign a statement the mother had made the previous day, but we've stopped them for now. We're heading to the airport to meet up with Joe. Get something from those images, you two. We'll call back in thirty minutes. Out.'

The Shetland line went dead.

And then, with little to add, Wolfgang had also called off. He'd leave the analysts to do what analysts do best.

He had filled the intervening thirty minutes with breakfast and some ablutions, whilst the police continued to scrape away at his shell. In the past half an hour they had brought a digger into his front garden and were lifting up any piece of spare lawn they could find. It would take an age to put that straight.

The second morning call had occurred when the Shetland team had a quorum. Sam had opened the chat by saying that Joe was now up to date. She then pressed Trish for anything from the satellite recce.

'Well, the latest imagery is interesting,' Trish had started.

'What?' Sam had come straight back grumpily.

'OK. There's nothing on the photos in the piece of real estate you describe, north of the track and west of the woman, other than a derelict. Which is odd. Unusual, actually. And that made us look harder. What sealed it for us was the track you mentioned doesn't die a natural death. It stops mid-bog ...'

'Tracks do that,' Jane interrupted this time. The Shetland team's satellite phone was clearly on speaker. Their voices gave a tinny echo. If they had any sense they would be sitting in the warmth of the van, or one of the cars, with the heaters on full blast.

'No.' It was Frank. 'This track stops dead, at a funny angle. It's as though someone has cut it. Like a quill at the end of a feather.'

There was a beat. Nobody filled it.

Trish took charge again.

'We think the image has been overlaid. No, sorry. We *know* the image has been overlaid. I've just sent through two JPEGs. The quality won't be good on your devices, but they should tell the story. The first is the most recent, but old, Google Earth.' Trish waited to allow time for people to access the imagery. Wolfgang opened both photos. One was a grey expanse of nothing – a marsh – with a derelict. The second was a grey expanse of nothing with a derelict, but included a red sharpie line.

Trish continued.

'The second is the latest mil-satellite overhead. I've etched it with a red marker. This follows the line Frank and I believe marks an anomalous boundary: a layer, where the older Google Earth image has been over-planted with a new image. The editing is mostly *very* clever, and in various places you really can't tell. But there are a number of instances where the join is not perfect. For example, the end of the track.'

There was a long pause.

'So you think someone has overlaid an older benign image onto the latest satellite photograph? To cover something up?' There was incredulity in Sam's voice.

'Yes,' Frank and Trish announced in tandem.

There was another pause.

'So someone is doctoring the imagery of this small patch of earth, every time there is a satellite pass?' Jane stated what they were all thinking. 'I've heard of this protocol being used for extremely sensitive places, such as US missile bases, and here in the UK, for example, over Faslane – to hide our subs. But ...' She didn't finish her sentence. 'That takes some reach.'

'We should order and look over all previous imagery. Going back as far as we can.' It was Frank. 'Maybe there was a time when the area wasn't deemed too sensitive to be photographed? If nothing else it might give you a building or some boundaries to work with?'

'Do that.' Sam had come straight back. 'We'll get onto Yell, quietly. If I were the YCA I'd have eyes on the between-island ferry. We'll call you when we get there. Anything else, anyone?'

Wolfgang wanted to mention that he'd found a backdoor into the CPS's server and had uncovered the Chief's defence file. The times the Chief was purportedly perpetrating grievous acts, he was actually in Nepal, meeting with the Chinese Minister for State Security – a meeting so secret that it couldn't be used in court to defend him. And, as the current locum 'C' was on the YCA's payroll, SIS wouldn't be prepared to vouch for their ex-boss. Sir Clive Morton would go to jail gagged by his own state secrets.

Wolfgang would bring that up at another, more convenient time.

The final call had just been concluded. The Shetland team were now on Yell.

To get them there securely, Sam had boxed clever.

Joe had taken the van on the small ferry – two of MI5 team were in the back. Nadia had followed on in one of the hire cars, taking a later ferry, which crossed a short sound every hour and a half. Sam and Jane, the ones whose faces would be known to the YCA, had paid a local fisherman to take them out on the water, before planting them on the opposite bank. The team had then come together: Sam, Jane, Joe, Nadia, Jack and Nigel. They had a white van, a hire car, two semi-automatic machine guns, some night viewing aids and an ambition to storm a building somewhere on a patch of 10 square kilometres of bog and marsh which didn't exist. They had no idea of the opposition, save a sonic ring and at least one man with a quad bike and a gun. But there were almost certainly more.

On the latest call Sam gave nothing of the plan away. Wolfgang wasn't sure if that was for security reasons, or she couldn't be bothered. He had the key timing though. If the Shetland team found the place – and could access it – they would hope to give Wolfgang a thirty-minute warning before they went in. His job was to patch the live feed through to CNN.

Wolfgang had wanted to be sure everyone understood the Americans' understanding of the plan.

'I have an open line with Holly. I've just spoken to her,' he said.

'Go on,' Sam replied.

'To be clear. They have a forty-minute reel. My understanding is they'd like at least twenty minutes airtime to set the scene, before they go live. And then they'll finish off with a final twenty minutes. As I understand it the reel is

509

ready now. Their preferred broadcast time is 10 pm, GMT. But there is some flex.' Wolfgang knew what Holly was after. And he knew that Sam could only deliver if they found the place, and if they could get across the threshold. He also understood that some of the YCA were old men and anything later than ten might be after their bedtime.

And, from his perspective, he wasn't sure he'd have a ceiling by then. If that were the case it would then be Frank's problem.

'Tell Holly she'll get what she gets. It might be all over by ten. If necessary you'll have to record what we get and she'll have to stick it in when she can.' Sam sounded frustrated. That wasn't unusual.

'Anything else. Anybody?' Sam finished with a growl.

Should I?

Yes.

'The Chief is innocent.' Wolfgang kept his revelation short. If Sam were interested and she thought they had time, he'd be asked for more.

'Go on.' It was Jane.

'The time and dates of the photographs match blanks in the Chief's diary ...'

'Yes.' It was an impatient Sam. Hurrying him along again.

'I've hacked the CPS. I've seen the Chief's defence notes. He was meeting with a very senior Chinese security official in those blanks – in Nepal. The meetings are too sensitive to be used in court,' Wolfgang said.

'Why won't SIS fill the gap? Give him a workable alibi?' It was Frank. They obviously all cared deeply for their former boss.

'Because the SIS's current leadership want him out of the way,' Sam said dryly.

There was another one of those pauses.

Then ...

'Leak it,' Sam said without emotion.

'But ...' Jane spluttered.

'Leak it, Wolfgang. Do it now. The boss can't defend himself without breaking a whole new set of laws. We can. Make it stick.' Sam was defiant. And she was managing to sound agitated and bored at the same time.

'But, Sam ...' It was Jane again.

'Do it, Wolfgang. Blame me. You and I made the decision independent of anyone else. Anyhow, we have to go.' And with that, Sam cut the line.

Wolfgang breathed in deeply through his nose. And then breathed out.

That meant he now had two jobs.

First was to ensure that, in a crisis, Frank could link the feed to Holly.

Second he was to think of a suitable strategy to release the Chief of SIS's secret itinerary to the UK press.

He was up for that.

Bridge over the Burn of Gossawater, Yell, Shetland

Joe Ledbetter nodded. Did he have any questions? No, he didn't. Sam Green's plan was as good as it was going to get.

She was an impressive, if prickly, woman. He had worked for and with a number of very capable women. A very impressive one had led the Service until the mid-90s, well within his tenure. Green was different, though. She was absolutely on her brief and he couldn't fault her judgement.

She was resourceful, tenacious and doggedly determined. Her reputation preceded her, and whilst some – mostly men – in the Service thought the stories about her were more community myth than fact, he was now certain everything he had ever heard was true.

And yet ... in a group he felt her confidence was veneer-thin. Doubtless, as a singleton agent, she could only be stopped by an immovable object ... or an accurately placed bullet. But as a leader of a group there was a touch of hesitancy. It was as though she was prepared to lay it all down, but was uncomfortable asking others to do the same.

As she set out her plan her opening line had been, 'Look, this is going to be dangerous. You're not paid for this. If you want to pull out, no one is going to judge you, least of all me.' It was heartfelt and honest. And she'd kept glancing across at Joe as she spoke. Which made sense. He was the highest ranking officer on the team. Jane a rank below him. But this operation was all about Sam Green. It was her territory. She was the powerhouse behind it – and she had the most field experience in this type of arena of any of them. Which was saying something, considering their age differences: he was fifty-four; Jane must be mid-forties; Green was late thirties, if that.

As things were he was more than happy to be ordered about by Green, though. Unarmed, there were lines he wouldn't cross, and Sam Green's plan reflected that, for all of them.

Almost.

Nadia, who he had a great deal of time for, was the only one who had asked for more responsibility. And, with reluctance, Sam had eventually accepted her offer.

In Green's mind Nadia would join Jane and Nigel. They were designated 'front diversion'. He and Jack were 'east diversion'. That left Sam, who was 'infiltration'. After she'd explained how it was going to work, Nadia had not been happy.

'You can't do this alone, Sam. What happens if you go down?' Nadia had raised a hand as she questioned Sam's plan. 'I'm coming with you. Two satellite phones. One in case of redundancy. You know it makes sense.'

Sam had remonstrated. Nadia had stood her ground. Eventually the plan had been changed. Infiltration would be a two-woman team.

And now they were ready to go.

'Check watches,' Sam barked. 'I make it 19.25.' She waited for everyone to check. Then, 'Remember. Unless you hear from me, east diversion kicks off at 21.30. South at 21.45.' Sam had glanced at Nadia. 'We go in at 22.00.'

There was a pause. Nobody said anything.

'Good.' Sam had taken one last look around the team. Her gaze had dwelt on his. He had given her a short nod. She did the same in return. 'OK, we're off,' Sam concluded.

And then she and Nadia, each carrying a small backpack, and Sam with the slung Sig Sauer, headed into the inky darkness.

'Are you OK?' Jane was at Joe's shoulder.

'We're fine. What about you?' Joe replied.

'OK, I think. Good luck.' She touched his forearm.

'You too, Jane,' he replied, 'Come on, Jack. We've got a diversion to effect.'

Jack put up a hand in recognition.

And then they both walked across to the hire car.

513

They weren't flushed with time. Everyone was in agreement that the derelict dwelling at Vigon (grid 482042 – the numbers tumbled from her brain) was as good a target as they were going to get. It was marked on the OS map, and was visible on the OS and Google satellite overlay, where you could pick out a roofless, three-roomed stone building with an attached sheep pen. It was on a small grass plain next to the sea, surrounded on three sides by rising bog – to all intents and purposes at the edge of nowhere and hidden from view, unless you wanted to find it. And the latest Langley imagery, which included the false layer, showed the same. In short they had no idea what they'd find when they got there. But the imagery was hiding something.

To avoid being seen, and hopefully circumventing any seismic array, she and Nadia were heading due west from the bridge where they'd left everyone. It was a 3-klick trek across extremely uncomfortable ground. When they could hear the sea, they'd turn north and follow the coastline for a further 5 klicks, by which time they'd be in overwatch above the derelict – or not – at Vigon. Sam had carried out a map recce of where she'd place the array if she were the enemy. She and Nadia were doing their best to avoid it.

Overall it was an 8-10 kilometre trek, at night, in difficult terrain. Even without rain – there was none forecast – the ground underfoot would be boggy. They would both fall over. Probably more than once. And whilst neither of them were carrying a great deal, they were loaded. And that made them top heavy and more likely to fall.

Leaving aside her arm which was throbbing away with the monotony of an out-of-reach kitchen fire alarm,

Sam knew she was fit enough. When they'd set out she had no idea whether Nadia would be.

'Have you ever been hill walking?' Sam had interrogated Nadia.

'Some.' Nadia responded with a single word. Sam liked that about her.

'What about 10 klicks in two hours on this terrain?' Sam had waved an arm about.

'Should be OK.'

And that was where they'd left it.

Now, 40 minutes in and just short of the first turn, Sam had no worries about Nadia's ability to cross lots of difficult terrain at night. She had matched Sam stride for stride. And hadn't yet, unlike Sam, taken a tumble. Thankfully Nadia didn't speak much. If she had, she'd have got short shrift. Sam wasn't one to chat whilst exercising. And she certainly didn't take encouragement well which, if things carried on the way they were, Nadia might be tempted to offer.

Sam stopped, and went down on one knee. Nadia, who was learning fast, did the same just behind her.

The only thing to break the penetrating silence was a light wind and the crashing of waves against rocks. It was coming from in front of them. Sam pulled the lightweight II (*image intensifier*) monocular, which hung around her neck, to her right eye. She turned it on.

There.

There was an obvious rise before a short fall which must lead to the 50-metre-high set of cliffs. They had reached RV2, the turning point. RV1 was the southern edge of Gossa Water, a bigger than pond-sized loch they had circumnavigated about twenty minutes ago. There were three more RVs to follow, before they reached the ridgeline overlooking Vigon.

She switched off the II and checked her watch.

It was 20.17. The eastern diversion, 6 klicks north east of them, would go live in fifty-eight minutes. The southern diversion, which would be somewhere around 2 klicks to their right, fifteen minutes later. She needed to get the chronology just right. She and Nadia couldn't afford to trip an array of any sorts before Joe and then Jane had done their bit. If her and Nadia's routes were barred by some form of security infrastructure, she wanted both diversions to have been played, or to be playing out, when they crossed any threshold. Three headaches were more complicated than one.

'You OK?' A whisper from Nadia. Sam turned. She could just about pick out facial features. Her ethnicity wasn't northern European. There was a touch of Southern belle in the tone of her skin; maybe even Indian subcontinent. That added to her attractiveness. She was a touch smaller than her, and lither, noting that Sam felt that she had been getting stockier by the year. Nadia would be a catch for some lucky person, that was for sure. Sam hoped that her attractive MI5 colleague was still in one piece this time tomorrow morning.

'Fine,' Sam replied. 'We go north from here, scouting within 50 metres of the coast.' She pointed unnecessarily. 'There are one or two hills, and we've got just under 5 klicks to the overwatch, assuming neither Jane nor Joe find an alternative target. Happy?'

'Sure,' Nadia replied.

'You've done this before. The walking.' It was no longer a question from Sam. It was a statement.

'A bit,' was Nadia's reply.

516

Sam snorted softly and nodded her head.
I bet you have.

Joe was in position. He and Jack had followed the route taken by the mother, south down the east side of Gloup Voe, across the river – where wet feet were the order of the day – and then north along the west side of the sea loch-come-fjord. It was pitch black and trekking an almost indistinguishable, very thin path, on a hillside which plummeted directly into the sea, was tough going. They had had to be more careful than they had originally assumed. And they had been slow. But, he had given them plenty of time, and had made what Sam Green had coined the 'FUP' with twenty minutes to spare.

He hadn't asked what FUP stood for. It was obviously a military term. But he knew where it was and he knew when he'd got there. Green's instructions had been clear. No comms unless the 'plan goes to shit'.

So far, his part of the plan hadn't gone to shit.

But it was early days.

The pair of them were in the lee of a very derelict building – more pile of bricks than wall – about 400 metres short of the metal-roofed hut the woman had spoken of. Joe could pick it out through a pair of II binos. They had a weighty thermal monocular as well. Jack was sporting that.

Joe understood both technologies. He had spent many a frustrating night sitting back from a window with eyes on a target – either a spot where an agent met other POIs (*persons of interest*), or fixated on a single human, watching and recording their every move.

His II gave an intermittent screen of green and black. It was never crystal clear. The intensity of the pixels changed as the evacuated tube continuously rehashed what it saw. Now, with heavy cloud cover and minimum light to amplify, he could just pick out the building in the far distance. It was a hazy, black object on the middle-distance horizon surrounded by other very dark shapes.

'What's the TI (*thermal imager*) giving us?' Joe asked Jack.

'Enough. The hot chimney is clear, as is the rising smoke. There's little else,' Jack replied.

'No sign of movement?' Joe asked.

'Nope. Not yet.'

Joe looked at his watch. It was 9.27 pm.

'Are you ready?' he asked.

'Good to go,' Jack replied.

The plan was straightforward. Their job was to walk west until stopped. The assumption was that the guard on a quad bike would intercept them. And he would be alerted by the seismic array which the mother had spotted.

Sam's order was to make some noise. But be realistic. Occupy the man. Make sure he reports in. But don't go as far as being taken. Pull out before then.

Before they'd left the drop off point, he and Jack had discussed strategy.

'We're walkers. Let's say ... we belong to a club. It's ...' Jack was making this up as he went along. 'It's a dark sky club. We're Airbnbing it on Yell. We've picked out this spot for some decent night sky and we're heading for a high point.' Jack had stuck a finger on the Google Map on Joe's phone.

'OK. But do you think that's enough to create the noise Green's after?' Joe hadn't been sure.

'Well, let's not take no for an answer. Right to roam and all that. What's he going to do, shoot us?'

Joe hadn't answered the question. Because he didn't want to. He had a wife and children. And a retirement plan which included a trip down the West Coast of the States.

In any case, they had no idea.

They had *absolutely* no idea.

So that was the plan.

It was about making a bit of noise.

The track which had led them around the loch and up onto the hill had petered out at the derelict. As they walked they were now making their way over grass clumps interspersed with bog. It was unpleasant going.

'There!' Jack said. 'The door's open.'

The light from inside the building was as bright as a lighthouse. The silhouette of a man was fleeting.

'Remember he's heading around the back to get his bike,' Joe said over his shoulder.

They kept walking. Checking.

Alert.

There.

They'd almost missed it. It was a stroke of luck that he'd spotted it.

A black beacon on a stick.

'Knock it over and stamp on it if you see one.' Sam's orders had been clear.

Joe made a small deviation, pulled the contraption out of the ground, laid it on the floor and stood on it. The plastic shield gave way instantly. What followed was the reassuring sound and the odd spark of electrics being submerged in peaty water.

Job one – done.

The noise of the quad bike refocused him. It cut through the night and sounded much closer than it was. It

519

had lights, like a car. And it was heading their way. Joe closed one eye to protect his night vision.

And still they kept walking.

Half a minute passed.

The guard and bike would be on them in another thirty seconds.

As they walked Jack took a couple of extra strides so he was shoulder to shoulder with Joe.

Guard and bike got larger as the engine got noisier.

And then they came to a halt, the smoke from the exhaust drifting through the bike's headlights.

The engine died.

And then the guard, who was chunky and wearing an unbuttoned wax jacket, was off the bike. He reached for the stock of his rifle, pulled it from its case, put the butt in his shoulder and held the pistol grip by his side.

He was right-handed. It was the sort of detail Joe was trained to observe.

'What the fuck are you doing?' The guard was a big man, but there was a touch of nerves in his voice. Joe reckoned he hadn't necessarily signed up for this. A night encounter with two determined walkers. Maybe they had the upper hand?

Joe raised a hand to his forehead, shielding his open eye.

'We might ask you the same?' Joe replied.

'This is private property, mate. You shouldn't be here.' The words came too quickly. The guard was twitchy.

Jack took a step forward.

'We have a right to roam. You know that.' Jack's voice was strong and clear, as if he were a Jedi disarming a couple of storm troopers. 'And, if you don't mind, I'd prefer it if you took your hand off the pistol grip of your weapon.'

It was difficult to gauge the man's reaction as his face was in shadow. But Joe still sensed unease.

It didn't matter. A squawk from a walkie-talkie broke the impasse. The guard reached for it from his belt.

'Foxtrot one, copy,' the man said into the machine.

There was a squawk in return.

'Let's continue, Jack,' Joe said loudly. 'These people can't stop us.'

And they both strode off, past the man on the walkie-talkie ... with the rifle.

'Oi! Fucking hell!' The shout followed. The guard's next conversation was into the walkie-talkie. 'I've got two walkers here. They're not turning around. Copy?' There was a touch of panic in the man's voice now.

'Oi! Stop, you fuckers!' the man shouted from behind them.

Joe and Jack kept walking.

And walking.

There was a walkie-talkie squawk. Then ...

BANG!

Joe instinctively dropped to the floor. He felt Jack do the same.

'You OK?' he shouted.

'I think so.' Jack's voice was wobbly. 'He effin' well shot at us!'

'Get up!' The man was on top of them now, his voice wavering. 'Get fucking up.'

The pair of them got to their feet. Joe was breathing deeply, his pulse pounding in his neck. He was too old for this – but his reaction surprised him.

There had been a shot. But they hadn't been shot at.

It was a warning, albeit a clumsy one.

Suddenly he felt a deep well of anger.

He turned square on to the guard, who had his rifle in his right hand and a walkie talkie in his left. Joe then deliberately took out his phone and switched on the camera. It was a gesture. He wanted to add to the man's discomfort.

The man shouted just as his left hand squawked.

'Putting that fucking phone away.' Again, there was fragility there. Joe knew people. He knew which buttons to press. It was his job.

Joe said nothing. Instead he purposefully dabbed at his phone.

'I said, put the fucking phone away!' The man's shout overrode another squawk.

'Your boss is calling.' Jack was beside Joe. He was pointing at the man's hand.

Well done, Jack.

They were both at it now …

… and this could go two ways.

'What?' the man spluttered.

'The walkie-talkie.' Jack pointed again whilst Joe pushed the phone at the man.

Something was going to give.

It did.

The man lifted the weapon. The end of the barrel was waving around. The three men were no more than 2 metres apart. At one point the weapon was focused on Jack. Another, on Joe.

As it swung nervously back to him, Joe grabbed the barrel and pulled it. As he did, he turned his body away from the pointy end. He'd last undergone self-defence training in the 90s, when he was a young pup. As a result the move was clunky. And fraught. The guard was strong and, on his own, Joe might well have lost the fight.

But Jack met the man's face, as it followed the trajectory of the rifle, with a flat hand. A rugby-straight arm. There was a *crunch* as bone met bone. The man's head lifted as he involuntarily let go of the gun. His hands reached for his face.

'Bugger, that hurt!' Jack shouted.

But Joe wasn't listening. He had the rifle and was lifting it by its barrel. And then, not as hard as he could, but hard enough, he brought the plastic stock down on the back of the man's head.

There was another *crunch* followed by a *groan*. The man then fell silent.

'Hello Foxtrot One, send report, copy?' The walkie talkie made a dull, damp squawk from the floor.

Jack leant forward, and with the better of his two hands, picked it up and reported in.

'Foxtrot One, all sorted here.' He paused, searching for the right response. 'Walkers now heading away. I scared them off with a shot over their heads. Copy?'

Jack's face glistened in the reflection in the lights of the quad bike.

'Copy.'

Both men stood upright. Both were breathing deeply.

'Was that enough noise?' Jack asked.

'It wasn't what I was expecting,' Joe replied.

'What do we do now?

I'm not sure.

'Are you ready?' Jane was looking at Nigel.

'As I'll ever be,' he replied.

They were sitting in the dark of the Nissan's cab. It was where they had been for the last two hours. Jane unnecessarily glanced at the digital clock on the van's dashboard. It hadn't changed much in the past thirty seconds.

Time to go.

Jane turned the van over. It started first time. She threw on the lights.

Move.

She drove sensibly down the track which passed a modern garage-type building on her left – to her right was the dwindling end of a sea loch. Up ahead at the corner a secondary track, made of stone and cement, headed north. That was as far as her foot recce had taken her. Beyond there the track wound up a shallow valley until, after about 2 kilometres, it stopped.

At an odd angle.

If you believed the Langley overhead.

They were at the junction now.

She pressed the indicator, a pointless exercise as they hadn't seen a single vehicle since they'd arrived at the bridge, and turned onto the track. They drove past a sign which read, 'PRIVATE PROPERTY. VIOLATORS WILL BE PROSECUTED'.

Both of them focused on the road and rising ground either side of it. They were looking for security devices. A camera pod. One of the seismic domes the woman had described. Anything which they might trip.

So far, nothing.

Jane drove on, the lights of the Nissan easily illuminating the route. They were a bright beacon in a sea of black. If the YCA had their ducks in a row, they'd know they had company by now.

'Anything?' Nigel asked.

Jane, who was leaning forward, her chin over the steering wheel, shook her head. She was concentrating too hard to answer.

On Sam's advice she had set the tachometer to zero. Trish had said the track met the additional image layer after 1.9 miles. They must be almost there. And the track looked as though it went on forever.

She glanced down at the gauge.

1.8 was about to turn into 1.9.

It did.

The track continued.

She drove.

2.0 miles.

To all intents and purposes they were now driving blind. There was no evidence from the imagery. But they were on rock, sand and cement.

The track existed. And it was in decent shape. You could easily get a 7.5 tonne lorry down here.

Hang on.

Ahead of them. 200 metres away.

A gate.

A new gate.

It was yellow. A single, horizontal, sturdy metal pole, with its pivot and counterbalance on the right. On the left, the pole rested in a Y-shaped metal groove. There was a hefty padlock. Either side was gently rising moorland. There was the odd balding fir tree. Beyond that everything merged to black.

Is there any other security apparatus?

Jane pulled the Nissan to a halt short of the gate.

She looked at Nigel. He looked back.

'Can you see anything?' she asked.

'Nope. It doesn't seem very well protected. If this was a big deal you would have thought the gate would be electronic and there'd be an intercom?'

Leaving the van running with its lights on, Jane picked a torch from on top of the dashboard and got out. Her breath clouded in front of her. She pulled up the collar of her coat.

Their job was to make a fuss. Provide a distraction. Twenty minutes' worth. They couldn't do it sitting in a van on the wrong side of a gate which led to who knew where.

She shone the torch around.

Nothing on and around the gate.

Left?

Nothing.

Right?

Nothing.

Wait.

The torch's beam caught a reflection halfway up a small tree. It was about 3 metres away.

There was a *clunk* behind her. Nigel had got out of the cab.

Jane ignored him. She had already leapt across a small ditch into the scrub. The terrain underfoot was awful. It was treacherous – she immediately felt sorry for the other two teams. But she persevered.

'What have you got?' It was Nigel.

'A reflection, possibly a lens, in this tree.' Jane was picking her route carefully. The torch's beam doing its own merry dance.

As she got to the tree, she bent over to get her head under a branch.

And there it was.

A low-light camera.

She was looking straight at it.

The lens shimmied, focussing, its movement caught her off guard and her heart did a blip.

Get a grip.

That's what she told herself.

What she felt was something a little less comfortable.

Jane used the torch to follow a wire which came out of the back of the camera. She tried to see where the wire went. No – she'd have to move.

She waddled around the tree, and then poked her head back in between two branches. There was a junction box. The wire from the camera went in, and two wires came out. One dropped straight into the ground. *Power.* The other snaked up the trunk of the tree to another box. On top of which was a stubby antenna.

They had seen her. Literally focused on her.

They knew she and Nigel were here.

What was their next move?

'Lights!' Nigel shouted from the track.

That's their next move.

She looked up the track and saw the beam of headlights sweeping across the sky. They'd be here in under a minute.

Jane stomped her way quickly back through the bog, clumsily jumped the ditch, and onto the road.

'You ready?' she asked. *I'm not sure I am.*

'I'll let you know in about five minutes,' Nigel replied.

Jane knew how he felt. And she was the experienced operator of the pair. Although, in her defence, she was still very messed up. That's why she thought Sam had given them the less problematic of the two diversions. The hope was they would never be more than a few metres from their escape vehicle.

The pair of them were standing in front of it now. The engine was still running and the headlights lit up the path ahead, which would soon be matched by the vehicle heading down the track towards them.

She felt her heart rate quicken. And her mouth dried.

She hoped she was up for this. Everything up until now had been in reaction to an event. Something happened. She had to do something in reply. It had all been intuitive.

This was different.

This was premeditated.

She had a chance to get away.

Hide in the back of the van.

Her leg started to shake. Just like it used to when, as a young woman, she had had to get on her feet and give a briefing. It was something she had overcome. And it was something which hadn't happened for an awfully long time.

But it was happening now.

Would she make it through this?

'I'm feeling a bit wobbly, Nigel. Can you fill any gaps?' Jane said honestly, as the lights of the vehicle crested the rise in front of them.

Nigel moved so that he was standing as close to Jane as he could without knocking her over. So much so she was convinced she could feel his bodily warmth through her jacket. She was certainly sharing the steam he was breathing out.

They stood there.

Side by side.

As planned Nigel had a notebook out. Jane had the questions.

She just wasn't sure she had the voice.

The vehicle was a 4x4. It was difficult to tell the make when you could only see the headlights. It came to a halt 10 metres short of the gate. Like the van, the engine was kept running and the lights left on.

Two people – no, two men – got out of the cab. They were dressed like gamekeepers. One was carrying a rifle. Sam would know the make and model. As she would the 4x4, even from just the headlights. Jane didn't, not that it mattered. A rifle was a rifle. But it didn't have a sight. And it would be awkward to use close to. Devastating at mid-range. More difficult odds at longer distances. They, of course, would need to turn the Nissan around. There was no room here, but there was a grubby offshoot track about 50 metres back. Could she reverse quickly?

Under fire?

Probably not.

They had a Sig in the van. Would they use it?

Probably not.

Her leg continued to shake.

The two men had sauntered up to the gate with the confidence of a platoon's worth. The gap between them and the men was 3 metres. Jane hoped to keep it at least that far.

'What are you doing here?' the man on the left, the one without the rifle, said. He was 180/185 tall. Big build. The other guy was shorter and had a belly on him.

But he also had the rifle.

'Where does this track lead?' Jane started with confidence, even though her tongue felt far too big for her mouth. They had rehearsed a series of questions. The first one was down.

'It's no business of yours.' The taller man paused. 'Answer my question ... please. What are you doing here?' The man's accent had a soft Scottish twang to it. His words lacked threat. But there was intent.

'Why has that man got a gun?' Jane asked. It wasn't in the brief. But it was a filler. The ambition was to give Sam and Nadia at least twenty minutes. She reckoned they were ninety seconds in.

The man with the rifle raised it. Slowly. The stock was at stomach height, the weapon horizontal to the ground. The aim – directly at her. It wasn't a traditional stance. But at 3 metres it didn't need to be.

Jane inwardly flinched. She started to say something, but stopped. Her shaking leg was out of control. The two men wouldn't be able to miss it.

'We're journalists.' Nigel answered the question. As he did he waved his notebook about. Immediately the barrel of the rifle changed its point of aim. Nigel was it now.

'And what do a pair of journalists want on *my* land, this time on a Saturday night in December. You must admit I have a right to be interested?'

There was certainty in the man's voice.

Nigel paused. Then, 'We've heard from the locals that something untoward is happening in the property ahead of us.' He pointed over the men to the horizon. He had kept his answer short. He was also playing for time.

'What sort of untoward things?' The man without the gun had now placed his hands on the horizontal pole, his shoulders forward. The gate reverberated a little as he did.

'There have been some abductions. On the mainland,' Nigel said.

Jane was both impressed and thankful for her MI5 colleague's intervention. And she was beginning to find her feet again. She felt a little more in control.

'Oh,' the man said. 'If that's the case, why aren't the police here?' The man raised his eyebrows. 'You have told the police?' He was humouring them now.

She and Nigel had been through this. They'd rehearsed the questioning – except with her leading.

'We have warned them that we're coming here. We're gathering evidence. And, with that in mind, can I take your name please?' Nigel made an effort to look as if he were about to write something down.

'No,' the man snapped back. And then with less tension, 'The police know who I am.' He changed tack. 'Which media outlet do you represent?'

Jane reckoned they were at four minutes. They had a while to go. She wasn't sure this was going to last much longer.

Nigel didn't answer the question. Instead, as it was with this particular ping-pong match, he asked another.

'We believe you are holding two young people in the house. Against their will.' No elaboration from Nigel.

The man stood up straight then. He turned to look at the second man. And then back at Nigel and Jane.

He stared at them for a second. And then, with real menace, said, 'Get off my land. Now.'

They were still *very* short of twenty minutes.

'Two women. Maybe a young woman and a man. In their early twenties. They were abducted on the mainland and brought here by truck.' It was Jane's turn. She was back on mission.

531

The man without the gun's face turned sour. She felt that if there hadn't been a gate between them, he might have lunged at her.

They had found a nerve.

'Get. Off. My. Land.' The words were squeezed out through gritted teeth.

She looked at Nigel. He looked at her. He shook his head.

'No,' Jane replied. 'Not until you answer our questions.'

And then they were reprieved. There was a noise from the man with the rifle's waist-belt. A walkie-talkie. He lowered the barrel, turned away from the gate and walked towards the car. Jane could hear the man's replies.

'OK. Sure. Shit. I'll speak with Don. Copy.' There was a concluding squawk. The man turned round and jogged back to 'Don'.

He whispered at the man without the rifle. Jane could hear every word.

'There's been an incident with Foxtrot 4. The alert system is down.'

The man who had been doing all the talking hadn't taken his eyes off Jane and Nigel. That didn't change when the shorter man whispered to him.

But his mouth turned into a snarl.

'Give me the rifle and turn the truck around. Now!' he barked.

The weapon was swiftly handed over and then, in a move which sent a spasm of terror through Jane, he easily vaulted the gate. There was less than a metre between them now.

'You've got two choices. Get off my land or ...' he threatened.

'Or what?' Nigel beat Jane to the answer.

The movement of the rifle was swift. The explosion in the weapon's chamber was piercing ...

BANG!

... and the cry from Nigel as he fell to the floor shattered any burgeoning resistance in Jane.

'What!? You've ...?' Jane was torn between finishing her sentence and attending to Nigel, who was moaning on the floor beside her.

'Get off my land.' The man's face was in hers. 'If I see the pair of you again your friend won't be so lucky.'

And then he re-vaulted the gate and walked purposefully to the 4x4 without giving them a second glance.

Jane bent down.

'Nigel?' Are you ...'

'Shit, my foot hurts. Shit!' Nigel replied between staccato breaths. 'How long?' he added.

'What?' Jane replied.

'How long did we keep them for?'

She looked at her watch.

'Eleven minutes.'

Not long enough.

'Can you manage?' Jane asked.

'Sure. I'll need to apply a tourniquet. But let's do that at the cut-off point.' Nigel had a hand on Jane's arm and was already wresting himself to his feet.

Chapter 21

Flemingstraße, Munich, Germany

Wolfgang could only presume things were going to plan in Scotland. Here, he wasn't quite so sure. Earlier on, as instructed by Sam, he'd given Holly the timings. He hadn't told her that the team had no idea whether or not they had found the YCA's property or, if they had, that they had managed to breach the defences and could guarantee a live feed. She'd come back to him half an hour later and told him that they would run a precautionary introduction at 21.45 GMT, with the aim of delivering the live feed as soon as it was available. Once the feed was finished, they would run the second part of the VT and then fill in with talking heads at the end. It wasn't perfect, but they got it.

It was 22.47, CET (*Central European Time*), thirteen minutes to ten in the UK.

And CCN was on it. He had their feed.

The opening title took up the left side of the screen: *Time to run the world?* On the right was a blow-up of an Elias Bosshart watch. The monogrammed 'YCA' was clearly visible. The accompanying music was a melodic 1930s southern Italian piano piece. Something a director would add to a black and white mafia scene. Not that he could hear much as his unwanted guests were now working hard on the door in the corner of the room. Dust hung like the lightest of snow showers. The smell was one of burnt material and overworked motors. His adversaries were minutes away from breaking down the door.

On his screen the anchor took over. Behind him was a mosaic of the eleven known members of the YCA. Two, the dead two, had a red line drawn through them.

'It's an unlikely story. Something from an Ian Fleming novel. But it's real. And it's happening in our lifetime. These men are behind a power cult, choosing and influencing governments, murdering – yes, I said murdering – their opponents at will. They have infiltrated politics across the world, they ...'

Wolfgang's attention was taken away from the anchor's introduction. He had a live mic open with Holly.

'What's happening, Wolfgang?' Her voice had an edge. She was under pressure.

She and I alike.

'I don't know. I've just taken a call from Jane. The man with her had been shot by one of the guards ...'

'What?' Holly shrieked. 'Is he OK?'

'I think so. I've tried Sam, but there's been nothing back. Nothing at all. Jane's under strict instructions not to approach the target. And now she has someone down, that's unlikely to happen. We're waiting on Sam. It's all we've got.'

There was a beat.

'Well, we're going to have to go to messages. And if we don't get some confirmation soon, we might have to pull,' Holly said.

'Got it.' Wolfgang swung his chair round. He could see a circular saw now. It was through the final layer of concrete. The noise and the dust was close to intolerable. It was all over his equipment. All over his clothes. It clogged his nostrils. And dried his throat.

If they broke in before he made the connection, even if Sam did have decent video, a couple of bullets into his servers and it would all be over. He could switch the delivery of the feed to Frank, but only once he'd made the connection between Sam and Holly. That was the only technology he had.

The noise of the saw stopped. It was blessed relief. And then he saw why. They were pouring water to cool the blade. It was gushing through the gap and onto the floor.

Bastards.

And then the noise started again.

'Wolfgang?' It was Frank.

'Yes,' Wolfgang replied.

'Anything?' Frank asked.

'No. Not yet. Just get ready to take control of the feed. *Verstehen*?'

'Yes. Are you OK?' Frank asked.

Wolfgang looked at the emerging hole in the wall.

He had maybe two minutes.

He glanced back to the CNN feed. There was an advert showing an electric car of some description. They all looked the same to him.

'Yes. I'm fine.'

Come on, Sam.

He looked back to the wall.

The pitch of the saw had changed. It had lost that low rumbling where he felt the machine was pushing hard, metal on metal. Now the sound was much higher. The blade was spinning much quicker. It was eating through the final layer of concrete. Centimetre by centimetre. One side and the top of a door-shaped gap had been completed. The saw was heading down the third side now. Towards the floor. Once there, a decent ram would knock it all down.

And it would all be over.

The speed of the saw was so mesmerising he almost missed his cue.

Scheisse!

It was a grainy image on his left screen. Glass. Like a small Eden Project. The scene was moving as the camera on the phone bounced around with the motion of its host.

Sam was there.

'Holly!' he shouted. 'Frank!' Wolfgang's fingers worked quickly. The connection between Scotland was made.

'Have you got it? Holly!' he shouted again.

'Yes, Wolfgang. Great!' Holly was delighted. 'We're on!'

Wolfgang didn't get a chance to complete his call to Frank. His fingers had made the necessary keystrokes and the link had been passed. But, at the same time, the wall had come down in an almighty *clump*. The push of air had caught him by surprise and he rocked forward.

He survived that.

In jubilation he had been about to shout a triumphant 'Frank!', when the 5.56mm NATO short round from the policeman's Haenel MK assault rifle ripped through his left shoulder, deviated down through his right lung before exiting and lodging into the polished concrete floor.

The first round didn't kill him.

But the second one did.

Vigon, Yell, Shetland

It was a struggle – it had been a struggle. And they hadn't really started yet. Who knew what was to come?

Keeping up with Sam across the rough, boggy terrain had been a nightmare. To avoid detection from obs

537

devices Sam had kept as close to the cliff edge as possible. It had been up hill and down dale, with Sam striding on as if it were a Sunday afternoon skip. Nadia had kept up, mind. And she had tried to appear as if it had been a breeze. But it hadn't. By the time they had reached the overwatch she was desperate for a five-minute hiatus.

Lying side by side, the damp ground providing a soft but cold bed, they'd just had time for that.

Just.

Their position didn't have as much height as they hoped. The building at Vigon – and there was a *proper* building at Vigon, which was a result – was only 5 metres lower than they were, and about 300 metres out. But it would do.

And what a sight it was.

Extraordinary didn't do it justice.

For a start there was a large helicopter on a circular pan.

'It's a Bristow S-92s. Used by our coastguard. Pretty indestructible,' Sam had said. She was looking through a monocular II sight. 'And it's not going anywhere in a hurry. Can you see?'

Nadia couldn't.

'Its blades are tied down. No one's flying in that without thirty minutes prep.'

Next to the helicopter were various sheds and something which looked like a large hosepipe on a reel; probably refuelling. Fifty metres further inland, and in a slight dip, was the main event, tastefully lit by a series of low-wattage arc lights.

It was something from Norman Foster's sketchbook. There was a huge, dome-shaped tubular frame, suspending large, diamond-shaped panes of glass; like a crystal and

538

steel turtle shell. Facing them, and only reaching halfway up the dome, was an entrance portal which would have suited an igloo. It was also made of metal and glass. In front of that was a tarmacked area which narrowed and led off to the right until it was hidden by a small hillock. Nadia assumed it was going in Jane and Nigel's direction. One way in; one way out.

There were two vehicles in the carpark. One was a Range Rover. The second, a Mercedes 4x4.

And then it got weird.

The dome was a shell, for sure.

It provided protection for a semi-derelict building, the crumbling stonework of which stopped at first-floor level, although Nadia sensed that at one point it probably reached higher. But there was also a further, inner building. A wood, or wood-clad, Scandinavian type affair. It made it to a second floor, on top of which was a flat roof. The inner wooden shell had a lot of glass, both on the second floor and with three large roof lights. Whatever it housed liked a lot of light. And there was some, albeit minor, light going on inside. The windows emitted a dull-orange hue, which flickered.

Further to the right was a smaller, second building. It was much more normal; wood clad, chalet-style. It was occupied – there was light from one of the windows. Parked next to it was a Ford Transit and four quad bikes. And there had originally been a pick-up of some description. It had taken off just as she and Sam had arrived at the overwatch.

'Security and staff.' Sam was pointing in the direction of the chalet. 'We'll approach via the helicopter, have a look behind the edifice, and establish a way in.' Sam was still looking, the monocular switching left then right, and back again. Without taking her eyes off the scene she added, 'Set up the rebro.'

Nadia took off her rucksack. As she did, a gust of wind stole its way through the neck of her jacket reaching where sweat had drenched her t-shirt. It reinforced how cold she was feeling now they were static.

She took out the Iridium relay, held down the 'on' button, and watched it boot up. She'd never used one before, other than rehearsing it on the ferry. It spoke to the satellite and provided a Wi-Fi hotspot with which, if you had the password, you could then access the Iridium network. She placed it behind on a small rise in the ground.

That will do.

Once it was up and running, she checked that her mobile had discovered the device.

'Phone check. I'm on,' Nadia said to Sam.

Without taking her eye off the monocular, Sam took her own phone out of her jacket pocket, glanced at it, put it back and said, 'On.'

'What do you think's happening?' Nadia closed the cord to her rucksack and threw it over her shoulder.

'Dunno,' Sam replied.

Nadia had her own pair of binos. She raised them to her eyes.

Nothing. Just the two buildings and the helicopter.

Sam dropped the monocular. She was about to say something when the sound of a gunshot rattled off to their right, from the direction of the access road.

'Fuck it. Let's go.' Sam was on her feet in an instant.

'But?' They were seven minutes out from H-hour. And Sam had been insistent: 'We don't change H-hour.'

'Now.'

Sam was changing H-hour ...

... and she didn't wait for any further remonstrations from Nadia. Crouched, and taking a long-weave down to the helicopter, she was on her way.

Nadia jumped to her feet and worked hard to catch her up. 'But never closer than 2 metres, when we're on the move'. Sam's instructions rang in her ears.

200 metres out.

Sam was weaving, still crouched. She then switched to a small indentation in the ground to run down.

Nadia followed.

100 metres.

Sam stopped. She immediately dropped to one knee. They were just short of the HLS.

Nadia went down. She was all eyes.

And then Sam surprised her. She quickly had the silenced Sauer in her shoulder, resting her cheek against the stock, pushing her eye onto the rubber of the sight. She steadied herself. Breathed slowly and deeply.

Nadia had no idea what Sam was doing.

Bang!

It was more like a *thud*. The noise of brick landing on a concrete floor. And it was aimed at the dome. Somewhere.

Sam moved her torso a fraction. She retook her aim. And went through the same motions.

Bang!

Another brick. Another floor.

Something else on the dome took a bullet.

Sam was up again. Weaving. Running. She was on the concrete pan now. She darted left, behind the helicopter. Nadia followed.

And then they went to ground.

It was a bloody big helicopter. Bigger than it looked from a distance. It was the size of a medium coach. It would take the whole of the YCA, some luggage, and still have room for a disco.

And Sam was on it, tapping on the underside of the fuselage, in front of the rear wheels.

Tap, tap, tap.

The sound changed. It was deeper where Sam was tapping now.

Tap, tap.

Still deep.

'Get back, with me,' Sam said as she stepped backwards.

They both moved to the edge of the pan.

Sam raised the rifle.

Bang! Bang!

Nadia couldn't stop herself from flinching. She was expecting the whole thing to explode and for them to be blown into the sea.

But nothing happened. Instead she heard the *hiss* of escaping gas. Sam unclipped the magazine from the Sauer and handed it to Nadia who, without being asked, pulled a fresh one from her pocket.

'What's that about?' Nadia asked as she pocketed the semi-used magazine. She didn't expect an answer.

'AVTUR rarely explodes if you rupture a fuel tank. But it does atomise. And escapes. So no smoking.' In the darkness Sam forced a smile. And then she was off again.

Really?

Nadia sighed, just a little, and chased after her.

It took them under a minute to get to the dome. Closer to it was a marvel. Thick stainless steel pipes and curved double-glazed panes. Inside was the stonework.

Between it and the dome the ground was covered in white pebbles. Above them and just on the other side of the stone was the wood of the secondary structure.

Sam squeezed herself next to a pane of glass and, with the Sauer pointing in the same direction, looked towards the igloo-entrance – and beyond that to the chalet. Nadia snuck in behind her.

There was a beat.

'Stay here,' Sam directed. And then she was off, around the back of the dome.

Nadia wasted no time. She took out the magazine Sam had given her and refilled it from spare ammunition in the same pocket.

Then she waited.

Nothing.

She raised the binos to her eyes.

The entrance was steel and glass, but inside she could now see a wooden porch.

She waited.

Nothing from the …

Wait.

There were headlights, off to the right, down the access track. Heading their way.

She could see the pick-up now. It pulled up sharp by the staff lodge. Two men got out. One was carrying a rifle. As they walked quickly to the entrance, the door opened – light spilling out, transforming relative pitch into not quite so pitch. A man emerged from the door.

There was a brief discussion.

The two men from the pick-up jogged over to the bank of quad bikes, fired two up and headed off to the left, their route quickly hidden by the dome. As they disappeared the beams of the quad bike's headlights flashed and scattered across the sky.

A minute later Sam was back. She slipped in front of Nadia.

'OK,' Sam said. 'There's at least one man in the chalet. There's one inside the dome, between the glass and the wall. He's round the side, running a console of sorts. I couldn't make much out.' Sam snatched a look in the direction of the chalet. 'If the woman heard the callsign right, then there are probably at least four "foxtrots" manning outposts. Maybe more. And there are another two guards, one armed, who just headed off on the bikes. That's at least eight men. Let's assume they're all armed.' Sam seemed to wait for a reaction. Nadia had nothing to say.

'Fire up your phone,' Sam ordered.

Nadia took her mobile out and, via the Iridium app, dialled into Wolfgang's server.

She waited a second. Two.

Three.

And then they had it.

'On,' she said.

'Good,' Sam replied. 'Let's go.'

There were four rules. Sam had explained them twice before they'd left the bridge. She'd used her fingers to count on the second run though.

'Follow me. Film everything. Any cover is good cover. Watch our backs.'

Film everything.

That meant – and she and Sam had practised with the Iridium link up earlier this evening – watching where she was going, keeping an eye on Sam, whilst at the same time ensuring her video was getting a decent feed. The world would be watching, Sam had added.

It had been complicated in rehearsal. It was doubly difficult now that adrenaline was spiking in her nerves.

They were at the dome's entrance. Sam peered round into the porch. She quickly pulled back.

'Double door. Keypad. Camera,' was Sam's staccato report.

There was a pause, as though her colleague was getting ready for something.

Sam shot a 'stay there' hand in Nadia's direction, took a breath and then quickly spun around the edge of the porch. A *bang!* followed.

Nadia waited.

A few seconds more.

Sam slipped back round the edge of the porch. She shook her head.

What now?

Sam was thinking.

'Follow me.' And Sam was off again in the direction they had come, away from the entrance. As the dome curved at its end, Sam stopped. Nadia followed suit, squeezing into a gap between metal struts.

Sam checked around, then turned to the lowest full pane of glass, placed the end of the silencer on the bottom corner of the glass, as close to the metal as she could, and fired.

Bang! Tinkle.

That was a louder sound.

The pane was holed at the bottom. The rest was paved.

Sam kicked at it. Twice. Three times, before it fell onto the white pebbles.

That was louder still.

'Come on!' she barked.

Nadia, always aware of the camera on her phone, followed on.

What will the world be thinking of this?

Breaking and entering, probably.

It was a squeeze for both of them. In the end Nadia had to take her bulky rucksack off and push it through the gap before her.

But she got through and gathered her rucksack. Sam was kneeling in a firing position, looking down towards the entrance.

'Done!' Nadia whispered a shout.

Without response, Sam was up and turned. She pushed past Nadia, following the gap between the dome and the stone wall away from the entrance. There was room for them provided they squeezed next to the wall – the glass and steel tapering as it rose.

They were down the far side of the dome in twenty seconds at which point Sam broke into a walk. And then slowed further still. The corner of the stone wall was just ahead of her. She raised a finger. And stopped. She went down on one knee. Nadia, having glanced behind, followed suit.

They waited for a few seconds ...

... and then Sam looked around the corner of the wall.

She was up on her feet. Quicker now. Nadia in pursuit. Ahead of them was a desk of sorts. It was though a chunk of the wall had been removed and the gap plastered and painted black. There was a chair facing the indentation and a set of screens at eye level secured to the wall. In front of that was a desk. On it was a keyboard, a mobile phone and an unopened Mars Bar.

The console was unmanned. But the back of the chair told a story. It had been left, swivelled away from them, towards the entrance.

'Get the camera on this.' Sam pointed at the screens. She then knelt beyond the console. 'Quickly.'

Nadia had the phone in one hand, sweeping. There were four screens. Each had numerous inset images, three of which were blank. *Sam's three shots*? The live ones looked to be security feeds of different parts of the dome and, presumably, inside the wooden building.

What's that?

She didn't have time to answer her own question.

A flash of movement to her left.

A man was at the turn. Half man, half stone wall. There was a pistol. He seemed caught between pulling back and taking a shot.

The pause did for him.

Bang!

The man fell to the floor … and immediately Sam was off.

'Get the pistol,' she shouted behind her.

What?

Nadia had all of this on film. She was sure of it. The man at the corner. The back of Sam's torso, her head, the rifle's barrel.

A momentary standoff.

A shot.

From Sam.

Death?

Nadia, after a brief pause as she reconciled what had just happened, sprinted after her, using her free hand to scoop up the pistol from the floor – the man was moaning,

547

which was a relief. She hoped the camera had picked that up too.

A few seconds later they were beside an entrance to the inner sanctum.

There was a wooden door. A brass handle. Nothing ornate. Perfectly ordinary. But sturdy.

Sam had a hand on it.

'Are you ready?' she said, her expression as intense as anything Nadia had ever seen. Her pupils were enormous, reducing her irises to a slither.

Nadia had no idea if she were ready. She had just witnessed someone shoot someone else, which was a first. And what she thought she had just glimpsed on the screen was incomprehensible. If that's what was going to face them now, she wasn't sure she could keep the camera still.

Sam gently pulled the door handle down. And pushed at it.

It opened.

She pushed a little more.

And a little more.

Sam slipped into the room. Nadia beside her.

Then it all became clear.

They had just gatecrashed a modern day version of the Hellfire Club.

And it was as grotesque as anything she could ever imagine.

There were seven men standing in a wide oval, filling most of the wooden structure. They were dressed in what could only be described as hessian dressing gowns, with hoods. They wore Jesus sandals and, and this was the inexplicable thing, they all wore crowns on top of their hoods made from animal heads – probably sheep or, at most, a small cow. All of them had their hands in the air, swaying and chanting to the action in the middle of the room.

There was music, an awful wassailing mix that grated at her ears. And there was a rock hearth with a fire. There were candles. Hundreds and hundreds of red candles. And, to one side, a long gnarled wooden table hosting nine silver goblets served by a large punch bowl.

But that wasn't it.

That wasn't the demonic act which thousands, maybe tens of thousands of people were now tuned into.

In the middle of the oval were two gagged naked women. They were on their backs, their heads twisting and turning in defiance. On top of them were two semi-naked men, save sandals and skulls, their gowns loose at the middle. There was writhing. And there was grunting.

Immense pain and sadness filled the tall room. Abhorrence and loathing mixed with the smell of incense. The feeling of hatred was overwhelming to Nadia. It was misogyny in a concentrated and directed way. Her immediate and completely uninformed view was that these men detested women. And they had to check that inner bitterness every day until a single weekend in December, every two years.

Then they could let it all out.

It was cultish.

And it *so* needed to stop.

Now.

Bang!

Sam shot the man closest to them in the leg. The target was a thick black calf.

As the man fell, one, then two, then all of the men, turned. The chanting stopped. And hands were dropped.

Nadia searched, but couldn't pick out any faces. They were all shrouded by the shadows cast from their hoods.

As the room's trance was broken and the men woke from their horrendous meditation, the awful music continued. The candles still burnt. And the two men in the middle of the room, oblivious to their predicament, continued to hate women in the most degrading way.

'Get those two to stop. Now!' Sam's trembling voice easily cut through the music.

As the black man writhed on the floor, there was an arrogant pause which was broken as one of the men off to their right stepped out of the rank of the oval. He strode purposefully towards them.

Bang!

He went down immediately, grabbing his leg. Sam quickly switched the barrel of the Sauer to another one of the hessian-clothed standing men – the one closest to them.

There was a different noise now. The black man on the floor – Nadia assumed it was Chibuike Grandom – and the second downed man were both groaning in pain.

'Get those ...' Sam didn't need to finish her instructions. One of the men on top in the centre of the now broken oval had noticed the change in atmosphere. He had stopped his abuse, and pulled off the girl. He looked bewildered ... and then angry. The poor woman, on the other hand; her eyes were wide and terrified.

Nadia's own rage was coalescing. As the naked man closest to her rose, pulling his gown closed and making sure his face was covered, she couldn't stop herself from pointing the pistol at him. She thrust it in his direction, the end of the barrel wiggling with the intensity of her anger. She tried her best to keep her other hand which was holding her phone still, but that was a problem.

She'd never fired a weapon in anger before.

Just now she was 'that' close to pulling the trigger.

'Take off your hoods!' Sam shouted.

There was no movement from the men. They stood steadfastly against the orders of an armed woman.

'Take off your fucking hoods!' As Sam shouted again, she took a couple of steps forward so she was standing over the man with the black legs. The hooded crowd sensed danger. En masse they tentatively stepped back.

But there was still no reaction.

Sam knelt, the Sauer remaining expertly pointing at the closest standing hessian-styled man. She pulled back the man's hood and motioned for Nadia to come forward. Nadia did as she was asked. And, once by Sam's side, she twisted the phone so it was pointing down.

The video would be clear: it was definitely Chibuike Grandom.

Sam stood. And stepped back from Grandom. Nadia followed.

'TAKE OFF YOUR FUCKING HOODS!' Sam screamed out the words. Her outrage pouring from deep inside.

One man twitched.

But nothing. Still no action.

The tension in the room was strong enough to blow the windows. The archaic music enhanced the mood. The gagged women were now both sitting up. They had turned to each other and, as if they were the best of friends, were now hugging each other.

Nadia's nerves were shot, her breathing erratic. Anything could happen – at any time. In some ways she feared – but in others she hoped – that Sam's next shot would be deadly.

Which looked set to happen.

Sam took a further step forward and theatrically rested her cheek against the stock of the rifle. And then closed her non-shooting eye.

'Take off your hood.' There was no shout this time. It was an announcement. A clear, direct order to the man closest to her. 'Don't misjudge me, fella,' she added.

A beat.

'Five ... four ... three ... two ...'

The man slowly raised his hands and pulled his hood back.

It was Marc Belmonte.

Two out of nine.

'Next.' Sam had moved the barrel to the left.

The hooded man twitched.

...

Nadia's reaction to the speed of the dash and lunge by the hessian-clad man off to their right, surprised her. His feet had already left the ground and his hands were outstretched. His movement displaced his animal-formed bone crown, and his hood had started to peel back from his face.

Nadia's body pivoted, the short barrel of the pistol followed.

And she fired.

It seemed like the most natural thing in the world. Whereas before tonight she might have flinched, or screamed, now there was no hesitation. She pulled the trigger of her newly acquired, and unsilenced, pistol.

BANG!

The noise cut through the sickening ambience of the room. It made her ears ring, and the *thump*, as the body of the man collapsed in agony on the floor, was one of the most satisfying things she had ever heard.

Sam was irrepressible. The barrel of her rifle didn't move, her aim wasn't broken. She just took a step backward and let the man fall to the floor in front of her. As soon as he was static, his hands reaching for the lower part of his torso where the hessian was already spotted with blood, Sam casually nudged the man's hood with a foot. And then nodded to Nadia.

Nadia, who still had the pistol pointing in the general direction of the men, outstretched her camera arm and let it dwell on the next face.

Jimmy Johnson Junior.

Sam wasn't resting. She nodded at her next target. And then started counting again.

'Five ...'

She didn't need to go any further. The man she was pointing at removed his hood.

It was Michael Connock.

'Those of you whose faces we've seen ...' Sam was directing again, '... move against the back wall. Girls, over here.' She flicked her head over her shoulder. 'The rest of you. Take off your hoods!' Sam had to raise her voice this time. The three men on the floor were a cacophony of suffering.

And Nadia was filming it all. The unhooded men, as they shuffled backwards. And the naked women as they stood, their gagged faces a damp painting of distress, quickly protecting their modesty with their hands.

To hasten things along Sam flicked the barrel of the Sauer from man to man. Four de-hoods later and they were one short of a full house.

The Duke of Nairnshire.

He must be the other man with a hole in his leg.

And Sam had taken a step towards him.

BANG, BANG, BANG!

Nadia had seen it in the movies. A volley of shots lifting and projecting a body – sharing the momentum of the bullets – which then fell in a clump a distance from its original position.

But she hadn't known if it were actually true, or just a cinematic myth.

She now knew, though.

She knew that the directors were making the right artistic choice. Bodies did rise, move and fall once they'd been hit.

Because Sam's did.

As Nadia dropped to the floor to avoid being a second target, her mouth formed an 'O', as an elongated 'nooooo' was expelled from her lungs. Surely, she was next? She had watched Sam's floppy body hit the stone wall, hesitate and then drop to the floor, the Sauer making a distressing *clang* as it smacked onto the wooden floor. Any moment now more bullets would fly.

In her moment of futility, she still turned towards the shooter. Her pistol following her line of sight. If she thought she had been overpoweringly angry at these detestable men, that paled in comparison to how she felt now. Now that she was Sam-less.

There he was.

As she spun, she saw him. A man. A guard. He was pointing his rifle at her. She was pulling her index finger towards her thumb. Closing around the trigger. The round in her pistol's chamber would fire soon.

But it would be too late.

The man was a professional. He would beat her to it.

The noise of the shooting which followed made Nadia want to bring her hands to her ears, crawl up in a ball and cry for her mum. It was all too much. Everything since they'd moved onto that old airfield had built up to this. It had been a maelstrom of emotion. Of success, of hard, intricate work, of travel, of camaraderie, of friendship, of trekking across a bog, of a helicopter exhaling explosive gas, of a building within a building which, in turn, held an abhorrent secret …

… and now, of death.

Hers.

Very likely.

Sam's?

She could see no other outcome.

The wait for the bullets which would rake through her was unbearable. The ringing in her ears, mind-numbing. The smell of lingering cordite was a deluge.

'Nadia!'

What?!

'Come on!'

What?!

It was Joe. And Jack. They were behind the guard, who was prostrate on the ground. Joe had stepped over his body and was heading her way.

'Come on! There are more guards!'

Joe was beside her now, moving beyond to where Sam's body lay in a pile. Jack was full inside the room, his own rifle pointing at the men with their backs to the far wall. His mouth open. His face drawn and pale. He was shouting at the naked girls to come to him.

But Nadia couldn't make it out. Everything was a blur.

She stood unsteadily. She looked to Sam. Joe was bent over her. She was ... dead?

'I can't leave her,' she said out loud to herself.

Joe had his hand on Sam's neck. He turned to Nadia and shook his head.

No.

No!

Joe stood, grabbed Nadia's arm and pulled her towards the door.

'Wait!' Nadia rasped. Bullets and smoke and Sam and her and the women and those horrible, detestable men. It was plastered onto one canvas.

But she wasn't done yet. This wasn't finished.

She broke from Joe's grip and walked quickly to the injured man on the floor whose face they hadn't yet seen. She pulled roughly at his hood. The phone's video took the shot. And then she jogged to Joe's side, glancing at Sam Green for the last time.

Did she blink?

No.

Absolutely no way.

It was too late, anyway. In the time it had taken for her to let the world see the last of the despicable YCA, Joe and Jack had taken off their jackets and thrown them over the young women. A few seconds later the five of them were already out of the building within a building, and into the dark of the night.

Epilogue

Fox and Duck Pub, Therfield, Hertfordshire, UK

Eight weeks later

It was a short walk from David's house to the pub. Jane had taken the bay window seat with views over the village green. It was a quintessentially English view. A large green, a pub sign suspended on a tall wooden pole, a minor road, and beyond that a row of thatched and red-tiled houses built in a different age, rising just high enough to peek over a privet hedge. Today, a low sun cast the pub's shadow across the green. Under it the grass retained its dusting of frost. Elsewhere the colours were vibrant and clear.

David was at the bar. Jane looked at him. He was shorter than she remembered, even from when she and Frank had burst in on his life, expecting solace and, in the end, receiving a free ship's pass to Rotterdam. He was dressed in pale mustard cords, a thick cotton chequered shirt and an olive green hacking jacket which was worn at the elbows. It wouldn't be long before Sally would need to administer some leather patches. And he was thinning on top; everywhere else, he was grey. She couldn't remember if that's the way he was three months ago. Possibly.

And her?

She was ... nothing really. A mess was an apt description, but that suggested movement. There hadn't been much of that. After a short series of police interviews in Lerwick, she and the MI5 team had driven back, via two ferries, to the Norfolk airfield. There, a Babylon/Box team had joined them for a couple of days of post-op recall. After that she had travelled on to her brother's.

At first she and the team were worried that the outcome of the airfield debrief interviews would be skewed. That their account of what had happened in Shetland would be misrepresented in favour of the YCA. She and Joe had asked for assurances that the interviewers were not affiliated to, on the payroll of, or associated with, the YCA. It was a bold, but necessary ask. Jane couldn't have countenanced a session with Marcus Trafford. Thankfully neither had turned up; indeed she had been told that Trafford was on gardening leave. She knew the SIS officers who had come. Likewise Joe had been happy with those from Thames House. After that it had gone smoothly.

Jane had penned her resignation over a glass of red wine the evening she'd arrived at her brother's house. She'd let it stew overnight, read it again in the morning, changing a couple of words, and then stuck it in the post. She had no intention of going back to work.

Christmas had been a boozy family affair. And since then, she'd spent her time redecorating her flat. She hadn't got round to thinking about what she might do next. Because she had no idea what that might look like.

In any case, why would anyone employ her? She was a wreck. She spent most of her waking hours in tears, or at the point of breaking down. Between sessions of nervous depression (yes, she had more pills for that), she was often on the loo. Coffee went straight through her. Anything with fibre in it sent her stomach into spasm before exiting as quickly as it had arrived. She'd lost more weight, to the point where she didn't have much more to lose – not without having to buy yet another wardrobe of clothes.

She was permanently listless. And always tired.

The doctors could find nothing biologically wrong. It was what it was. And it seemed that time was the only thing which might bring her house to order. She'd see. She had been somewhere like here before, after Vietnam. That had eventually begun to rectify itself. She'd even gone back into the field. She'd survived Bosnia. Things had been getting back to normal ... until her phone call from the Chief. And the bloody mess which followed.

David was at the table now. He had a pint of beer in a straight glass in one hand and a smaller glass and a can of coke in the other. He placed them on the wood-topped table and sat down next to her.

'I've ordered two winter ploughmans,' he said, forcing a smile at the end of his announcement.

'Winter?' Jane asked, without much humour.

'I think you get thick soup rather than a porkpie.'

Jane nodded, closed her eyes, and then opened them again.

They'd covered the 'how are you' piece on the short walk over from his house. David had sounded as miserable as she was. She had feigned 'recovering from a tough cold', as to why she appeared so dreadful. She was convinced that David had seen through her disguise, but hadn't pressed.

He raised his glass.

'Cheers, Jane,' he said.

She raised hers and immediately felt the rising of tears. She reached into her handbag and pulled out a pretty handkerchief which was screwed up into an already damp ball. As she dabbed at her eyes, she looked back out the window. A small group of starlings were messing about on the grass. Life for them went on.

David touched her arm.

She looked at him.

There was a moment.

'I need to know as much as you can tell me,' he said. 'And I've all the time in the world.'

She sniffed. Smiled, looked for her glass and the can, and filled one with the other.

'You've kept up with the news?' she asked, hoping that David would talk for a bit as she gathered herself into something which might be considered a functioning human.

'I've got that the Chief has been released without charge, but has not returned to his post. Not yet, anyway,' David said, over the top of his pint.

Jane nodded.

'And a number of high-profile billionaires have either been arrested, or are being investigated, for a wide range of crimes. In a number of countries.' He paused, and smiled again. 'That's on the back of what has been classified as the most watched, or subsequently streamed, TV news segment in the history of global video media.'

Jane nodded and took a swig of her drink.

She had forced herself to watch the CNN extended clip.

The original one, which had been live-streamed from Nadia's phone on a standard ten-second delay, had been adequately desensitised on the night by an adept editor. No graphic sexual violence had been broadcast that night. Where shots had been fired, images were blurred. But the intent was clear. The faces of the men, though. They had been available for everyone to see – as it happened.

CNN had released a more graphic version on their YouTube channel. There, only the faces of the women had been pixelated.

Jane, on the other hand, had seen the whole, unexpurgated twenty-seven-minute clip.

It was horrible. Disgusting. Unwatchable for the most part.

But she had sat through it. Eyes open.

It was one of the reasons she was in the state she was. But she didn't regret it.

She needed to know. To witness everything. It was her version of a child visiting the morgue to see a dead parent. The psychiatrists would always be split on what was the wise choice. See Mum? Or no? Jane had her own view. She had to know for sure. Otherwise it would plague her forever.

They had been silent for a while. David was halfway down his pint. He had a thin layer of white foam on his top lip. And was making no attempt to remove it. Maybe he felt as inert as she did? That it was too much effort for his tongue to make a quick sweep?

She understood.

David coughed a small cough into his hand, the foam inadvertently removed. And he smiled again.

'We both know that Fordingly has been arrested. That the current government is in crisis. And that we might be heading for a general election,' David added.

Jane nodded again. She was going to say something, but was stopped by one of the bar staff laden with soup and cheese and bread. Room was made by moving a stack of beer mats, and questions about condiments were asked and answered. Cutlery was delivered on a second pass.

'Is the YCA broken?' David asked. 'I need to know.'

Jane had tried the soup. It was red and thick. And it was too hot for her just now.

She put her spoon down.

Took a breath.

And started.

'All nine members of the YCA got off the island after we left. The Langley satellite images were disguised with a false overlay, so we didn't know that there was a modern quay down from the main house – if you can call it the main house. There was a decent RIB on standby. They were transported to the main island, and from there took a number of what can only have been emergency routes back to mainland Scotland. Some made it out of the country. Others were arrested at various airports and docks.'

Jane paused to eat something. David hadn't touched his plate.

She continued.

'The two men who were raping the women were Sheikh Rashid bin Nahzan and Kirill Semenov. We've lost Semenov. He's disappeared, probably into Belarus. There is an international arrest warrant out for him. The sheikh is awaiting extradition from the UAE.' There was a beat. 'Michael Connock and Edward Grinstead, the Duke of Nairnshire, are both in UK custody. Marc Belmonte hobbled all the way to Paris, where he was arrested on arrival. Chibuke Grandom is at large in West Africa … somewhere. He has been struck from the Nigerian premiership. Elias Bosshart is under house arrest in his Swiss chalet in Verbier. And I guess you know that Edouard Freemantle was murdered on his South African ranch last week by a bunch of local vigilantes. That made the news everywhere.' Jane drew breath. She then cut off a piece of cheese from the large block on her plate.

David started to mouth something. And then stopped. Instead he took another sip of his beer. He then asked, 'And Connock's empire?'

'I'm a week out of date,' Jane said. 'I get my updates from Frank who, you'll be pleased to hear, has stuck at his job. Unlike me,' she added self-deprecatingly. 'We always speak on a Friday, after work. He breaks every security protocol and tells me everything.'

David had picked up his soup spoon and was prodding at the bowl.

Jane continued.

'There's nothing out in the media, but we understand that there's been an international agreement for Connock's media portfolio to be broken into country-sized packages. The UK government will announce next week that it will seize control of all of his empire's associated UK media: video, satellite, internet and print. That is until they can find a suitable buyer, or buyers. It will be an unprecedented move. They're trying to get the deals done in the next few weeks; certainly before the general election which may be as early as the first of April.'

She paused again. She had a piece of bread in one hand. She looked at it and gently shook her head. She knew the danger. If she ate it she'd either be immediately ill, or feel rubbish tomorrow. She put it back on her plate.

David was slowly getting through his soup. He paused to ask another question.

'So it looks like the YCA has been dismembered?' He didn't wait for Jane to answer. 'Do we know who they really were? What was their point?'

Jane let out a light sardonic laugh. And she took a sip of coke to wet her lips.

'It's blood crazy,' she said. 'The house, the hall, call it what you will – Vigon, the original croft – has a special place in Shetland mythology. Sorry, that's not fair on Shetland.' Jane sighed, took a breath and carried on. 'There's this manuscript written in 500 and something. The Box team found it in the Duke of Nairnshire's mainland estate. Apparently it was in a bomb-proof box which may well have been taken to Vigon in the helicopter and brought back on the RIB. It's soaked in Viking nonsense and some other Scandinavian mythology. But there's no actual reference to anything which you might consider to be original Norse. It's been verified, or non-verified to be precise, by a professor in Oslo. In short, it's a stand-alone, Shetland script written by some ancient laird who wanted to place himself way above the locals.' She knew she sounded bitter.

She had every right to be bitter.

It *was* crazy. Madness. A parchment of vile instructions which, in the wrong hands, would lead to the formation of something like the YCA.

David was getting close to the bottom of his soup. He was using his bread to mop up the dregs.

'And it dictated that during the winter solstice the great and the good do what they want to whomever they wanted?' he asked.

'Every second year since 500 and something,' Jane added.

'When did it start?' David asked.

'In its current incarnation, just after the war. Second World War, that is. Previous to that there are no records, as such. But there are rumours. It's work in progress. The Box have a team on it,' Jane said.

A parchment of vile instructions.

It hit her then. And something broke. And the tears came.

Jane retrieved the hanky from up the sleeve of her cardigan.

It did a particularly poor job.

David offered a red with white spots, man-sized cloth from his own pocket.

That worked better.

'I'm sorry,' Jane said from behind David's handkerchief.

'Please, please don't worry,' he replied.

'It's just ... well, Sam was right all along.' Jane cried some more. David placed a hand gently on her shoulder. 'She said it must be more than just money and power ...' Jane wobbled her words through heaving shoulders. 'That if it wasn't actual religion, it was something similar.'

David shuffled closer to her. He put his arm around her shoulders. Jane continued to weep.

'I miss her *so* much!' Jane almost shouted it out.

'Me too, Jane. Me too.'

Jane's head was now against David's shoulder. They were gently rocking together.

'Have we found her body?' David asked.

She sniffed.

It was *the* perplexing question.

They had all scrutinised the video.

Analysts from both organisations had offered comment. All they had was, from what they could tell, Sam had died in Vigon. The bullet wounds were there to be seen. Joe had taken her pulse. Nadia was convinced of it.

Sam had been murdered in a spray of bullets ...

... but her body wasn't in the building when the police had arrived.

And none of the YCA in police custody had offered any explanation.

The collective story from those under arrest was that they had dressed quickly, and were then escorted from the building down to the quay by some guards.

Sam Green's body had been left where it had fallen. And no one was able to, or prepared to offer any explanation as to where the body had been taken. Or why.

It was all too terrible for Jane to think about. She had seen it on the video. And immediately dismissed it …

… until the retelling of the Vigon manuscript to David just now. It had been the one part of the torrid story she had managed to keep hidden from herself.

She sniffed. And sniffed again.

David let her shoulders go. He looked at her. She at him. They both managed a smile. He moved back to where he was originally sitting, placing both hands under his thighs.

'And Wolfgang?' he asked.

This was a little easier for her.

A little.

She squeezed out a pathetic smile.

'Originally the German police reported that he had died of a heart attack whilst they were storming his property. However, the BND team which was subsequently tasked to review the case have confirmed that he had been shot twice. Murdered by a YCA-sponsored SWAT team in his own cellar.' She wiped her face again.

God, I must be bloody blotchy.

David breathed out through his nose.

'And the MI5 team? I've purposely not spoken with Joe,' David asked.

'They're fine. Nigel needed surgery on his foot. The guard who shot him has been arrested and charged. But, the team are all back at work … which is good.' She was feeling a little better.

She took another swig of her coke.

'And you, Jane? What will you do now?' David asked kindly.

She looked out of the window again. The starlings had gone. They had been chased away by a woman walking a black Lab. It was just about to pee on the bottom of the pole which held the pub sign aloft.

She knew she was in no fit state to work. That was for sure. But, similarly, sitting still wasn't the right thing either. There were only so many apartment walls she could paint.

She was going to have to do something.

She looked at David. Her face probably matched her tummy, which was beginning to object to being fed. It was, like her, anxious.

Jane prepared herself. She squeezed the end of her nose between two fingers.

She had decided. She knew all along. She just hadn't said it out loud.

'I'm going to find Sam's body. Then I'm going to bury her somewhere peaceful. And then I'm going to drink a bottle of very decent red wine.'

The Sam Green Series So Far:

Unsuspecting Hero

Sam Green's life is in danger of imploding. Suffering from post-traumatic stress disorder after horrific injuries and personal tragedy in Afghanistan, she escapes to The Isle of Mull hoping to convalesce. A chance find on the island's shores interrupts her rehabilitation and launches her on a journey to West Africa and on a collision course with forces and adversaries she cannot begin to comprehend.

Meanwhile in London, MI6/SIS is facing down a biological threat that could kill thousands and inflame an already smouldering religious war. Time is not on anyone's side and Sam's determination to face her past and control her future, regardless of the risks, looks likely to end in disaster. Fate conspires to bring Sam into the centre of an international conspiracy where she alone has the power to influence world-changing events. Blind to her new-found role, is her military training and complete disregard for her own safety enough to prevent the imminent devastation?

Fuelling the Fire

Why are so many passenger planes falling from the sky? Why are two ex-CIA agents training terrorists in the Yemeni desert? Why is a religious cult transferring millions of dollars to unattributable bank accounts around the world? Are these events connected? If they are, is this the mother of all conspiracies?

MI6 analyst, Sam Green, desperately wants to establish why her only surviving relative died in the latest plane crash. But can she put aside her grief and make sense of it all? Or is the clock ticking just too quickly, even for her?

The Innocence of Trust

Sam Green's been promoted. She's now working out of Moscow as an SIS 'case officer' and hates it. She loathes her boss, feels out-of-place among SIS's elite and loses her only Russian informant to a bomb that also had her name on it.

On the verge of jacking it all in, Sam promises a beautiful stranger that she will find her boyfriend's murderer. That promise propels her into a web of top-level industrial crime and savage international terrorism. With reliable friends and colleagues in very short supply, Sam starts something she cannot stop. And this time, she's going to need more than an expert analyst's eye and a complete disregard for her own safety to prevent the most lethal terror plot since 9/11.

For Good Men To Do Nothing

Someone's messing with the Global Positioning System and no one knows who, or why. The CIA has intelligence of a major terror attack planned for the Middle East, but they have no idea of when and where. And the ultra right-wing Christian sect, The Church of the White Cross, is back doing what it does best: laying down carnage and inflaming anti-Muslim hatred.

Sam Green's been fired from SIS/MI6 for being a maverick operator and is trying to get her life back together. Skiing on a shoestring in Austria, she spots a face in the crowd. And it's a face that doesn't want to be recognised. But it knows she knows - and that can't be allowed.

Then someone lets slip the dogs of war.

Sam's back; this time without SIS support. Pursued from Europe to Venezuela, via The Bahamas and Miami, her enemies are seemingly one step ahead. With a single act of terror the world could be plunged into a religious war that would last for decades. With only the help of her old German hacking pal, Wolfgang, together can they prevent Armageddon?

On The Back Foot To Hell

A new, undefined terror is spreading across the globe. Indiscriminate, low-level acts of violence have hit all five continents - and it's getting worse. The world's security services are at a loss. Who is behind the upsurge in violence? Where will the next attack take place? Will it ever stop?

Sam Green, now a lowly supermarket till girl in a small town in England, is oblivious to world events. She has her own inner demons to fight and they're consuming her every spare moment. All too soon those demons will take on human form. And then she will be faced with two choices: run or fight.

In Naples, Italy, a young Welsh student is innocently researching a link between The Mafia and the history of art. And two thousand miles away in Moscow, Russian intelligence services are struggling to contain a new terror cell that threatens nuclear catastrophe. Are all these things connected? If so, can someone force order from chaos? Sam has managed before. But now there are too many obstacles, the biggest of which are those plaguing her own mind.

Blood Red Earth

There's trouble brewing in East Asia. The Korean peninsula is heading for peaceful reconciliation, and not everyone wants that. Wider still, the communist old guard in China, Vietnam and Cuba is losing its grip - and that can't be allowed to happen.

Sam Green's former Secret Intelligence Service boss, Jane Baker, was on the case. But she's disappeared in mysterious circumstances. Back in London, an MI5 officer uncovers a potential conspiracy at the highest levels of the UK's intelligence services - but who can he turn to? Meanwhile the CIA has just lost their latest North Korean defector in Croatia, and soon they're going to lose a whole lot more.

Could this all be linked?

Unaware of these events, Sam's restless. She's just about recovered from her terrible ordeal in Switzerland and needs to spread her wings. Jane was last seen in Cambodia and that's a good enough start point for Sam. Little does she know her latest journey will literally place her on board a train to destruction. And this time she may well lose more than she ever knew she cared about.

The Belmonte Paradox

The last thing Sam expected was a phone call. She was convalescing. Heading to Greece and the winter sun. He contacted her. Someone she didn't know, but someone who knew of her. And that presented her with a dilemma.

A thousand miles away in sleepy Gloucestershire, a security guard at a disused nuclear power station spots something untoward. Ex-military, he can't discard previously taught skills, and risks everything to find out more. At the same time a Serbian undergrad has lost her journalist brother. He's in trouble and very soon she's fighting for her own life, as well as his.

And a French spy has a theory. He believes the western world is not as we see it. Governments are not in charge - other forces are. Forces which have scant regard for order and calm.

Sam makes a decision, one she may well live to regret. It takes her to northern Europe, back to the Balkans and eventually into sub-Saharan Africa. She's using her instincts; lifting up rocks and disturbing nests. And people are getting killed. This time the job is huge - and it's too big for her. This time she might have to rely on more than her old SIS pals to get the job done. But this time there may not be enough … time.

Or try Roland's first non-Sam Green novel …

Of Black Bulls and White Horses

Emily Copeland is a young teacher at an inner city school. And she's good at it. One Christmas her mother shares a long held secret of a teenage affair with a French fisherman. Months later her mother is killed in a hit and run and Emily's life is dislodged from its axis.

With the school summer holidays approaching, Emily decides on a cathartic journey to revisit the French seaside village where, all those years ago, her mother enjoyed her summer fling. Clutching a series of old holiday snaps, she sets off with the ambition of closure. However, the Camargue - where the mighty Rhône meets the Mediterranean - holds deep secrets. It's a lawless place of cowboys and gipsies, of mudflats, lakes and meandering tributaries … and of black bulls and white horses.

Emily's journey soon ends up being more than just a rehearsal of her mum's past. As she traces her footsteps, the romantic memories she unearths of a previous summer paint an altogether more sinister picture of the present. And Emily's trip turns out to be one of enlightenment and of deceit; and of abuse and of greed. Ultimately it's a story that ends in love ... and death.

Printed in Great Britain
by Amazon